PITCHER Perfect

a novel

TESSA BAILEY

AVON

An Imprint of HarperCollins*Publishers*

HarperCollins books may be purchased for educational, business, or sales promotional use. For information, please email the Special Markets Department at SPsales@harpercollins.com.

Avon, Avon & logo, and Avon Books & logo are registered trademarks of HarperCollins Publishers in the United States of America and other countries.

FIRST EDITION

Interior text design by Diahann Sturge-Campbell

Baseball bat illustration © chuprakov_yuri/Stock.Adobe.com

Library of Congress Cataloging-in-Publication Data has been applied for.

ISBN 978-0-06-338083-7
ISBN 978-0-06-338082-0 (simultaneous hardcover edition)

25 26 27 28 29 RTLO 10 9 8 7 6 5 4 3 2 1

ACKNOWLEDGMENTS

I did not expect Robbie Corrigan aka Orgasm Donor #1 to get his own book. Believe me. But one thing about me is that God forbid a secondary character show an ounce of depth, they will demand a story until they get one. This time, I believe that fatal flaw of mine paid off, because I can no longer imagine a world without Robbie Corrigan. Mailer's moment is coming, too . . . it's just a little ways down the road.

That being said, this book is dedicated to female athletes who are getting more and more well-deserved recognition lately. Athletes like Ilona Maher, Simone Biles, and Caitlin Clark have been ruling my social media timelines, strong and uncompromising while under tremendous pressure. They gave me inspiration for Skylar Page, starting with her opening "fuck you" and ending with her finding balance with a partner who understands, appreciates, and encourages her in the same way he wants/needs to be encouraged.

After all, balance, respect, and understanding go hand in hand with love. I'm so proud to share these characters, Robbie and Skylar, who demonstrate those qualities . . .

After a little push and pull, of course.

Love, Tessa

PITCHER
Perfect

CHAPTER ONE

Skylar Page sat cross-legged on her twin-sized bed enjoying the moments before sunrise. That stillness just before dawn when Boston would begin to stir outside of her window, sounds and scents penetrating the brick walls of her studio apartment. For now, it was just her and the quiet thoughts she needed to envision the day ahead, calculate travel times, and prioritize errands.

After taking a medium gulp of coffee, she opened her white leather planner, her gaze bouncing between underlined reminders and to-do lists, releasing a satisfied sigh over the carefully blue-inked letters. There was nothing like knowing exactly what the day, week, and year had in store.

Currently, it was Saturday morning and she planned on pampering Future Skylar by knocking out some tasks over the weekend—in between practices, of course.

First up—

Her phone rang.

Brow creased, she transferred her attention to the lit-up iPhone where it sat beside her thigh on the raspberry-colored comforter.

Elton, her brother, was calling? At 7:00 A.M. on a Saturday?

Immediately, her heart kicked into a sprint. No one called this time of day with good news. Was something wrong with one of their parents?

Skylar answered on speakerphone, then gripped her knees. "What's wrong?"

"Nothing. What's wrong with *you*?"

That wasn't the tone of someone in the middle of an emergency. Her relieved exhale shifted the pages of her planner. "Why are you calling so early?"

"Because I'm on my way to pick you up."

Furiously, she flipped through a mental calendar, followed by the physical one in front of her, wondering if she'd missed a significant date. Had they made breakfast plans and she'd simply forgotten? That would be a massive rarity for Skylar, but maybe an email had gone to spam. "We're not going to visit Mom and Dad until next Sunday. Did you mix up the dates for spring break?"

"Nope. This is something else."

Skylar waited for her older brother to elaborate, but there was nothing but the sound of his turn signal ticking in the background. "Explain or I'm hanging up!" she shouted at Elton, the way only a sibling could do. Technically, they were only related by marriage, but they bickered like it was their birthright. "I'm in the middle of something."

"Shut up. You're writing in your planner."

"I wasn't writing anything," she mumbled. "I was admiring what's already there."

"Whatever you do, don't put *planner gazing* in your dating profile." She heard a shift of clothing. "I've got some good and bad news, sister of mine. Which one do you want first?"

"The bad news. Obviously."

"Whatever you scribbled down in your planner for this morning? Canceled."

"Hanging up on you seems like a good idea."

"Wait for the good news," Elton rushed to say. "You're pitching this morning."

A beat of silence passed. "That's it? I pitch every morning."

"Not against the Boston Bearcats, you don't."

Slow blink. "Elton, when did you start taking edibles?"

A deep, husky laugh reached her ears from the other end of the call. One that didn't belong to her brother. No, she knew that laugh like she knew the raised seams of a softball. And her heart was back to pumping, her gaze boring into the phone like she could see the source of that laughter through her blank screen. That perfect sound belonged to Madden Donahue, her long-standing crush . . . and her brother's best friend. "Madden is with you?"

"Who else is going to catch your pitches?" Elton responded.

Skylar picked her way backward through the wild conversation, her concentration splintered just knowing *Madden* was apparently on his way to *her* apartment. Snatching up the phone, she jogged to the bathroom, set the device on the sink, and found her toothbrush, applying a swipe of Crest. "Okay, wait. Did you say I was pitching against the Bearcats?" she asked, just before sticking the brush into her mouth, scrubbing.

"Correct."

"As in, the professional hockey team?"

"Yup."

Her incredulity reflected back at her from the mirror. "How and why?"

Elton had the nerve to sound impatient. "I'll explain on the way. How soon can you be downstairs? We're here."

She rinsed and spit as quietly as possible, barely refraining from chucking the phone into the toilet. "Ten minutes."

"Five."

"Ten, shithead." She yanked her long brown hair up into a ponytail. "You're lucky I only set aside this morning to work on next week's to-do list."

"Do me a favor."

"In *addition* to this one?" she sputtered, running to her bedroom closet and hunkering down in front of the stackable drawer holding her multitude of sports bras.

"Yeah. When you get into the car, sit as far away from me as possible just in case sucking is contagious."

"I'm going to sit close enough to choke you to death. You won't even see it coming."

"Choke me after the game. Save your energy for pitching."

"We'll see."

Nightshirt off. Quick underwear change.

Sports bra on. Yoga pants up.

Socks.

It was that weird turning point between winter and spring when the temperature was chilly in the morning and absolutely baked Boston in the afternoon, so Skylar wasted a full minute trying to decide between a tank top or a sweatshirt, finally pulling on both. Then she snatched up her sneakers, keys, phone, and her softball glove where it sat on a shelf of honor by the front door. A minute later, she sailed out of the building, flashing her brother the middle finger through the windshield of his car, a gesture that he gleefully returned.

"Hi, Madden," she said, climbing into the back seat. "That bird wasn't for you."

She watched his profile for that signature lip twitch, her stomach turning over when she got it. "Good morning, Skylar."

"Why *doesn't* Madden get flipped off?" Elton complained while pulling into traffic. "You've known him too long to be polite."

Heat crawled up the back of Skylar's neck, carrying into her cheeks, so she ducked down to lace up her sneakers—and hopefully hide her infatuation at the same time. "I don't know. It probably has something to do with the fact that he's a decent human being. You should be taking notes."

"Take note of this." Elton hit the brakes and Skylar almost tumbled off the seat.

"Hey!" She rubbed her noggin where it had connected with the back of the driver's seat. "Are you trying to injure me right before the season?"

"That was too far," Madden said evenly. "She could get hurt."

Elton continued to drive, unperturbed. "You're right. Then who would pitch this morning?"

Madden grunted.

It took all of Skylar's concentration not to hurl herself down onto the seat in a full body swoon. And to keep her eyes from cataloging the breadth of Madden's catcher shoulders, that little whorl where his dark hair ended just above the nape of his neck, the utter stillness of him. The solid dependability he'd projected from the moment he arrived to live with their next-door neighbor when Skylar was fifteen.

Elton and Skylar both lived in Boston now, but they'd lived most of their lives in Cumberland, Rhode Island. The summer she earned her learner's permit, the elderly Irishwoman who lived beside their two-story colonial had knocked on their door to introduce her grandson, Madden, who'd come all the way from Belfast to visit her in Cumberland for the summer.

For some reason, he'd never actually left Rhode Island.

Or her heart—which he'd owned since the moment his guarded eyes met hers.

"Um." She ordered the fluttering in her chest to cease its torture. "Are you going to explain why we're randomly playing ball with a pro hockey team?"

"If you insist." Elton sighed. "Couple weeks back, I took Bubba to the dog park." Bubba was her brother's beloved bichon frise, which he'd inherited from an ex-girlfriend who'd realized after adopting Bubba that she was allergic to dogs—and Elton, too. "While I was at the dog run, I met this girl."

"I had a feeling this is where our story would begin," Skylar inserted dryly.

"Things were going well—or so I thought. She gave me her number. Then four hockey players showed up and started hassling me about it. Fine, whatever. She's taken. I get it." Elton rolled to a stop at a red light, glanced back at Skylar over his shoulder. "Then they start talking shit about baseball."

Skylar turned to stone. "Excuse me?"

"They said it's boring. Easy. Not a real sport. Background noise for a nap."

She opened her mouth, but the outrage prevented actual words from coming out.

"I know," her brother said, regardless. "Naturally, I challenged them to a game."

"Who else is coming?"

"Few of our old teammates from Brown, plus a couple of guys I met at spring training last week in Florida." Elton and Madden had both played baseball for Brown and were now preparing to enter the minor leagues in May. "They were driving distance and pissed off enough by my story to give up their Saturday."

"I haven't thrown a baseball in a few months. Only a softball." Skylar stretched her fingers in her lap. "Not since the last time we were home."

"That's why we're getting to the field early. So you can warm up that arm." Elton chuckled. "I can't wait to see their faces when you throw your first pitch."

Madden made a sound of agreement that sent a wave of warmth through her chest.

"Speaking of going home . . ." She strove to sound casual. "Madden, you're coming to Rhode Island for spring break, right?"

He turned his head just enough to send her a sidelong glance. "You think I'd miss the Page Stakes?"

"No." She laughed breathlessly. "Of course not."

She ignored her brother's watchful gaze in the rearview, schooling her features and quickly tightening her ponytail. On the inside, though, was another story.

A full week with Madden.

Anticipation sparked in her wrists, her fingertips.

Maybe Madden would finally start looking at Skylar and see more than Elton's tomboy younger sister? Please, universe? After all, she was now a senior at Boston University and dude, she cleaned up *nice*. Pretty nice.

Decent, at the very least.

There had been times over the past six years when she'd thought maybe, just maybe, Madden was looking at her as if he found her attractive, but she usually just had ketchup on her face. The annual Page Stakes might be the perfect opportunity to show her brother's best friend that she'd become a capable woman, not the nosy tagalong from days of yore. Maybe she could even convince him to be her teammate at the yearly competition?

"So . . ." Skylar slid her hand into her glove, crushing the worn leather with the opposite hand. "Speaking of the Page Stakes, have the teams been locked in?"

"Uh, are you fully awake yet, Sky? The teams are always set in stone. Otherwise, how would Team Foul Balls be defending champs?" Elton and Madden exchanged a quick fist bump over the console. "Mom and Dad pair up. You and Eve round out the teams," Elton continued, referencing Skylar's best friend who still resided in their hometown. "That's how it has always been. Don't fuck with tradition."

"Wouldn't it be fun to shake things up, though?"

"No," Elton replied without missing a beat. "Stay in your lane."

Skylar sniffed. "I'm going to throw the game this morning just to spite you."

"Sure." Her brother's skepticism was on full display in the rearview. "When you meet these assholes, you'll want to beat them as much as I do."

For once, Elton was right.

The trio arrived at the Langone Park ball field on Boston's North End fifteen minutes later. Skylar must have subconsciously assumed she was being pranked by Elton—and it would be far from the first time—so she was a little stunned to find an assembly of giants awaiting them in the overcast distance.

"Holy shit," she murmured, slowly climbing out of the car, hand in glove. "Those are the actual Bearcats, aren't they? You weren't lying."

Elton barked a laugh. "You think I could come up with a lie that creative?"

"No, you're right. You're not that smart."

Madden, clearly amused, tucked his tongue into his cheek and looked down. "The Page Stakes are going to be extra interesting this year."

This was her opening. "Come on, Mad. Abandon ship while you still can and join Team Skylar. I've been fine-tuning my talent show performance—"

Elton elbowed her in the side, knocking her off-balance. "Quit poaching my teammate."

"Offer's on the table, big guy," she whispered, patting Madden on the shoulder. Forcing herself not to squeeze or run her palm down the hills and valleys of his triceps. Had he been working out extra hard lately?

Madden laughed in that low, chugging way of his, then joined Elton picking his way across the ball field. As they walked, car doors began slamming in the parking lot and soon enough, they were flanked on all sides by various baseball players carrying bats, some of whom Skylar recognized from her brother's former squad at Brown. Others were unfamiliar. The ones she'd never met perused her curiously, as if wondering what the hell a girl was doing at this national summit of penis power.

She hid an eye roll.

Her pitching would speak for itself. It always did.

Usually.

The scouts from Brown passed on you, didn't they?

Much to her parents'—die-hard Brown alums—everlasting disappointment.

Skylar cleared her throat of discomfort and notched her chin higher, a conversation taking place among the hockey players reaching her ears, carried on the morning air.

"You should have seen this girl I brought home last night. Legs up to her fucking eyeballs," said one of them to the group. A mountainous redhead in a wrinkled shirt and the cockiest posture to ever exist. Chest puffed, chin up. A standing manspread. "I had to peel her off me this morning so I wouldn't be late and she's already blowing up my phone."

"You going to call her later?"

"Only if she brings a friend next time. I like a little variety."

The ensuing laughter soured Skylar's stomach. Then and there, she decided to pitch as though life itself was hanging in the balance. A hockey player with a shaved head scoffed, shoving the offensive jackass and, along with the group, they simultaneously realized their opponents had arrived. The handful of Bearcats went from playful to intimidating in the blink of an eye, bristled jaws flexing, arms crossing over their huge pro athlete chests.

The one who'd been bragging about his exploits didn't even have the grace to look embarrassed over being caught talking about women like they were trading cards, though he visibly jolted upon realizing a lady was among them, his copper head ticking to one side, an interested gaze narrowing in on Skylar, a shaft of sunlight briefly highlighting the green moss hodgepodge of his eyes.

Fuck you, she mouthed at him.

A smile spread across his bearded face.

Oh. She couldn't *wait* to strike this guy out.

This one's for the girls.

CHAPTER TWO

Target acquired.

The drop-dead gorgeous brunette was looking at him as though she'd like to vivisect him with a spoon, but, wow, that disdain only made her huge brown eyes sparkle. God, they were remarkable. Rich and deep, complementing the ponytail that blew in the wind. Hints of sunlight from the overcast sky washed over her fresh face and she had the look of someone who'd just woken up. Kind of messy and cranky.

Apparently, he found that combination . . . fucking adorable.

The rich quality of her skin appeared sunbaked, possibly from playing an outdoor sport. She wasn't short by any means, in fact she was probably bordering on five foot nine, but positioned as she was in a sea of big, ugly baseball players, she was a princess that needed to be rescued.

Robbie Corrigan was just the man for the job.

"We win, you show up to our next home game in our jerseys," his Bearcats teammate, best friend, and roommate Mailer was saying.

"And *when* you lose?" Elton the Dipshit scoffed.

Robbie struggled to tear his attention away from the bristling brunette. Honestly, he could have gone on cataloging her attributes all damn day, but his hatred for baseball had brought the entire Bearcats squad to this park on a Saturday morning to settle some beef. Standing there in a stupor over a girl wasn't going to

cut the mustard. Beef. Mustard. *Can't believe I skipped breakfast.*
"How about this?" Robbie barked. "Your prize is you don't get
your asses kicked." He looked past Elton to the group standing
at his back. "Obviously, the lady would not be included in an ass
kicking of any kind."

The girl in question didn't even take a beat. "Aw shucks, that's
so sweet." She wrinkled her freckled nose. "But I think I'll stick
around and give you the junk punch you so clearly deserve."

Amusement flared in Robbie's chest. "Fair enough."

She smiled at him without her eyes losing an ounce of their
malice—impressive—all while grinding her fist into her glove.

This bloodthirsty baseball chick was not his type. At least, he
didn't think so. It had been a long time since he'd had to *try* with
women. Or bother with anyone who wanted more than a good
time. And they fell into his lap these days. They had in college,
too. Instant popularity with the opposite sex was the second-
best thing about being a hockey player. The first best part was
playing hockey, obviously.

On their nights off, he and Mailer went to the club, booked the
VIP section, and no other effort was required. Pulling this girl,
whose first words to him had been "fuck you," would probably
require a great deal of effort. It might even be impossible.

Why the hell couldn't he stop staring at her?

Mailer elbowed Robbie in the ribs, pointing to a figure approaching the baseball field from the direction of the dog park.
Was that Chloe? Sig Gauthier's future stepsister?

Yeah, it was. An English bulldog trotted behind her on a
leash, looking half asleep.

"Hey, *Elton*," Chloe shouted, sounding decidedly pissed.

"Chloe!" every hockey player in attendance said in unison.
After all, the girl was a ray of sunshine. It was impossible not to
like her. She cheered for the Bearcats on the sideline like democ-

racy was at stake, slandering the referee with an unexpectedly colorful vocabulary every chance she got. Mad respect. Everyone knew she and Sig were together, even if they refused to admit it publicly. Despite that, Robbie and Mailer flirted with Chloe as often as possible, hoping to force Sig into owning up to the relationship, but Sig hadn't pulled that trigger quite yet.

Now, collectively, the Bearcats surged toward Chloe to welcome her, as well as bring her into the fold of hockey players where she was safe from baseball cooties.

She whipped up a hand to stop them, her ire directed squarely at Elton.

"Uh-oh," Mailer muttered, frowning. "Hold up a second, what is Chloe doing here?"

"That's what I would like to know," Chloe said through her teeth.

"I invited her," Elton answered Mailer with a smug grin. "She's here to cheer us on."

"Excuse me?" Chloe sputtered, sounding like her vocal cords were being suppressed.

"Excuse her?" Robbie echoed, intending to hold down the fort until Sig arrived to provide backup for Chloe—which he would. It was only a matter of time before—

And yup.

There was Sig. Coming in hot from the parking lot, visibly ready to blow.

Chloe, unaware that Sig had arrived, was turning pink. "Did you invite me here under the false pretense of a doggy date, just so you could piss off my friends?"

"I don't know, did I?" Elton winked at the Bearcats. "And did it work?"

Were they evolved enough not to take that bait?

No. No, they were not.

Hockey players converged on baseball players, everyone arguing at the tops of their lungs. Gloves were thrown down into the dirt. Off to the right, there was a heavy sigh and the rustle of chain-link, Burgess inserting himself in the middle of the fray with an air of exasperated patience. "Just a reminder that we're all adults here," said Sir Savage, the legendary Bearcats captain and reigning hero of the planet. "Let's take a second to locate our maturity."

"Some of us never had any to begin with," Elton drawled, taking a step closer to Chloe. "Obviously she figured that out and made a better choice."

Sig loomed behind Chloe, fury causing him to vibrate. "Get any closer to her and I will use your kneecaps for batting practice."

Some people had the ability to predict the weather by looking at the sky. Or determine the direction of the wind by holding up a blade of grass. Robbie Corrigan could smell a brawl coming a mile away—and the air was beginning to get ripe for flying fists.

Without any conscious thought, he found himself edging toward the brunette.

Because God help everyone if her beautiful face caught one of those fists. He'd even let her punch him in the junk if it meant she stayed out of the fray. It would hurt, but he'd recover. Eventually.

As slyly as possible, Robbie reached through an opening among the group of baseball players and nudged Brown Eyes. "Psst." He jerked his chin in the opposite direction of the brewing altercation. "Come on. Let's go."

What? she mouthed, incredulous.

"Move. Before you get hurt," he whispered.

"I'll hurt *you*," she whispered back, furiously.

From five yards away, she'd been interesting to look at. Obviously pretty.

Up close?

Her scowl made him wonder how much a bouquet of long stem roses cost.

"You wore Crocs to play baseball?" murmured the brunette while looking down at Robbie's feet. "Are you serious?"

"When I want to play a real sport, sweetheart, I put on skates."

"I could do a lot of interesting things with a blade right about now."

"You're kind of violent, aren't you?"

She gave him another one of those evil smiles in response.

By insulting baseball, he'd probably just ruined his chances of taking this girl out, but he never backed down from a challenge. Hence this Saturday morning face-off that literally no one asked for.

"I wasn't going to play," Sig was saying in the middle of removing his jacket, which only meant one thing to Robbie. It was time to kick someone's ass. "But the possibility of hitting you with a line drive between the eyes is too tempting."

Elton scoffed. "My sister, Skylar, is pitching and she's D1 all-American. You're welcome to try."

Sister.

Skylar.

She was the sister of *Elton*? The jackass Robbie had been feuding with?

They didn't even appear to be related.

But clearly, they were, in some form or fashion.

Excellent.

His shot with Skylar was basically nonexistent now.

But as he watched the blush spread along her cheekbones, the way she ducked her head, as if shy about her brother's open admiration, Robbie decided he was still going to try like hell. A Division 1 all-American pitcher who made fun of his shoes and implied she'd like to stab him with a hockey skate?

Hot. That was fucking hot.

Even hotter? When she stomped her way through the base-ball players to reach her brother, slapping him in the chest with her glove. Hard. "Idiot. Can't believe you pulled something like that," she hissed, referring to the glaring reality that he'd brought Chloe to the field just to piss off the Bearcats.

Skylar hit Elton once more—Robbie almost swooned—before heading for the pitching mound and calling over her shoulder, "I'm telling Mom."

Elton trailed after her. "You better not."

CHAPTER THREE

If only Redbeard would stop grinning at Skylar, she could enjoy pitching into the steady glove that belonged to Madden, the man of her dreams. Taking out the hockey player's teeth with a line drive would be effective, too, but violence would probably only give the Bearcats what they wanted. Brawling was likely their comfort zone.

So, she'd pitch.

That's what Skylar did. That's where she found her answers, her solace. By mentally running through a list of strategies, based on an abundance of factors, mainly the hitter's preferences and strengths. Had they swung at her last fastball? Were they desperate for a hit after striking out during their first three at bats? The mechanics of her windup were like a needle falling perfectly into the groove of a record; her pitch was the music. Her form never changed. She had it down to a science. There were no unknowns or last-second changes.

Sure, this morning, she was pitching a baseball, which meant a different windup, an overhand throw, but she knew baseball almost as well as she knew softball. After all, she'd grown up playing with the boys, and later, at age twelve, when her long-divorced mother had met her recently single soon-to-be stepfather at a youth baseball tournament, she'd learned to play ball with her new fourteen-year-old brother. And down the road, Madden.

Athletics were what had bonded her newly combined family.

They never stopped moving, training, trying out for the best travel teams. Performing, competing, winning.

That's what she did. That's how she belonged.

Lean forward. A practiced intake of breath.

Straighten. Judge the distance, the position of the hitter.

Another breath.

A twist of her foot on the mound.

Knee up, arm back, ball into the strike zone.

Sound filtered in from both dugouts. Elton's friends—at least, the ones who didn't know her prior to this morning—were slack-jawed. The Bearcats punched one another in the shoulders, shouting variations of "oh shit." Madden nodded at her in approval, stood, and threw back the practice pitch. Skylar tried not to be obvious about savoring the vibration down her arm, but it had been a while since she'd received a throw from Mad.

It hit different, okay?

"Has anyone here ever played this godforsaken sport?" shouted one of the hockey giants to the rest of his scruffy teammates, who all definitely looked like they'd rather be on the couch scratching their unmentionables. "All right, one of you lead off. The other goes second. Just get on base and I'll bat you in."

"Gauthier with the baseball lingo," someone said. "I think I just sprouted wood."

"Really? Because I fucking lost mine."

Redbeard's grin finally, rapidly, dropped and he socked the guy who'd lost his boner in the shoulder. "There's a lady present, jackass."

"Sorry, Chloe," yawned his friend.

"What? Nah, Chloe is used to our bullshit." She could feel Redbeard staring at her from the assemblage of hockey dudes. "I was talking about the pitcher. She's feeling me."

A jolt of surprise ran from Skylar's shoulder down to her fingertips.

He was . . . talking about *her*?

She'd been the target of myriad intimidation strategies, but this one took the cake.

Skylar resented being taken out of her pitching zone, but this shithead needed to be put in his place. "No, I'm not," she called sweetly.

Redbeard went back to smiling. "You will be."

"Only if I have to check for a pulse after the game," Skylar said, doing her best to sound bored. "Because we're about to murder you."

"Trust me, I've got a pulse, sweetie. You're making it race."

Heat scaled the sides of her face, forcing Skylar to yank down the brim of her cap to hide her complexion. If her brother caught her blushing, the absolute *roasting* he'd deliver after the game would be the stuff of legends. It wasn't that she found the hockey dickhead attractive or anything, she'd just never had someone show her this kind of blatant interest.

Or any interest at all, to be honest.

Her resting bitch face *probably* wasn't encouraging anyone, either.

Still, this guy's overtures were all to get in her head. *Don't fall for it.*

"Are you just trying to psych me out?" she asked. "You are, aren't you?"

"Holy shit." Redbeard frowned. "It's almost like . . . she doesn't know she's hot."

A teammate slapped him on the shoulder, though he barely flinched at the assault. "You better marry her before she finds out she could do way better."

"I know, right?" Then to her, "Can't wait to tell the grandkids how we met, Skylar."

"Hey." Elton strode past her toward first base. "Stop talking to my sister."

Redbeard's head dropped back on a loud groan. "Why does every attractive woman have to be somebody's sister?"

What exactly did *that* mean?

Skylar shook herself, refusing to spare this man another thought. She had a batter to strike out—and her first victim went down easy. It wasn't polite to revel in another player's walk of shame back to the dugout, so she settled for trading a smirk with Madden.

The second batter managed to get on base, but only because a teammate advised him to bunt. That Bearcat, the third to approach home plate, confused Skylar, just a touch, because while he appeared to be incredibly cocky, he also gave her the almighty chin dip of respect. Interesting. Actually, she recognized this one from television. Sig Gauthier, right? Yeah. Cool. It wasn't every morning she got to strike out a celebrity.

Her first pitch found its target.

Unlike the last guy, however, this one adjusted his stance, dropped his elbow slightly, clearly having studied her first throw. *You want a piece of me, hockey boy?*

Skylar toggled the ball behind her back, preparing to throw a curve, took a breath, and went through motions that were second nature, pitched—

And he actually caught a piece of it.

Everyone looked up as the ball sailed into the right outfield and Sig took off.

But as Sig was rounding first base, all hell broke loose.

The English bulldog accompanying the blonde named Chloe streaked like a rotund comet across the diamond, his pretty owner hot on his heels, crying out the name *Pierre*. As if that wasn't odd enough, Sig abandoned his run for second base and sprinted after them, all the way into the outfield, the trio disappearing into the tree line and leaving everyone in attendance speechless.

Almost everyone, anyway.

Redbeard probably couldn't even pronounce the word "silence."

"I'll pick up where he left off," he shouted, swaggering to home plate and picking up the discarded bat, tapping it against the white diamond, before settling it on his oxlike shoulder. "Next batter, right?"

"Doesn't anyone want to go check on them?" Skylar asked.

Redbeard glanced back at his dugout for a consensus, getting a handful of shrugs and headshakes in return. "Nah." He gave a practice swing. "If Sig can't handle that problem, none of us can."

As a fellow athlete, she appreciated teammates knowing one another so well, but she didn't allow that to show on her face. "Fine." She started to drop into her stance. "I'll happily demoralize you."

Some appreciative *ohhhhh*s carried over from the baseball player dugout.

"Yeah. About that." Redbeard lowered the bat and straightened, taking Skylar out of her rhythm—which he seemed to realize. Had he been watching her so closely? "I was thinking, Rocket. Why don't you and I place a little side bet?"

"No."

"At least hear me out," he said, chuckling.

"I've heard more than enough from you."

"I'm better one-on-one." He winked. "Happy to prove it."

"Earlier, it sounded like you prefer one on *two*."

Another chorus of *ohhhhh*s from his teammates.

He inclined his head, eyes twinkling, yet verging on regretful. "Touché."

"Take his head off already, Sky," complained Elton.

Redbeard was undeterred. "Permission to approach the mound, Your Honor."

Skylar came very close to launching a pitch into the man's eye socket. This whole situation was infuriating, right down to the sexism and entitlement. Could she handle herself? Yes. That didn't mean she should be required to. Odds were, he wouldn't be giving this same flirtatious treatment to a male pitcher, would he? Singling him out in front of everyone for his own amusement?

If it wasn't for Madden standing up and slowly removing his catcher's mask, appearing on the verge of decking Redbeard, she would have whittled the hockey player down to size in front of both teams and gotten on with her day. But her pulse started to race with reckless joy at the possibility that Madden was jealous. Over her.

Could he be? Like, *actually*, actually?

Hope almost caused her to float.

Was giving this insufferable hockey player the time of day worth getting Madden's attention? After years of pining in silence?

Bet your butt.

"Permission granted to approach the mound," she blurted, finding her voice.

"*What?*" Elton sputtered behind her. "Skylar, I have an appointment at the groomer's this afternoon. Don't drag this out."

"For you or the dog?" she hissed back at her brother.

"Very funny."

"Give me one second!"

When she turned back around, Redbeard was standing directly in front of her, his shaggy hair waving in the wind, that mouth in a lopsided smile. Tall and thick as one of the trees she used to climb in her backyard during the summer. And all right, fine, he was . . . handsome. Very handsome. In a shit-eating, takes-nothing-seriously jock kind of way.

Not even close to her type. Light-years away.

But when she leaned casually to one side and found Madden glaring at them, a new game plan started to take shape. Instead of waiting for Madden to notice her, maybe she'd give him a tiny nudge, even if allowing this douche to get away with his antics was irritating, to say the least.

"What is the side bet?" Skylar tilted her head back to meet his eyes—a rarity for her at five nine, but this guy had to be over six foot four. "Be quick."

"Nice to meet you, too. I'm Robbie."

"I didn't say it was nice to meet you," she scoffed. "Name the terms."

Robbie, apparently, narrowed his gaze, giving the briefest of looks back over his shoulder. "Why are you suddenly humoring me?"

"Maybe I like to gamble."

His eyes tracked down to where the ball was fisted in her grip. Stayed there a beat. When he met her gaze again, he was a hint more serious than before, giving her a glimpse of what he might be like in a hockey game. Focused, driven, competitive. "You've got a whole operation going on here and you don't like anything or anyone getting in the way of it. Definitely not the gambling type."

"Good baseball players can't be gamblers? Ever heard of Pete Rose?"

An appreciative spark lit his moss-green eyes. "Fair point." He studied her for a beat longer, before shifting to the opposite foot. "If I make it on base, you let me take you out for coffee after the game."

Skylar pretended to choke. "After what I heard you say about last night's date? No way. I'm not interested in being your next one-night stand." Insecurity got the better of her within a split second. "Not that . . . you'd want that. With me. I wasn't implying you were interested like that." *He looks so confused. Shut up.* "Anyway, I don't even drink coffee, I drink orange juice."

"Okay, Tom Brady," he said slowly. "I'm sure we can manage to track down some OJ. Are you saying yes to the bet?"

She was already regretting this. Why not stick to the original plan and wait for that magical future moment when Madden eventually saw what was right in front of him?

So what if it took another decade?

A sad trombone slide came from the direction of the parking lot. Or possibly her mind.

Face the facts, Skylar. Her plucky tagalong role wasn't working. And yearning this hard, this long? It hurt.

Perhaps she could make the bet. But still win and avoid the date.

That alone could be enough to nudge Madden.

"Fine." She coughed into her wrist. "Whatever. You're on."

A few seconds ticked by, his eyebrows steadily drawing together. "Are you only agreeing to this bet because you think I don't have a snowball's chance in hell of getting on base?"

She shrugged. "Maybe."

With a wink, he walked backward a few steps, before turning and jogging the remaining distance to the batter's box, picking up the bat again. "Gentlemen, please serve as witnesses," boomed his obnoxiously deep voice. "If I make it on base, me and the pitcher have a coffee and orange juice date at a TBD location."

Madden spat, yanked his face mask back into place, and dropped to his haunches.

She wasn't imagining this, right? Mad was jealous over her.

"I'm not worried," Elton drawled. "She won't let you make it on base."

No. She wouldn't. She had far too much pride for that.

But Redbeard had done her a favor by being so publicly annoying. He'd declared her datable to anyone who would listen—including Madden—and maybe, just maybe, gotten her brother's best friend to see her in a different light.

No one expected Robbie to lean into her next fastball.

Which, she realized afterward, was a huge miscalculation on her part.

Of course, this hockey bruiser didn't mind a fastball to the shoulder.

In fact, he seemed to enjoy having his strength tested.

"Nope." Elton threw down his glove and strode toward the batter. "That was fucking cheap. You are not taking out my sister."

Robbie ran his tongue along the inside of his bottom lip, smiled. "The terms were clear, man." His attention ticked to Skylar. "Pulp or no pulp, Rocket?"

Elton landed the first punch.

Robbie's head whipped back, but he stood his ground.

And socked her brother square in the nose, staggering him back several yards.

Everyone converged at once, fists flying.

Including Skylar. No one punched her brother, except for her.

Before she could enter the ruckus, Robbie ducked his way out of the brawl with a supreme air of nonchalance, as if he hadn't been the one to instigate it. He bent his knees, tossed her into a fireman's hold over his shoulder, ignoring the way she pounded on his concrete-reinforced back, trying to free herself so she could get a piece of at least one Bearcat. "Put me down," she shouted through her teeth.

"Let me save you," he called up to her, making an *oof* sound when she punched him in the butt. "If someone accidentally hit you, this would go from a friendly Saturday morning brawl to an emergency room visit for a lot of baseball players."

"You started it!"

"Your brother threw the first punch."

"You deserved it."

"Maybe so, Rocket, but let's focus on what's important."

"Like what?"

"Look where I'm standing."

Skylar twisted around to judge their location.

His feet were planted firmly on first base.

He'd won the bet.

She sagged in defeat.

CHAPTER FOUR

Robbie turned to Skylar from where he stood at the counter of Café Lil Italy, totally unconcerned about the ugly, blue-black swell forming around his right eye. "You never told me, Rocket. Pulp or no pulp?"

"No pulp," Skylar responded, thoroughly dazed.

"Do you want anything to eat?"

"No." She swung her backpack around to the front, fingers poised to unzip the front pocket. "I have money."

He ignored that. Obviously. Was probably one of those guys who frequently shrugged and said, *What can I say? I'm traditional.*

How. How did she get here?

"I got it. You want to grab us a table?" With a wry smile playing around his lips, Robbie sent a nod toward the street. "Since we're on the clock and all."

Skylar turned, walked stiffly toward the only open table, which happened to be the farthest one from the front of the shop, taking off her backpack and plopping into the wooden chair. God, she did not have time for this. Now she would never get a head start on packing for Rhode Island or get the cracked screen fixed on her phone. No meal prepping would be done. This guy had her in the weeds.

Skylar should have continued pitching her game, no detours, no harebrained impulses. She never should have let him approach the mound. Look where that rare impulsivity had gotten her.

Drinking orange juice with a chauvinist hockey player while her brother waited outside in the car like some deranged chaperone, icing his own nose and eye bruises, inflicted on him by her date. Just a typical Saturday.

More interestingly, Madden sat in the passenger seat, and he hadn't spoken on the short drive to the coffee shop. Not a totally remarkable event, since he was a man of few words, but Skylar couldn't help but wish she could read his mind.

How did he feel about her being on this date?

As someone who'd usually felt like an outsider in her blended family, Skylar had always related to Madden, even considering him a kindred spirit of sorts, since he'd learned how to live in a new place with different traditions—coming from Ireland to Cumberland—just like Skylar had done at age twelve when her mother married Doug. Madden had become even more of an outsider midway through high school when his kidney disease progressed and he'd gone on dialysis, before eventually receiving a kidney from an anonymous donor, something she'd always sensed he had a hard time coming to terms with. Not knowing.

She wanted so badly to be close enough with Madden to finally ask him about that part of his life, but they'd never made the transition from friends to confidants.

Today, however, possibilities existed where none had before. The bubble of hope expanded just in time for Robbie to set down a coffee mug of orange juice in front of her and fall into the opposite chair, halfway through unwrapping what looked like a bacon, egg, and cheese on a bagel. And it didn't go unnoticed by Skylar that he slipped a second one into the pocket of his black Bearcats fleece for later. "Do you mind if I eat?"

"Be my guest."

"Thanks." A third of the breakfast sandwich was gone in one bite. "So, tell me about yourself."

Original. "No thanks."

"Besides pitch like a Hall of Famer, what are you into?"

"Cannibalism."

Robbie chuckled into his second robust bite, leaned back into a sprawl, and studied her while he chewed. "Are you mean to everyone or just me?"

Skylar crossed her arms and propped them on the table. "Are you surprised I'm a little standoffish after you made a joke out of me in front of everyone, then punched my brother in the face?" She exhaled toward the ceiling. "You better hope Elton's black eye is gone before we visit my parents next week or Mother is going to be pissed. She taught me everything I know about cannibalism. You're big. You could feed us for a month."

"See, now I can't tell if you're joking or not."

"I'm not," she deadpanned.

"I see." He tossed the remainder of the sandwich into his mouth, chewing briefly and swallowing the bite in an audible gulp. Briefly, *very* briefly, her attention was drawn to the network of throat muscles that strained inside the raised collar of his fleece. Nice, but she wasn't interested. "How did I make a joke out of you?"

Skylar blinked at him. "Are you serious?"

"Yes." How galling that he appeared authentically puzzled. "I thought I was doing the opposite."

"How?"

"I don't know. By hyping you up."

It took every ounce of her maturity not to mimic that dopey statement in his distinctive baritone. "I don't need to be hyped up, you presumptuous dickwad. My arm does that for me." She drummed the fingers of her right hand in the crook of her left elbow. "I was there to pitch. I should have been treated like any other pitcher. Did you stop to think how uncomfortable it would be for a woman to be in the company of two dozen guys while being objectified so openly like that?"

Was it satisfying to watch her explanation sink in? Yes. It was.

Unfortunately, the way his skin drained of color, his eyes closing briefly, as if silently berating himself, was annoyingly . . . endearing? Perhaps that wasn't the right word, but it was becoming steadily obvious that he hadn't *intended* to embarrass her. Or make her uncomfortable. Not that he got a free pass. He didn't. "Wow. I'm sorry." He balled up the foil in which his sandwich had come wrapped, bouncing it off his own forehead. "I didn't think of it that way."

"Whatever." She uncrossed her arms, scooped up her mug of orange juice, and took a hearty gulp. "I already hated your guts by that point, anyway."

"Because you overheard what I said when you arrived at the field?" He dropped his head back on a groan. "I knew it."

"Why else would I have mouthed the words 'fuck you' before introductions were made?"

"I don't know, I just figured you hate redheads."

"I do. But only when they're named Robbie."

"Very specific of you."

"It's who I am."

"Tell me more about who you are." When Skylar only rolled her eyes at him and pretended to stab herself in the neck with an invisible knife, Robbie swiped a hand through his mess of windblown hair, a tattoo peeking out from the sleeve of his fleece, which appeared to be the outline of an island. "All right, I can see I'm starting from a deficit with you. The first period hasn't even started yet and I'm losing by five."

"Eight."

"Cool. Cool." He spread his hands. "I like women. Women like me. Usually. I'm not going to apologize for that, but . . .

the shit I was saying when you arrived at the field . . . I guess it sounds a lot worse in hindsight."

Skylar was getting tired of scolding him like a cranky school principal. "I'm not here to lecture you about your treatment of women." She gave him a bright smile. "You're going to learn your lesson all on your own someday and that's good enough for me."

Robbie shivered. "You're kind of dark, Rocket, you know that?"

"Pretty standard for a cannibal."

He huffed a laugh, shook his head. "Damn. I would give my left—"

"Slow down. Think about your words."

"*Arm.* I was going to say arm. I would give it up to rewind this morning and start over." Gingerly, he touched his damaged eye. "It still would have ended in a brawl, but maybe if I had done things differently, you'd be giving me a legitimate shot right now."

"Probably not."

"Why?" He seemed genuinely curious. "Just because I punched your brother?"

An amused sound snuck out against her will. "You know, that usually does put a damper on a courtship, but no."

Skylar opened her mouth to continue and somehow, *unbelievably*, her deepest, longest kept secret almost came flying out. Why? Why to *this* guy, especially? Maybe because her nonrelationship with Madden had been at the forefront of her mind all morning? Or because this conversation felt weirdly personal and reflective even though she'd only met this man a few hours ago?

More astute than she'd given him credit for, Robbie leaned in. "What were you going to say?"

"Literally nothing."

"It was *some*thing."

"I was going to ask you about hockey, so you could start talking about it and I could just zone out."

"Oh, come on. Have you ever been to a game?"

"No," she said robotically. "Tell me everything. I'm riveted—"

A chime coming from Skylar's phone interrupted her.

She assumed that was her brother checking in, but when she dug her phone out of the front pocket of her backpack, there was a text from Eve, instead.

> Bad news, babe. Two of my bartenders quit to follow their Bitcoin dreams and I'm going to be covering their shifts all next week. Big crowds for spring break. As much as it pains me to break tradition, I don't think I can be your teammate this year for the Page Stakes. I'm so sorry. I miss you madly. X

"Crap," Skylar breathed. Having so many of her plans obliterated in the space of a few hours had rendered her off-balance. Ignoring the observant way Robbie watched her, she drained her orange juice, wishing for once that it contained some tequila.

"What happened?"

She plunked down her mug. "How much time is left on this date?"

"Sixteen minutes."

"Oh Jesus. Fine." She hastily tightened her ponytail. "My mother, Vivica, married Elton's dad when I was twelve and they met at an elite baseball club tournament, where they were each the loudest parent in the stands—a title that is not easily won. Imagine the two most competitive, high-functioning people you know getting married. That's them. They had their wedding reception at a rock climbing facility." She took a bracing breath.

"To commemorate the blending of our families, they hold this competition at our home in Rhode Island called the Page Stakes. It's a series of races—swimming, climbing, and more. The winner takes home a trophy I made in seventh grade out of Popsicle sticks and a Pepsi can. It's called the Page Cup." She took a breath, surprised Robbie didn't appear to be bewildered like most people were when she told them about the psychotic family event. "My parents are one team. I pair up with my best friend, Eve. Elton and Madden round out the teams."

"Madden is . . ."

Her voice softened against her will. "The catcher. From earlier."

Robbie's face didn't change, but disappointment lowered the wattage of his moss-green eyes. "I thought I noticed a little something there."

Skylar's pulse started to accelerate, just having her secret this close to the surface. "A little something where?"

"All right. Let's see." He scooted his chair closer, as if hunkering down for the nitty-gritty. "He's not your man or he wouldn't have let you come on this date, so . . ."

"'My man'? Could you, like, try and evolve a little, Redbeard?"

"Sorry, but if you were my girlfriend, I'd be very not okay with some other guy buying you orange juice. I'd boycott oranges for the rest of my life."

"Believe me, this is a problem you'll never have to worry about."

"Yeah, I can see that." He hung his head for a moment, before meeting her gaze again, a little more of the spark gone. "Are you into him, or what?"

On reflex, she glanced toward the street where Elton and Madden were idling at the curb with their hazard lights on. Thanks to the afternoon sun, she couldn't discern their faces through the window, nor did she know if they could see this far into the restaurant, but Skylar couldn't deny that the possibility of Madden watching her go on a date made her feel . . . visible and coveted. And she didn't feel like that very often outside of sports.

Never, actually.

"You are into him." Robbie's throat bobbed, his laugh lacking some of its earlier boom. "But you're not *with* him."

"Yeah," she said quietly, before she could stop herself. "Fine. You cracked the case."

CHAPTER FIVE

Robbie tried like hell not to show the defeat currently lancing him in the gut.

She loved this fucking catcher named Madden. He could tell. When she'd said his name earlier, it was the first time her brown eyes lost their spite. Speaking about him now was causing her to shift in her seat, fidget with the mug of orange juice. Robbie was a side character who'd walked into a love story already in progress.

One girl wasn't going to work out for him. *One*. So what?

So she was gorgeous and funny and athletically talented and took no shit. So she made jokes about cannibalism without blinking and the weight of her had felt really goddamn good thrown over his shoulder. So she was competitive and seemed to value her family, even while poking fun at them.

So what?

The bacon, egg, and cheese bagel was now a ten-ton boulder sitting in his stomach.

He should really get up and make a hasty exit, take the hard lesson she'd given him about his treatment of women and forget this ever happened. But he couldn't quite bring himself to stand up and leave. Something about never seeing this person again was giving him a very distinct burn behind his Adam's apple. Had that ever happened before?

No.

Plus, hey, he still had ten minutes on the clock. He couldn't give her dickhead brother the satisfaction of ending the date early, right?

Mostly, though, Robbie just really *liked* sitting across from her. Skylar smelled like soap and orange juice and her voice had this husky pitch that made him wonder what she said when she was close to coming. *Stay there. Right there. Don't move. Harder.*

Apparently, Robbie was never going to find out.

"What's your plan?" he prompted, even though he desperately wanted to change the subject. That was the hockey player in him, though. Embracing the shit show.

Skylar's chin came up, interest shifting her beautiful features, irritation clearing from her brow. *Oh Jesus.* She was even more beautiful when she didn't want to slice off his balls. What had he even said to evoke such a change? Right. *What's your plan?*

"Plan?" she echoed.

"Yeah. For pulling the catcher."

"I'm not trying to pull him. I'm trying to . . ."

"Marry him. Have his babies." Robbie gave her a sympathetic wince. "Hate to break it to you, Rocket. If you want those things, you have to pull him first."

"Well." Skylar twisted the mug in front of her, appearing more than a little thrown. Man, it was so endearing the way she flushed to the roots of her hair. "There wasn't a softball league in my town growing up, so I played baseball. It wasn't until much later, freshman year of high school, that my parents started driving me the twenty miles to play club softball on a girls' team, but by then I was one of the guys. Those friend groups among the girls were formed and they were so . . . good at wearing the right clothes and sliding into DMs."

"You preferred sliding into bases."

That earned him his first laugh from Skylar Page—and it

forever changed him. It was as unique as the rest of her. That slightly sunburned nose wrinkled and she gave sort of a mini lurch, no sound coming out at first, but then a tremulous gasp filled the space between them. "That was terrible."

"It had the desired result." Every second that drained from the clock now was like an explosion in his ears. "All right, so you're not good with men."

She groaned. "I can't believe I'm telling you this."

"Maybe you sense that I'm the perfect person to help."

Help?

What the actual fuck are you doing? Robbie wasn't even 100 percent sure yet, the idea was coming to him in flashes, like the goal teasing him with glimpses between a hoard of shifting defenders. All he knew was that if Skylar walked out of that restaurant and he didn't have a way to see her again, he'd regret it more than the time he tried bleaching his hair and eyebrows blond in middle school using Clorox. He still had the chemical burn on his scalp and a lifetime of nightmares ahead.

Speaking of nightmares, right now, as he looked at Skylar, every crude thing he'd ever said in the locker room was coming back to him in hideous waves, turning his stomach to soup. *He* wouldn't even recommend that Skylar date him. Maybe helping her with the catcher was the only way he could realistically remain in her orbit. Maybe watching her win another man over was going to serve as punishment for the way Robbie himself had been treating women lately.

Because he'd been raised a lot better than that, hadn't he?

Yeah. Talk about an understatement.

His parents were still happily married and living on Long Island. They wore matching polo shirts to the golf course. They'd just gotten a pizza oven installed in the backyard and they texted him a picture every single time they used it, their smiling faces cut off and out of frame in some haphazard selfie. By example, they'd taught him what a healthy, respectful relationship looked like. To say nothing of the numerous lessons his grandfather Nick had taught him before—

Robbie cleared his throat so hard, Skylar jolted.

Come on, guy. He knew better than to think about his grandfather in public.

He ducked his head to hide the flash of grief.

Bottom line, he'd let his bachelor behavior escalate, drunk on the access to women that his career and gladiator physique afforded him. And he'd been taught better.

Skylar was squinting a skeptical eye at him. "How would *you* help me?"

Great question. Just figure out a way to see her again and go from there.

When would he see her, though? She'd just finished telling him she'd be in Rhode Island next week for some bizarre family Olympics. Two weeks from now, he'd be nothing but a distant memory—

Wait.

Wait.

"Don't you need a new teammate for the Page . . ."

"Stakes? Yes." She leaned forward, then way back in her chair. As if she comprehended where he was going with this line of questioning but wasn't sure if Robbie was quite that crazy. Spoiler alert: he was. "Why?"

He spread his arms wide. "Look no further."

"That punch knocked your common sense loose. *Looser,* I should say. You're proposing we compete together, as a team, in the Page Stakes?" She shook her head slowly, one corner of her mouth lifting with secret amusement. "Honestly? You have no idea what you'd be in for. I should let you come, just to watch your dawning horror."

Robbie scratched his beard. "Your family is that fucked-up, huh?"

"My dad wakes us up with a trumpet. He keeps a local nurse on speed dial, just in case any of us require medical attention."

"I'm in."

"What . . . is wrong with you?"

"Same thing that's wrong with you. I'm competitive to a fault. I don't care if the prize is a Pepsi can, I want to win it." *With you.* "And in the process . . ." He tried to shrug off the warning twist in his chest, but he didn't quite succeed. "We make your catcher a little jealous. Let him see who and what he's missing."

Skylar studied Robbie's face long and hard, probably double-checking that she wasn't being had. Then she stared off into the distance, cogs turning behind her incredible eyes. "Do you think . . . that would really work? I mean, he *did* seem a little jealous when you sexually harassed me at the baseball field."

"Christ. Talk about a wake-up call," Robbie muttered, the words "sexual harassment" echoing in his ears. "We've only got about two minutes left, so I'll lay it out for you. I'll come to Rhode Island and help you win this guy . . ." Speaking of nurses, he needed one to treat the burning in his esophagus right about now. "I owe you. I want to make up for what happened this morning."

Skylar tilted her head, as if maybe she was caught off guard by his earnestness, but still not quite sold. On him *or* the idea. "What would I tell my family?"

"That I'm your . . . love interest. Obviously. That's how we're going to make this assho— the catcher, I mean, jealous."

Briefly, she covered her face, clearly in disbelief to be considering this proposed charade. "Even if I could convince my parents that I'm suddenly the girl who brings home her boyfriend, who I've never told them about, do you really think Elton is going to buy that? What about Madden? You think they'll buy the story that we had some miraculous turnaround in our relationship after thirty minutes in a coffee shop where neither one of us drank coffee?"

"I can be convincing." He cocked a challenging eyebrow. "Can you?"

She hissed a sound. "Don't do that."

"Do what?" he asked, innocently.

"Prod my competitive side."

Robbie almost had her. He was *this close* to being allowed to go with Skylar to Rhode Island and help her win another man. Sure, he'd get to spend time with this amazing girl and beat some baseball players' asses. Watching her pine for another man would be fucking awful, but there was no turning back now. He wasn't lying when he said this morning had been a wake-up call and he not only wanted to leave this girl with a better impression of him, he wanted to remind himself of the person Grandpa Nick had helped raise. Someone who treated everyone with respect.

When had he gone so far off course?

"Moment of truth, Skylar. Are you in or out?"

She glanced toward the street, her teeth furiously chewing her bottom lip.

Were his palms sweating? Yeah. Profusely. After all, she could say no to this asinine idea and walk out the door without looking back. Frankly, it terrified him how easily she could do that. In fact, she probably *should* do that, because she had exactly zero reasons to trust him.

Give her one.

Without giving himself the opportunity to talk himself out of it, Robbie took the wallet out of his back pocket and slid an old photograph out of the billfold. He hesitated only a moment before setting it down in front of her, making sure his voice was even before he started talking. "This is my grandfather Nick. He is . . . he *was* the most important person in the world to me. I swear on his memory that I'm going to help you do this. I'll take it seriously." He tried not to be obvious about the long breath he had to take. "I also swear on his memory to mop the floor with your brother at the Page Stakes."

Skylar snorted on her way to burying her head in her hands. "God knows I'm not getting Madden's attention on my own," she murmured, almost to herself.

Robbie carefully put the picture back in his wallet and waited.

Dug his fingertips into his thighs as she started to speak. "I—"

The door of the coffee shop flew open. "Sky, let's go," Elton barked from the entrance. "Time's up."

She stood on reflex, then seemed annoyed about it.

Robbie stood, too, intending to walk her to the car, no matter which decision she made. Wanting every last second, if this was going to be the final time he saw her.

"Hey," he started, stepping back so she could lead the way to the door—

"Look." She wet her lips, looking up at Robbie. Paused for a five count, as if trying to read his mind, then whispered, "Maybe this is the worst thing I've ever agreed to, but I'm in." She snuck a peek at his lips. "Might as well lay the groundwork now, right?"

Robbie heard the words coming out of her mouth, but he was still somehow completely caught off guard when Skylar fisted the front of his fleece and drew him down for a kiss. A quick press of warm, plush lips against his own, a moment of lingering where she searched his eyes, tick, tick, tick, followed by her elevating onto her tiptoes to kiss him more fully . . . except this time he was ready. Barely, thanks to his fucking heart drumming in his ears, but he managed to cup the back of her head and savor the second lock of their mouths, the featherlight alignment of her athlete's body against his, the dizzying waft of soap and orange juice, the twitch and rise of his dick, the sifting of his fingers through her hair, the levitation of his body into the sky—

She sank her teeth into his bottom lip and tugged, giving him a warning look.

"If you mess this up, I will mess *you* up."

"Understood," he managed, winded.

"I'll be in touch."

With that, she turned and sauntered out of the shop, right past her bewildered brother, who was splitting his shock between Skylar and Robbie, but Robbie was reeling too severely to gloat for once in his life. All he could do was stare at Skylar's retreating form and attempt to ground himself, until Elton finally allowed the door to swing closed, street sounds cutting off abruptly, leaving only the pounding of Robbie's pulse.

"What a woman," Robbie whispered, rubbing the center of his chest.

He'd just signed himself up for hell.

But Skylar? She was worth it.

CHAPTER SIX

"You're what?"

"You heard me, Dina."

"Did I?" Skylar's pitching coach stepped in front of her, blocking her view of the net where she'd been aiming. "Because I think you just told me you're taking a fake boyfriend to your parents' house for a week."

Skylar wouldn't waste time living in regret over telling Dina what had happened that morning at Café Lil Italy. There were no secrets between a girl and her pitching coach. Was she a member of the team? Yes. Her position tended to keep her isolated a lot of the time, however. During games, while everyone was in the dugout, she was either on the mound or in the bullpen. At practice, like now, she trained on a different section of the field, had her own coach, her own game schedule and recovery techniques.

Dina, a former all-American collegiate pitcher in her own right, stood at an impressive six foot two, the messy bun at the top of her head giving her those final two inches, and her ability to spit from the mound into a bucket at home plate was her claim to fame—and rightly so.

"Because I've met your parents, Sky, and they're too quick on the uptake to fall for something like that. They're going to see through you a mile away."

Dina made a good point.

An excellent point.

One Skylar hadn't taken into enough consideration. She might be able to fool her parents for an afternoon, but for a whole-ass *week*? If she'd stopped to think about everything this ruse would entail, she would have said no. She and Robbie—whom she barely knew!—would have to share a bedroom. They'd have to hold hands and kiss. Tell stories about each other. Make goo-goo eyes.

God, she'd have to *smile* at him. Laugh at his jokes.

Relying on her next pitch to keep her from spiraling, Skylar leaned forward, took a centering breath, locked in on the strike zone, led hard with her left leg, and let fly, sending the late-breaking rise ball into the back of the net . . . which wasn't half as satisfying as listening to the ball hit Madden's glove.

Madden.

The reason she'd agreed to this totally unethical scheme.

Absently, she put up her glove to accept a catch from Dina, taking her position at the mound once more. She wasn't seeing the net, though. She'd traveled into her mind's eye where she, Elton, Madden, and Eve were swimming in the backyard of her childhood home. Madden in the shade with a book, quietly observing everything over the wind rustling pages. Elton on the phone with a girl, trying to convince her to come over. Eve sunning herself in the daring sophistication of her black, vintage-style one-piece. Everyone so comfortable in their lane, except for Skylar, sixteen, who hadn't been able to find a bathing suit at the mall that was exactly the right balance of modest, practical, and cute, so she'd donned the Speedo one-piece with the racer back that her mother wore to water aerobics. And paired it with some board shorts Elton hadn't worn since the fifth grade.

She didn't know how to get Madden's attention. She didn't know how to get *anyone's* attention, even that of her parents, by any other means but her athleticism, so that's what she did.

She swam laps, hoping Madden would notice her perfect form. She'd been practicing. When that didn't work, it was backflips off the diving board, dunking on the floating basketball hoop. She smack-talked her brother, as per usual, trying to be funny, but looking back, she could see she'd only ever known how to be one of the guys.

Now, at twenty-two, it wasn't as though she couldn't dress up and apply makeup, if she so felt like it, but the impostor syndrome never quite left her alone.

Skylar was not naturally graceful and sexy like Eve.

She couldn't pair the perfect outfit, like Elton's revolving-door girlfriends.

Flirting? Might as well ask her to perform an appendectomy in a blindfold.

Since starting at BU she'd gone on dates, usually set up by her teammates or one of her brother's friends. Some of them went well, others were awkward, at which time she'd defaulted to talking sports and ended up with drinking buddies instead of a boyfriend. A couple of times her dates had ended in sex that started off feeling really good, but somewhere in the middle, everything started going too fast, no plan, no practice helping herself have an orgasm with a partner, and the men never seemed inclined to give any input, so the whole business of sex had sort of been back-burnered for a while.

Sex would be good with Madden.

She knew that in her soul. He was the most patient, intuitive person she knew. It wouldn't be a frantic dash to the ending with him. He'd talk to her, take his time, because he knew her. Cared about her.

But if Skylar was being honest with herself, she'd stopped attempting to draw Madden's eye because she wasn't so sure *she'd* satisfy *him*. Or be the person *he* needed.

How could she with so little experience?

Was Robbie "Redbeard" Corrigan her chance to get some?

"You've been midwindup for ten minutes, Sky. You mind focusing?"

Skylar went through her breathing routine, fired her arm in a reverse circle, and let fly. Pow. A little high, but into the net nonetheless. "You're the one talking my ear off."

"Excuse me," Dina sputtered. "It's not every day my star pitcher lands a phony boyfriend. Thank you for being interesting for once."

"You're welcome," Skylar said, catching Dina's toss. "So you don't think there's a snowball's chance in hell of me pulling it off, huh?"

"Correct." Dina laughed and shook her head, appearing distracted by a flock of birds flying overhead. "Not unless you do some serious practice first. Practice wins games. I don't need to tell you that."

"Practice wins games. Planning leads to execution." Skylar slowly turned to face the pitching coach, also known as the woman with Skylar's dream job. The one she dreamed of calling her own one day. "You're right. I need practice."

"Are we talking about boys or baseball now?"

Skylar was already making a detailed itinerary to present to Robbie.

Flirting instructions. Kissing practice. Goo-goo eyes training.

Robbie. She'd found herself thinking about him on her train ride to the field, remembering how genuinely contrite he'd looked when apologizing over the scene at the baseball game/ brawl. How he'd gotten a little choked up talking about his grandfather.

How his huge body had shuddered when she kissed him.

Had she actually . . . *affected* him? Or was he just surprised?

Probably the latter, since she'd had no practice.

Not yet, anyway.

ROBBIE SCRUBBED AT his wet hair and beard with a towel, parking himself on a bench in front of his locker. Around him, his Bearcats teammates were in various stages of showering and getting dressed to go home after practice. Today had been a light one, thankfully, as playoffs started at the end of April and now was not the time for anyone to get injured. But even a light practice in this profession meant his whole body ached.

And he loved it.

The more pains and strains, the better. That's what he'd signed up for.

If his morale light was a little dim over the veteran players ganging up on him for every tiny mistake he made out on the ice, so be it. All part of being a rookie.

When did the constant teasing and berating end, though?

Robbie shook off the sinking feeling. *Be positive. Smile through it.*

In addition to his usual full-body throb this evening, his shoulder was still on fire from leaning into Skylar's pitch. Instead of reaching into his duffel bag to dig out a T-shirt, he reached up and touched the sore spot now, smiling at the memory of her flinching back on the mound, hands covering her mouth, almost like she didn't fully relish the idea of murdering him with a fastball. So romantic.

Mailer sat down heavily a few feet away, shoving his feet into a pair of rubber slides. "What's for dinner tonight, Mom?"

Finally, Robbie pulled on his white T-shirt, followed by his favorite hoodie, which—incidentally—said ORGASM DONOR across the front. "There are three Stouffer's lasagnas in the fridge. We each get one. Rock paper scissors for the third."

"Why don't we just split the third one?" Mailer asked.

"Too easy."

His roommate snorted. "Everything is a competition with you."

"Yeah. Well." Robbie spoke without thinking, visions of a certain brunette spinning in his head like an army of tops. "Turns out that's going to work to my advantage." A wet towel was launched at Robbie's head, soaking the shoulder of his hoodie with shower water before he could duck. "What the hell, man?"

Mailer didn't look the least bit remorseful. "Stop being cryptic. You've been like this all day. Just tell me how the fucking date went."

"No." Robbie sniffed. "I don't kiss and tell anymore."

"Does that mean you kissed her?"

"I'm not going to confirm or deny." All right, apparently it took more than a lecture and one afternoon to evolve, because the truth was tap-dancing on his tongue. Not necessarily because he wanted to brag, like he usually did, but . . . he felt kind of victorious for pulling off a kiss with Skylar Page. That alone had to be harder than making it from one end of Boston to the other without hitting traffic. "But if I were going to do either of those things, I would confirm."

Mailer slammed his locker shut with a hoot. "Even for you, that's impressive. She went from wanting to harvest your bones to kissing you?"

"She still might harvest my bones. Violence is part of her mystique."

"You know what?" Mailer stood, pointing at Robbie with the look of a proud papa on his face. "You get the extra lasagna tonight."

"Seriously?" Robbie pretended to well up. "You're too good to me."

His roommate pointed to his own ORGASM DONOR sweatshirt.

"Hey. I wouldn't want to match hoodies with anyone else." He heaved his hockey bag onto his shoulder. "You can tell me your game plan on the ride home."

"My game plan for what?"

"The pitcher. If she's coming over tonight, I'll charge my noise-canceling headphones."

Skylar being discussed like a random hookup caused a bad taste to filter into Robbie's mouth. "Nah, it isn't like that."

Mailer snorted. "Right."

"It's not."

"What's it like?" The smugness slowly ebbed from his friend's face, replaced by abject horror. "Wait, are you trying to date this girl or something?"

"No," Robbie scoffed, zipping up his bag. Then . . . "Maybe. Sort of."

A suspicious pause ensued. "How do you sort of date somebody?"

Robbie didn't know how to explain the situation without sounding pathetic or reckless, so he laughed long and hard until Mailer had no choice but to join in. "Remember the catcher from this morning's game?" He wiped tears—of mirth?—from his eyes. "She's in love with him. We're going to pretend to date, so she can make him jealous."

Mailer's laughter abruptly cut off. "What the fuck did you say?"

Sig appeared at the end of the locker row. "Yeah. What?"

Burgess came into view beside Sig. "Against my better judgment, I, too, would like some context."

Of course, this was how Robbie finally got the vets to pay attention to him.

It had to be *this*.

"It's not a big deal. I'm just helping her out," Robbie started.

Sig raised an eyebrow. "Why?"

"Well, for starters, I acted like a presumptuous dickwad at the game this morning. Her words, not mine. I made her uncomfortable." Grandpa Nick would have been ashamed of him. He couldn't say that part out loud. "This felt like the least I could do."

"I'd say an apology is the least you could do," Burgess pointed out. "Pretending to date to make another guy jealous sounds above and beyond the typical mea culpa."

"Mea *what*?" Robbie griped. "Stop talking like you're in the Bible."

Burgess nearly stared a hole through Robbie's face.

"Sir Savage is right, though," Sig chimed in. "You could have apologized, bought her a coffee—"

"Orange juice."

"—and walked away whistling. Why are you *really* doing this?"

"You better not like her," Mailer said. "Do you *like* her? In a more than sex way?"

"Yup," Robbie said, dragging miserable hands down his face, accompanied by a long, drawn-out groan. "How did this happen?"

Mailer backed away from him. "Wow. You think you know someone."

"Wasn't it you who asked the new general manager out for sushi this week?" Robbie hurried to point out.

His roommate's expression didn't change, but he visibly winced at the mention of Reese Bauer, a take-no-prisoners type with big ambitions who'd recently assumed the GM spot in the wake of her father's departure. Mailer's eyeballs had nearly popped out of his head when she'd walked into their first team meeting less than a week ago. "I don't want to talk about it."

"Convenient."

Sig and Burgess traded a withering look. "All right, Corrigan." Sig sighed. "We've established this is a ridiculous situation you've put yourself in—"

"More ridiculous than spending every waking moment with your future stepsister?"

"Shut up," Sig snapped. "We're not talking about me. This is about you."

"Convenient."

"Yeah. Convenient," Mailer said, backing Robbie up, even though he was still openly disgusted that Robbie liked someone. "Word of the day."

"What is the actual plan, Corrigan?" Sig persisted. "A date or two? Just a nudge to get this catcher to pay attention?"

"I'm spending next week in Rhode Island with her family for a series of wilderness competitions. He'll be there. All of us are duking it out over a Pepsi can trophy. Normal, everyday shit."

Burgess's laughter boomed through the entirety of the locker room, while Sig and Mailer donned various expressions of incredulity.

"I'm not even going to address the wilderness competition thing, but suffice it to say? What the fuck. Let's focus on the rest. You're helping her land another guy," Sig enunciated. "But *you* like her, Corrigan."

While this happened to be one of the most demoralizing moments of Robbie's life, it was a necessary splash of cold water to the face. This plan he'd proposed to Skylar *was* crazy. If he liked her now, how much was he going to like her after a week? What the hell had he been thinking?

"Back out," Mailer said, slashing a hand through the air. "Tell her you're moving to France."

"She'll know I didn't move. We play hockey on television, bro."

Mailer shrugged. "Wear a disguise."

"Okay, are we done here? I need to eat two lasagnas."

"No, we're not done." Burgess stepped closer, poking Robbie in the collarbone with a finger that could have passed for a sandwich roll from Subway. "Next week is a light week, the lull before playoffs, but we've still got practice."

"I'm going to drive in for practice!"

"Fine. But you think you'll be worth a damn in playoffs if you're moping because the girl you like is with someone else?" Sir Savage shook his head. "This is bad."

"I concur, Captain." Sig sighed.

"I'm not backing out. She needs the help." Robbie begged himself to leave it at that, but obviously that line drive to the shoulder had knocked loose his sense of self-preservation. "I can't have her writing me off as some womanizing asshole. I don't think I realized that's who I'm becoming until she wouldn't even give me a chance. The worst part is, Grandpa Nick used to talk about this all the time. He said I'd meet a girl one day and she'd read me like a book, including the chapters that came before her. I didn't listen. So . . . yeah. This is kind of my way of making it up to my grandfather, too."

The other three men stayed quiet for way too long.

Sig and Burgess had twin expressions of grudging sympathy.

Mailer continued to look horrified.

"If you insist on doing this, you need to go in with the right mindset," Sig said, quieter now. "The last thing you want is to love someone if they don't return the feeling, you know?" Sig dipped his chin. "It's fake. You have to remember that."

Hope was beginning to transform Mailer's features. As though he was realizing he might not lose his nightly wingman after all. "Once you're done shaking off this psychosis, I'll be right here waiting with a variety of women to console you."

Wow. That didn't sound all that appealing, suddenly. *Should I be scared right now?* "So, just to recap, Mailer. You're not hot for the new GM anymore?"

Flinch. "Again, I don't want to talk about it."

Robbie rolled his eyes. "All right, look. I'm not suffering from some delusion that she'll change her mind and want me instead. You should see her talk about him." He laughed, but the sound verged on deflated. "She'll never talk about me like that. I've managed my expectations. I will come out of this unscathed. And more importantly, single."

Mailer bashed his fist against the locker and cheered.

Sig and Burgess looked dubious.

Robbie managed to keep his smile intact through two lasagnas and three episodes of *Reacher*, but when he got into bed that night and stared at the ceiling, seeing nothing but challenging brown eyes, the smile was long gone.

CHAPTER SEVEN

"I can't believe I'm doing this."

Skylar idled outside of a luxury high-rise in East Cambridge, her fingers clutched tightly around the steering wheel. Those digits only stiffened when Robbie Corrigan emerged through the double glass doors with a bag thrown over his shoulder, the picture of casual in loose, navy-blue sweatpants, slides, and a hoodie. A black ballcap was pulled low over his forehead, his red hair fanned out around the sides. He scanned the circular driveway in front of the building where plenty of other drivers waited to ferry residents to work on the other side of the Longfellow Bridge.

When he spotted her, he took off his hat and executed a quick bow, before slapping the ballcap back down over his messy bed head.

Skylar shook her head at him, but at the same time, she was noticing how the wind blew the material of his sweatpants up against his thickly muscled thighs. How the strap of his duffel bag journeyed between two hefty pecs, needlessly making them more prominent. She'd been pondering those pecs, more than she should have, because her breasts had made the unfortunate mistake of grazing them when she kissed him in a fit of temporary madness. They were hard as iron.

And all that pec pondering had led to mouth reminiscing.

It was a very nice mouth.

A very smoothly confident mouth that obviously got a lot of exercise.

Instead of stopping at the passenger door, Robbie swaggered past the window of her white 2017 Honda Accord, knocked on the trunk, and waited.

Waited for what?

A . . . hug, maybe? Should she get out and give him one?

Don't you dare acknowledge that ticklish strain in your nipples.

"Are you going to open the trunk or does our journey end here, Rocket?" Robbie shouted through the rear windshield.

"Oh!" Red-faced, she sprung the trunk open, slapping at the air-conditioning controls to turn up the air. "Sorry," she muttered a moment later, when he sprawled into the seat beside her, taking up way more space than anyone who'd ever occupied that side of the Honda. Dina could never. And those thighs were even more prolific up close.

Had he smelled like this on Saturday? Like musk and cinnamon?

No, she would have remembered. How long would her car smell like this after their week together ended? For some reason, knowing any part of him might linger was . . . daunting? Why?

Didn't matter.

Main takeaway: as far as fake boyfriends went, she could do a lot worse.

"Hey," he said, grinning at her from beneath the brim of his hat. "Miss me?"

"No, but I'm looking forward to it."

He let out one of those brief cracks of laughter. "This is so us, right? Starting off this adventure with contempt. Setting the tone."

Skylar implored the ceiling for patience, then put the Honda into drive. "Are you going to be this annoying the whole hour and a half drive?"

He flashed his teeth. "I'll put my unique charm on the back burner for now. We're going to need the full ninety minutes for you to educate me on your town, your family. You." She felt his attention travel down the side of her profile. "If we're going to be convincing, I'll need to know more than just the casual details."

Skylar had a lot more to discuss with him than backstory on this trip, but she needed to work up the courage first. "You live in a nice building."

"Yeah, thanks. Mailer and I went in on a condo together."

"Mailer, as in . . ."

"My teammate, wingman, buddy. Henry Mailer. We have separate bathrooms—that's the key to a successful marriage."

"I'll try and remember that." She glanced over at him. "Is it common for a professional athlete to have a roommate?"

"It's more common than you think. First year in the league, nothing feels stable enough yet to put down roots. Everyone upstairs is watching to see if you live up to expectations." He made himself more comfortable in the seat. "Mailer and I have a deal that whoever moves out first has to pay the other back for their half of the condo. Just in case one of us gets traded. Or . . . other horrible things that shan't be named."

"Like a career-ending injury?"

He clutched at his chest. "Jesus, woman. You of all people should know you're not supposed to put that possibility out into the universe."

"Sorry," she muttered, genuinely chagrined, because he was right. She did know better. She blamed her lack of tact on the topic weighing heavily on her mind. How she'd bring it up. How he would react. "For what it's worth, you've obviously had numerous blows to the head and you're still playing."

"Good point," he said without missing a beat. "Mailer and I also co-own a truck, but he has custody this week."

"This sounds like a totally normal friendship with healthy boundaries."

"Thank you for noticing," he said, smiling unironically. "What about you? What's your living situation?"

"I live alone." She rolled her lips inward to wet them. "I'm kind of meticulous when it comes to my surroundings. I need things to be in their place. For instance, I can't fall asleep if someone else is watching television in the living room. I just need everything and everyone to be settled and in their place in order to relax. It made the first year of college, when I was living in the dorm, pretty difficult."

"Yeah, I can imagine." He was watching her thoughtfully, as if running back through that explanation more than once. "A messy outdoor competition must be pretty hard for you, then."

"No joke."

"Why do you compete in these games, then?"

"I don't really have a choice. When you meet my parents, you'll understand." Skylar accelerated to join the flow of traffic on I-95. "My stepdad's name is Doug, by the way. My mother is Vivica. They both grew up in Rhode Island." A tickle of discomfort made itself known in her throat, spreading as she spoke. "They both attended Brown, though they didn't meet until much later in life. Everyone in my family, including Elton, has attended Brown. Except me."

"You wanted to shake things up?"

It took her a breath to respond. "No, I didn't get accepted."

"Oh." Robbie shifted his attention to the windshield, as if he knew she didn't want to be scrutinized in that moment. "Guess they made a mistake, so."

"You don't have to say that," Skylar rushed to say, deftly blocking the feeling of gratitude. Nope. She'd blown her opportunity and she needed to own that. "Anyway, unlike me, you are googleable. I memorized your bio on the Bearcats website, so I know you grew up on Long Island. Attended Quinnipiac. Drafted in the second round last year by the Bearcats. Can eat a breakfast sandwich in three bites."

"I can eat a breakfast sandwich in *one* bite. I was being polite."

She made an interested sound. "Could there be a gentleman lurking in there after all?"

"If there is, I doubt we're going to find out this week." He reached up and took hold of the handle over the door. "Not when there's an aluminum can trophy on the line."

"That's the spirit." She realized her lips were turned upward at the corners, but the fledgling smile froze in place when she remembered the plan she'd formulated. Was this her opening to bring it up? Was he going to hear this idea and immediately ask her to turn around, drive him back to East Cambridge? Because Skylar had worked on her proposal in the shower and the whole thing sounded a lot crazier out loud than it looked on paper. *Everything* looked better on paper. "So, I have a tiny little proposition for you, Redbeard . . ."

"Thank God you said something. Yes, I'm hungry. I'll stop anywhere."

"In a while. It's something else."

"Fire away."

"Okay." She flexed her fingers on the wheel. "Okay, I just want to preempt this by saying, you can decline. Obviously. No hard feelings. If you say no, we'll just move on and pretend like this never happened."

He turned in the seat to face her. "Holy shit, I'm so intrigued right now."

"It's definitely intriguing. I'll give it that." Deep breaths. In, out. "The objective of this week is not only to win the Page Stakes, but to make Madden notice me, right? Well, here's the thing. What if he actually *does*? Notice me." Needing something to do with her hands, she fiddled with the radio, flipping through various Sirius XM stations and landing on some alternative. "I don't know how to seal the deal. I'm not great at flirting. My, um . . . physical encounters with guys have been kind of awkward. So even if we *do* manage to get Madden's attention, I have no idea how to keep it."

Robbie was quiet for a full ten seconds. "Okay, like, this is serious. You're being serious. You don't think you're enough to keep someone's attention."

He sounded so incredulous. Why? "I mean, I haven't kept anyone's attention before, so . . . the proof is in the pudding, isn't it?"

"Maybe *you* just haven't liked any of the guys enough to bother. Have you thought about that?"

Did he sound a little pissed off? No. He was likely just irritated that she'd lured him on this trip under one pretense, then sprung a totally new game plan. "Whatever the reason is that I've been single my whole life, I just want to make sure I'm ready. *Really* ready. In case this ruse works. You know?"

"Where do I come in?"

"Well . . ." The temperature of Skylar's skin started to elevate, her scalp prickling. "We've established that you like women and women like you. Hooking up is pretty much your specialty." In her periphery, she noticed Robbie's shoulders slump ever so slightly, but couldn't imagine why. He'd bragged about this exact truth a matter of days ago. "Maybe you could teach me to do the things . . . that women do to attract you?"

She glanced over to gauge his reaction, but found his expression blank. The only telling movement was the heavy rise and fall of his chest. "I thought . . . I mean, I want to be *better* than how I've been, Rocket—"

"Oh, I hope you didn't misunderstand me before," she rushed

to say. "There's no shame in having as many partners as you want, as long as they're treated with respect, you know? And, um . . . well. There's also no reason all that experience and knowledge in your head couldn't be harnessed for the greater good, right?"

"Greater good," Robbie repeated slowly. "Meaning . . . ?"

"Meaning, if you say yes to . . . teaching me some moves, the best part is that you won't— you *don't* get attached. It's guilt free." Skylar gave a rueful laugh. "And come on, it's for a worthy cause."

Brow puckered, Robbie stared out at the highway, his white-knuckled fist gripping the strap of his seat belt. Uh-oh. Any second now he'd ask to be taken home. "I strongly disagree with the way you're making yourself sound like a charity case, Skylar," he said instead. "And I don't . . . I don't *want* you to have moves that other girls have."

"Why?"

"I don't know!" When she only raised an eyebrow at him, he visibly searched for a qualifying statement. "You have your own moves. You just haven't located them yet."

"Let's say I believe that. *How* am I going to locate them?"

Robbie swallowed loudly. "WWBD," he said to himself. "WWBD."

Skylar did a double take. "What does that mean?"

"What would Burgess do? I'm trying to imagine him in this situation."

"And?"

"Turns out it only works for hockey. I got nothing."

All right, clearly he wasn't comfortable with the idea of teaching her how to operate around men. *Drop it. Now.* Pushing too hard on something like this would make her behavior as bad as Robbie's that day at the baseball field. "Should I stop at Dunkin' or Denny's?"

Now it was Robbie's turn to do a double take. "That's it? We're done talking about this?"

"Yes. Easy as that."

"Oh, sure, easy. Right."

"Dunkin' or—"

"What kind of moves are we talking about? Flirting and . . . what?"

Skylar took a very heavy gulp. Braced. "If you open my glove compartment, there's a white leather planner. There's a slip of paper folded in the middle. It's an . . . itinerary. Of potential lessons, so to speak."

He almost broke the glove compartment getting it open. Seeing her beloved planner in Robbie's hands gave her a warm, unexpected flip in her stomach. No one had ever touched that planner, save her, and his long, blunt—and somewhat crooked—fingers looked so masculine tracing along the softness of the spine, the breath caught in her throat.

What is wrong with you?

Skylar gripped the wheel and ordered her pulse back into its usual rhythm, but the sound of him unfolding the paper shot it sky-high again.

CHAPTER EIGHT

Robbie stared down at the neatly lettered timeline in front of him.

It was a five-day calendar of the current week. Each day, there was a new lesson, and each lesson had been penned in a different color.

Such innocent teals and pinks for writing phrases like:

SUNDAY: Flirting
MONDAY: Date Night Practice
TUESDAY: Making Out
WEDNESDAY: Blow Job Workshop
THURSDAY: Main Event (Maybe)

Fucking. That meant fucking. Maybe.

Son. Of a bitch.

This was the hottest thing he'd ever laid eyes on. Besides Skylar. And his dick was acting accordingly, turning to stone in his sweatpants, perspiration starting to bead at the hairline hidden beneath his ballcap. *Let me get this straight.* If he went along with this plan to be her professor of love, every day for the next week, he would not only be allowed to perform these activities with Skylar, he would be encouraged to do them.

Teach *her* how to do them.

He didn't deserve to be this incredible woman's sex tutor.

At all. Like *at all*.

Which is why there was a catch. A huge one.

He'd be teaching her all this for the benefit of another dude.

So . . . at the end of the day, was this *heaven* or *hell*?

Jesus, though. Even knowing hell might lie on the other side of this five-day crash course, he couldn't stop himself. Not a chance in hell. Even the idea of flirting with her was making his balls throb, let alone a *blow job workshop*.

Had a more magical phrase ever been uttered?

And dammit, even knowing these skills would eventually be put to use on someone else, he hated the possibility of her going through life thinking she was . . . less than. In any way. An ache that had started to form at the beginning of the conversation intensified now.

I have to show her she's the holy grail. She needs to know.

The fact that Skylar, a Division 1 all-American who could cut him off at the knees with a well-timed insult, had *any* doubt in herself at all made Robbie wonder.

Where the hell had that self-doubt come from?

"You're very quiet over there."

"Sorry, I've never seen blow jobs on an itinerary before."

Ever so slightly, she winced. "I grew up around my brother's friends. I know how much those skills are valued. But we can skip that one if—"

His booming laughter almost caused her to crash the car. "No, no. It stays."

Skylar blinked over at him. "Wait, so you're in? You'll help me?"

Robbie could practically hear Sig, Burgess, and Mailer shouting at him to say no immediately, turn back now before it was too late and Robbie ended up falling for this girl. Because he was halfway there already and this sexy list almost guaranteed he'd be wrapped around her little finger by the end of the week.

Don't do it, imaginary Mailer hissed at him. *Come back. Let's go clubbing.*

Show me a single man alive who would say no to this.

That's fair. Mailer again. *Just remain objective. Don't be in it for anything but the sex.*

"Okay, got it," Robbie said.

"Got what?"

"I meant, yes. I'm in."

When Skylar put the car in park and the engine abruptly cut out, Robbie almost had a heart attack. He'd thought they were still on the fucking highway.

Nope. They were in the parking lot of a Dunkin'.

This dirty calendar had blown a fuse in his brain.

"Should we start now?" Skylar asked, blowing another one. *Pew. Pew.*

"Here?"

"What's the matter?" She pursed her lips at him. "You've never flirted in a Dunkin' Donuts parking lot before?"

Funny how she didn't seem to realize the way she naturally challenged him *was* flirting. The best kind, apparently, because his whole body started to thrum. "Go on." Robbie jerked his chin toward the rear of the car. "I'll meet you at the trunk."

"As long as you don't stuff me inside of it."

"Not until I get my blow job."

Skylar giggled on her way out of the car and Robbie's breath hitched in response, his gaze zeroing in on that tiny little gap that formed between her jeans and the small of her back when she exited. A miniature handle he wanted to slide his fingers into to tug her back into the vehicle and kiss her senseless. That wasn't happening until Tuesday, though, according to the schedule, and he wasn't going to push his luck.

She knocked on the rear window. "What are you doing in there?"

Answer: waiting for his erection to go away. It was one thing to flirt in a Dunkin' parking lot. It was quite another to do it at full mast in broad daylight. Problem was, his brain had made it to the end of the itinerary to "Main Event (Maybe)" and now every part of his body was sweating. Would they have to fabricate some excuse to leave her family and hump it out in a parking lot somewhere, his jeans around his knees, her panties torn down the middle, the car rocking steadily faster?

Goddamn.

Wherever this ended up (maybe) taking place, he'd bring his A-game.

She'd be a changed woman afterward.

And somehow, some way, he'd make sure he wasn't too much of a changed man.

"I give up," Robbie muttered when his dick adopted a heartbeat. Giving himself a junk adjustment, he climbed out of the passenger side. Quick glance down to make sure the thing wasn't pointing east like a weathervane, then he put as much swagger into his step as humanly possible, rolling to a stop in front of a curious-looking Skylar where she leaned back against the trunk, watching his approach. "It's the first of the month, Rocket. Time to pay up." He eased into her personal space, using his knuckle to tilt her head back. "You've been living in my head rent-free."

She blinked, lips parting.

Nailed it.

A laugh burst out of her, the force of it causing her legs to lose their balance, her butt landing on the rear bumper. The girl was literally shaking.

"No, you didn't," she gasped, holding her ribs.

"What?"

"I hope you're happy. You've disgraced this hallowed Dunkin' Donuts parking lot." Skylar sailed through another round of laughter. "I can't believe you used a pickup line on me."

"Pickup lines exist for a reason," Robbie defended. "A man has to start somewhere. You're lucky I didn't ask to buy you a coffee, because I like you a latte. I thought about it."

She was laughing so hard at this point, her eyes were starting to turn glassy.

This wasn't going well. At all.

Robbie loved the sound of her laugh, but he didn't take her shocked amusement as a good sign when they were supposed to be flirting. Time to turn it up a notch. Which he hadn't been required to do in . . . ever. And something inside of him, possibly his competitive nature or maybe just an intense need to appeal to this woman, had Robbie leaning down and hovering his mouth a hair away from Skylar's. Close enough to taste orange juice on her breath. "You're fucking beautiful all the time, but especially when you laugh."

Ironically, her mirth died down, brown eyes running a curious lap around his face. "I'm already confused about flirting. So far, according to you, it's either cheesy or intense. Isn't it supposed to fall somewhere in between?"

"It's a mixture of both. Making you laugh, but also making sure you know . . ."

"Know what?"

An exhale hissed out of him. "That I'd like to wake up tomorrow with your knees imprinted on my mattress."

Her chest dipped. "Any girl's knees, you mean."

No. He didn't. But this was her way of reminding him of the barrier between them, wasn't it? This wasn't real, no matter how much he wanted it to be. She was there to learn from him, not to make an actual connection. Still . . . "If we're going to be convincing this week, maybe you just have to pretend I'm talking about you, Skylar. All the time."

She thought about that, no idea it was the truth. "Yeah, you're probably right."

Taking her wrist, Robbie tugged her off the bumper. "Come on, let's go get breakfast." He twined their fingers together, ignoring the lump that welled in his throat over how right it felt, and guided her toward the Dunkin' entrance. "Pretend we're a couple. We'll keep working on flirting."

Skylar's wide-eyed gaze brushed over their joined hands. "Okay."

"It's your turn for a pickup line, so start thinking."

"The pressure is on," she muttered, following him into the air-conditioned shop, the coffee- and sugar-scented air enveloping them on all sides, "Smooth Operator" drifting out of the unseen speakers. There was nobody in line, so they walked up to the register hand in hand. Skylar ordered an orange juice and a chocolate glaze, while Robbie ordered three breakfast sandwiches and a large coffee, cream and sugar, please and thank you.

The young man working behind the counter handed Skylar her donut right away and she took a bite while they stepped aside and waited for Robbie's food to be ready.

"Okay, I think I've got a pickup line. Be forewarned, it might be terrible."

Robbie tried not to stare at her mouth as she chewed, knowing full well it would taste like chocolate oranges. Still sweating in all the places. "Let's hear it, Rocket."

She swallowed her bite, squared her shoulders like she was preparing to throw a pitch. "If you were this donut I'm eating, you'd already be inside me."

Immediately, he choked on his spit, dissolving into a coughing fit right there in the middle of Dunkin'. "Holy shit, girl," he managed.

"That bad?"

More sweating. His waistband tuck job wasn't going to last. But his own suffering became an afterthought in the face of Skylar's growing embarrassment. "Bad? *What?* That was *hot.*" *Just please don't say that ever again to anyone but me. Please.* "Don't quote me on this, but I think you might be a natural."

She rolled her eyes. "Shut up."

"I won't shut up. That was advanced."

"Well . . ." She shrugged, a little cockier now. "I was raised around a lot of boys."

"Believe me, you do them proud. I almost choked on my tongue." Completely forgetting himself, Robbie reached up and brushed a speck of glaze from the corner of Skylar's mouth. "Now, say it again, but give me body language at the same time."

"What kind?"

Never having explained flirting out loud before, Robbie took a moment to think. About what he'd die to have Skylar do to him. What would make him hot. Or hotter, as it were. "Look at my mouth when you say it. Touch me in some way."

She nodded for a few seconds, then stopped. "Touch you how? Give me an example."

Gladly.

Looking her in the eye, he moved closer, smoothing back some wayward hair that curled near her right temple. Then he let his fingers skim down, down to her neck, right behind her ear, just the barest hint of his fingertips connecting with her smooth skin, gratified when he left goose bumps in his wake. "No one should ever touch you like this, unless you asked, okay?"

"I know," she half whispered, studying him with a small wrinkle in her brow.

"If someone ever does that, you come find me. I'll go find them."

"Not if I kill them first."

Lips twitching reluctantly, he let his hand drop away, all five digits continuing to tingle. "Good."

After a beat, Skylar raised her hand and repeated the action identically, which Robbie found so endearing it was almost painful, because he didn't have those little flyaway hairs at his temple, but who cared? Who gave two shits when her touch was trailing down the cords of his neck and her gaze was locked on his mouth. God, it was a struggle not to breathe like he'd just played a full period of hockey without substitutions.

"If you were this donut I'm eating, you'd already be inside me," she murmured, surprising him by dipping her fingertips past the collar of his hoodie, tugging lightly on one of the strings playfully, before letting her hand fall to her side once again. "How was that?"

"Really good," he rasped, abdomen flexed tighter than a drum.

A voice was shouting in the back of his head, probably some kind of warning that he was already getting in too deep with Skylar, feelings-wise. And the voice only got louder—

"Robbie, they're calling your number." She waved a hand in front of his eyes. "Your pile of sandwiches is ready."

"Oh. Yeah." He turned on a heel and stumbled to the counter, wincing when the man behind the counter gave him a knowing smirk.

This trip was off to a fine start.

CHAPTER NINE

As Skylar took the exit off 95 that would take them to Cumberland and her family home, a familiar knot started to form in the dead middle of her stomach. It wasn't the kind of knot that tied itself around her intestines before she pitched a game. Nor was it the type of low, confusing knot she'd experienced back in the roadside Dunkin' Donuts during her first official flirting lesson.

Right up until now, she'd been thinking almost exclusively about the latter knot. How tight it had cinched when Robbie said, *No one should ever touch you like this, unless you asked, okay?* And then proceeded to hype her up over that cringey pickup line.

This guy . . . surprised her?

A lot of things about today were surprising her. Like how comfortable the occasional silence was between them as they drove. How she felt ever so slightly more confident in herself as a potential romantic partner for someone since he showed up—a very different kind of confidence than the type she'd developed as an athlete. The kind she'd pretended not to want for a really long time, usually while sitting on her couch Friday nights wondering if she was missing out on an important part of being young. Or if she was too uptight to relax and allow herself to be in a mood for flirting. Romance.

And as she put her Honda in park in the driveway of her parents' giant, log-cabin-style home, nestled among the trees, the third type of knot started to harden and fossilize in her midsection— and Skylar was glad not to be alone.

When she made no move to exit the car, Robbie looked at her. "You good?"

"Yeah."

"Really? You've been holding my hand for the last mile. I'm not complaining," he rushed to add. "They might have to amputate due to an extended loss of circulation, but at least it's my left hand. I can probably still play hockey with some minor adjustments—"

His words sunk in gradually through the anxiousness and she let go of him abruptly. "Oh. God. Sorry."

"It's okay." He closed that hand into a tight fist. "Are you worried about pulling this dating ruse off?"

"Of course, I am. But mainly . . ." She pulled in a breath, searching the windows of the house for signs of life. "My family is a lot."

"We're here for a wilderness competition, Rocket. I gathered that."

Weirdly pleased that he'd kept up, a brief smile tilted her lips, even if the tightness in her chest had started to gather again. "I told you how this is a second marriage for my parents, right? I was so little when my mother divorced my biological father, I don't even remember what he was like in person. He moved back to the West Coast to be closer to family and over the years, we sort of drifted. Our communication slowed down throughout high school and now it's almost nonexistent, even if he still sends birthday cards. But sometimes . . . I wonder if I'm more like him than Doug and Vivica. Elton."

He didn't say anything right away. "Keep going."

"Well." She slicked a hand down her ponytail. "I *am* competitive, just like them. You know this. But I don't always feel like I gelled as easily as the three of them did."

"Why not?"

They weren't even inside yet and she could see the memorabilia on the walls. Vivica even owned a set of Brown pot holders. "Us getting into Brown was all my parents talked about for the first six years of their marriage. Elton sailed right in, no problem. Played ball for them and graduated with honors. I . . . didn't get in. I totally bumbled the interview with my admissions counselor. Even with two alumni parents and a star athlete for a brother, I got rejected." Skylar swallowed. "When I come here for this competition now, sometimes I feel like I'm trying to prove I belong in the fold, despite . . . leaving it."

Again, Robbie was silent for a handful of seconds. Then, "Jesus Christ, Skylar. You're attending Boston University. That's not exactly clown college."

"I know. I *know* it's a great school. But it's not Brown. You'll see what I mean."

"You're a perfectionist. Obviously getting a rejection is going to sting like hell, but, hey . . . I've been rejected, too."

"By women?"

"God, no. By hockey teams." He unhooked his seat belt, so he could turn more of his big body in her direction. "When I was in high school, I couldn't break into the AAA division for three long years. My teammates and best friends moved up, but I continued to be held back. I nearly quit at one point." His eyes softened. "Once after a particularly brutal tryout, Grandpa Nick took me to fly kites. All three of them caught the air at different times, even though he let them go all at once. That's always stuck with me, you know? We all catch the air at different times."

It was a rare thing, Skylar being captured so thoroughly by another person's enthusiasm that she momentarily forgot to worry or fret about the time. What *else* she could be doing. There was just Robbie and his eager expression, waiting to see if his words had made an impact—

The front door of the house blew open.

Her father, Doug Page, exited with his trumpet aloft, heralding Skylar and Robbie's arrival with a boisterous rendition of the "Star-Spangled Banner" while Vivica, her mother, hustled out into the open behind him carrying a half watermelon full of tinier balled melons impaled by toothpicks. They stopped at the edge of the porch, beaming down at the car in matching red polo shirts and chinos.

"Oh my God," Robbie said without moving his mouth. "Are they AI?"

"No, but they are about to be freakishly nice to you. Don't buy it. They are just sizing up the competition." Skylar smiled and waved through the windshield, while gathering her phone and keys. "From this point forward everything—and I mean everything—you say will be used against you. Do you understand?"

"Show no weaknesses. Ten four."

"Right. So . . ." The pulse at the base of her neck beat like a hummingbird's wings. "From here on out, we're a couple."

"We're *the* couple."

"Robbie." She put a hand on his arm before he could open the passenger door, a sweeping sense of responsibility pillowing in her stomach. "If this gets to be too weird or too much . . . either the competition or the pretending . . . I won't hold it against you to bail, okay?"

"Yes, you would."

"Yes, I would."

He reached across the front of the car and traced Skylar's

cheekbone with his thumb, his mossy eyes seeming to catalog her features one by one. "See? I know you already, don't I?"

"Wow." She peeked at her parents out of the corner of her eye, noting they were riveted, and nuzzled her cheek into Robbie's palm. "You might have missed your calling as a professional fake boyfriend."

"Fake. Yeah." Chuckling, he took his hand back. "Shall we?"

"Let the psychological warfare commence."

They climbed out of the car at the same time, meeting at the front bumper where Robbie clasped her suddenly clammy hand tightly within his larger one, squeezing it reassuringly. "Hey, Mom. Hey, Dad." Skylar took a deep breath. "This is Robbie."

"Robbie!" Vivica exclaimed, setting down the watermelon on a wicker coffee table and sailing down the stairs, her toned and tanned arms outstretched. She wrapped them around Skylar and inhaled deeply, rocking her daughter, so similar in build and coloring, side to side. And Skylar hugged Vivica back, absorbing the affection, knowing the love was genuine, but also so unsure how to nurture it. "It is such a pleasure to meet you," Vivica said, breaking the embrace with Skylar to grasp Robbie's hand. "Welcome to our home—and the ninth annual Page Stakes!"

"Thanks for having me—"

"We should have known our little Skylar wouldn't take last year's loss to Team Foul Balls lying down," boomed Doug, chest puffed. "She went and joined forces with a professional athlete, did she? Fight fire with fire! She got that from me."

"Sadly, none of our competitions involve skates and a stick," her mother said with a sweetly sympathetic smile. "Do you have any *useful* outdoor skills?"

"Here we go," Skylar muttered, poised to defend him, like a good fake girlfriend.

"Oh, I do." Robbie sniffed. "But I'm not telling *you* what they are."

Her parents traded an impressed look. "We've got a live one, honey."

Doug rubbed his hands together. "Ooh-wee. This is going to be interesting."

"That's one way to describe her canoodling with the dude who gave me a sore nose and a black eye," called Elton, appearing in the side yard. Madden sauntered closer in Elton's wake, that characteristic broodiness thickening his energy. He seemed to be looking through the assembled group, searching for something that he didn't find, but then again, that's how he always looked— and Skylar *loved* how he looked. Sturdy and patient and somber and eternal. That was Madden.

"Looks like it's healing nicely," Robbie commented as Skylar's brother drew even with the group, Madden arriving seconds later, but hanging toward the back, quiet as ever.

Feeling Robbie's gaze on her profile, Skylar realized she was staring at her longtime crush and shook herself. "First of all, Elton, the word 'canoodling' isn't for you. Drop it from your vocabulary. Second, please enlighten Mom and Dad as to who threw the first punch."

Elton waved off the request. "Irrelevant."

"Spoiler alert. It was Elton," Skylar stage-whispered to her parents.

"Only because he was harassing my sister." Robbie's hand flinched inside of hers at the reminder of the morning they met. For some silly reason, she decided to give him a reassuring squeeze this time. After all, wasn't he here to make up for his behavior that day? "What is he doing here?" Elton burst out, as if an explanation was long overdue. "Bad enough you kissed him right in front of me, Sky. I've actually considered bleaching my eyeballs, by the way—"

"Don't do it," Robbie rasped. "Trust me."

Elton scowled. "Now you're what? *Official?*"

"That's right," Robbie responded, his gaze level.

"And your first official date is observing the Page Stakes?"

"He's not observing." Skylar lifted her chin. "He's my team-mate."

Madden's head jerked up, his blue eyes concerned. "What about Eve?"

"Eve has to work through spring break." No help for it. Sky-lar's tone turned to velvet when addressing Madden. "She can't make it this year."

Her brother's best friend didn't like hearing that at all. Of course he didn't. He was compassionate and thoughtful. He wouldn't want Eve missing their one chance for the four child-hood friends to be together every year, right? "I'll go see her," Madden said, breaking from the group. "Maybe I can cover some shifts."

"Don't even think about it, man. We're defending champs," Elton called after Madden. "Get your head in the game."

"Gosh. Have you always been this empathetic, Elt?" Skylar mused.

Robbie chuckled at her sarcasm.

Everyone looked sharply at Robbie.

Down at Skylar's and Robbie's connected hands.

Then at one another.

"Isn't there a rule stating that any changes to the teams have to be reported in advance?" Elton asked. "A few hours before the opening ceremony doesn't count."

Vivica inclined her head. "The change was reported before-hand. Your sister emailed me days ago."

"And you didn't tell me?" Elton was appalled.

"And lose the element of surprise?" Doug scoffed. "We need to take every available advantage." He rubbed at his lower back with the hand not holding the trumpet. "We no longer have youth on our side, you know."

Skylar and Elton traded a smirk.

"Uh-uh. You're not going to play that old and feeble card, so we underestimate you. It didn't work last year and it won't work now." Elton exhaled up at the sky. "So the hockey player is around for the whole week, huh?"

"Afraid so." Robbie tugged Skylar into his side. "Longer if I'm lucky."

"Gross." Her brother gave Robbie a disgusted once-over. "Don't think we won't be having the 'hurt my sister and die' talk."

"Looking forward to it," Robbie said without so much as a blink.

Elton rubbed the corner of his eye with a knuckle while muttering under his breath something about *getting himself into this mess*, before wearily stalking up the porch steps into the house. "Thank God Sky's bedroom is the farthest one from mine."

When her parents and Madden turned and followed him, Robbie leaned over to whisper in her ear. "We're going to be in one bedroom? Singular?"

Skylar studied his face for signs of early regrets but saw only pure, unadulterated hope. Like he was actually *holding his breath* for confirmation they'd be staying in the same room. This man was a grade A horndog, through and through. "You seem even less bothered by sharing a bed than you were about the blow job workshop."

"Facts."

"We're sticking to the schedule."

"I'll stick it to whatever you want."

A laugh snuck out, so she shoved him for the sake of balance. "*Robbie.*"

He allowed himself to stumble back, never losing his grin. "Yeah?"

Skylar shook her head at him, then said, "As far as introductions go with my crazy family, that one was pretty decent."

A combination of relief and pleasure moved across his features. "We got this in the bag, Rocket."

"Don't get cocky yet, Redbeard," she said, ascending backward up the steps. "There will be curveballs."

There was something she couldn't quite read about his tone when he said, "I'm ready."

CHAPTER TEN

Walking into Skylar's childhood bedroom was like stepping into a time capsule.

Replace the baseball posters with hockey and it could have been *his* room—if it wasn't for the subtle feminine touches, like the lamp on her bedside table with a shade made of feathers. The light teal pintuck comforter. A vanity in the corner with a little stool in front of it, adjacent to a shoe rack filled with muddy cleats in various sizes.

She must have noticed Robbie's eye drawn to the cleats, because she sighed. "It's so weird, I know. I can never throw them out, even when they're falling apart."

"No, I'm the same with skates."

"Are you?"

"Sure. Hard to toss something that was with you through a whole season of wins and losses. They hold all the sweat and blood. They're yours."

Skylar slid him a surprised look. "Exactly."

He'd never dated a fellow athlete before. If he recalled correctly, one of his high school girlfriends had been on the soccer team, but high school soccer was a far cry from the heights Skylar had reached. That took a lot of drive and ambition. Qualities he was extra familiar with. Now, as he stood shoulder to shoulder with Skylar, relating to her, Robbie tried to remember what he usually spoke about to women. Surely, they talked about *something* other than the logistics of where the bone down would be taking place. Right?

It was possible that he'd simply never tried to get to know anyone as well as he wanted to know Skylar.

"What's your pregame ritual?" he asked now.

"Whoa. Personal."

"We're going to be sharing a bedroom for a week. Might as well start getting personal now."

She squinted an eye. "Should we lay some ground rules for that, by the way? I mean, we're not *actually* together."

Out of nowhere, there was a rock stuck in his windpipe.

"I know you're going to be passing on some tips and tricks," she continued. "But we're here for a purpose."

Robbie did his best to maintain his affable expression, even though his lungs felt deprived of oxygen. "I don't exactly need a reminder after you nearly fainted at the sight of ol' Madden in the front yard. Should I be carrying smelling salts on me at all times?"

"Am I that obvious?" Skylar winced.

"Yes." He cleared his throat. *Stop now before you start to sound jealous.*

Was he jealous?

Come on, guy. You've been jealous since the coffee shop.

The sick feeling in his belly worsened now, minute to minute. "If you want ground rules, lay them. Otherwise, we'll stick to your calendar. You tell me what is a yes or a no." He looked her in the eye. "I know how to listen, Skylar."

They maintained eye contact for several seconds, him impressing on her that she was safe and in control, her searching him with surprise for the second time since they'd walked into the room. "My pregame ritual is listening—in my AirPods—to Whitney Houston sing the national anthem at the Super Bowl in

1991," she blurted, seeming a little shocked that she'd admitted it out loud, but also excited to share. "Have you seen it?"

"I . . . don't know."

"You would know," she said, full of passion.

"Then I haven't."

"Try it someday, before a game. It's the best live performance by anyone. Ever. It makes me want to go out and pitch the innings of my life. It makes me want . . ."

"Immortality."

"Yeah." Skylar breathed a laugh that left a smile on her face and it hit Robbie, right in that moment, that there was definitely no one more beautiful than her in the fucking world. "Yeah, it sounds weird, but I want to leave something like that behind."

"I throw up before every game," he said, distracted enough by her sparkling eyes to ruin the moment. Or he might have ruined it if Skylar was someone else. But she wasn't. She was a person who'd pushed their body to limits it couldn't handle and . . . visibly understood.

Damn. I have to find me a woman who doesn't get grossed out by throwing up.

You did.

She's right here.

And she's in love with someone else.

"Wow. Interesting choice to bring up pregame rituals when that is yours."

"I should have lied and said I listen to Lil' Wayne," he managed on a chuckle, feeling more than a little winded.

"Why didn't you lie?"

Mildly insulted, he drew back. "I wouldn't tell you I know how to listen to yes and no, then lie to you in the same breath."

Skylar scrutinized him from a distance that had definitely grown smaller since they walked into the room. Who had moved closer? And when? "Maybe it's premature to say this, but I'm not sure anymore that . . . you're exactly who I thought you were."

It wasn't easy, but Robbie managed not to show on his face how relieved he was to hear that. How . . . honored. "Thank God for that."

Skylar seemed to realize their bodies were about to brush and stepped back, quipping, "To be fair, you've still got a *long* way to go."

Robbie scrubbed at his beard. "Oh, yeah. Obviously."

"Was that flirting just now?" she asked, after a beat, clearly thrown that their proximity hadn't registered earlier. He'd been close enough to kiss her.

God, I'd die to kiss her.

"If so, you're getting better at it," Robbie said. "I couldn't even tell you were trying."

"I wasn't," she said, mostly to herself, her brows drawing together. "Trying, that is."

Maybe . . . she didn't have to try.

Maybe she was a little bit attracted to him?

Normally, women being attracted to Robbie was a given, but not with Skylar. This new possibility that the chemical reaction he experienced in her presence might go both ways was the best news he'd received since getting drafted by the Bearcats.

It was also dangerous.

Robbie was already falling for Skylar. The only thing keeping him realistic and grounded about his chances was the fact that she loved someone else. But if he had attraction on his side? Hope opened doors. Hope made him feel like he had a shot.

And he didn't. So he needed to keep his eyes wide open.

"I'll go get the bags out of the car," he managed on his way into the hallway. "You want your planner?"

That threw her. She opened her mouth, closed it. "Yes, please."

He turned and went before he could reach too much into the silent appreciation arranging her features.

THE OPENING CEREMONY was a cookout in the backyard, thankfully. Robbie had been entertaining visions of blood sacrifices and the summoning of ancient deities, so the sizzle of burgers on the grill was a welcome sound, instead of his own tormented screams.

In attendance were the usual suspects from the earlier front yard introductions, henceforth known as the following:

Team Silver Hair = Doug and Vivica (another obvious ploy to dupe everyone into counting them out because of their age; not happening).

Team Foul Balls = Madden and Elton (a joke they'd obviously come up with as teenagers; it hadn't aged well).

Team Skeeve = Skylar and Eve (a combination of their names that they clearly hadn't chosen, but it had stuck nonetheless).

The six of them stood around the firepit in the backyard, sizing one another up, quietly conferring with their counterparts and sipping straight water. No one was consuming a drop of alcohol, which would have made the gathering a shoo-in for the most boring cookout of all time, except it wasn't. Not at all.

For one, Skylar was there.

And two, this was Robbie's chance to properly get a read on Madden.

Did the big, quiet dude with the Irish brogue like her back? Was he into Skylar and merely prevented from pursuing her due to his best-friend status with Elton? If so, he was a lot more noble than Robbie, because Robbie would have gone for her anyway, damn the consequences.

Problem was, Madden wasn't an easy read. His expression rarely shifted from silent observation. He definitely looked at

Skylar every once in a while, that attention lingering long enough for tension to build in Robbie's neck, but beyond an open flicker of curiosity from the guy now and again, Robbie couldn't glean much else.

Now was a good time to remind himself he was supposed to *want* Madden to notice Skylar. As more than a kid sister. As the beautiful woman she was. That was the goal. That's why he'd volunteered to be there this week. He'd come to Cumberland to help Skylar land this man. He needed to focus on making that happen instead of wondering about the what-ifs; for example, what if Madden wasn't interested?

Would she . . . could she . . . turn her attention to Robbie?

Better squash that hope now before it grows teeth.

A flame licked out of the firepit in Skylar's direction and Robbie moved without thinking, hooking an arm around the small of her back and walking them backward and out of the literal line of fire. "Careful," he said, looking down into her startled face.

"Thanks," she said, wetting her lips. Her attention drifted over his shoulder to the others. "Maybe you should let me go now. Everyone is staring."

"Maybe that's exactly why I shouldn't."

"Ohhh. Okay, good point." Damn, she was the perfect height. Tall enough that he wouldn't have to bend his knees to kiss her. Short enough that she had to tip her face up to make eye contact, the sunset bathing her smooth cheeks, picking up hints of gold hidden in the depths of her brown eyes. "Time for another round of flirting practice?"

Robbie waggled his brows. "Thought you'd never ask."

She started to relax more and more in his loose hold, her fingers even lifting to toy with the buttons of the white polo shirt he'd thrown on. "Look at me go. I'm touching, like you taught me."

Like you taught me.

Was it sick to be turned on by that phrasing?

Suddenly, he was picturing Skylar beneath him in the queen-sized bed they were sharing, both of them naked while he pumped home, his hands shaking as they pressed her knees open, their mouths slanting, panting.

Did I make you hard just like you taught me?

Even in the fantasy, his response was incoherent.

"You were the token suck-up in class, weren't you?" Robbie asked, his voice a lot grittier than before. Hard to blame him when they were still fucking like animals in his mind, Skylar on top now, her ponytail coming loose, hips bucking—

"Every single time," she answered, sniffing. "And you were the class clown, I'm guessing?"

Come on, man. Focus.

She asked for help. Give it to her.

"Smile at me a little," he leaned down to murmur against her forehead. "You look like you're telling me to go jump in the lake."

Her mouth softened gradually, along with her eyes. "I wouldn't mind seeing that."

Robbie shrugged. "I'm a strong swimmer."

"Hopefully that will come in handy." Her fingertips moved higher to the collar of his polo, smoothing it out, and he almost saw stars when the pad of her pinkie finger grazed the skin below his ear. Felt that minor touch all the way in his stomach, nearly causing him to groan. "The main purpose of the opening ceremony is to go over the rules and receive the first challenge."

He blinked to clear his sudden double vision. "Who designs the challenges?"

"My parents."

Robbie hadn't been expecting that, although it hadn't occurred to him to wonder who came up with the events. He'd had too much else on his mind; namely, the girl in front of him who was going to have a black belt in flirting by the end of the night, if they continued like this. "They get to plan the challenges, even though they're competing?" Robbie asked, using his thumb to smooth down those curly hairs at her temple.

Did her eyes get kind of drowsy when he rubbed her temples or was that just wishful thinking? "It's the one advantage we give them due to their age," Skylar said, tamping down a yawn, then looking around to make sure no one saw it.

"Generous of you," he quipped quietly, rubbing with a little more pressure.

"You might have to stop doing that."

"Why?"

"It's putting me to sleep when I need to be alert." She gave a rapid shake of her head and caught his wrist, starting to pull it away. But something—or someone—behind Robbie must have been watching because she brought his wrist to her mouth and kissed his pulse, before letting it go, blissfully unaware that she'd just sent it haywire.

"Did he see that?" Robbie asked. It was that or start moaning.

She searched his face a moment before nodding. "I can't tell what Madden thinks about all this. You being here."

"You've known him a long time. You don't feel comfortable asking him?"

"No," she said on a burst of breath. Then, more troubled, "No."

"Not yet," Robbie said, wanting to make her feel better. Encouraged.

Gratitude danced briefly across her face. "Right. Not yet."

She seemed at a loss for what to do with her hands now that they were still standing close, but not touching, so Robbie wound the fingers of his right hand through her left ones, stroking his thumb along the base of her wrist, gratified to see her pupils dilate slightly. Chemistry. He had that with her, if nothing else.

"Speaking of sleep," Skylar said, sounding a touch out of breath, "I'm probably not going to get any this week. I've shared a bed before, but mostly as a kid at sleepovers or with my teammates at travel tournaments. And never someone your size."

"Thank you." He winked down at her. "It is remarkable in size."

"I'm talking about your overall body size. Not your penis."

"We'll have to talk about it eventually, Rocket. It's on the calendar."

"We'll cross the dick bridge when we get to it."

Robbie coughed a laugh. "Can Dick Bridge be our new team name?"

"No, but we *should* have a new team name, right? Team Skeeve only makes sense when it's me and Eve." Decision visibly made, Skylar's hold on his hand tightened and she turned, pulling Robbie back in the direction of the firepit.

He dug in his heels. "You're hot enough without catching on fire, Rocket."

She shot him a glance, insult loading, but realized at the last second that everyone had ceased their conversations to watch them interact. "Thanks, Redbeard."

"Redbeard and Rocket," mused Vivica, elbowing a watchful Doug. "Cute."

"Is it, though?" Elton tilted his head, obnoxiously. "*Is it?*"

Skylar pursed her lips. "Maybe *you* should catch on fire, Elt."

"I'd prefer that over watching you two canoodle."

"Mom, can we start deducting points every time Elton uses the word 'canoodle'?"

Elton made a face, but Robbie only noticed it in his periphery, because he was watching Madden. And Madden was watching him back with a frown.

Okay. Looked like they had his attention.

Robbie ignored the sinking sensation in his stomach.

"Speaking of point deductions," said Doug, commandeering the conversation in a booming manner that reminded Robbie of a radio DJ. "Honey, would you like to remind everyone of the rules of engagement? You do it so eloquently."

"Thank you, dear. Yes, I would." Vivica folded her hands at her waist, her gaze sharpening to a point. "No sabotaging whatsoever. I'm looking at you, Elton and Skylar. If anyone is caught tampering with alarm clocks or equipment, both offenders get an automatic DQ. No bribing the Page Stakes committee for a more desirable challenge. They are set in stone and stored in a secure location."

"They're taped to the back of the bread machine my mother never uses," Skylar said out of the side of her mouth.

"Each evening, the following day's challenge will be left on the refrigerator, beneath my Brown University Alumni magnet." Doug and Vivica traded a proud look. "And last but not least, no laxatives in anyone's cereal, Skylar. Remember 2019."

"He looked a little backed up," Skylar replied innocently. "I was trying to help."

"You nearly helped my spleen exit my body." Elton looked around the group, visibly haunted. "You're not supposed to use the whole bottle."

"Oops."

With a final reproving glance at her children, Vivica produced two laminated sheets, handing one to Elton and the other to Skylar with a flourish. Eager to find out what they'd be up against, Robbie stepped up behind Skylar and scanned the first challenge from over her shoulder.

Challenge One: Blindfolded Blitz

"Don't worry, I'll explain it later," she said for his ears alone. Then louder, "It should be a cinch." Skylar adopted a casual backward lean against Robbie's chest. So casual he wondered if she realized she'd done it at all. "We won't even break a sweat."

Her brother shrugged, handing the list to Madden, who—goddammit—had to tear his attention off Skylar in order to take it. "Easy peasy."

Vivica laughed. "Tell yourself whatever helps you sleep at night, but we all remember the ER visit of 2021. You needed seventeen stitches, right, Madden?"

"Yes, ma'am."

Vivica high-fived her husband. "That's what I thought."

These people were intense.

Skylar turned to face Robbie, dropping her voice to a whisper. "We should probably get to bed early tonight."

Spend alone time with Skylar, no Madden in sight?

"Sign me up."

She started to back toward the house, holding the laminated challenge to her chest, her bravado so bold, scholars would write odes in its honor one day. "One last thing," she called to her family. "We're changing our team name to Rocket and Redbeard."

Elton doubled over and made a retching sound.

Robbie and Skylar fist-bumped on their way into the house.

"Come on." They walked side by side down the hallway toward her bedroom. "The longer we spend around them, the more they'll get in our heads."

"You're right," Robbie said. "We need some team bonding time. I've got just the thing."

"No."

"It was worth a shot."

CHAPTER ELEVEN

Shirtless men didn't faze Skylar. Usually.

She'd grown up with a brother who'd stumbled into the kitchen in his boxers most mornings, plunging his paw into the closest cereal box. His friends were always swimming in their backyard, oftentimes in very translucent underwear, not to mention pantsing each other every chance they got. She'd seen a lot of shrinkage in her day. Lots of butts. A bare chest didn't even rate. Usually.

Robbie Corrigan, professional hockey player, didn't have just any chest.

Or abdomen.

Or arms.

Nothing about him was typical.

He was a thick, stacked, red-bearded giant. In her bedroom.

And she was watching him pull on sleep sweatpants in the mirror of her vanity when her back was supposed to be turned.

Obviously, she'd had a lot of doubts about their scheme to get Madden to notice her—and she still did. Tonight at the cookout, however, she hadn't expected to feel so much like a united front. As much as she loved and adored Eve, Skylar inevitably felt like the odd one out at the Page Stakes every year. The underdog. The pest. The one who hadn't quite lived up to the lofty expectations set forth by her overachiever family. Robbie talked a lot of shit, had an overwhelming amount of confidence, and didn't seem at all fazed by his sudden entrée into their zany family competition.

Something about his ability to roll with the punches? It allowed her to stress less and focus more. It was . . . not awful.

Maybe *he* wasn't awful.

Maybe they even had a chance to win?

"What are you thinking about so hard over there, Rocket?"

Her chin jerked up to find him watching her in the vanity mirror, those superhuman hands perched on his hips, chest still blessedly bare. She could appreciate him objectively, right? One athlete to another. He kept himself in peak physical condition.

Good for him.

Good for half the women in Boston, too.

Skylar cleared the confusing twinge from her throat. "I was just pondering."

He leaned back against the dresser on the opposite side of the room, crossing his arms, his biceps and triceps competing for attention. "Care to share?"

"Uh . . ." *Stop looking at the V.* "I was thinking about the competition tomorrow. I've done this event before and on the surface, it might sound kind of silly. But it's not. It's actually pretty hard. We need to have a game plan."

"I'm going to be blindfolded. You'll lead me through the headphones."

"I—" She wrinkled her nose. "Why are you automatically the blindfolded one?"

"A couple of reasons." He uncrossed his arms in order to count on his fingers. "One, there's no way I'll be able to sit still during *any* competition. Just thinking about it makes me squirm." He shuddered. "And two, you could step in a gopher hole and twist your ankle or some shit and I wouldn't be able to handle it, especially considering I'd be the one giving you directions."

Okay, *that* she hadn't seen coming. As soon as his words sank in, her right eye started to twitch. "You're worried I'm going to get hurt?"

He studied her in silence. "Why do I feel like I just stepped in it?"

"Because you did." Slowly, Skylar skirted around the edge of the bed in his direction. "Remember when you asked me on a date during the baseball game? Same thing, Redbeard." Stopping in front of him, she poked him between those hard pecs. "If we want a chance to win, you have to quit treating me like less of a competitor because I'm a girl."

"I hear what you're saying, but . . ." His attention dragged along the curve of her right hip and back up her center to the notch of her throat. "I can't pretend you're not softer, shorter, and a hell of a lot prettier than me."

A warm, unexpected wind wafted through her chest, but she couldn't help but be skeptical. After all, *soft* and *pretty* were adjectives that hadn't been used to describe her many times in her life. She wasn't sure she totally liked them, either, despite the giddy rush currently sneaking through her bloodstream. "Is this another round of flirting practice?" she asked, suspiciously.

"Nope. Those are just facts."

"W-well," she said, floundering momentarily. "Keep your flirtations to yourself, unless we are actively engaged in practice, as set forth in the schedule."

"My bad, Rocket." A corner of his lips twitched. "Bottom line is, I would like to be blindfolded. I'm indestructible. I can tape up and play on anything short of a broken limb."

"So can I. I have."

"I'm not saying I don't believe you, but . . ."

A light bulb went off in Skylar's head. "The problem is you don't trust me. As a teammate. Not yet." Her attention hit a snag when Robbie stroked five fingers through his beard, as if settling in to listen to her explanation. What was the texture of that beard? What would it feel like against her cheeks and chin if—no, *when* they kissed? They were going to kiss, eventually. She'd blocked out a whole hour of time on Tuesday for exactly that. The fact that her blood pumped faster at the thought was alarming, to say the least. "Um. I think the best thing we can do to prepare for tomorrow is establish trust. As teammates, I mean."

"As opposed to . . ."

"Trusting you as a man. Or a boyfriend. It would be a cold day in hell."

He shoved off the dresser, his face a mask of disbelief. "Excuse me? Are you implying that I wouldn't be a trustworthy boyfriend?"

"I'm not implying anything. I'm stating facts, just like you."

"Jesus, Skylar. *My* facts were flattering." He paced right, then left, spearing her with a hard look all the while. "Granted, I haven't been in a serious relationship, but if I was, if I liked someone enough to make her my girlfriend, I'd make sure I was all in. I wouldn't do it halfway. When I commit to something, I do it a thousand percent."

"All right." Guilt somersaulted into her belly. "I shouldn't have said that."

"Shouldn't have *said* it? Or shouldn't have assumed I'd be a ratbag boyfriend?"

A small hesitation, followed by a wince. "Said it," she whispered.

"Wow." He shook his head slowly. "A man recounts a hookup to his teammates *one time* and he's branded for life."

"One time or *every* time?"

"Semantics."

"Semantics," she echoed, mimicking his baritone. "Let's table the discussion on the ethics of locker room talk for now. My point is we need to build some teammate-style trust. Otherwise, how are you going to have any confidence in my instructions tomorrow?"

A red eyebrow zipped upward. "You're letting me do the blindfolded part?"

"Only because I feel a little bit guilty for implying that you'd be a ratbag boyfriend." She pinched her fingers together and held them up to prove her guilt was scant, at best. "But the guilt is against my will."

"Aha. You hurt my feelings *and* you get to avoid injury. This sounds abundantly fair."

The guilt wasn't so scant anymore. Was she being a bad teammate? Or too judgmental? Did everyone else keep the truth to themselves to be more likable and why couldn't she seem to pull that off? "Maybe this is why I'm so bad at dating. I'm too blunt. Or honest. Or—"

"Hey, hey. No. Stop that." Robbie clasped her shoulders in his huge hands and a weird tingle shot all the way down to her knees. "I'm only kidding around. If a guy can't handle your bluntness, maybe that's a good sign that he's uncomfortable with honesty and you should run in the other direction, huh?"

The sudden wave of gratitude and belonging came as such a surprise, Skylar took a full five seconds to nod. "Okay. Thanks."

His gaze dipped to her mouth, his bare chest expanding. "Welcome."

Musk and cinnamon and . . . was it the taste of bare flesh coming off his torso and throat? Whatever it was, the trifecta made her eyelids feel heavy. Made her wonder again about how his beard would feel in her fingers. Or dragging sideways along her collarbone.

When his hands dropped from her shoulders, they both stepped back, visibly regrouping. After what? What had happened, exactly?

Was she *attracted* to Robbie?

Surely not.

Just the dry spell talking.

Skylar did her best to circle her focus back to the task at hand. Despite Robbie's assurances, she couldn't help wanting to make up for what she'd said. Was there a way to gain some trust in each other and smooth over the awkwardness she'd caused?

Her eyes landed on her closet.

Maybe.

"I have an idea."

He dragged his bottom lip through his teeth. "Skip to Thursday on the calendar?"

"Nope." *Ignore the way your skin is heating.* "I'm going to let you read a page out of my diary. From when I was thirteen."

"Shut up." His jaw fell open. "I should make you feel guilty more often."

"Don't get too excited. You have to share something embarrassing with me, too." She was careful not to brush their bodies together as she moved past him to the closet. "It's a trust exercise."

"Ah." Robbie sighed dramatically. "If only I'd ever done anything embarrassing . . ."

"I'm sure you'll dredge something up," she said, while rummaging through a clear plastic storage container that held school projects dating back to middle school.

The bedsprings groaned as he sat down. "I'll have to dig deep."

"Doubt it," she muttered.

"I heard that, Rocket."

She almost—*almost*—apologized again for being so mean, but

swallowed the sorry when she emerged from the closet to find him grinning and rubbing his hands together. "Are you picking the material? Or can I open to any random page?"

"Any random page will do. They're equally humiliating, I'm sure."

"Hand it over, girl. Let's go."

His visible excitement somehow made it easier than it should have been to hand over the small pink book. As soon as the diary was in his possession, Robbie cleared his throat as if preparing to deliver the Gettysburg Address and flipped to a section in the dead center. "June seventh, two thousand sixteen." He smoothed a palm down the page filled with loopy blue printing. "Oh, we have some daisy doodles in the corner. *Very* nice."

She slapped her hands over her face. "Shut up and read."

"'A lot of people have crushes on celebrities, but I feel like my crush on Kit Harington is totally different. I think if we met, he would get me. He would know I'm different. He would stop signing autographs and stare at me.'"

"Good lord."

"Oh, it's good all right." He bit his lip to trap a laugh. "A *Game of Thrones* girl, were you?"

Skylar groaned. "How much longer is this page?"

The man was enjoying himself way too much. "Well, you have three lines of overlapping hearts here, which must be some kind of code. Heart heart heart *heart* heart heart *heart*. Am I pronouncing that right?"

"Just skip the hearts, smart-ass," she said, picking up a pillow and hitting him with it.

"'Kit would come to my softball game and everyone would be like OMG. My parents would just have to effing deal with it.'" Robbie lost it on that part, collapsing backward onto the bed with his sides shaking. "'Kit would tell Elton to stop making fun of me. Or else.'" He closed the diary, biting his lip until it turned white. "Tragically, that's the end of the page."

"Thankfully, you mean."

"You better hide this before I read the rest and make it my whole personality." He made her tug on the diary three times before releasing it. "Are you ready for my embarrassing contribution? I managed to recall the one incident of my lifetime where I wasn't obscenely cool."

"Don't leave me in suspense."

He sat up and reached for his phone, which he'd left charging on the surface of her dresser. After a few moments of scrolling through his photo library, he handed her the device. "Mailer took this video of me in the shower."

She snatched back her hand. "Whoa, whoa, whoa."

"Relax, you won't see anything." He tossed the phone in her direction where it landed with a *pfff* on the bedding. "But let me know if you want to. A team shower sounds like a good trust building exercise, too."

"Challenge yourself to not be gross for ten minutes."

His only response was to grin and stack his hands beneath his head, turning himself into a muscle buffet right before her very eyes. Not to mention the very unmissable ridge raising the leg of his sweatpants. A popular dish, surely. Who wouldn't pile their plate high with that—

"You going to hit play, Rocket?"

"What? Yeah." She picked up the phone, chagrined to find her hand was a little sweaty. "I'm terrified, but here goes . . ."

It took a full ten seconds for Skylar to figure out what she was hearing.

"That's *you* singing in the shower?"

"That's me."

Her mouth fell open, spine zipping straight. "Hold on, you're actually kind of a good singer. How is this embarrassing . . . ?"

It finally registered that he was singing "Get'cha Head in the Game" from the original *High School Musical* soundtrack.

"Oh." Skylar tumbled sideways onto the row of pillows, her breath knocked out of her in a whooshing laugh. "Ohhhh *nooooo*."

He took the phone back, presumably hitting pause, because the sound of his passionate crooning no longer filled the air, though her eyes were too tear-filled to confirm.

"What do you think?" Robbie asked, his voice coming from above. "Did this trust building exercise work?"

Skylar's laugh cut out when she opened her eyes, finding his face inches from her own, his expression one of rapt fascination. Why? Because she was laughing?

"Yeah," she said, winded, sitting up quickly. "Yes, I'd say it worked. You?"

"Sure."

Neither one of them said anything for several seconds, during which it became very clear they were not only having a good time together, they were having a good time together *on a bed*. In their sleep clothes.

"Do you want me to sleep on the floor?" he asked, gruffly.

"No. We're . . . we can be mature about this. Don't be silly."

His attention swept her body, a ripple going through his jaw. "I don't know, Rocket. I still think I should."

Why was her pulse going so fast? "Okay. Why?"

"I'm worried I'll be half asleep and . . . touch you without thinking." He huffed a sound. "I mean, Christ. It takes concentration not to touch you when I'm *awake*."

The bedding started to feel different against her skin. Softer. More alluring.

Bad.

Fine. Maybe she could admit to being . . . attracted to Robbie. Nothing too unusual about that. He was a hot professional athlete who probably appealed to most women who crossed his path. It stung to be one of thousands, but she couldn't do anything about it now. Except to remember that the attraction was physical in nature only. She didn't have grand, once-in-a-lifetime, momentous feelings for anyone but Madden. That's why Robbie was here in the first place. Luckily, she'd found someone she found attractive to help weed through her insecurities with men, but that's all this could be. That's all she *wanted* it to be.

And most importantly, that's all he was offering. He definitely couldn't wait to get back to his carousel of one-night stands.

"Yeah." Finally, she nodded in agreement, tossing him a pillow and the spare blanket folded on the end of her bed. "You're right. Maybe it's best if you sleep on the floor."

ROBBIE COULDN'T SLEEP.

Not because he was bedding down on the floor. Although trying to catch some z's while Skylar was within reaching distance, breathing softly in her little tank top and shorts . . . not easy. Not easy at all. He'd lost count of how many times she'd checked him out while completing their trust exercise, those gorgeous brown eyes glued to his abs like she was on a stakeout. Did she realize every thought in her head played out on her face?

Did she realize he loved that so much?

Would she care?

Robbie dragged a frustrated hand down his face and focused on the second reason he couldn't sleep—he'd only eaten one dinner. A small one, at that. The objective of tonight's cookout had been to size up the competition and find out tomorrow's challenge. Being the newcomer, he'd hesitated to be too forward and ask for a second helping, but Jesus. One measly burger for dinner?

Giving up on falling asleep, Robbie got up and quietly left Skylar's room.

"One burger. What am I?" he muttered, now on his way down the dark hallway. "A toddler?"

Robbie turned the corner into the kitchen and drew up short. Slumped forward at the white-and-gray marble island was Elton, his gaze locked on the phone in front of him. A picture on it showed a smiling young woman with black curly hair and a medal around her neck. In the space of two seconds, before Elton noticed Robbie's arrival, Robbie witnessed something other than irritation or exasperation on the baseball player's face for the first time. Heavy, hollow sorrow. That's what it was.

He tried to back out of the kitchen before Elton clocked him, but it was too late. The other man's jaw hardened and with a swipe of his thumb, he darkened the phone.

"What do you want?" Elton asked.

"Like, four times the amount of food I ate earlier." Robbie slipped behind Elton and made a move for the refrigerator, opening the freezer first. That was where his favorite foods were usually hiding. "Does your mom keep any Stouffer's lasagnas in the house?"

"Pretty much everything in this house is from the farmers market."

Robbie blanched. "Aha. So this is going to be the real test of survival, is it?" He reached in and found a frozen bag of cauliflower crinkle fries. What the *fuck*? "Feeding me normal-sized portions until I'm too weak to compete."

"You'll get used to it," Elton said, sounding as though he was fighting off weariness.

Even though he had an intense dislike for this prick, Robbie couldn't quite stem the impulse to break up the sadness he could still feel lingering in the air. Laugh through the pain, that's what he'd been taught. Being the class clown growing up had turned the tide from being laughed *at* to being laughed *with*. Was his court jester personality also the reason a lot of his veteran teammates constantly rolled their eyes at him?

Yeah.

Too late to change now, though, right?

Robbie gave up on the freezer and opened the fridge, a little surprised to find himself checking for orange juice before locating food for himself. The no-pulp kind Skylar liked. Why didn't they have any on hand for the morning? Mentally planning a trip to the store before she woke up, Robbie sighed in relief when he saw a plastic-wrapped platter of leftover burgers, buns and all. "I assure you, I will never get used to regular human portions of food. When I was a kid, I got kicked out of summer camp for breaking into the cafeteria in the middle of the night." He set the plate down on the counter and whipped off the plastic like a magician revealing a rabbit. "They found me with my face submerged in a five-gallon tub of corn chowder. That's how I got my summer camp nickname. Robbie Corn-igan."

"Wow. Sounds like you've always been a pain in the ass."

"You've got that right," Robbie said around a mouthful of meaty goodness. "Like recognizes like, I guess."

He put his hand out for a fist bump.

Elton gave it a withering look.

"If you thought this was going to be a bonding moment, I hate to break it to you, it's not." Elton turned in the stool to face Robbie, rearing back a little when he caught Robbie inserting an entire slider into his gob before he'd even finished the last one. "Jesus, man."

"I'm ftarbing!"

Elton made a flippant gesture toward the fridge. "At least put some fucking ketchup on them. They're completely dry. If you choke, I'm not Heimliching you."

Robbie swallowed. "I've had to learn how to Heimlich myself. I'm a pro."

"Wow. I had no idea my sister had lowered her standards quite this much."

"Lucky me," Robbie said, grinning.

Elton scrutinized Robbie in the dim kitchen light, brow puckered, his fingers drumming on the island. "I can't believe I'm going to ask you this, but what are your intentions with my sister?"

Robbie took a huge bite, so he could buy himself enough time to formulate an answer. Because, yeah, that wasn't an easy question. In a perfect world, one where he hadn't presented himself to Skylar as a misogynist asshole from the jump, he'd be trying to date her. Only her. Yeah. Skylar was a once-in-a-lifetime girl. He'd probably be painting his body in BU colors to cheer her on at softball games by now. That was, if she hadn't—correctly—pegged him as a player who took nothing and no one seriously.

The burgers sprouted thorns in his stomach.

There was very little chance he could convince her of the opposite now. She'd made up her mind. But Robbie couldn't very well spill the truth to Elton. That he'd come here to atone for his behavior with Skylar.

And he *definitely* couldn't tell Elton they were fake dating to attract his best friend.

Robbie decided to stick as close to the truth as he could, under the circumstances. "I like your sister. A lot. I'm just trying to spend as much time around her as possible."

Elton processed that with an air of skepticism. "Are you sure you're not just here to incite me?"

"You think I'd go to all this effort just to piss off a baseball player?"

Skylar's brother raised an eyebrow.

"Fine, I guess that suspicion is justified." God, if he could just go back and rewind the last week of his life, he would do it in a heartbeat. Make a better impression on Skylar. Even on her brother. Now he was in the familiar position of trying to convince people he wasn't a total shit show of a human being, which seemed to be his default situation. When would he learn his lesson?

Now.

You're learning it right now.

You mouthed off one too many times and now you can't have the girl.

"I'm not here with the sole intention of pissing you off, man. That's just a bonus." Robbie could no longer find his smile and the burgers had lost their appeal, so he commenced wrapping them back up in plastic. "I didn't expect Skylar. She's clever, funny, driven, cool, and . . . God, she's fucking beautiful." Had his stomach gotten stuck in his windpipe? "I'm here for her. No other reason. She's reason enough."

When he looked up at Elton, the other man appeared caught off guard. He recovered quickly, however. "That's not what I asked. What are your intentions?"

Make her fall for me instead of Madden.

That's what his heart begged him to say. To believe.

But that possibility was so far-fetched, giving it oxygen would be pathetic.

"Treat her right. Make her laugh. Help her win." Robbie forced a chuckle. "Hope she doesn't realize she's way out of my league."

A rumble emanated from Elton's chest. "I punched you in the face last week for disrespecting my sister, but . . . she *can* take care of herself. We all take care of ourselves. Individually. I'm not going to step on that." Elton stood, moving forward to place himself toe-to-toe and eyeball-to-eyeball with Robbie, who—obviously—held his ground like a motherfucking hockey player should, fists bunched and ready to swing if necessary. "But I heard the same shit she heard at the baseball field. Bragging about your hookup from the night before." Robbie tried not to openly flinch, but he didn't quite keep the lid on his reaction. He'd been so sick about Skylar overhearing him, the fact that Elton heard, as well, hadn't quite occurred to him. Until now. "If I ever find out you're talking about my sister like that, I will put you in the emergency room."

I'd die first. That's what his gut urged him to say out loud. Why would this guy believe him, though? Those women he'd been speaking so openly and inappropriately about . . . they hadn't knocked him on his ass and given him heart palpitations, the way Skylar did, but they'd deserved the same respect, hadn't they?

"I'd never talk about her like that," Robbie rasped, more truth slipping out than intended. "The thought of it makes me sick."

Elton's brows drew together at that, as if not sure how to read Robbie. Which was fair, since his reasons for being there were not straightforward to anyone but him and Skylar. "Good," Elton said finally, jabbing a finger into Robbie's shoulder. "Just consider yourself on notice, Corrigan."

Robbie nodded curtly. "Copy that."

As soon as Elton stomped out of the room, Robbie sat heavily in the stool he'd vacated. In dire need of a distraction, he turned around a picture frame on the counter, revealing a family photo. Doug and Vivica, along with their children. Arms resting on one another's shoulders, standing in front of a sign welcoming them to the Grand Canyon.

Elton totally at ease, with a buzz cut and a smirk, captured in the middle of goofing off. A much younger Skylar, as solemn-eyed as he knew her to be, but relaxed. Less tense.

The baseball mitt on her hand made his stupid heart squeeze. Even at the Grand Canyon.

As someone who never went anywhere without a hockey stick, he got it.

He got . . . her.

But as much as he wanted to carry on cataloging things about Skylar from the past, he couldn't help but notice something else about the snapshot.

Everyone pictured wore a Brown University T-shirt. Even Skylar.

Robbie glanced up from the photo, seeing the pennant framed on the wall in the living room for the first time. The blanket folded up neatly on the couch. All red and brown, the colors of the apparent sacred family alma mater.

Nothing for BU anywhere?

Robbie went back to his place on the floor in Skylar's room with a frown on his face . . . and he didn't fall asleep for a very long time.

CHAPTER TWELVE

Skylar woke up to an empty pile of bedding on her floor and a text from Robbie.

> Gone for rations. Be back soon.

"Rations?" she echoed through a yawn, stretching on her way to her suitcase, where she'd left it sitting in the corner. Still groggy, she flung the luggage onto the bed and unzipped, reaching into the mesh pocket for underwear and a sports bra. The sun had yet to rise and the house remained mostly quiet, except for her father, who was puttering around in the kitchen counting down the minutes until trumpet-blowing time. Didn't matter that everyone was already awake this particular morning—he'd probably blow it regardless just to put everyone on their guard.

Looking out the window, she could see her mother and Elton sharing a cup of coffee on the back porch, comfortable in their companionship. A familiar scene in which she was rarely included. The few times she'd joined her stepbrother and mother for their morning chat during the Page Stakes, they'd talked mostly about their experiences at Brown, his and her former professors, news from the alumni board, of which they were both members.

Of course, they didn't *exclusively* talk about the college, but it was an easy segue into other topics. That bond made it easy for Vivica to relate to Elton in a way she couldn't seem to relate to

Skylar. As an all-American student athlete, academics were a huge part of Skylar's life, but talking about her courses inevitably drew comparisons to the Brown curriculum. Criticisms, too. And at some point, Skylar had decided to avoid morning coffee sessions with Doug, Vivica, and Elton because they left her feeling deflated. Like someone standing just outside of the inner circle.

Now, Eve, her Page Stakes teammate, was a great friend. However, she'd raised herself in difficult circumstances, and as the daughter of the town pariah, Eve had grown up with a tough outer shell that Skylar couldn't always penetrate. *Not* the warm, fuzzy type—and not everyone *had* to be. Her quiet strength and no-nonsense pragmatism were some of the reasons Skylar loved Eve. Now that she'd taken over her father's strip club and turned it into a burlesque lounge, she had some hefty responsibilities, too, meaning Skylar's best friend was now emotionally and physically distant. Something that hadn't really registered until last night when Robbie, as her new teammate, had been so . . . there. Ready for anything. *With* her.

Which also made Skylar wonder if she was missing something with Eve. Had *she* not been present enough for her best friend?

In the bathroom, Skylar sat down on the closed toilet lid and called Eve.

Four rings. Voicemail.

"Hello, you've reached Eve, lady proprietor of the Gilded Garden. Lucky you. Leave a message and make it brief. I don't have all day."

Beep.

With a fond half smile on her face, Skylar left a message. "Hey, I know you're super busy this week, just wondering if you had time for coffee. Would love to catch up. If I don't hear from you, I'll just show up at the lounge later this week. When you least expect it. Boo."

Deep in thought, Skylar took a quiet shower, dressed, and brushed her teeth. Fashioned her wet hair into a braid and, for old times' sake, slid her feet into an old pair of cleats that still held clumps of dirt from senior year of high school.

Then she tucked her planner into the back waistband of her yoga pants and snuck outside to pitch. The sound of her spikes on the front porch steps was familiar enough to raise a pebble in her throat, as was the rusted lock on the shed adjacent to the house, where the sporting goods were kept. The black wire bucket of dirty softballs that waited for Skylar made her sigh with pleasure. And after dragging out the nine-pocket practice target she'd been using since middle school, she got to work.

Relax into stance, breathe, wind up, release.

Relax into stance, breathe, wind up, release.

It would be so easy to let herself become distracted. To think about the Page Stakes kicking off this afternoon, the pressure of competition, the high expectations of her family, even when they were only battling against one another. It would be so easy to think about the man who'd slept on her floor last night, mumbling in his slumber about forechecks, his face softened by sleep. How she'd lost her battle with curiosity and reached down in the middle of the night to test the texture of his beard. Just a teeny, little finger graze.

Why did it have to be the perfect combination of bristly and smooth?

Women must love it.

Skylar missed the target completely on her next pitch, the ball disappearing into the trees. "Damn."

"Brought my glove, if you'd rather pitch to a human" came the voice behind her.

Madden.

She hadn't heard him approaching from the house next door, which had been passed down to him following the death of his aunt.

Skylar's stomach tied itself into seventeen complicated knots. A familiar feeling, considering this was a familiar scene plucked straight out of her high school years. One she looked forward to reliving on an annual basis during the Page Stakes. Pitching to Madden's steady glove, experiencing that ripple of approval across his furrowed brow whenever she landed a strike. His quiet strength. The sense of camaraderie.

Just the two of them, no Elton to tease and remind her she was the annoying younger sister. Perfect.

Oddly, her fingers tingled where she held the next ball, the memory of Robbie's soft bristles making itself known at the least opportune moment.

Not now.

Forcing herself to play it cool, she tossed a smile over her shoulder. "Sure, thanks."

Madden nodded in that slow, easy manner of his, striding past her to the target, moving it aside and taking its place in front of the towering oak she'd christened the Pitching Tree long ago.

Skylar shook the nerves out of her arm and threw a decent pitch, the imaginary umpire in her head calling it *low and inside.*

Retrieving another ball from the bucket, she bobbled it in her hand a moment, trying to work up the courage to start a conversation. Considering how long they'd known each other, exchanging words shouldn't be so hard, right? There was normally a buffer of some kind. Or they just played in silence in the name of concentration. But this was her week to get his attention, to break free of the patterns that made her nothing more than Elton's little sister in Madden's eyes. *Seize your chance.*

"Is it nice being back in your aunt's house for the week?" Skylar asked.

Nice job bringing up his deceased aunt. Ask about his absent parents next.

Madden stood and returned the ball, her glove receiving it with a *slonk*. "It is nice, yeah." She wasn't sure he'd elaborate, but after a moment he kept going. "I forget some of the smaller things about her. Like the dishes she kept everywhere for candy. Every once in a while, I find a hair curler stuck in a couch cushion or behind a stack of books." He hunkered back down, punching the center of his glove. "Good reminders."

"Those are good," she murmured, swallowing the twinge in her throat.

Another pitch. A perfect throw back in Skylar's direction.

Odd how conversation didn't seem to come easily between them. Obviously, they just needed more time alone. To get comfortable with each other.

Obviously.

"Listen, Skylar," Madden said, kind of abruptly. "About this hockey fella."

Skylar froze in the process of dropping into her stance. Madden was asking about Robbie. They'd *already* gotten his attention? Her suspicion that he'd been bothered by Robbie's interest in her at the game last week had been correct.

Holy shit, it was happening.

She flipped her braid over her shoulder, nonchalant as possible. "What about him?"

"Do you actually like this guy, or what?" He rolled a shoulder, appearing to choose his words carefully. "Something seems off."

Uh-oh. "Off . . . how?"

He studied her through narrowed eyes. "Can't put my finger on it, really." A thoughtful pause. "You don't date often, now suddenly you're moving very quickly, bringing him here to meet your parents and all."

Skylar kept her expression neutral. "Well . . ." Okay, was Madden jealous or merely skeptical of her relationship with Robbie? He was impossible to read. Why couldn't he just demand she break things off with Robbie and give him a chance, instead? "I probably wouldn't have invited him to meet my parents so soon, but Eve couldn't make it."

For some reason, Madden's eyes darkened dramatically at the mention of her best friend. "Right." He looked down, scuffing the dirt with his boot. "Eve."

"But I do really like him," Skylar finished quickly. *Too* quickly?

Madden's head came up again, brow drawn. "I see."

Skylar held her breath. This is where Madden expressed his sudden realization that it had always been her—

"Jesus, I could eat another ten of these fucking sandwiches" came Robbie's voice behind her, accompanied by his footsteps up the driveway. "That place in town called the Whistle Stop? It's a banger. Restaurant and food market all wrapped into one. Cleaned them out of Stouffer's lasagnas, if anybody wants one."

It took Skylar a moment to turn around, because she couldn't figure out why Robbie's interruption came as a . . . relief? But she was forced to put that weird reaction aside for later when Robbie stopped beside her, setting down the brown paper bags he'd apparently carried half a mile . . . and leaned down to kiss her.

A firm, possessive kiss, his fingers sliding into her semidamp hair to cradle the back of her head, loosening her braid and tugging her head back, giving him the angle he needed to slant a second, hungrier kiss against her lips, the pleasing scratch of his beard on her chin and cheeks causing a very distinct tumble in her stomach, her eyelashes fluttering and closing against her will, the ball dropping out of her glove into the dirt.

For several seconds, she forgot their location. Their audience.

The kiss dragged her unwillingly into a semiconscious state where she couldn't help but be fascinated by the sensuality of Robbie's movements, their lips locked together in a firm draw, a low growl in his throat making her nipples feel tight—

"Brought you some orange juice, Rocket," he rasped, pulling away and dropping a lighter kiss on her nose and forehead, though it wasn't lost on her that his pupils were the size of salad plates. "No pulp."

"Yuh?" She blinked to bring her surroundings back into focus, but life remained 50 percent blurry. God, he was a great kisser. Too good. "What?"

"Orange juice." He nudged her forehead with his own. "Got you some."

Mouth so close. "Oh."

He dragged the pad of his thumb down the center of her bottom lip while wincing. "Got you a bagel, too, but I ate it. Sorry about that. My appetite is a problem." They maintained eye contact for another several beats, before Robbie cleared his throat and cast a glance toward . . . Madden? Had his presence actually slipped her mind momentarily? If so, that would be a first. "Morning, Madden." Robbie rubbed his knuckles against the small of her back. "Thanks for keeping Skylar company."

"No worries." Madden watched them closely, especially the movements of Robbie's hand. "I enjoyed catching for you, as usual, Sky."

At the use of the nickname, Robbie's knuckles paused at the base of her spine. "Great. But I've got it from here."

Skylar did a double take. "You've got what?"

"I'll catch for you," Robbie explained.

Madden's head tilted with rare amusement. "Will you now?"

"Yup." Jaw set with determination, Robbie walked to Madden and held out his hand. "Mind if I borrow that glove?"

"Sure thing, mate."

Robbie appeared a little thrown when Madden handed the glove over without hesitation, but he sniffed and stuck his hand inside, nonetheless. "The fit isn't great. My hand is a little too big." Then louder, while looking at Skylar, "Hand. Way too big."

"Maybe you shouldn't do this, Robbie," Skylar called. "You've got playoffs coming up and everything—"

"If you'll recall, I scored our first date by leaning into one of your pitches."

"You're right about that," Madden said dryly. "Destructiveness seems to be a pattern for you."

Robbie bowed, before dropping to his haunches. "Thank you."

Madden shook his head and backed up.

Skylar watched the scene play out with fascination. Was Robbie an incredible actor? Or were these two men butting heads over her?

Had to be the former.

Robbie was only there to help her. And in conjunction with that kiss? His possessive boyfriend act was convincing as all getout. He was totally earning that stolen bagel.

"Don't hold back, Sky," Madden said.

Robbie appeared to be grinding his jaw. "Yeah, let's go, Rocket." He punched the center of the glove. "My nickname is better."

"If you say so."

"Okay, are you really ready?" Skylar called the question, falling into her stance only when Robbie nodded. *Breathe, wind up, pitch.*

She landed it in the dead center of the mitt. But only because

Robbie shifted the target slightly to the right at the last second, compensating for the trajectory.

He didn't even flinch. He simply stood and threw back the ball.

"Well." Madden slow clapped. "I underestimated you."

"Don't let it happen again." Robbie sniffed.

Doug Page stepped out onto the porch, then, drawing the threesome's attention, the sound of his trumpet splintering the cool, spring morning air.

"Let the games begin," he hooted, lowering the instrument.

"Looks like they already have," Madden remarked, backing toward his aunt's house. "See you all at the field."

"Yes, you will," Robbie called, swaggering toward Skylar.

The closer he got to the makeshift pitching mound, the more obvious his pale complexion became. "Let's get you some ice."

"Good idea," he croaked, shaking out his right hand.

CHAPTER THIRTEEN

No doubt about it. This family was psychotic.

Robbie stood blindfolded at the edge of the field, listening to Skylar recite the rules in the provided earpiece.

"Okay, remember. There are four flags. You have to collect them *all* to cross the finish line. In all the kerfuffle, you're going to lose count—"

"I won't lose count."

"You will. I'll keep track, too. Just focus on my instructions and remember to trust me, one hundred percent. Okay?"

He thought of that page in her diary. "As you wish, Mrs. Kit Harington."

"Never. Never say that again."

Robbie grinned, lifting his blindfold just enough to observe Elton beside him at the starting line, stretching his hamstrings like he was preparing to run the Boston Marathon. "What are the rules on bodychecking?"

Skylar sputtered in his ear. "What?"

"Is there a rule preventing me from knocking your brother on his ass?"

"God, you're such a hockey player," she groaned.

"Yes or no."

"Technically?" A long pause. "No, but—"

"Great." Robbie rubbed his hands together. "It's in the bag."

"Don't you dare knock my mother over."

"I'll do my best, Rocket, but I'm blindfolded, remember?"

Was that . . . ? Yes, that was definitely the sound of Skylar's grinding teeth.

And speaking of teeth, Robbie's molars gnashed involuntarily. Returning from the store this morning to find Skylar and Madden in such a cozy scene was the equivalent of getting coldcocked by a heavyweight boxer.

A pitcher and a catcher.

Perfect counterparts.

His mission to help bring Skylar and Madden together had momentarily slipped his mind. His one-track brain had ordered him to *kiss her now*, to warn Madden away from Skylar, instead of showing the man what a desirable woman he could have for himself if he just paid attention and made the slightest effort.

Yeah, Robbie hadn't been thinking of that. He'd just reacted.

He'd allowed himself to want Skylar for himself. Just for a moment.

But those moments were coming way too frequently now to be anything but dangerous when she inevitably started dating Madden. There was no other outcome here. She was too incredible. Madden would pull his head out of his ass sooner or later and see Skylar for the ultimate catch that she was. *So knock your jealous bullshit the hell off.*

Unfortunately, the more time he spent with her, the harder ignoring these possessive feelings became.

"Two minutes to the whistle, Redbeard. Get your game face on."

"I never take it off." He drummed his fingers against the outside of his thigh. "Is this a bad time to talk about our date tonight?"

"Yes," Elton said to Robbie's right, sounding like he'd just licked a lemon.

Robbie turned his back to Elton and dropped his voice for Skylar's ears alone. "Monday is dating practice. It's on the calendar. Plus, I saw it written in your planner and underlined four times."

A sound seemed to catch in Skylar's throat. "Why were you looking in my planner?"

"I couldn't sleep and thought it might help—and it did. I found it kind of . . . soothing."

She didn't immediately respond. "How is it soothing?"

"You slant all your words the exact same direction. If your planner was a clock, they'd be pointing at the two. Then you've got all these seasonally themed tapes. I don't even know where someone goes to buy that shit."

"Online, mostly. But there are also stationery shops . . ."

"Is there one you like in Boston?"

"Why?"

Robbie lifted his blindfold just a tad and peered into the sun, trying to see Skylar across the field, but at that distance she was nothing but an outline. "Maybe I'll get my own planner." He yanked the blindfold back down. "We can have a planner party."

"I can only imagine the kind of debauchery you'd schedule in that planner. Do you even need to pencil in an orgy? Seems like you'd remember."

A sour layer coated his tongue. "You know, Skylar, most nights I'm at hockey practice. Passed out at home *after* hockey practice. In an Epson salt bath. Or eating lasagna with Mailer. I'm not always out haunting clubs looking for women."

"You only do that three times a week."

Robbie snorted. "Twice, tops."

I can't see myself doing it anymore, he almost added. *Not after you.* Yeah, when he got back to Boston, he'd talk to Mailer about knocking off the irreverent bachelor lifestyle. Maybe . . . who knows. Maybe Skylar and Madden wouldn't work out. She'd bump into Robbie at the park after the breakup and he'd be extra jacked, since this was his fantasy. She'd be, like, *What have you been up to?* And he'd say, *Not clubbing, that's what. I volunteer at hospitals now in my spare time.*

Then she'd whip out her adorable little planner and schedule in a date with him.

A real one.

For now, however, if all he got was a fake one, he'd damn well take it.

"So, we're definitely on for tonight?" Robbie asked, peering down at the grass through the tiny sliver of daylight at the bottom of his blindfold and finding the white starting line that had been spraypainted on the grass. "Take me somewhere the portion sizes can feed a family. Or one Robbie."

"I might know a place," she mumbled. "But I'm not going to be in the mood for a date if we lose."

He dropped into a runner's stance, adrenaline beginning to simmer. "Roger that, Rocket."

"Ten seconds. Are you ready?"

"Born ready."

"The first flag is an easy one. Straight ahead about twenty yards. No obstacles in your way." The shriek of the whistle echoed across the field and Robbie lunged forward into the open field. "Go, go, go."

"I'm going. Start telling me how to get to the next one."

"Okay, once you pocket the first flag, number two is a hard cut to the left, maybe fifteen yards. Here's the thing, my mom's *and* Elton's second flags are right beside it, so you're going to have company."

Robbie snagged flag one and changed directions. This was going to be easy as pie. "Is anyone or anything in my path?"

"No, but my mom is coming in hot. Be prepared."

Prepared for what? How bad—

A sharp elbow caught him in the ribs, followed by a maniacal cackle. Next, what Robbie suspected was a foot tripped his ass and he went sprawling forward into the grass.

"Oops," Skylar said in his ear. "Told you."

He was already back on his feet, dismayed to find he'd lost his sense of direction. "Jesus Christ." He turned in a disoriented circle. "Where . . . ?"

"Listen for my airhorn," Skylar said. "Face the finish line again."

A deafening honk came from a football field away. He twisted around and continued on his way. "Got it. Where's the flag now?"

"Take five big steps to the left. It's there."

A second later, he seized the flag. "When did you get a freaking airhorn?"

"Worry about it later, my mom already has three flags."

"*What?* Where's my next one?"

"From your current position, take eight paces forward." She sucked in a breath. "Be warned, you might encounter Elton. His zig might intersect with your zag."

"Looking forward to it."

"Come on, Robbie. Your black eye was just beginning to fade."

Robbie heard approaching footsteps a split second before he sensed a presence. His instinct was to lower his shoulder and flip Skylar's brother. Or increase his pace and take him to the boards, but there were no boards in the middle of the open field and he really wanted that date with Skylar tonight, so he waltzed with Elton instead. Clasped the other man's left hand in his own, planted a hand on his shoulder, and started counting off one two three, one two three . . .

"What the hell are you doing?"

"Not pissing off your sister."

A frustrated curse. "I don't know which direction I'm facing now!"

"That might have been my ulterior motive." Robbie released Elton and ducked by him, knowing exactly where he was in the field, because he'd kept track of his box steps. "Those church dances just paid off, Rocket."

"I can't believe what I just witnessed. Slow down, you're almost to the third flag. There. Stop. No, feel your way along the grass to the right . . ."

"Got it."

"Yes! Okay, dead run toward my airhorn. Nothing is in your way. The last flag is right in front of the finish line."

"Yeah, but where is your mom? I'm terrified."

"She slipped in some mud."

"Oh shit. Does she need help?"

"Hell no! It could be a trap! Just keep running."

Robbie and Skylar won the first Page Stakes event.

On the other side of the finish line, Robbie doubled over with his hands on his knees, judging he'd have a bruise on his side the size of Atlanta by evening. The pain was well worth it when he tore off his blindfold to find Skylar running in his direction, laughing, her braid bouncing side to side on her shoulders.

"You were amazing! We won!"

Time moved in slow motion as she jumped into his arms, her warm laugh bubbling in his ear. And eventually sighing into his neck when he banded both arms around her and held, locking her curves tight to his frame, his eyes rolling blissfully into the back of his head over the way she fit him, absorbing the perfect feeling of the girl who was going to get away.

"Hey," Robbie murmured into her hair, allowing his fingertips to travel down the length of her braid and tug lightly. "That wasn't so bad at all."

She leaned away to meet his eyes. "It'll get harder as we go."

Robbie tucked her face back into his neck, not ready to put her down yet. Or ever. "Yeah. I know it will."

They were slowly flanked by a muddy Vivica and a disappointed-looking Doug and Elton. Madden stood at the edge of the group.

"I suppose congratulations are in order." Doug sniffed, shaking Robbie's hand. "Bear in mind, the first challenge is the easiest."

"That's right." Vivica wiped off her face with a moist towelette, somehow collecting all the mud in a single pass. "Tomorrow is rock climbing!"

Robbie waited for the others to wander off and lick their wounds before looking Skylar in the eye. "Is now a good time to tell you I'm deathly afraid of heights?"

CHAPTER FOURTEEN

Women really, *really* liked her fake boyfriend.

On some level, Skylar had assumed this to be the case. Robbie Corrigan was a professional athlete, which automatically gave him a certain mystique. Not to mention, he had the physique to show for bashing bodies on the ice for over a decade. Throw in his good-time grin and the uniquely messy coiffure of red hair—beard to match—and the guy turned heads. A lot of them.

Pretty much every single one in this Cheesecake Factory.

Which didn't make Skylar *uncomfortable*. Not one bit. If she didn't *love* thinking about how the same thing must happen every time Robbie walked into a bar or nightclub or, hell, even the supermarket, that was purely her amused exasperation talking. What he did back in Boston didn't concern her.

If that were true, though, then why did the queasy weight in her stomach grow more intense every time a woman smiled at him?

Probably because Robbie's easy confidence in himself as a catch only drew attention to the fact that she was not. What did they even look like together? In her hoodie and sneakers, she probably didn't resemble the kind of woman he normally dated . . . sorry, *took home*. She'd taken out her wet braid earlier and her hair was wavy, complete with requisite flyaways. Her makeup consisted of Chapstick and a sunburn.

She probably needed way more help than this man could give her.

Skylar and Robbie approached the hostess station and two more sets of female eyes widened. "Oh. Um. Welcome to the Cheesecake Factory." One of the young women gathered two menus in her visibly unsteady hands. "Two for dinner?"

"Yup." Robbie slung a casual arm across Skylar's shoulders. "Just me and my girl."

"That's so cute," breathed the menu carrier.

"Hear that, Rocket? We're cute together." He pulled her closer while addressing the hostess. "Could you seat us somewhere with a big table? I'm going to be ordering more than one entrée. We'll need space."

"And an extra chair for his ego, please," Skylar added.

The hostess's lips twitched. "I'm sure that won't be a problem. Follow me."

They were led to a booth that could easily fit six people. "This ought to do," Robbie said, tossing the hostess a wink that sent a blush to the roots of her hair. And he didn't even seem to notice. "After you," he said to Skylar, gesturing for her to slide into the booth.

Instead of sitting himself on the other side, he scooted in right next to her, his big, warm body crowding her into the wall, that arm back around her shoulders.

At first Skylar was too stunned by how nice it felt to be held to say anything, but when the hostess sailed off and they were left alone, she found her voice.

"I'm far from a dating expert, but I don't think this is how people sit on a date. This isn't even how a *couple* usually sits on a date."

"Really? This is how I'd sit with you if we were a couple."

"I'm not practicing to be in a couple."

A muscle hopped in his cheek—a total contradiction to the humor in his eyes. "Aren't you?"

Skylar's mouth snapped shut. He had a point.

The waiter chose that moment to arrive with a breadbasket and Skylar stared at the contents, trying to imagine sitting in a restaurant with Madden's arm around her. Would he be comfortable with public displays of affection? No. She didn't think so. Still, maybe with the right girl, he wouldn't mind. And she *was* the right girl for him.

The zip of excitement Skylar typically experienced over a Madden daydream didn't land quite as hard as it usually did. There was an explanation, though. Robbie took up so much room, his hard body and big mouth such a distracting presence, how could she concentrate on anything else?

He'd already housed four pieces of bread in the time it took her to articulate her thoughts.

"Do you want any?" he asked, midchew.

"No, thanks. I don't want to lose a hand."

"Sorry, I just need to take the edge off. Your mom served fruit salad for lunch, Skylar. In my world, fruit is a garnish." He dragged the final slice of brown bread through the tab of butter and swallowed it whole. "Okay. I'm ready for dating practice."

Skylar squared her shoulders, ready to take the lesson seriously. When and where else would she get an opportunity like this with someone so experienced? "Okay, so . . . we make small talk, right? How is this different from flirting?"

"For one, it's way harder," Robbie started. "Because you're trying to eat and be cute at the same time."

"Is that the goal?" She raised a brow. "To be cute?"

His gaze ran an appreciative lap around her face. "You've already got the cute part covered," he said, gruffly. "Let's focus on small talk."

Don't fidget because he called you cute. He probably calls a multitude of women cute on a weekly basis. "So, um." Skylar turned slightly in his embrace, her right knee grazing his left one, pressing and staying. Touching equaled flirting, right? He'd taught her that. "You've met my zany family. Tell me about yours. Tell me about . . . you."

"Me," he repeated, stroking his beard, as though mentally pinpointing where to start. "I'm from—"

"Where did your phobia of heights come from?"

He choked on a sound. "Don't look now, but you might have accidentally turned off the small talk highway."

"Sorry." Her face flamed. "I'm paying attention. I am. It's also in the back of my mind that we have to figure out how we're going to win tomorrow when you might not be able to climb."

"Oh, I *definitely* won't be able to climb."

It was very easy to see he hated disappointing her. The lines around his mouth were tight and he was no longer making eye contact. Which was why she refused to give him a hard time about it. Or poke fun. "Your phobia is that bad?"

"Afraid so, Rocket."

She ducked down until he had no choice but to look at her. "Do you want to tell me where it came from?"

Tension played itself out in the muscles of his powerful arm, which he still had draped along her shoulders. "It's not some traumatic story or anything—" He let a slow exhale seep out of him, grief dancing briefly in the mossy depths of his eyes. "It just reminds me of my grandfather."

Skylar allowed her surprise to settle. "Okay. How?"

He cleared his throat. "He used to take me to Sands Point Preserve. It's this spot on Long Island with hiking trails. It's on the coast and there's this small beach below the cliffs where we'd fly kites. Constantly. When my grandfather was younger, he competed in competitions all over the island, so he had this serious love of kites. One of the last times we flew them together, his got hung up in a tree that was . . ." He used his hand to demonstrate an angle. "Sort of growing out of the side of the cliff. His favorite yellow box kite got stuck in the branches, so I went up to get it. And, Jesus, I couldn't do it. As soon as I got up there and saw the ground below, I got dizzy and nauseous. Sweaty palms, hyperventilating."

"Wow."

"Yeah, wow. I'm not sure if I had a forgotten experience when I was little or I was just born with the phobia, but it's real and it's severe." Did he realize he'd pulled her closer? His words were stirring the flyaways at her temples. "My grandfather passed away shortly after that. The kite is still in that goddamn tree, if you can believe it. I check every time I go home for a visit. And I have this . . ."

When he didn't continue, she nudged his leg with her own. "What?"

"It's ridiculous, but as long as his kite is stuck in that tree, I'll have this weird sense of things being unfinished. Or unresolved. Like he's out there somewhere missing that damn kite."

Skylar didn't think it was ridiculous at all. Not even close. In fact, she'd resigned herself to having that very same feeling ever since getting her rejection letter from Brown and not fulfilling the expectations of her parents. She'd never bring their lives full circle. Nothing would ever make sense. "Do you think your grandfather would want you to feel that way?"

"I don't know. I've wondered about that. He was the type to push me to be better, so at the very least, he'd probably give me shit for making him wait."

The fact that she'd disliked Robbie on sight and now . . . related to him so thoroughly was a kick in the ass. A reminder not to judge people too quickly in the future, especially this guy. "Sounds like he'd fit right in with my family."

"You might be right."

They studied each other for several beats, only breaking the mutual stare when the waiter arrived to take their order. Chicken parmesan with spaghetti, empanadas, and carrot cake for Robbie. A club sandwich and fries for Skylar.

"What did you mean your grandfather pushed you to be better?" she asked, once the waiter had departed. "Was he a hockey player?"

"No one in my family plays hockey but me. They excel at talking shit in the stands, though, and that skill should never be underestimated in my sport." A rueful smile played on Robbie's lips, as if reminiscing. Yeah, Skylar found herself looking at his mouth way longer than was appropriate. His jawline and throat, too. All the food chewing was paying off in a big way. "So, when I was in elementary school, I got bullied. A lot."

Shock snapped her to attention. "You?"

"You're seriously surprised? You've noticed the color of my hair, right? At that age, anything different about you makes you a target—*especially* on Long Island." He ran five fingers through the hair in question, leaving it in tangled disarray. "I used to take it to heart, come home crying. But my grandfather taught me to laugh off the pain. Let the insults and name-calling roll off my back." He huffed a laugh. "That strategy has definitely served me well lately. Being a rookie and all."

"Starting at the bottom again," she murmured.

"Yeah. The vets make sure you know that's where you are— the bottom." His thick shoulder jerked. "It's a rite of passage, I guess."

Forcing a newbie to earn their stripes via unfair treatment or harsher judgment was an unfortunate reality in the sports world, though Skylar suspected it was more intense in men's hockey than softball. BU's softball program was a fostering environment. Team bonding was not only encouraged, but facilitated by the coaching staff. Based on the way Robbie shifted his position, as if uncomfortable where the conversation was leading, she got the feeling the Bearcats didn't have those same systems as firmly in place.

"But that treatment from the vets really bothers you."

He opened his mouth, closing it before he could say anything. "Nah, it's fine." He chuckled finally, amusement lines fanning out from the corners of his eyes. "It's all in good fun—and it's starting to get better, little by little. I just need to put in a few years of work and they'll start taking me seriously. As a person and as a player." He waved his free hand. "I'm no different than anyone else who came before me, right?"

No. *Not* right. He'd struck a chord. "*Everyone* is different. Our experiences make us that way." Skylar hesitated, surprised to find herself wanting to share something with Robbie that she hadn't shared with anyone, except for Dina. Aspirations for her future career behind the scenes. "Part of the reason I want to go into coaching someday is that no two players are the same, and I don't always see that taken into consideration. Yell the same directive at three players and get three different results. One of them will shut down, one will die trying to follow instructions, the third one will raise hell, yell back. That's why the best coaches—and teammates, for that matter—recognize strengths and weaknesses in a person and coach to those qualities."

Did his eyes seem a little glazed, or . . . ? "God, you're so fucking smart."

The unexpected compliment caused pressure to gather in her chest. "I . . . thanks."

"You're going to be a badass coach. Makes me want to grow a ponytail and try out for your squad."

She rolled her eyes to hide a smile. "You wouldn't make it

ten minutes without trying to pick up every girl on the field, Redbeard."

"The hell I wouldn't," he said, affronted. "Look at me. I've learned the error of my ways." Slowly, he reached over, settled a hand on her knee and squeezed, causing a very distressing tingle at the juncture of her thighs, an acceleration of her pulse. Oh my. Oh no, what was *that* reaction about? "And anyway, I've only got a thing for pitchers, don't I?"

Skylar put her most concerted effort into not looking down at the trapezius muscles peeking out of the collar of Robbie's T-shirt. And not thinking about the casual power of his outstretched thighs beneath the table. How all of him seemed to be poised. Waiting. "Is this another round of flirting practice?" she asked, so quietly her voice was almost swallowed by the din of the restaurant.

"Flirting practice." His expression didn't budge. "Sure, that's what we'll call it."

Stop. Stop looking at his mouth. "I don't think I'm cut out for small talk."

"Says who?" He leaned in while wetting that mouth she was not supposed to be staring at like it was her club sandwich arriving early but . . . wow, he had the sexiest lips. As much as she didn't want to admit it, the texture and give and temperature of them had been plaguing her brain since they'd kissed this morning. Obviously, she hadn't kissed anyone for so long, she'd entered a state of shock.

Right.

"I think you're cut out for a lot of things, Skylar."

"I'm afraid to ask what you mean."

"Afraid of the answer?" His hand on her knee slid ever so slowly to midthigh, massaging, and she couldn't believe . . .

couldn't believe the moisture gathering in the seam of her flesh. In a Cheesecake Factory. With Robbie. Not Madden.

"Yes," she whispered.

His voice was like sandpaper against her ear now. "Afraid you might want to skip forward to make out day?"

Oh. *God.*

It has been so long, cried her libido, sounding like a granny.

"Me?" she asked, breathily. "No, I'm not worried I'll want to skip forward."

"Are you sure?" He tilted his head, examining her mouth like a lion sizing up a mouse. "If I know your strengths and weaknesses, I can coach to those qualities."

"Wow." She tried to give him a look of stern disappointment but couldn't quite keep the amusement out of her tone. Was she having fun with this guy and getting turned on at the same time? She'd never experienced that combination before. Hadn't really believed it possible. *Keep it going. You're learning from him.* "You have no shame," she said lightly, tracing the hand on her thigh with the pad of her index finger, watching his eyes darken dramatically. "Using my own methodology to trick me into making out with you."

"I'm not smart enough to trick you," he said, those blunt fingers lingering on the inside of her knee, moving in a gentle circle that continued to stir something far from gentle inside of her. "I wouldn't even try."

"Ironically, that proves you *are* smart."

They smiled at each other in the low light, Skylar exasperated to find she had to work hard to control her breathing. To control the need to grab a fist of that red hair and drag his mouth down to hers, sealing them together. Forget skipping to Tuesday, she should be more concerned about Thursday coming early. As in, welcome to the main event. Yeah, good thing they were in public, because she could easily go for some of that right now. Purely because her body hadn't been joined with a man's body in such a long time. She'd been picturing her next time with Madden, daydreaming about his careful hands on her skin, but right now? Robbie and his thickly honed body seemed to be taking up *a lot* of air. Too much air to picture anyone or anything else in her mind's eye.

That had to be the only reason she wanted to climb onto Robbie's lap and feel his sex through her jeans. Against her own. Rubbing herself against him there while his tongue stroked in her mouth. And God, that made her disloyal, didn't it?

Not only to Madden, the idea of them, but to her own plans. Her goals.

Because her eagerness was a little too much to consider Robbie merely . . . practice.

She needed some time to get ahold of herself.

Thankfully, plate after plate of food were steadily being set down on their table, forcing Robbie to remove his hand from her thigh and release her from his embrace, though he seemed reluctant to do so. Was he . . . enjoying their "date" as much as she was?

When she would normally keep that kind of worry to herself, something about Robbie made her feel okay about voicing it. Maybe it was his self-deprecating humor or the fact that he'd never judged her request for guidance with men. Whatever the reason, she didn't hesitate. "What are you thinking about?" she asked, weirdly positive he'd tell her the truth. Geez, that certainty was comforting.

"It's killing me that I might let you down tomorrow, Rocket," he said.

"We haven't lost yet," Skylar reassured him, picking up a fry and waving it around like a conductor's baton. "I'm just waiting for inspiration to strike."

They sat side by side for a full minute, Robbie plowing through his chicken parmesan like it had deeply offended him, before the idea came to Skylar.

"Coach to a player's strengths and weaknesses, right?"

Robbie said something unintelligible around a mouthful of pasta.

She popped the fry into her mouth, suddenly eager for the morning challenge to arrive. "I've got a plan."

CHAPTER FIFTEEN

Robbie woke up with the hard-on of the century.

Not exactly newsworthy—that's how he woke up most mornings, but he was usually in the privacy of his own apartment, not on the floor of his fake girlfriend's idyllic childhood home. He reached under the blanket and wrapped his fist around his dick, anyway, trying to judge the appropriateness of beating himself off while Skylar slept a few feet away.

Relieving himself right here and now would definitely cross a boundary.

Wow. Look at me, all ethical and whatnot.

Skylar rolled over in bed, one of her bare thighs coming into view above, all smooth and toned and kissed by the beginnings of the sunrise. Christ, he would give up jerking off for a year for the privilege of licking her knee to pussy, spreading her legs wide on the bed, and just going to motherfucking town on her with his tongue. Last night, she'd made it clear she could use some sexual attention, if not verbally, then by how she'd reacted to his hand on her thigh. Squirming and blushing in the booth of the Cheesecake Factory, staring at his mouth and throat and forearms. Pulse erratic at the base of her neck.

She needed something Robbie knew how to give—and give good.

No wonder he was stiffer than a flagpole in January.

But having a painful erection was a hell of a lot better than having his chest ache, the way it had throughout their "date" last night. Wasn't it? Even though they'd technically been on one date already, back in Boston, he'd still underestimated how fulfilling it would be to sit with her in a restaurant, arm around her shoulders . . . and talk.

Skylar had worried about being a good date? Making small talk?

What she had to offer was so much better than that. She was passionate and honest and insightful. She listened, offered valuable opinions. Sitting in that booth, surrounded by hundreds of diners, he'd sworn they were on their own deserted island. A place where they could say anything and not be judged, only understood. He'd told her about his grandfather's kite. No one knew how much that three feet of yellow nylon being stuck in the tree bothered him. Only her. And that shame felt so safe in her hands, he wanted Skylar to store all his insecurities and secrets and fears now.

The sound of her yawning and stretching made Robbie close his eyes, picturing himself in the bed beside her, instead of lying on the floor. He'd sip her upper lip, followed by the bottom one, while his fingertips slowly teased her nipples, keeping up the treatment until her thighs started to squirm, wordlessly asking for pressure, friction, a more intimate touch, and he'd slide his hand into her panties, hitting her with a deep kiss at the same time. Grip her pussy hard to let her know he'd heard that plea loud and clear. He'd work it in his palm and whisper for permission to finger fuck—

"You awake?" she asked through a second yawn.

"Huh? Yeah," he rasped into the stillness, visions of them still vivid and glorious on the backs of his eyelids. "Happy making out day, Rocket."

She hummed. "Don't get any ideas, Redbeard. I haven't brushed my teeth yet."

Robbie smiled through the pain. There was no one else like her, huh? No games. No pretense. Just real and earnest. "Do you mind me asking when this make out session will take place? Like, before or after I humiliate myself at the rock climbing wall?"

"Maybe we should wait until after you've been humbled. I'll be less intimidated."

Robbie sat up immediately, propping his chin on his hands on the edge of the mattress. "Intimidated?"

She turned on her side, half her face nestled into the pillow. That thigh was still exposed in the sheets, though, and his dick was extremely aware of that spot where thigh turned into hip. His palm itched to span the entirety of that curve, squeeze it, drag his thumb along the slope of her hip bone. Eventually, he'd slide his hand around to that ass, hold it steady while he—

Robbie severed his own train of thought when he noticed the tips of her ears darken while she tried to come up with an explanation for him.

She truly expected to be intimidated. This bothered her.

Why did it suddenly feel like elves were sawing his jugular?

I don't like when things bother her.

"You're going to think I'm . . . stiff," Skylar said, finally. "No, I *am* stiff in those situations."

He made a skeptical face. "No, I'm pretty sure I'm going to be the stiff one."

"You know what I mean."

Yeah, he did. Her worry didn't make sense to him, though. "Skylar, when I kissed you yesterday in the front yard, you fucking melted. You weren't stiff whatsoever." She blinked, appearing to think back to the prior morning. "If you really think you're stiff with men, maybe it's something they're doing wrong, not you."

"Both of them?"

"Both of what?"

"Both guys I've . . . hooked up with."

"You've only hooked up with two guys? *Ever?*"

"Can you yell it a little louder so my parents and brother hear you?"

"Sorry, I just . . . sorry." Encountering the alarming, sudden urge to weep, Robbie briefly pressed his face into the mattress, before lifting his head again. "Honey. I was probably awkward the first *eight* times I was with a woman. You've only been in the situation twice."

Brown eyes narrowed. "Keep talking."

"I'd rather you keep talking. Tell me what you didn't like about it."

Skylar shifted a little, as if to get more comfortable in the sheets. Did she like talking to him, too? Was he not totally blowing this cool sleepover moment? "It moved too fast. I didn't even have a chance to get used to the foreplay. I wasn't given any time to find my rhythm. It was just a sweaty, frantic mess."

"So, you didn't . . ."

"Didn't what?"

"Orgasm."

"Oh. God, no. They didn't even call me afterward."

"I mean, I'm not defending them, but they probably didn't call because they were embarrassed. If you'd hooked up with me when I was eighteen, I could have easily been a sweaty, frantic guy. It takes us a while to figure out what the fuck we're doing."

"And now you know."

"Yes, Skylar. I know." His cock was deeply, deeply invested in this conversation, having turned uncomfortably heavy in his sweatpants. "I hear what you're saying. You want to take your time. You want . . . a man to take his time."

"That doesn't seem like a lot to ask."

"It's not." His abs were starting to burn from being flexed too long, just to combat the rough pull of need in his balls. *Deep breaths.* "When we practice making out—or anything else on the calendar, for that matter—you'll get all the time you need. If you just want to kiss, that's what we'll do." Robbie gave in to the impulse to reach up and trace the outside of her thigh with a single fingertip, trailing it from hip to knee, then back, listening to the acceleration of her breath in the quiet room. "If you want to tease me through my clothes, I'll do my best to live through it. Or you could find out . . ."

He shut his unholy speech down before it went out of bounds, but she didn't seem happy about it. "Or I could find out what?" A slow blink. "Don't censor yourself with me. Just say it. I could find out what?"

"How it feels to have your cunt eaten by a man who gets it dripping first."

Her eyelids fluttered, those lips parting but no sound coming out.

"Was that too much?" he asked after a full ten seconds of silence.

"I guess not." She drew the word out, followed by a swallow. "Because here I am, trying to mentally rearrange some things in my planner so we have more time."

Robbie exhaled. "Attagirl."

Skylar sat up slowly, seeming a little disoriented, and his gaze was drawn several places at once. Her dark hair, flattened on one side, haywire on the other. So stinking cute that a knot formed behind his Adam's apple. Then . . . oh Jesus. The plushness of her mouth after sleep. Her braless tits swayed inside the twisted tank top, nipples stiff and poking the cotton, which he decided to take as a compliment toward his dirty talk.

All of him needed all of her.

Badly.

Was she even remotely on the same page?

"Can you give it to me?"

Go time.

Robbie got to his knees, already wetting his lips. "Now? I thought you'd never ask—"

"About my planner? Sorry, can you hand it to me? It's on the dresser."

"Oh. Yeah." He crossed a forearm over his erection, attempting to hide it and push the goddamn thing down at the same time. With his free hand, he swiped the little white planner off the dresser and settled it in her lap, which, incidentally, is where he wanted his face. "Here you go."

Resigned to the agony, Robbie propped his chin on a fist and watched Skylar leaf through her planner, finding the sound and structure of her days incredibly soothing, despite the situation in his sweatpants. When she found the little, lined box containing a list of the day's activities, he leaned forward to read them.

1. Pitch (1 hr)
2. Breakfast
3. Shower
4. Rock climbing challenge
5. MOP
6. Dinner with Eve

MISC. NOTES: Robbie spending night in Boston (practice). Borrowing my car.

"Hey. *I'm* in there." He couldn't control the grin that spread his mouth. Their schedules were intertwined. "When did you write that?"

"You told me on the ride here, so I wrote it in when we arrived."

"Cool. You're still okay with my using your car?"

"Yes."

"Great." He jerked his chin at the tiny book. "I assume MOP stands for making out practice. How much time will we have?"

"It depends when you're leaving to reach Boston."

"Around four, I'd say."

"Oooh. We might have to reschedule MOP."

"No. We're not rescheduling MOP. We're MOP'ing."

A corner of her mouth wiggled. Almost like she was pleased to know he wanted to make out with her. Did this girl own a fucking mirror, or what? Any man worth his salt would kill for a shot. "We're only going to have about twenty minutes between getting back from rock climbing and you leaving for practice."

Robbie scoffed. "I can make magic happen in half that time, Rocket."

"Really? Maybe I should be calling *you* Rocket."

"Nah, you're going to be calling me Big Daddy later," Robbie boasted, forgetting all about his erection and standing up while scratching his chest hair. At least, he forgot about it until Skylar's eyes grew three times in size. "Shit." He turned to face the opposite direction and glanced down to get an accurate picture of what she'd seen. Good God, he looked like he had a torpedo in his pants. "Sorry about that."

"I-I . . ." She struggled for words. "When did it get like that?"

"I woke up like this."

"And you were just carrying on a normal conversation with it?"

"Uh, yeah. It's a skill we're all required to learn during puberty, Skylar. These things have a mind of their own."

"Well . . ." Was she breathing harder than before? "What are you planning to do about it?"

"Honestly?" He looked back at Skylar over his shoulder, inordinately pleased to find her attention locked on his ass. "Wait until you go out to pitch, then . . ."

Two beats of silence passed. "Then what?"

That whispered question had Robbie's forehead wrinkling, his gaze seeking her out once again over his shoulder, his cock thickening that final, painful degree when she looked flushed and . . . interested? Excited? "You want details?"

Her nod was slight, but it was there.

Pulses were firing at the speed of light all over his body. Wrists, neck, chest. His dick had been hard so long without being attended to, his stomach was beginning to hurt from keeping the weight of his sex hoisted. From keeping the pressure locked inside, not letting it out. And so he gave in to the need, gritting his teeth and gripping himself through his sweatpants, heat prickling up his spine at the sound of her gasp.

"Details . . ." he muttered thickly, sweat beads beginning to pop up on his chest, upper lip. "I was going to lock your door, track down some tissue, lie back down. Spit on my palm a couple of times and . . . try and not grunt too loudly while I stroke one out."

Her pupils dilated. "You grunt when you do it?"

"Yeah." He raked the heel of his hand down to the thickened ridge, cupping his balls and jostling them lightly, before massaging back up to the tip. Ahhh, fuck. So good. Ten times better than usual because Skylar was in the room while he did it, her voice the soundtrack to his lust. "I think so. I'm not really focused on the sounds I'm making."

"Oh."

"Oh what?"

"I don't know. When I watch . . . porn?" Her voice was slightly muffled, as if she'd covered her face. "That's my favorite part. When the guy groans."

Damn, he was learning some invaluable lessons about her this morning. A treasure trove of Skylar-isms that he would put to incredible use, if and when he was afforded the opportunity. "Why?"

"I don't know. I guess . . . the girl always seems to be faking it, but the guy . . . when he groans, he seems to be authentically enjoying himself. It's hot."

Robbie's chest was heaving like he'd just swum the Potomac. "You wouldn't be fake moaning with me. I'd probably have to cover your mouth to keep you quiet."

A shuddering breath from Skylar.

Fuck it.

She'd given him this opening. He wasn't going to pass it up.

"Do you want to watch me fuck myself, Skylar?"

An audible swallow. "Yeah. Yes, please."

Oh my God. "Are you sure? I don't want you to be uncomfortable around me."

Actually, that might physically kill him. Messing up the bond they were building.

"I'm sur—"

"Great. Good." He turned, his knees almost losing power at the way her attention zeroed in on his cock, her eyelids sagging, fingers digging into the bedding. And when he sat down on the left edge of the mattress, leaned back onto his left elbow, took out his dick in his right fist, and settled it against his abdomen, her mouth formed an O that did remarkable things for his ego. "I'm going to spit on my hand now."

She nodded, cheeks bloomed with pink spots.

Robbie spat in his palm.

Before he could bring the natural lubricant where it needed to go, Skylar snagged his wrist, brought his hand to her mouth . . . and spit in his palm. All while looking him in the eye.

Coming without touching himself became a very distinct possibility in that moment.

"Christ," he said hoarsely, fisting his cock before he could humiliate himself. One slide of his clenched fingers was like throwing a match into a puddle of kerosene, though, and he just went for broke, groaning behind his gritted teeth, watching her face while he masturbated. "You like having your spit on my dick, baby?"

Son of a bitch, she was mesmerized. "Yes."

"Ohhh. Fuck." He pumped his fist faster. "No one's ever watched me do this before."

"Really?" Her smile was drowsy, horny. "I'm the first?"

First girl he could fall in love with, too.

Don't say that out loud.

Don't even think it. So dangerous.

"What are you fantasizing about?" she asked. Closer than before? Was that her breath on his shoulder? Lord. "While you do it."

"I don't have to fantasize about anything," he said in stops and starts, the pleasure beginning to hit an overwhelming high. "Not when you're lying there with no bra. Your fucking thighs . . ."

She shifted the legs in question, rasping them on the sheets. "My thighs?"

Too close now. Filter gone. "I'm thinking of my spit all over them. How I'll lick it on there to help my hips slide when I'm riding you into the goddamn ground."

A hitched moan from Skylar was the absolute end of him. His

balls tightened, wrenching a groan from the pit of his stomach, and he got off in his frenzied hand, his thighs jerking against the edge of the mattress, his head tipped back, mouth wide, while he captured as much moisture as possible in his moving fist, the rest of it seeping out around his knuckles. During what he thought was that final wave of pleasure, he looked over at Skylar's perked-up nipples and blew another hard rope, then another, his whole body collapsing back onto the bed, gasping for fucking air.

Whoa.

Whoa, what the hell?

Sex had never been so . . . satisfying. And she hadn't even *touched* him.

Okay. Yeah. I'm in deep-ass trouble here.

Robbie shook himself free of the lingering bliss of relief and studied Skylar, trying to figure out where she was landing on all this. Was she regretting the intimacy? Was she still processing what happened? *What?* Her eyes were glazed and glued to a spot in the near distance, those sexy nipples still in perfect peaks. Thus, his brain said horny.

Deciding to trust that assessment, Robbie leaned over and brushed their lips together, that zing of connection winging around his chest like a majestic bald eagle only driving home the fact that, yeah, he was screwed. "Do you want me to take care of you?" Entranced by those chips of gold in her eyes, he cupped the side of her face with his clean hand, keeping their lips close. So close. "No fake moans with me. With us."

Us.

That word visibly grabbed her attention. In a good or bad way, he couldn't tell.

Not right away.

But when she bounded off the bed and crouched down in front of her suitcase, pulling out clothes and backing toward the door? He concluded . . . bad.

She didn't want an us.

She wanted Skylar and Madden.

Not Skylar and Robbie.

"Hey, listen," he said, voice gravelly as he yanked his sweatpants up to cover himself. "I didn't mean to—"

"It's fine. I just need to pitch. I'm late to pitch."

He swallowed a handful of tacks. "Okay. I'll see you after."

And then she was gone, leaving Robbie to stare at the closed door.

CHAPTER SIXTEEN

Skylar stared at her parents as they gave instructions for the rock climbing challenge. Doug's mouth was moving, expounding on his journey to becoming a certified climber while everyone else baked bread during Covid, but Skylar was only catching every seventh or eighth word. Ever since Robbie . . . did that. On her bed. Just did it right there. A low, horny hum had been taking up most of her ear function.

She'd gone through the motions while harnessing up and preparing for the climb, her brain moving at half the usual speed. Slogging. Making robot beeps. Could anyone blame her? How was she supposed to live with that mental imagery?

Look. She'd shared a bathroom with her brother starting at age twelve. As she'd reached later teenhood, that period of time in their respective youths when he'd taken forty-five-minute showers had made a lot more sense.

Unfortunately, by then, it had been too late to start hiding her loofa, but she digressed. Male masturbation wasn't some exotic idea. She knew it occurred with great frequency. Had even overheard her brother's friends talking about it from time to time. She'd just never expected to see someone doing it two feet away.

And enjoying it so much.

Talking to her—*about* her—while he enjoyed it so much.

Time to face facts. Robbie's hotness was beginning to be a

problem. Madden was standing ten yards to her left, reconnoitering with Elton about strategy for the challenge, and Skylar could focus on nothing but the memory of Robbie's corded forearm shifting and flexing while he stroked himself. The way his neck strained. The glazed quality of his eyes.

The way he'd lifted his hips on a particularly thorough stroke, making a choked sound. Panting.

How he'd reached completion to thoughts of them. Together.

I'm thinking of my spit all over them. How I'll lick it on there to help my hips slide when I'm riding you into the goddamn ground.

Brain cells were pouring out of her nostrils at this point.

Panicked, she zoned out and attempted to picture Madden in the same position on the edge of her childhood bed, pleasuring himself while she watched . . . and she couldn't even imagine it. Madden would never speak to her like that, would he? Had he spent too many years thinking of her as Elton's little sister to be that . . . blunt and unabashed and sexual in her presence?

Because . . . oof. She liked it.

A lot.

Robbie gave her a subtle nudge in the ribs. "Look alive, Rocket."

"I'm alive. I'm ready."

"You're as red as my hair."

"It's . . . the preclimb adrenaline. It's beginning to surge—"

"Right." Sighing, he faced his thick body toward Skylar, leaning down to whisper in the hair above her ear, the action blowing a warm shiver down her spine. An even more heightened sense of awareness than before. One that she really didn't *want.* "Look, I'm sorry about earlier. I shouldn't have done that in front of you."

"I asked you to do it." God, her voice sounded husky.

"Maybe so, but we deviated from your schedule. I knew better than to do that. You told me we were sticking to the plan." He slid her a glance. "Now you look like you've just returned from an alien encounter."

"That's not so far off." She cut him off before he could respond. "Don't you dare make a joke about the Milky Way."

"How?" He stared. "How did you know?"

She pursed her lips at him. "I told you, I played on the boys' team in middle school. Fluid jokes are part of the deal."

"You never told me the boys were being inappropriate, Skylar," Vivica said, coming up behind them unexpectedly, dismay written all over her face. "I would have said something to the coach."

"It's okay, Mom." Skylar waved off her mother's concern, even though it felt nice to have Vivica focus on her feelings. A rarity. "The guys probably would have just laid it on thicker."

Robbie choked. Turned white from holding his breath.

Vivica didn't seem to notice. "That kind of thing can really affect someone's performance." She rolled an irritable shoulder. "They're lucky it didn't."

"Right." Skylar exhaled. "My performance is what matters most."

"Hell, yeah, it is," Elton said, hands on hips, staring up at the rock face. "Ask the scout from Brown."

Three members of her family snorted, passing a knowing look among their trio. Even if her mother frowned after only a few seconds of mirth and gave the men a reproving look, Skylar still felt that comment in the deepest pit of her stomach.

"Honey." Doug sent his wife a tight smile. "Wasn't it Mark Twain that said, 'The two most important days in your life are the day you were born and the day you find out why'?"

"Yes, it was," Vivica confirmed with a squeeze of Skylar's shoulder. "Words to live by. And she does, to the best of her ability. That is all any parent could ask for."

"Thanks," Skylar said with a fleeting smile, just wanting the conversation to be over, please, for the love of everything holy. When Vivica walked away to go consult with Doug, Skylar let out the breath she'd been holding and all at once, became aware of Robbie's bewildered scrutiny.

"Holy shit, that was unhinged. Are you good?" Robbie asked, seeing way more than was comfortable. How had this man been a part of her life so briefly and already knew her triggers? The tension with her family regarding her shortcomings. Her scheduling quirks. He'd picked up on her so fast.

It was as comforting as it was scary.

"Yeah." When he raised an eyebrow at her, his concern obvious, Skylar repeated herself, quieter this time, grateful for his presence despite her growing concern that she and Robbie were getting too close, too fast. "Yes."

After a moment of scrutiny, he nodded. "Great. Because I've got two things to say. One. Nothing is *ever* going to be more important than you, regardless of how you perform. Got that?"

"Yes," she managed, pulse tripping.

"Good." He studied her for a moment, as if to confirm, before bracing. "And two . . . I can't even look at that rock wall without getting sick."

Still flustered from the first part of that statement, she worked to recover. "Just stick to the plan."

"The plan is not foolproof."

"It's the best we've got."

His mouth flattened into a grim line, signs of seasickness beginning to creep into his complexion. Such a range of moods in one morning. Worry. Humor. Apprehension. Sensuality . . . with a mesmerizing side of helplessness at the end. When his muscles tensed up and his shaft darkened and he'd groaned, that fist picking up speed—

"Skylar," Robbie said, his laugh more like a scrape.

"What?"

"Have I ever told you that whatever you're thinking shows on your face?"

Impossible. She was a pitcher. A poker face was essential, and she'd sharpened the skill like a knife over the last decade. Dina remarked on it all the time. Was it possible that Robbie alone could discern her thoughts so easily without a word? No. Absolutely not. "What am I thinking about?"

"Not the challenge," he snorted.

"Oh?"

"*My* O. That's what you're thinking about." He closed the already scant distance between them while running his tongue along his lower lip. "Guess it's only fair since all I can think about is getting one out of you."

"Oh."

He hummed low in his throat. "There's that word again." His pupils had nearly eclipsed the green of his irises at this point. "I'll give you as many as you can fucking stand, Skylar. Swear to God, just set me loose."

There was no breath remaining in Skylar's lungs when her parents blew the air horn.

Birds screeched out of the trees overhead, plunging her back into reality with a wheezing gasp, her spine snapping to attention. A monumental feat considering heat rolled through the lowest region of her belly like thunder, her skin hot and clammy. Another vision of Robbie hitting his peak threatened to garner her brain power once again, but she managed to stave it off with a wave of determination. *Focus.*

"Okay, teams," boomed her father, turning sideways to indicate six ropes hanging from the cliff overhead. At the end of each one was a harness. "As we communicated in the challenge sheet, one member of the team will ascend to the top of the peak and retrieve the flag, bringing it down to their partner. That partner will then climb to the same spot and plant the flag. First team to stake their team colors in the soil wins. Are the instructions clear?"

"Yes, sir," Madden and Elton said, approaching the line and attaching it to their harness with the metal carabiner, testing the hold. Skylar joined them, doing the same. Meanwhile, Robbie stayed where he was, the trench between his brows growing deeper by the second.

Her father frowned at Robbie. "Aren't you going to attach yourself to the line, son?"

"Actually, no. He's not," Skylar answered on his behalf. "The rules stated that the first player must ascend to the top of the peak. But it didn't specify how."

Doug and Vivica traded a puzzled look. "I think it was abundantly clear that both players are required to climb," blustered Doug.

"We read it differently, Dad," Skylar said breezily.

"Wow. This is the first year you've felt the need to cheat, Sky," Elton cut in. "But don't worry, I'm sure it has nothing to do with your new partner."

"Eat a dick, Elton," she chirped back without missing a beat.

"Skylar!" Vivica was not pleased. "Language!"

Robbie's appreciative laughter, however, cracked behind her, stealing a very immature giggle from Skylar's throat. In her defense, there was usually no one on her side. Skylar versus the unrelenting torture of her older brother who never seemed to be admonished for teasing her. That was normal. During the rare times she'd broken down and cried when the sibling rivalry had gotten out of hand, her parents had ordered her in no uncertain terms to suck it up.

You're tough, Sky.

You're tougher than this.

This will only make you tougher.

Robbie standing behind her, laughing at her insult, might be a small thing to some people. But it was big and wonderful to her. She looked back at him over her shoulder to give him an appreciative smile, which, for some reason, made him appear . . . winded? Like he'd been socked in the gut? Clearly, his fear of heights was rearing its ugly head.

As SOON AS Doug blew the whistle, Robbie started to sprint.

Last night, he and Skylar had devised a plan—a terrible one, honestly, but his phobia of heights had left them little choice. In this outlandish scenario, he would run west as fast as possible to the path leading to the top of the rock face, which was a good quarter mile of uneven terrain away, thus avoiding the actual climb. He'd retrieve the flag from the top of the cliff, hopefully without spewing his guts, before running back and tagging in Skylar for her leg of the climb.

Not a foolproof plan. His muscles were already tensing at the prospect of seeing the ground from such a high height. And as he wove through trees and leapt over fallen branches, he could think of nothing but Skylar's smile. How she'd looked at him right before the whistle blew. Like he was some kind of hero.

Something told him he was about to disprove that theory.

It burned like hell that Madden was probably halfway up the rock face by now, no fear holding him back. As if the guy needed one more advantage.

Robbie spied the path and turned on a dime, running full speed up the gradual incline, passing a hiking couple who were startled by the sudden appearance of a six-foot-five man with a warrior's physique. It called into focus exactly how bananas this entire competition happened to be. No time to dwell on that, however, as he'd nearly reached the top of the cliff . . .

That's when the dizziness started to set in, his stomach elevating toward his mouth.

The pace of his run slowed without a command from his brain, suddenly feeling as if he'd slung his equipment bag over each shoulder. Heavy. Lethargic. Blurry. Everything blurred, the ground growing less stable beneath his feet the closer he came toward the red flag where it sat buried in the ground. Too close to the edge. Way too close.

Robbie got down on his knees and started to crawl, desperately trying to avoid looking into the distance where he could see the tops of trees, a reservoir, the view making it obvious he was elevated. His temples started to throb, acid spearing up his chest, and he stopped feeling the earth beneath his hands, his knees.

Somewhere in the whirlwind of warnings being issued by his brain—*danger, danger*—he saw his grandfather at the bottom of the cliff back on Long Island, waiting for him to untangle the yellow box kite from the tree. Robbie hadn't been able to retrieve that kite, either, and though Grandpa Nick had hidden his disappointment well, he'd hated driving away and leaving it there. His favorite kite. Stuck in the tree overlooking the Atlantic forever, because he'd died before he'd gotten it back. Robbie could still see it blowing in the breeze.

He opened his eyes just in time to see Madden crest the top of the cliff and snatch up his team's flag, giving Robbie a look of sympathy before disappearing from view once again. Robbie, who couldn't make himself move any closer to the edge without either blacking out or having a nervous breakdown.

Skylar replaced the mental image of his grandfather at the base of the drop and all he could do was lay his head down and wait for the nausea to pass.

CHAPTER SEVENTEEN

Robbie Corrigan was not good at losing.

He was an even worse loser when he dragged Skylar down with him.

The ride back to the house was as close as one could get to hell. Parents up front humming out of tune to KC and the Sunshine Band, Elton in the back seat swiping Tinder matches . . . and Skylar sandwiched between him and Madden—who hadn't turned the color of a tomato and nearly swallowed his tongue due to a thirty-foot drop—in the middle row.

Madden looked deep in thought, as always, like some kind of hulking-ass poet, but Robbie wasn't buying the act. Every time Madden's thigh brushed Skylar's, he knew exactly what he was doing. Driving nails into Robbie's composure, that's what. There were three rows in this tank of an SUV. Why hadn't Madden sat in the far back seat with Elton?

Same reason as Robbie, most likely. They couldn't fit through the opening. And since Skylar would rather shave off her eyebrows than sit beside a gloating Elton, the middle row was the only option for all of them.

Three had never been more of a crowd.

Robbie wanted to put his arm around Skylar and make it clear any rogue thigh brushing was not welcome, but he didn't deserve the privilege after such a humiliating show of fear back during the climb. She had to be wondering why she'd trusted him enough to bring him on as a teammate. And now he had to drive back to Boston for practice, leaving her within striking distance of Madden aka Sad Boi Mad.

God, she looked so fucking pretty, too. Sun-kissed and a little disheveled, the glow of her skin standing out against her white tank top.

Madden had to be noticing by now.

Robbie glanced over at the other man, positive he'd find him checking out Skylar and vice versa—but he was surprised instead to find Skylar looking at *him*. Robbie.

"You're dwelling," she whispered.

"Dwelling?" He feigned confusion. "On what?"

Exasperation only made her more beautiful. "Not handling the height very well," she explained, as if teaching a toddler his ABCs. "You have to shake it off."

"I already have. It has long been shooketh."

"Come on. You won't even *look* at me."

"I'm looking right *at* you."

"Those are my boobs, Redbeard."

Robbie snorted, waved her off. Stared out the rear passenger window. "I'm just trying to lock in for practice tonight."

She hummed. In the window's reflection, he noticed her looking down at her fingers.

"What?" he asked.

"Nothing."

"What?"

"*Nothing*. I just . . . wish you weren't going."

His head swiveled around so fast, he gave himself a crick. "Why not?"

A pink blush coasted upward toward her hairline.

Oh. Okay. Damn, he was slow on the uptake sometimes.

Skylar was obviously trying to flirt with him in front of Madden and he was dropping the ball. But Jesus, he didn't have much selflessness in his tank right now. Hardly any.

Find some.

"Yeah, I don't want to leave, either," he said quietly, kissing her forehead. "I don't want to leave you for a single minute, actually," Robbie added, in a rush of honesty, feeling Madden's gaze on them as Robbie executed what was beginning to feel less and less like deception. At least on his end. Skylar still wanted to have Madden's babies.

They'd produce brooding pitchers with big eyes and a cautious nature.

Meanwhile, if Robbie and Skylar procreated and combined their competitive streaks and mutual mischief, their children would probably set shit on fire and howl at the moon.

Robbie flicked Madden a glance before he could completely hide his envy. Skylar saw it and tilted her head, considering him, then Madden.

As if she'd forgotten the catcher was sitting there, nearly plastered to her side?

Wishful thinking, at *best*.

"Home sweet home," called Doug from the front seat.

"Please take off your dirty shoes before going inside," Vivica said absently, before she twisted in her seat to regard the occupants of the van. "Everyone has plans tonight, as I understand it, so we won't bother cooking. Every man for himself."

"What?" Elton piped up from the back seat. "I don't have plans."

"Loser," Skylar said, without hesitation, tugging up one corner of Robbie's mouth.

Dammit, she was so cool.

They would have had so much fun together. If she wasn't in love with someone else and he hadn't outed himself as a womanizer on day one—a fair title, honestly. That's what he'd been for years. She was right to set her sights elsewhere. Obviously. Although something inside of him was starting to . . . feel a lot less inclined to let her go.

Or help her attract Madden.

Also known as the only goddamn reason he was in Rhode Island.

No. His teammates had warned him about this.

Getting attached. Wanting Skylar for himself.

Don't reach for something you can't have.

"Sorry, I, uh . . ." Robbie took off his seat belt, his earlier queasiness threatening to return. "I better grab my things and get on the road. Don't want to be late for practice."

Madden had already climbed out of the van before Robbie finished speaking. Skylar continued to regard him for two, three breaths, then exited, as well, Robbie close behind. He didn't stop on his way into the house. Something weird was happening inside of his chest and he needed to get out of there, before it sprouted spikes and sank them in.

He kicked off his sneakers to the right of the front door and entered the house, beelining for Skylar's back bedroom. Indecision and frustration crowded in on him from all sides. He didn't want to leave her there with Madden. He also knew it was dangerous to stay and absorb more of what he couldn't have.

As soon as he reached the bedroom, he unplugged his cell phone charger and stuffed it into his bag, intending to hit the bathroom next where he would collect his toothbrush—

The bedroom door snicked shut.

Skylar stood just inside the door.

"You're not coming back, are you?"

Once she said it out loud, he acknowledged it to himself. That's exactly what his instincts were demanding he do. Get out while he could. Get out before he fell in love with her.

Was he too late?

"I don't know," he said, finally, in response to her question.

"It was one challenge, Robbie. You're overreacting."

He almost laughed. She thought his wanting to bail was all about the climb. No. That might have sparked this epiphany, but his reason for blowing this joint was a lot more complicated than embarrassment over not being able to accept a loss.

Skylar crossed the bedroom and sat heavily on the edge of her mattress, looking down at her palms, as if she'd never seen them before.

He had.

He'd studied those pitching calluses in the predawn light for the last two days when he couldn't sleep, his gaze continually drawn to her fingers, slack in sleep, dangling over the side of the bed. As if she'd dozed off in the act of reaching for him.

"Please, don't do this, okay?" Skylar said now, looking up at him, so openly vulnerable his lungs suddenly grew twice their weight. "Today was the first Page Stakes where I felt like I was on a team. Around my family." She was silent for a moment. "Maybe anywhere, really. Pitching is so solitary, even when you're surrounded by teammates. I know my family is intense and the Page Stakes are wacky, but I feel like we have a chance. I feel . . . I don't want you to go."

Don't you dare read anything into that.

"I have practice, Skylar."

"I'm not trying to keep you from practice. I'm talking about in the morning. Are you going to come back or stay in Boston?"

Robbie didn't respond. How could he?

One choice disappointed her. The other one had the potential to devastate him.

"I'll text you after practice."

"Bullshit."

"Skylar . . ." *I overestimated my ability to hand you over to someone else. Someone better.* With that truth ringing in his head, he turned to leave.

Before he could open the bedroom door, Skylar's hand twisted in the back of his T-shirt, holding him in place. "Wait."

All at once, he couldn't gather a breath, his chest tight with the need to turn around and look at her. Soak her in again.

Don't do it.

"Thank you for coming. For staying as long as you did," she said, getting herself together. Enough to sound a little formal, but sincere. "I'm sorry it has to end like this."

End.

End?

That's what he would do by leaving. End this, end *them* for good. Leaving before his part in the bargain was fulfilled. Not only his role as her fake boyfriend, but . . . the itinerary would never be completed. Jesus, if he left here without giving her making out day, at the very least, no greater crime would ever be committed. From now until the end of time.

"Why aren't you leaving?" she whispered.

For a full three seconds, time and movement suspended, her words turning the air sluggish, even while his pulse started to beat a thousand miles an hour. Briefly, white light bled into the edges of his vision, his grip around the handle of his duffel growing less and less sure. In the end, it was the promise of her taste, the silkiness of her hair in his hands. The chance to burn himself into her brain, the way she'd done to him.

"I can't fucking leave without knowing what it's like to kiss you . . ." he said through his teeth. "When it's just for us. Not for anyone else. Not for show."

Clearly sensing his hesitation to go, the conflict being waged inside of him, Skylar maintained her hold on his shirt, using it to pull herself closer, closer, while he held his breath, letting it out on a big shudder when she went up on her toes, pressing her open mouth to the back of his neck and releasing a warm exhale.

"Go on. Show me how to make out, Robbie."

Heat and hunger trampled through him. Juggernauts. "*Skylar.*"

Her right hand traveled slowly along his rib cage to the front of his body, pausing momentarily at the top of his abdominal muscles, before her fingers curled inward and her touch dropped away entirely. Leaving him sick. "Sorry, if you want to go, I won't stop—"

Robbie dropped his bag and spun around in one swift movement, catching her face in between his hands, his mouth coming down on hers, their lips barely meeting before opening for each other, his tongue dipping into her mouth and stroking slowly, a breathy sound falling from both of them. One of uncertainty and hunger, all rolled into one.

He wanted to back her up, make her lose her balance onto the bed.

Get on top of her.

Kiss her until she forgot her name and location and started begging him to fuck.

He could do it. He could cover her mouth and bang her rough as hell, right under her father's roof, make her squeal into his palm. Christ, he *needed* to know what her pussy felt like. How fast it dampened and how tight it clenched when she got excited. How well his cock would fit. Whether or not she liked to be pinned and flipped over and manhandled.

Making out was a far cry from sex, though.

Get yourself together.

She had asked to be taught. Not debauched.

"Come here," he growled, breaking the kiss and leading her over to the dresser, turning her around so she could look in the mirror, Robbie looming behind her. That ass tucked into his lap like a motherfucking dream and although he tilted his hips slightly to get his dick tight between those ass cheeks, he grit his teeth and ignored the urge to yank down her yoga pants and panties, the way he wanted. "Look at yourself. In the mirror."

"What?" Her neck seemed to lack power suddenly, her head briefly lolling to the right, before straightening up. "O-oh. Okay."

"You told me before that sex happens too quickly, right? That you never get time to find a rhythm." He fisted her hair and pulled to the left, exposing her neck, his open mouth dragging up the full length, not stopping until he reached her ear and groaned against the smooth shell of it. "We're working on foreplay, Rocket. That's the purpose of making out. You can demand what you need. You can ask for the things that will get you ready."

Already, her eyes were glassy, her tits rising and shuddering back down in the neckline of her tank top. "I can ask. Demand."

"That's right." Never breaking eye contact, he planted his lips on the side of her neck, suctioning, razing his teeth and lapping at the spot almost crudely, all while his hand kept a firm grip on her hair. In charge of her, yeah. In charge of the situation, most definitely. But most importantly, impressing on her that she had a right to speak out loud. To express what she needed.

Express it with me.

Temporarily.

Robbie fought through the steep drop of his stomach. "Do you like that?"

"Yes," she said, lips barely moving. "Yeah, I like it."

"Then ask for more."

"More," she gasped, her mouth falling wide when he bit the spot that connected her shoulder and neck, raking his teeth up to her ear and breathing hard there. Yanking her hips up and tighter to his lap, looking her in the eye while he humped her once, twice, three times, rattling the dresser. "More, more, more," she said, teeth chattering.

Robbie whirled Skylar around to face him, unsurprised when her thighs wound around his waist like vines around a pole, their frenzied mouths meeting to fuck, tongues and lips and teeth clashing in the most sensual battle, his hands finding and massaging her juicy ass, squeezing until she whimpered and let her head fall back, giving him her neck again, shaking in his arms when he attacked it, laving and sucking and kissing.

"That's what you need, isn't it?" He cracked his palm against the right cheek of her backside, baring his teeth against her mouth as she gasped. "Yeah, it is. Tell me that college girl pussy isn't getting wet right now." Her thigh muscles rippled around him, her stomach hollowing, lust and censure warring in her eyes, though lust was clearly winning. "That's how it is, Skylar. I talk fucking dirty."

"I like it," she managed.

"I *know* you like it or you wouldn't be rubbing your cunt on my lap."

"*Robbie.*"

He pressed a wicked grin against her mouth, snagging a hard kiss. "If only it was Thursday, right? I'd have your knees over my fucking shoulders by now."

God. God.

This wasn't making out. This was more.

Everything between them felt like *more*.

He walked her backward until he had her flattened against the door, his hips pumping once out of pure desperation to connect to her, to Skylar, to imprint her body with his, to leave a fucking mark. To own her. Give her ownership over him—

No. No, she didn't want that. You're screwing yourself, Corrigan.

Slow down, slow down, slow down.

"Slow down," he said thickly against her mouth. "Too fast. Too much."

I'm at the point of no return.

"Please keep kissing me."

Fuck it. A little longer.

"Okay, baby. Okay." A slanting of lips, followed by the slowest, most perfect twist of hard on soft, an unbelievable rush of surprise and pleasure inside of him over how they anticipated each other's movements, rough for rough, savoring for savoring. The taste and texture and scent of her broke into his brain like a burglar and ransacked the place, his heart thumping crazily in his rib cage. *I could kiss you for the rest of my life.*

That was the thought that had Robbie breaking away, struggling for breath.

Struggling not to look at her and start their engines again, mauling her mouth until tomorrow came and went, Robbie ordered himself to let her down carefully, both of them panting as he backed up, putting distance between them that he hated as much as he needed, purely for his own self-preservation.

"That's enough . . . for now."

She blew a piece of hair out of her face and his heart turned over. "Huh."

Leaving Skylar breathing hard, dazed and flushed against the door, was the hardest thing he'd ever done in his life, including NHL training camp, but he managed to pick up his bag and get out the door with his heart still inside of his chest.

"Bye, Skylar," he rasped, unable to resist kissing her temple on the way into the hall.

"Bye, Robbie."

It only took him half a mile to realize he'd been dead wrong. His heart—and apparently all his common sense—had been left behind in Rhode Island.

What the hell did he do now?

CHAPTER EIGHTEEN

Skylar parted the hanging beads leading into the underground burlesque club, a swanky, swoony, old-fashioned melody guiding her toward the performance area. The Gilded Garden was smoky, but not from cigarettes. The fog machine positioned at the entrance to the club was Skylar's favorite of Eve's ideas. *I want people to feel like they're walking through a screen and stepping back into the past.*

You definitely nailed it, Eve.

As soon as Skylar emerged from the fog, the lights turned a citrine blue, and she was surrounded by Roaring Twenties decor. Black-and-white pictures of performers in various stages of near undress hung along the hallway walls, showcased by golden art deco frames. The entire ceiling was made up of pink feather plumes that hung down, close enough to tickle Skylar's forehead if she went up on her toes. A familiar brassy and crystal chandelier hung at the end of the hallway, beckoning customers forward, along with the sensual hibiscus fragrance, to the mouth of the club where the stage and tables were nestled into the sapphire darkness.

Skylar wasn't a club person. She was the "drink a gallon of water, get a lot of sleep, and wake up refreshed" type. But she envied the creativity it took to start with Eve's father's no-frills strip club and build something like the Gilded Garden out of it. To have a vision for something so fantastical and make it happen.

Her surroundings only drove home the fact that Skylar and Eve had opposing personalities. Perhaps they never even would have been friends, except for the day in middle school Skylar had overheard Joe Logan asking Eve if she planned on stripping at her father's club after graduation, because he'd be first in line to pay the cover charge. Skylar might have left her defense of Eve as a simple *shut up and leave her alone, Joe.*

Then she'd witnessed Joe pinch Eve's butt.

Skylar decked him, instead.

Well worth the three-day suspension during which Eve had arrived at the front door of the Page household with a stack of Skylar's homework. She'd gone and collected it from all of Skylar's teachers, saving Skylar from having to do the legwork upon her return to school.

"Are we even?" Eve had asked, stone-faced.

Skylar had propped her shoulder against the doorjamb, pretending to think about it. "No, I'm pretty sure I still owe you. I've wanted to punch that fucker for years."

They'd been inseparable from that day forward.

Eve attended all of Skylar's softball games, though she read a book in the stands and didn't participate in the chants or cheers. Skylar did her homework with Eve in the office of the strip club, too, from time to time, though she'd wisely omitted that truth from her parents.

Skylar crossed the half-full lounge to the ornate black-and-gold bar, intending to order a Sprite. Somehow the words "vodka tonic" came out of her mouth, instead.

And didn't she deserve a stiff drink or two after this afternoon?

Robbie was not coming back.

She knew that in her gut, the way she knew the sound of a home run as soon as it connected with the bat. The knowledge that she'd given up a home run usually filled her with the same type of hollow dread. This felt different, however. Not simply disappointment in herself and a growing drive to do better next time. More like a horrible sense that she'd missed something or hadn't paid enough attention. The feeling also happened to be more concentrated in her chest than usual, too. A horribly uncomfortable sensation that made her desperate to numb the feeling. Or better yet, get rid of it entirely.

Not easy when she could still feel Robbie's fist in her hair, his lips skating up the side of her neck. The possessive way he'd licked her. Kissed her. *Bit* her.

"What the heck," Skylar whispered into her first sip of the lime-laced cocktail. Thank God for the way it burned on the way down, distracting her from the heat she still felt everywhere else. *Annoying* heat that only seemed to multiply her confusion.

Why did she have to be so attracted to Robbie?

Did he kiss every girl like that? In a way that was starved and conflicted at the same time? What had caused his sudden need to leave (apart from her highly functioning dysfunctional family, that is)? And most importantly, why did the thought of never seeing him again put her in a state of mourning?

God, she almost felt . . . disoriented from the sudden loss of his chuckle—

"Skylar," someone said to her right. "Hey."

No, not someone. Madden.

Madden was there. In the Gilded Garden. His dark hair had turned blue black in the lighting, his jaw set with tension, along with his wide shoulders. So handsome. Almost . . . debonair in black jeans and a fitted white T-shirt.

When a weighted flop would normally happen in her belly at the sight of him, so tall and intense, now Skylar only experienced a tiny zing that translated mostly as . . . fondness? The events of the day had obviously taken a lot out of her if she was too spent to get excited at the sight of her forever crush in such a romantic setting, right? The alcohol could be to blame, too, of course.

"What are you doing here?" she asked Madden.

He shoved both hands into the pockets of his slacks. "Elton mentioned you were coming to see Eve tonight."

"Okay . . ."

"I thought I might join you."

Two, three seconds ticked by during which she tried to make sense of that answer. Had he come . . . because he wanted to spend time with her? As a friend? Or . . . more?

She didn't have time to dissect his behavior because he pulled out a hammered brass stool for her, then himself, signaling the bartender with a curt nod. Somehow the man seemed to know his drink by heart, sliding a frothy beer in front of Madden within seconds. Was the guy a psychic or something? Or had Madden been here before?

"Robbie left for practice tonight, so?"

A little chisel hammered her in the throat. "Yes. Playoffs start next week, so they're mostly resting, but not enough to lose their conditioning."

Madden took a thoughtful sip of his pint, that characteristic furrow locked to his brow. "Would you say things are going well between the two of you?"

Skylar's pulse started to race, but she couldn't tell why. Because Madden was showing interest in her love life and finally seeing her as an adult? Or because her relationship with Robbie was a fabrication and she'd have to lie? "I don't . . . know, actually," she said, finding she spoke the truth. "How did it seem to you?"

It seemed to take him an hour to respond, and she couldn't help but compare Madden's thoughtful manner to Robbie's instantaneous quips. "Sure, isn't it natural for me to feel protective of you, Skylar? I've known you years. And this Robbie . . ."

He paused. "The sports world is small and in Boston, it's even smaller. People talk. Men talk. I'm sorry, but Robbie has something of a reputation. With women."

Skylar already knew that. Hearing it out loud, knowing Robbie's playerhood was a definitive fact, lined her stomach with lead, nonetheless. "Yes, I'm aware."

Madden nodded, apparently satisfied. "I couldn't let it pass without saying something to you. You're not likely to listen to Elton." Ever so briefly, his eyes twinkled. "For good reason. He can be a right arse, as you well know."

A laugh bloomed in her throat. Suddenly, there she was, drinking alcohol with this devastatingly hot and mysterious man, in a smoky burlesque club. It was an odd moment of clarity—*oh, I'm truly an adult*—that she probably should have experienced long before now, considering she'd been through almost four years of college. But still. This was a sex situation. A situation where the right moves could lead to sex. With Madden.

The possibility flooded her with panic.

Too fast. This is moving too fast.

She hadn't even finished her lessons with Robbie.

Dammit, Robbie. Are you coming back?

"There was something else I wanted to speak with you about, Skylar," Madden said, cutting the distance between them in half. Before she could stop herself, she twisted forward in her seat so she wouldn't be facing him and drained half of her vodka tonic. *Why are you wasting this opportunity, you clown?* "It's somewhat delicate . . ."

I've finally realized I'm in love with you. That's what he was going to say.

"I'm going to run to the ladies' room—"

"I've been brought up to professional level. I'm going to catch for the Yankees."

Skylar sucked in a breath.

Surprise, elation, and a sense of melancholy crammed into her throat, all at once, and she found herself blinking back a layer of shocked tears. "*What?*" Without overthinking the impulse, she hopped off her chair and wrapped both arms around him. "Oh my God. Congratulations. Oh my God!"

He cleared his throat. Patted her gently on the back. "Caught a scout's eye while training for triple A and . . . well, it's the perfect storm of the New York catcher getting injured and them verging on busting the salary cap. They needed someone moderately inexpensive, but good."

"That's amazing. Amazing!" Skylar released him, only to shove him full in the chest. "The fucking *Yankees*, though? Seriously?"

A rich laugh came tumbling out of him. "I wasn't given much choice in the matter."

"Still," she said, shivering. "Don't expect me to wear pinstripes at your games."

"I wouldn't dream of it." Gradually, his amusement faded. "Elton doesn't know yet. I'm worried he's going to feel . . ."

"Left behind," she finished, his reluctance to celebrate finally registering.

"Yeah. Exactly that."

Skylar deflated slightly under the weight of understanding. She had a love-hate relationship with her brother. They would forever fight like siblings. Competitive ones, at that. And she knew Elton would most likely see Madden's success as a negative reflection of himself. It would be brief, though. She had enough faith in him to know that. "He'll beat himself up for not being in stride with you, like always. But one day, he'll realize this is what motivated him to be better. And long before that, he'll put aside his own shit and support you. Give him a chance. He's only an ass, like, ninety-two percent of the time."

Tension slowly bled from Madden's face as she spoke. "I can't wait to see what you do with your talent, Skylar. You were always impressive as a pitcher, but you're . . . surprising as a person, too."

What did that mean?

And why did she just want to take it at face value and move on, instead of dissecting every syllable and equating his sentiments to love, the way she did before?

"Thank you," she whispered, feeling kind of dizzy. Sad. Adrift.

Madden tilted his head and started to say something but was interrupted by the crackle of a PA system. "Ladies and gentlemen," purred a low voice, the music lifting in volume, a spotlight appearing in a perfect circle in the center of the stage. "You're in for a rare treat. Performing tonight for the first time, the mistress of the Gilded Garden herself. Put your hands together for the electrifying Eve."

Glass shattered.

Close enough to Skylar that she flinched away from the sound, only to realize it was Madden's beer glass. That it had broken right there in his hand. She stared at him in shock, before gaping at the stage. What to address first? The fact that Madden apparently didn't know his own strength? Or the fact that Eve was performing—something she claimed she would never do?

There she was, however, standing in the center of the spotlight, her waist-length blond hair covering her breasts, an oversized feather fan shielding her lower body.

Plus a teasing smile—and that was all.

Truthfully, she looked like a mischievous angel. Beautiful. If Eve hadn't spent their entire friendship vowing she would never perform, because she refused to fulfill the expectations of everyone they'd grown up with—whether they were low or high—Skylar would be thrilled for her. But Skylar recalled all those conversations well. Recalled the relentless bullying Eve had faced at school, due to her father owning the strip club, a source of local vitriol. And so this sudden appearance of her best friend onstage worried her. Not because there was anything wrong with performing burlesque. Even Skylar, who was inexperienced in the art form, had witnessed its empowering and beautiful nature.

No, she was worried because for Eve, performing was out of character.

Unexpected.

Before Skylar could come up with a plan to address both issues confronting her, Madden was off like a shot. One moment, he was slicing through the crowd, the next he was onstage, throwing Eve over his shoulder and continuing through the blue velvet curtain without so much as a hitch in his stride.

Skylar's drink remained suspended in the air for two more seconds before she plonked it down on the bar and jogged after Madden and Eve, leaping through the curtain to find her best friend glaring at Madden, feather fan clutched to the front of her body.

"How dare you, Mads. How *dare* you."

A single word scraped from his throat. "Why?"

No change in expression from Eve. "Because I wanted to."

Madden made a sound. "Don't lie to me."

"Guys . . ." Feeling oddly as though she was interrupting something, Skylar took a few steps in their direction. "Why don't we go talk in Eve's office?"

"No," Eve blurted, eyes widening. A rare glimpse of nerves from her usually deadpan best friend. "No, we can talk here."

"Why?" Madden asked, gaze narrowing. "What's in your office?"

Eve said nothing.

A beat passed.

Madden turned on a heel and strode farther backstage, paying no mind to the scattering of scantily clad burlesque dancers, toward the office. He didn't have far to go, either, only fifteen yards or so and he was nearly ripping the hinges off a door marked "Manager," while Eve and Skylar hustled forward in his wake.

The last thing Skylar expected to see on the other side of the door was two little kids.

A boy and a girl. Both of them roughly the age of five.

Were they . . . twins? Yes.

One of them played on an iPad, one colored in a Barbie coloring book.

Madden jerked to a stop, as if he'd hit a brick wall.

The kids barely glanced up from their activities at the three newly arrived adults.

Face pale, Eve reached past Madden and closed the office door.

"Are you happy?" Eve wanted to know.

Madden said nothing. Only stared.

"They are my sister's kids," Eve said, quiet and firm, visibly keeping herself calm. Poised. "Lark and Landon. They're mine now."

"Eve . . ." Madden sputtered. "How?"

"It's a long story and I don't have time to tell it tonight." She caught Skylar's eye and Skylar watched a shadow of guilt dance across Eve's expression. Because of her tone, maybe. Or because major life changes had obviously taken place and she hadn't even called her best friend. Whatever the reason for her guilt, Eve visibly forced herself to soften, though she refused to look at Madden. "I'm selling this place to take care of them. There's a prospective buyer but . . . he's hesitant. I haven't had a chance to build the clientele since I turned it into the lounge. I've only gotten the doors open, so . . ." She closed her eyes. "I thought if

I performed, word would get around. You know every asshole in this town will show up to see me humbled. If that's what I have to do to get butts in seats, so be it—"

Madden turned and put his fist through a wall.

While this action made Skylar gasp, Eve, weirdly, didn't seem the least bit surprised. "I'd like you to leave, Mads," she said after a gulping breath.

The catcher paced one way, then the other, before giving Eve one final, hard look and kicking his way through the emergency exit. Skylar gaped. What was *that* behavior about?

Skylar was off-balance and worried on Eve's behalf, but Madden was . . . *incensed.*

"Skylar . . ." Eve trailed off while reaching for the silk robe hanging on a nearby chair, finally dropping the fan that hid her brief lingerie and pulling on the garment. She swiped at her eyes and took a long breath, before giving Skylar a quick but crushing hug. "Can we meet up in a day or so? I know you left me a message, but . . . I need to work up a little more courage to talk about this."

Skylar banded her arms around her best friend, empathy and alarm and love for Eve making her eyes damp. "Of course. You know where to find me."

"Throwing balls at a tree, probably," Eve said on an abrupt laugh, her gaze straying toward the exit door. "I'll call you. We'll meet somewhere . . . where we won't be interrupted."

"You sure you're okay?"

Eve winked, fanned herself with the feather fan, but the corner of her mouth quivered in an almost unnoticeable way. "I'm always okay, babe."

Skylar left through the same door as Madden, though he was nowhere to be seen. Feeling disconnected from reality, Skylar circled back around to the front of the establishment while tapping through the process of calling an Uber. Seeing that she had a fifteen-minute wait, she sat on the carved stone bench outside, absently murmuring hello to customers as they walked inside, wondering if they were about to see Eve dance.

While she'd been in the club, the moon had grown clearer behind the surrounding trees, a slight chill flavoring the air. None of the seductive music could be heard from within the Gilded Garden. Only silence. Only the heavy thunking of her own heart. And loneliness started to creep in.

It would be so easy to talk to Robbie, with his perfect balance of humor and honesty, about what had just happened. Wouldn't it?

Skylar chewed her lip for a moment, judging he'd finished practice and returned home by now. Would it be weird to call him? She'd watched him masturbate this morning, after all. That tended to reduce any and all formalities. If she was being honest with herself, her main concern was that he wouldn't answer.

Don't be a wimp. If Eve could give up her dream to raise two kids at age twenty-two, Skylar could call a dude.

Not allowing herself another second of stalling, Skylar called Robbie.

What greeted her ears was a full-on party. No, a *rager.*

Women and men and music and squeals of laughter.

The clinking of glasses.

She could hardly hear Robbie's voice over the pandemonium. "Skylar?" shouted his deep voice. "Rocket, you there?"

Calling herself ten kinds of stupid, she hung up without saying a word.

CHAPTER NINETEEN

Two Hours Earlier

Robbie couldn't put a puck in the back of the net to save his life.

Either he was off his game, or someone had shrunk the goal to fuck with him.

His skates were too tight. The arena was warmer than usual, right?

Waiting for Coach to shut up and blow the whistle, he almost threw his stick in a burst of impatience. *Come on.* The only way to stop thinking about her was to play. Why did everything have to move in slow motion today of all days? He ground his teeth down hard into his mouthpiece, closed his eyes, and gave in to the inevitability of Skylar's face and voice and scent materializing in his mind.

Today was the first Page Stakes where I felt like I was on a team.

All the trophies and medals and cups he's won throughout his life and that might be the most memorable honor he'd ever been given. Having that girl tell him she liked having him on her side. That she felt less alone.

And he'd left.

He'd left with no intention of going back.

"Wake up, shit for brains," one of his teammates made the mistake of saying on his way past Robbie, a cheap hit from behind nearly causing a distracted Robbie to lose his balance. Apparently, the whistle had blown to resume play—and now he was about to blow, too. He'd always been taught to keep his anger suppressed. To laugh everything off. But nothing was funny today. Not a goddamn thing.

His gloves and stick were on the ice before he could register his own actions. It took him three seconds to catch up with the teammate who'd hit him, grab him by the back of his jersey, spin him around, and sucker punch him in the jaw. Everything exploded into motion at once. The whistle blew, shrill and prolonged, skates moved in their direction, hands twisting in Robbie's jersey to pull him back, but not before the guy returned the favor in the form of a right cross.

God, it felt incredible. The pain, the distraction, the well-deserved punishment.

He wanted to bleed.

Sig was suddenly in front of Robbie, holding him back, his expression one of pure confusion. Of course, it would be. Everyone laughed at Robbie and he never took offense. He locked down the disappointment, grinned, and kept moving.

Not today.

Maybe not ever again.

Skylar would be cheering him on, too, wouldn't she? Wasn't she the one who encouraged him to stop suppressing his anger and discontent? To demand respect from his teammates? Punching someone probably wasn't what she had in mind, but this was hockey. They had their own methods of getting a point across.

"What the hell is wrong with you?" Sig gritted, wrestling with Robbie.

"Call me shit for brains again," Robbie shouted over his shoulder. "You'll be watching the playoffs from your hospital bed."

"Hey." Burgess skated between the struggling players, blocking Robbie's view of the offender. "He's your teammate. That's enough."

"Oh, really? Am *I* on the team, too?" Robbie growled, pushing Sig off and ceasing his attempts to get past him and land another punch. "That doesn't seem to keep everyone from fucking with *me*."

Sig rolled his eyes. "You fuck with *everyone*, Corrigan."

"It's good-natured! I don't question anyone's intellect. I don't disregard anyone." He took his helmet off and threw it against the glass. "Roll your eyes at me one more time, Sig, I swear to Christ, you're next."

Sig's eyebrows disappeared into his own helmet.

You could have heard a pin drop.

God bless Mailer, though, he finally made it from the other side of the ice and now stood shoulder to shoulder with Robbie, throwing his stick and gloves down, ready to take on the whole team if his roommate asked. "I'll fight anyone but Burgess," Mailer said out of the corner of his mouth. "That's the man."

"Obviously," Robbie spat.

Burgess sighed. "In the locker room, Corrigan. Now."

"Great. Fine. Gods don't need to practice anyway."

"We're talking about *practice*," Mailer drawled, giving Robbie a subtle elbow in the ribs. "Listen, we're about to lose this fight, but that's fine. I've got, like, fifteen girls coming over tonight and the fridge is full of whipped cream cans."

Nausea rolled in Robbie's stomach.

Since when did a whipped cream party sound so fucking horrible?

Daydreaming about all the dents he was going to put in the lockers with his fists, Robbie skated off the ice while giving the teammate who'd punched him the middle finger and headed down the tunnel, leaving stunned silence in his wake. That was the one thing that sucked about hockey—skates preventing him from stomping.

As soon as he reached the team rooms, his skates came off and Robbie was in the middle of bashing his left one up against a cinder block wall when Sig and Burgess arrived, looking grim, but kind of . . . sympathetic, too—and sympathy was the last thing Robbie wanted from anyone tonight.

"Couldn't you guys have let the fight go on a little longer?"

"And risk injuring two players, right before playoffs?" Burgess methodically removed his gloves. "I don't think so."

Sig straddled the bench and sat quietly for a handful of seconds, watching Robbie break the blade off his skate and throw the remaining boot down on the ground, kicking it into a locker. "This is about the pitcher, isn't it? You didn't listen to us."

"I'm not required to listen to you," Robbie bit off. "Jesus, I'm sick of being spoken down to because I'm a rookie. How about you people give me the respect I should have earned just by getting here? *Getting here* is hard enough."

Burgess shrugged. "Fine."

"You could have just asked for some respect sooner."

Robbie stared. "I hate you both."

"No, you don't," Sig countered patiently. "What happened? Did you tell this girl you're down bad for her yet?"

"You told me not to!"

"You're not required to listen to us," Burgess pointed out. "You just said so yourself."

Robbie picked up his other still intact skate and slammed it against the wall.

It was either the skate or his head.

The two veterans sat in silence while he got the frustration out of his system, waiting for an explanation, which didn't come for another full minute, when Robbie exhausted himself, slumped against the wall, and slid down the cinder blocks onto his padded ass.

"She's in love with someone else. I can't compete with their . . . history. I can't compete with him. He's like you two. He's someone people take seriously. I'm nothing but some immature player to her. She knew all the worst shit about me before we even met. She'd never go there. She shouldn't. Even *I* want better for her . . . than me."

Burgess looked kind of pissed. "Where is the man from five minutes ago who claimed he deserved respect for getting here because just *getting here* is hard?"

"He wore himself out. He wants a bath and a lasagna."

"Okay, let's start over." Sig raked both hands through his hair. Man, that guy had such good hair. A normal color, too. So unfair. *Life was so unfair.* "You went there to pretend date the pitcher so she could catch this other guy's eye. How is that going?"

"I've noticed him noticing her a lot more. Checking her out. How could anyone *not* check her out? She's drop-dead gorgeous, even in sweats." He thought for a second. "Maybe *especially* in sweats. *God.*"

"Do you only want her because he wants her?" Burgess asked. "That's a thing."

"Nope. I'd much rather he didn't. I'd saw off an arm."

"Okay." Sig chuckled. "You'd saw off an arm for this guy not to notice her, but you're willing to just accept defeat? Get back up there and *win*, man. At the very least, give it everything you've got. Unless you want to see their marriage notice in the *Globe* and wonder what would have happened if you'd tried."

Marriage notice? "I feel sick."

"Deep breaths." Burgess had been acting a lot fatherlier lately. He was a father, but ever since he'd hooked up with his daughter's au pair, he'd been more . . . nurturing. In like a super grudging kind of way, but still. "In through your nose, out through your mouth."

Robbie did as he was instructed, eventually calming the storm in his belly caused by the mental image of Skylar and Madden walking down the aisle of a church together. "Is it always this hard when you meet the one?"

"Yes," Sig and Burgess said in unison.

"Did you ever think life would be easier if you'd just never met her to begin with?"

"No." Again, in unison.

"Yeah, me neither. She makes me feel like me. The me that isn't pretending to be someone or something else. Is that stupid?" He didn't wait for an answer. "It's like she's *showing* me . . . who I am. And I'm just really scared she's going to leave once she's done. Once she's done making me fall in love with her . . . oh fuck." That four-letter word—"love"—hit the back of his head like a sack of bricks and he dropped his head into his hands. "Fuck. *Fuck*."

"Really sneaks up on you, doesn't it?" Burgess rumbled.

"Damn right." There was a shadow of something nostalgic, possibly even wistful in Sig's eyes as he stood up. "I'm only going to talk about this once, all right?" He let out a breath. "Whenever I doubt myself with . . . a girl, I ask myself one question."

"What is it?" Robbie croaked.

"If there is anyone else in the world who'd work harder to make her happy. As long as the answer to that is no, you're the right man." He cleared his throat hard. "So what's your answer?"

Robbie had no clue. At first, anyway.

Until now, he hadn't allowed himself to think that far ahead.

Did he know how to make a woman happy? In bed, yeah. He knew very well how to do that, though he didn't exactly love thinking about being in the sack with anyone anymore. He'd rather sleep on the hard floor beside Skylar's bed without a chance of sex than accept a sure thing from anyone else. Eye-opening, to say the least, but he'd felt that way since the morning they'd met. Just . . . *boom.*

He'd been hit by some irreversible magic. Permanently down for the count.

But can you make her happy?

"I don't know," he said.

"Think harder, then," complained Burgess.

"Okay. Jesus." Robbie massaged his temples, running down the mental list of everything he'd learned about Skylar. "She likes orange juice with no pulp. She likes making lists. She's obsessed with her planner. Even uses these cute little stickers and colorful tapes . . ."

Sig and Burgess stared back at him, stone-faced.

Robbie cleared his throat and stopped circling around the important stuff. Just put himself out there by proving how deeply she'd scored him. "She's brave. She's funny. She's got this . . . heart of an athlete, but it's not just winning and competing, she really understands the mentality it takes, how that should be cultivated and coached. She wants to coach . . . no, she *will* and she'll be excellent at it. If you gave her a whistle and told her to coach hockey, she'd figure out a strategy by the second period. No lie. She doesn't take anyone's shit, but she . . . knows when to pull back and support someone, too. She just wants her family to love her unconditionally. She wants to be loved for being great at softball, but she wants to know she'd be loved *without* being great at it, too. I don't know . . . I don't know if she has that foundation. She should." His heart was starting to beat in a near-painful way. He was indignant and proud and aching all at the same time. "She didn't get into Brown. *So what?*"

With all those words hanging in the atmosphere, echoing back to Robbie in his ears, he suddenly knew. He had to try. He had to try to make Skylar fall in love with him, instead of Madden.

He also knew exactly where to start.

"Get back to Rhode Island and *try*, Corrigan," Sig said, correctly interpreting Robbie's silence as an epiphany. "You might never get this chance again."

ROBBIE DIDN'T GET back to the apartment until late.

After practice, he'd showered, changed, and made a stop, promptly getting stuck in the Sox game traffic on the way to his place. By the time he dragged himself into the elevator and hit the button for his floor, he just wanted to crawl into bed and sleep long enough to reset his brain. After all, he'd be driving back to Rhode Island first thing in the morning to win over the woman of his dreams. Rest was key.

He forgot all about the whipped cream party until he walked into it.

"What in . . . oh. Oh no." Robbie slapped his hand over his eyes to prevent himself from seeing the scene in his living room twice. "Mailer!"

"Welcome home, buddy."

"Don't talk to me until you have some clothes on," Robbie barked.

"Hold on." Two seconds passed. "Okay, I'm covered."

"In something that *isn't* edible."

"Oh."

Robbie used his free hand to reach back and grip the door handle, reopening it and backing himself in two lunges into the hallway, refusing to drop his hand from his eyes until the door was closed, muffling Drake by ten or so octaves. He paced while waiting for Mailer to emerge, debating whether to tell Skylar about this. Probably, yeah. He'd definitely want to know if she'd seen four *men* in whipped cream bikinis, even if they were taking turns making out with her friend, instead of her.

"I still wouldn't like it," he muttered, his stride hitching.

He wouldn't like his girlfriend in that situation. Period.

That was the moment Robbie decided he'd never put himself in a position like that ever again. End of story. If by some stroke of epic luck, Skylar decided to give him a chance, a real one, he wouldn't be responsible for a single second of insecurity. Take it to the bank.

His phone vibrated in his pocket. Assuming it was his best friend calling from inside the den of iniquity, he answered without hesitation. "I'm waiting."

Silence greeted him. Thick silence. The opposite of what was coming from the other side of the apartment door. Quickly, he checked the screen—and his heart collided with his stomach. "Skylar?" Of course, Mailer selected that moment to open the door, releasing the unholy soundtrack of debauchery into the air. No, no, no. "Rocket, you there?"

The call ended.

Irritation ripped up the middle of his throat. *"FUCK."*

"Hey." Mailer yawned on his way into the hallway, a towel wrapped around his waist, rubbing his knuckles in his chest hair. "Where have you been? There were more ladies here, but even I can't handle that many at once. Yet. A little more practice and who knows—"

"I think I need to move out."

Mailer snorted, obviously not believing him. "Shut up."

"I'm serious." The announcement hadn't been planned, but that phone call had just made a hard-to-navigate situation even worse. With every second that ticked by, Robbie was more positive that finding a new place to live was the right thing to do. Not only for this fairy-tale relationship he was definitely crazy

184 · TESSA BAILEY

for pursuing, but . . . for himself. It took meeting Skylar to realize how much respect he'd been lacking for himself and others. His treatment of women was a big part of that, wasn't it? Yeah, he'd been ignoring those lessons he'd learned growing up, trading them for a good time. Only thinking about himself.

No more. Especially if he wanted Skylar. And he did.

Badly.

Time to grow up.

He'd explain what she heard on the phone when they were face-to-face, so he could look her in the eye. She'd see he was telling the truth. Right now, he had to make his best friend understand the changes that were taking place inside of him.

"It's not you," Robbie said. "It's . . . me."

Mailer did a double take. "Wow."

"That didn't come out how it sounded, man. You know I love you. I've just been doing some soul-searching, I guess, and—"

"Bullshit. You can admit it's the pitcher." Mailer crossed his arms. "Admit you like her."

"Yeah. Yeah, I do. A fucking lot." Irritation caused his voice to get louder. "Why wouldn't I want to admit that?"

"Because we were supposed to be the ones who didn't get trapped. We've talked about this a thousand times. We were going to be the smart ones who stayed free while all the other idiots got tied up with engagement photo shoots and making babies. Babies all look the same. We've gone over this!"

Robbie shoved his friend, but it was half-hearted, because who liked letting down their best friend? "Oh yeah, those conversations we had after like *nine beers*?"

Mailer pushed him back. "Are you saying you didn't mean any of it?"

"At the time, maybe I did, but I didn't know what it was going to feel like to meet Skylar yet. Okay? She's the thing making me feel free, not the thing taking away my freedom." He cursed under his breath. "Love isn't what we thought it was, okay?"

"*Love?*" Mailer covered his face with both hands. "Christ. It's worse than I imagined."

"Yeah, no shit! It is pretty fucking bad, because she wants someone else and I'm trying to make something happen. Feels horrific, if I'm being honest, you dick."

"Well, I'm sorry it feels horrific, cock wad."

"Thank you!"

"You're welcome."

They shoved each other once more each.

Took a moment to regroup.

"At least come in for a beer."

"Oh my God. No. I don't want to see any girls in whipped cream bikinis. I only want to see Skylar in sweatpants."

"You've been brainwashed," Mailer whispered.

"What happened to you liking the new general manager, anyway? For a week, you couldn't stop talking about her. Now you're doubling down on this playboy lifestyle like it's your job."

Mailer's face lost some of its color. "I asked her out. She told me she doesn't date boys, she dates men. Then she closed her office door in my face and emailed me a copy of the organization's nonfraternization policy."

Robbie knew better than to show even a hint of sympathy. "Wow. She must be blind, because you're a king."

"I know, right?" There was some definite embarrassment mingled with a healthy heap of disappointment in Mailer's expression, but he quickly banished it. "Anyway, it's fine." He jerked a head toward the apartment door. "I've got a deep enough roster, don't I?"

Funny, Mailer didn't look all that excited to go back into the apartment, either.

"You really going to move out?"

"Afraid so. But we'll still have lasagna nights. At least twice a week."

"Three and you've got a deal."

"Sold."

They fist-bumped.

It turned into a hug.

"Look. We don't have to figure the living situation out tonight. I'm just going to head back to Rhode Island, so you can pick up where you left off."

"Great," Mailer muttered, making no move to enter the apartment. "Thanks."

"Yeah." After a brief hesitation, Robbie backed toward the elevator. "See you in a few days, man. Bye."

"Bye." Right before Robbie stepped into the elevator, Mailer shouted, "You got this, man. I believe in you."

The elevator closed on Robbie's grateful, if dubious, grin.

CHAPTER TWENTY

Breakfast was a quiet affair.

The inside of Skylar's head was not.

She stared down at her planner, which sat open beside her bowl of overnight oats. Already this morning, she'd pitched to the tree for an hour, showered, paced, and, most of all, tried to figure out what to tell everyone about Robbie.

He wasn't coming back, meaning she no longer had a teammate.

Calling Eve to act as a temporary replacement was not an option. Not with everything she had on her plate, the imagined weight of which had kept Skylar awake half the night, trying to think of ways to help. She also knew getting Eve to accept any form of help would be the biggest obstacle. Eve didn't take assistance very well. Waiting for Eve to ask for that help would be hard, but Skylar knew from experience there wasn't another choice.

For now, the only option was to compete solo in the family competition. An unprecedented twist in Page Stakes lore, to be whispered about for years to come.

Elton would have a field day with this. She could already hear her brother's smug comments. No doubt, everything out of his mouth for the next two days would be variations of *I told you so.* Her parents were allergic to expressing sympathy, so they'd feed her a bunch of platitudes, like *What doesn't kill you makes you stronger.* Or *You'll be smarter next time. You've been given the gift of insight.*

The other four people at the dining room table—Elton, Madden, and her parents, three of whom were wearing Brown University T-shirts—were beginning to notice her silence, so Skylar took a tasteless bite of cold oats and scribbled something unnecessary into her planner. She tried not to think about what Robbie was doing right now. Or who. It was approaching 8:00 A.M., meaning he was probably spread-eagle in a tangle of women, sleeping with a smile on his face.

Had he even enjoyed the time they spent together?

Or had he spent the whole time dreaming of wild nights in Boston?

Sensing eyes on her profile, Skylar turned to find Madden watching her with brows drawn, his own breakfast untouched in front of him, as well. He raised an eyebrow at her, as if to say, *Are you okay?*

Skylar nodded. *Tell them your news,* she mouthed.

He thought for a moment, then gave a curt shake of his head. Looked away.

The clock ticked.

The silence continued.

They were all waiting for Robbie to appear. According to the laminated schedule that had been posted on the refrigerator this morning, today's challenge was the swim across the reservoir— and it started early. As if on cue, both her über punctual parents checked their waterproof watches and exchanged a knowing glance, clearly beginning to grow stressed by the missing competitor.

She'd run out of time.

"Um." Skylar closed her planner. "I guess you're wondering where Robbie is. I might . . . well, I might have some unfortunate news about that, but I'm not *complaining*. Okay? I can compete by mysel—"

The screen door of the house opened and in walked Robbie. In a Boston University T-shirt.

Disbelief streaked through Skylar, followed by relief. Gratitude.

Warmth. It swept downward from the crown of her head to her feet.

"Good morning, you family full of lunatics," Robbie said conversationally, approaching the table. So casual, but his eyes were locked on Skylar, as if trying to get a read. "Miss me?"

"No," Elton responded, without his usual venom. He was looking at Robbie's shirt, his forehead puckered in thought. Skylar was staring at it, too, with a growing knot in her jugular, her hands dropping into her lap and curling into fists. Silently as possible, she attempted to take a giant breath but found it difficult to draw air. In a house filled with Brown paraphernalia, here was Robbie rocking BU merch, her school being represented for the very first time in this home. She'd never even worn anything from BU around her parents, except for her softball uniform, wanting to avoid reminders of their disappointment.

"Nice shirt," Madden said, lips quirked behind his folded hands, though his tone was hard to read. Was that approval or sarcasm?

"Thanks." Until now, Skylar hadn't noticed the stack of plastic-wrapped shirts Robbie carried under his arm, but when he started dealing them around the table like blackjack cards, Skylar officially couldn't breathe. "I bought one for everybody."

"Oh." Her parents traded a startled look. "We're—"

"Big Brown fans. Which is cool, but there are no rules against supporting two teams, right? I mean exceptions have to be made when your kid is the star pitcher. You going to eat that, Rocket?"

Before Skylar knew what was happening, Robbie scooped her off the wooden bench, sat down, and settled her sideways in his lap, proceeding to down her entire bowl of overnight oats in exactly four bites.

In just thirty seconds, her world turned itself upside down.

Or right side up?

No idea.

Before Robbie walked into the house, she'd been exposed and unsteady and lonely, ready to reveal a weakness to people who didn't tolerate them, already at her usual deficit of *Didn't get into Brown*. Half a minute later, there she sat in the sun, her entire body surrounded in warmth and support, reassured as she watched Robbie unapologetically eat the remainder of everyone's meals. He'd stunned them into silence.

He'd stunned Skylar.

Frankly, at that moment, she didn't care if he'd slept with half of Boston last night.

She laid her head on Robbie's shoulder and closed her eyes, anyway.

"Did you already get your pitching in this morning?" he asked, rubbing the middle of her back. As if no one was watching. As if they were the only two people at the table.

"Yes." Skylar studied him a little more closely. "Is that a black eye?"

He hummed. "My last one was beginning to fade. Had to get a replacement."

"I'll be happy to replace it next time," Elton voiced from across the table. "But, uh . . . welcome back. I guess. I wasn't looking forward to watching my sister try and swim both legs of the race."

"Today's challenge is swimming? And you've got a Long Island kid on your team?" Robbie winked down at Skylar. "It's in the bag."

IT WAS PROBABLY better they didn't have any time alone between breakfast and the hike to the lake for the swimming challenge. While Skylar helped clean up breakfast and tried to pretend her hands weren't shaking, Robbie quickly changed into swim trunks in her bedroom. Elton and her parents headed outside, Madden lingering by the sink, looking like he wanted to speak with her. Yet all she could do was watch her bedroom door, waiting for Robbie to emerge. Robbie, who'd definitely been with other women last night—nay, *every* night of his proud bachelor life . . . and still, she could only wonder if they would continue her lessons or if he'd forgotten about them in a blur of beautiful babes.

Skylar shook herself.

Focused on Madden.

Stop getting distracted from your goal.

"Um . . ." She folded up the dish towel in her hands. "Why didn't you want to tell them about the Yankees? It's *good* news, Mads."

"Right. Yes, 'course it is. I will share it, eventually." He coughed into his fist. "Did a lot of thinking last night, though, and I'm wondering, do you think it's an opportunity to help Eve—"

"Ready to go," Robbie said, entering the kitchen the way a runner slides into home base, wrapping an arm around Skylar's waist and hauling her up against him, bending her backward slightly and planting a kiss on her mouth. Mere inches from Madden. And *that's* what she should have been thinking about. Madden's reaction. Not the delightful friction of Robbie's beard on her chin. The way he could lift her so effortlessly onto her toes and didn't hesitate to be physical with her. So confident she'd want it—and she did. Mouth so good. Good, good mouth. Mmmm. "You didn't answer me before. Did you miss me?" Robbie asked.

"Yes."

"Good. Now ask me the same question."

"I forgot the question."

"Ask me if I missed you."

"Did you?"

"I got a speeding ticket on my way back to you." His fingers threaded into her hair, gently tilting her head and slanting his lips down in the opposite direction, groaning into a slow, thorough kiss that turned her legs to mush. "I hassled someone into punching me to distract me from missing you and it didn't even work."

Goose bumps. Everywhere. *What is happening to me?* "That's a shame."

"Look at me. Look." He framed her face in his hands and pressed their foreheads together. "After practice, I raided the BU campus bookshop for merch. After that, I went to my apartment and Mailer was having a party. But I left, Skylar. I saw a couple of random butts and I left right away. I didn't even appreciate those butts. I just wanted to get back here to *your* butt. You believe me, right?" Not waiting for a response, he rolled their foreheads together. Kissed her hard once, twice. "I slept in my car at the end of your driveway. I didn't want to come in and wake you up. Actually, that's a lie. I did want to come in and wake you up, but I was feeling some kind of way, missing you like that, and I would have ended up on top of you. I'm fucking *dying* to be on top of you, Skylar. You dying for that?"

The fog parted momentarily. Madden. Oh my God.

Was he still standing there, hearing all this?

Skylar's head swiveled right.

They were alone. How long had they been alone?

Who was Robbie benefiting with this speech?

"He left when you said you missed me." He searched her eyes. "Did you mean it?"

"Yes." Nine avenues of thought merged into a traffic jam. "Wait, I have so many questions."

"About last night? Ask." He dropped his hands from her face and backed up, straightening his shoulders as if swearing on a Bible in court. "Ask me anything. I recorded my drive on my GPS so I could show you I was on the road. Not partying—"

"No. No, I believe you about that."

His slow grin could have powered the entire state of Rhode Island. "You do?"

"Yeah." She opened her mouth, closed it. "What reason do you have to lie?" Saying the next part felt . . . oddly like a lie, but she couldn't figure out why. "You don't owe me an explanation. We're not actually together. It's . . . just for show. Right?" One after another, strings pulled taut in her chest. "Which is why I'm wondering why you said all that when Madden wasn't even standing here."

"Oh my God. Okay." He dragged both hands down his face. "Here's a lesson for you, Rocket. A guy doesn't choose to spend a week with a girl's deranged family unless he's into her. Like, *really* fucking into her. Maybe I lied to myself about doing this for noble reasons—and yeah, fine, that was part of it. I wanted to show you and myself I'm not a tool." He took a shuddering breath. "But at the heart of it, Skylar, I wanted so badly to be with you. I was afraid of not seeing you again. And now?" He laughed without humor. "Now, I'm petrified of that. I couldn't actually do it."

The superhighway of her mind had become a ten-car pileup. "I . . . what?"

Robbie grabbed her shoulders, leaned down until they were

eye level. "I want to be your boyfriend. I don't want to be the reason Madden pulls his head out of his ass and notices you. I want to be the reason I pull *my* head out of my ass."

"So much butt talk this morning," she said, dazed.

"Just a cheeky little coincidence. Did you hear anything I said?"

"Yes, I'm trying to decide if you need medical attention." Gently, she took him by the elbows. "Exactly how hard did you get punched in the face last night?"

He stared at her with incomprehension.

Even though her heart was heavy and racing from the effect of his words, she pasted on an incredulous smile, because no. No, she couldn't just accept them at face value. Even if he truly meant them right now, he would regret giving up his lifestyle. He'd look back and claim he was in a fugue state. "You're just going to give up clubs and women and whipped cream—"

"You heard that, did you?" he asked, weakly.

"You're going to give that up for one girl. Who doesn't even know how to give head."

"Ready and willing to work on that, Sky. Right now, if possible."

A light bulb went off. "Maybe that's what this is about. You're not used to delayed gratification and I'm the one putting you through it." She nodded sagely, positive she had the issue all worked out, although not so sure anymore she wanted a cut-and-dried explanation. *I got a speeding ticket on my way back to you.* "I'm sure if we sleep together, you'll get over this fleeting interest in being my boyfriend."

"Well." His jaw popped. "You've got me all figured out, don't you?"

"I'm not . . ." She wet lips that were rapidly drying out. "The last thing I want to do is hurt your feelings, especially after y-you showed up here in a Boston University T-shirt and you . . ." Her voice fell to a whisper out of necessity. Talking was suddenly difficult. "I'll never forget you did that. I mean, ever. You're actually my hero right now."

His eyelids slid closed. "Skylar."

"The possibility I'm hurting you is giving me the worst stomachache. I guess I'm just worried you'll change your mind after some time passes."

His nostrils flared. "I won't."

"I never wanted to change you."

"*I'm* changing me."

"Robbie . . ."

"Okay." Resigned, he nodded. Planted both hands on his hips and regrouped. "Okay, I hear what you're saying. You need time to believe I'm for real. That's fair, even though I hate it." He'd never looked this serious. Not since she'd met him. "Just tell me you have feelings for me. Tell me I'm not crazy."

Oh God. This was like leaping over a ravine full of crocodiles. Admitting she had feelings for him would only encourage him to pursue this relationship—one that would absolutely lead to her getting hurt when he eventually decided to go back to his wild bachelor ways. Hurt was putting it mildly, too. He'd cut her off at the knees, wouldn't he? Yes. Because she *had* been developing feelings for him. Sneaky ones. They'd been nipping at her heels since day one. Now they were fully grown, biting her everywhere. Stealing chunks of her preconceived notions about Robbie. Chunks of what might have been her resistance.

"I have feelings for you," she whispered.

He remained still as a statue for long moments, before the breath came whooshing out of him, his big body falling forward, hands planting on his knees. "Holy shit. I was only giving myself ten to one odds." It took him some time to straighten and slow his breathing down and all Skylar could do was watch in fascination. This reaction . . . it was all for her? "What about him?" Robbie's voice had dropped way down in pitch, his eyelids hooded as he observed Skylar closely, seeming to hold his breath again. "You still got feelings for him?"

"I don't know," she said, truthfully. And hey, "I don't know" was a huge downgrade from a couple of weeks ago when she would have willingly thrown herself in front of a train for Madden. She'd just never expected the train to have unruly red hair and an appetite that rivaled the passengers of a medium-sized cruise ship.

The fact that her feelings had been massively—and troublingly—downgraded didn't seem to satisfy Robbie in the slightest, however. In fact, his jealous expression as he backed her up against the kitchen counter made her shiver, her neck losing any semblance of strength, head falling back when he spoke against her ear. "Give me ten minutes in the dark with your panties off and you'll know. I'll get you over him underneath me."

Several brain cells fried themselves like eggs on a skillet.

"It's, um . . ." She twisted her hands in the sides of his shirt, struggling to form coherent thoughts when he was raking his open mouth up and back in the slope of her neck. *Feels so good.* "It's Wednesday. Main Event parenthesis Maybe isn't until tomorrow."

"Believe me, I know."

"Today is BJ Workshop day."

He hooked an arm under her knee and drew it up to his hip, higher, higher, only allowing her center to graze his erection, light encounters until she gasped, trying to get closer. To rub on him. "Oh, believe me, I know that, too." He made an almost humorously desperate sound into her neck. "God in heaven, please just get me *alone* with this girl."

The lines were quickly blurring here.

What had started off as lessons to help her be more confident with men was turning into . . . something else. A guideline for giving pleasure to each other. But where would all this leave her when Robbie inevitably came to his senses?

"Can we just keep them . . . lessons for now? Can they stay what they always were?"

His mouth paused on her neck and this time, she visibly injured something inside of him, which was not her intention. She simply didn't know how else to protect herself. Keep this gorgeous sought-after hockey god interested indefinitely when she'd never been able to retain interest from men in the past? In what world?

Protect yourself. That's all you're doing.

"Yeah. Lessons," Robbie said, voice like gravel, reluctantly disengaging from her as the air horn went off outside. "Whatever you need to tell yourself until you're ready to think of me as more than a player."

Skylar wanted badly to correct him. Tell him that's not how she thought of him.

Truthfully, though . . . she did. She had for their entire acquaintance. It was something she'd just accepted, classifying her jealousy as silly and useless.

Was it even possible to change her perception of him now?

But if he could make her heart race just by walking through the door, didn't she owe it to herself to . . . try?

CHAPTER TWENTY-ONE

The only thing making Robbie feel better as he, Elton, and Doug stood at the edge of the lake, preparing to swim to the opposite shore, was he *easily* looked the best shirtless. His standout physique was little consolation, however, because Madden and Skylar were standing shoulder to shoulder on the other side of the lake and Skylar was in a bathing suit. A black one-piece Speedo, obviously. That was so her.

No nonsense.

Buy the most aerodynamic swimsuit on the market.

No bells and whistles.

Somehow, she managed to make it hotter than a string bikini.

The one silver lining here was that he had an incentive to swim as fast as humanly possible to get to the other side of the lake and break up Skylar and Madden's little huddle, preferably before she remembered all the reasons she was in love with Madden. Maybe Robbie should be grateful that Skylar had answered *I don't know* when asked if she still had feelings for the catcher, but guess what? He wasn't.

Robbie needed the answer to be a hard no, like, yesterday. Last year, even.

As soon as he'd made the conscious decision to fight for her, all the possessiveness and hunger and admiration and fear he'd been keeping contained broke free. Now he was a teeming tangle of issues, all of which revolved around her, yet she was also the fucking antidote? Love was a bitch, man. It didn't even make sense.

If there is anyone else in the world who'd work harder to make her happy. As long as the answer to that is no, you're the right man.

The answer to that question was even more solid this morning after witnessing Skylar's reaction to the Boston University shirts. She'd needed those symbols of support. He'd noticed that and acted on it. Maybe he'd only done one small thing so far, but it counted, right? She'd tucked her face into his neck afterward. He could still feel it there.

"You boys ready to lose?" Doug said, dropping into a runner's stance, preparing to sprint toward the water. "I was the captain of the swim team my senior year." His tone sounded . . . forced? "I swim this lake every morning in the summertime."

Elton patted his father on the back. "We'll try to keep up, Dad."

"Don't patronize me," snapped the older man.

Concern crept into Elton's expression. "Is everything okay?"

"Fine and dandy." Doug straightened, spearing Robbie with a look. "What point were you trying to make with those T-shirts, son? You think I can't afford to buy my own shirts?"

Most guys would avoid an argument with the father of their potential girlfriend at all costs. Most guys weren't Robbie. He didn't know how to avoid an argument to save his life. Especially this one. "I know you can afford it. That's what makes it all the more confusing that you don't already have one. Or *ten*."

"Meaning what?"

"Meaning, your house looks like the gift shop at Brown. Not a goddamn pennant or bobblehead for BU anywhere." He raised an eyebrow. "How do you think that makes Skylar feel?"

The older man waved him off. "Oh, stop. She knows it's our family alma mater. She's tougher than that."

"Yeah. She is. So imagine someone that tough and high-achieving gets rejected and has to be reminded of it every single day. Everyone is tough *to a point*."

"Who made you her spokesperson?" Elton wanted to know.

Robbie rolled a tense shoulder. "I'm not qualified to be anyone's spokesperson, but I'll tell you this. When I notice something making her sad, you can bet your ass I'm going to say something about it. That's my girl."

God, it felt so good to say that out loud. Even if it wasn't true yet.

Felt true, though. Felt as real as the sky overhead.

"Ridiculous." Doug sniffed, his voice lacking the conviction from before. His robust frame seemed to be hunching in on itself, his usual confidence carrying away on the breeze. "Why hasn't she said something if it bothers her so much?"

"Probably because complaining is a sign of weakness in your house."

Elton and Doug blustered enough to start a dust storm. "Who asked you?"

"*You* did!" Robbie countered.

Obviously, Vivica chose that moment to blow the air horn.

"Goddammit." Elton sighed.

They all ran for the water at once, Robbie yelping at the temperature. "Jesus Christ, that's cold."

"Isn't ice your thing?"

"Yeah, when I'm insulated by pads."

That was the final exchange before the three men were cutting through the water with freestyle strokes. Robbie took the lead after thirty seconds to the soundtrack of cursing in his wake. Not only was he motivated as hell to make it to the other side of that lake to reclaim his still technically fake girlfriend, but he'd also gone to surfing camp three summers in a row in Long Beach, so his skills were on point. Throw in the fact that he'd blown the climbing challenge and Robbie had something to prove. Thankfully, he did, reaching the other side of the lake long before the other two men.

There was Skylar in her no-bullshit bathing suit, waiting for him with that exhilarated thrill of competition on her face, holding out her hand to get tagged. Instead of tagging her with a hand slap, he snagged her hand, bringing it to his mouth and kissing her palm.

"Got us the lead. Bring it home, Rocket."

Color warmed her complexion. "On it."

She splashed into the lake and dove into a seamless freestyle stroke, tan arms slicing through blue. He was so mesmerized by her graceful movements, he barely paid attention when Elton and Doug reached shore, tagged their partners, and immediately started to argue about who had gotten there first. Robbie tuned them out, shouting encouragement to Skylar once she reached the halfway point and still had the lead.

Something happened, though, toward the middle of the reservoir. Something that didn't make sense.

She slowed down.

Madden gained on Skylar, then little by little, he passed her.

Meanwhile, Vivica was in a distant third and appeared to be swimming in the wrong direction. But Robbie's attention remained locked on Skylar and when she stopped swimming completely and her head disappeared under the surface, his fucking soul left his body.

"*Skylar,*" he shouted.

She had a cramp. She'd gotten dizzy and lost consciousness.

Jaws is real and he's in the reservoir.

Bad. Bad. Something bad.

Robbie's brain snapped into survival mode and he quickly scoped out the surrounding shoreline, trying to judge if there

202 · TESSA BAILEY

was a closer entry point into the lake to her location—and there was. There was. He broke into a sprint without taking his focus off the spot where she'd gone down—

She emerged from the water and Robbie made a broken sound, but he didn't slow down, not one iota, because she was visibly struggling.

"What the fuck. *What the fuck*," he chanted, finally reaching the closest section of the beach and barreling full speed into the water, breaking into a swim as soon as the water got waist-deep. He didn't allow himself to speculate on what was wrong with Skylar or what could happen if he didn't get there in time. No. Just go. *Go.*

It seemed like an hour had passed by the time he reached Skylar, when in reality it had probably been under three minutes. She flailed in the water with an expression of pure fatigue, followed by the relief of seeing him.

Robbie, she mouthed without sound.

"I've got you." He turned her around, banding an arm across her collarbone, and immediately reversed direction back to shore, adrenaline moving like lightning through his veins. "Breathe, Skylar. I've got you."

"I don't know what happened." Her teeth were chattering, no doubt from fear, as well as the water temperature. "My leg cramped and I tried to . . . push through it but I got so tired trying to compensate . . ."

"Okay. I figured it was something like that. Deep breaths. You're going to be fine."

"I didn't think anyone would see me," she whispered, breath hitching.

"Really, Rocket?" Robbie labored through a few inhales, exhales. A few violent clenches of his heart. "Don't you know I never stop looking at you?"

She wrapped herself around his arm, holding on so tight, his throat constricted. By now, Skylar's parents and Elton had become alerted to the emergency. Elton was currently swimming in their direction with an obvious sense of urgency, Doug and Vivica waiting on the shore holding each other and looking terrified.

Robbie could relate. Now that Skylar was safely in his arms, angry cymbals smashed together in his head. Visions of what could have happened plagued him. By the time he was able to put his feet down and carry Skylar the remaining distance to land in his arms, the blood vessels behind his eyes were on the verge of bursting.

"Towels! *Get her some towels.*"

Madden appeared, holding a stack of striped beach towels in his arms, his concern for Skylar obvious and at that moment, Robbie didn't have the capacity to be jealous. Later, maybe. Right now, as he held a shivering Skylar to his body while everyone wrapped towels around her, he was racked with residual fear—and frankly, outrage. Not over the competition itself, but the fact that it stood in place of emotional bonding. The kind he was starting to sense more and more that Skylar needed.

"Never again. She's *never* doing the swimming challenge again. Or any other dangerous ones. Is everyone listening to me?" Having cocooned her as much as possible in various shades of terrycloth, Robbie caught her in a bear hug. "Please stop shaking. Please stop shaking."

"I'm okay."

"I'm not. You almost drowned because the Pages can't sit in the living room and play charades like a normal family." He looked all three Pages in the eye, one by one. "The need to continually prove herself is going to get her *killed.*"

"Hold on just a damn second—" Doug blustered.

"The games feed our competitive spirit. They're *ours*," Vivica insisted, but her eyes held a note of worry as she regarded her daughter. "Skylar, you enjoy them, don't you?"

"I don't know," Skylar said hesitantly, her voice muffled by Robbie's neck. "I guess I don't know anymore."

Several seconds of silence passed.

Madden observed the ground, while Elton stared at his sister, as if trying to solve a puzzle. And Robbie was caught off guard by his own concern for the family. All of them. Maybe he'd been insensitive by pointing out the fatal Page flaws this morning. He didn't regret it, though. His concern was Skylar and anything that had the potential to hurt her, physically or emotionally, needed to be addressed.

This is what Sig meant. About no one working harder to make her happy. I get it.

Holy shit. I'm capable of learning.

"We talk about these games all year, Sky," Elton said finally, appearing baffled, but veering toward concerned, like his mother. "We look forward to them."

In Robbie's arms, Skylar's chest was beginning to shudder up and down, her wide eyes flitting between the members of her family. Ah shit, he'd put her in a bad position. And what if he was wrong, to boot? Had he imagined Skylar's forced enjoyment of this yearly competition? Had he dreamed her exhaustive need to keep up, prove herself, when all she needed was someone to hug her and say *I love you, win or lose*?

"I used to love them," Skylar murmured, finally. "Maybe I still do, because we do them together, but I feel useless when I lose. I feel useless when I don't do everything at the highest level. And maintain it."

"You could never be useless," Vivica breathed, visibly horrified.

"We've always believed in pushing our children," Doug tacked on, though his voice held a note of uncertainty. "It's what bonded us in the first place. Instilling a drive to succeed, not merely compete."

"She has *already* succeeded," Robbie said firmly, drawing her tighter to his chest. "Everyone needs to have their hard work acknowledged once in a while. That's why we have the ESPY Awards." He pressed his mouth to her hair. "Speaking of which, will you be my date this year? Mailer looks like shit in a dress."

Caught off guard, Skylar laughed, and warmth flooded Robbie's body. Enough to drown in. "I'll think about it."

"Fair enough."

"Skylar . . ." Doug cleared his throat so hard, a flock of birds went screeching from a nearby tree. "We're very proud of you, if we haven't made that clear." His attention lingered on the Boston University T-shirt hanging from Robbie's back pocket. "In hindsight, I see we've missed an opportunity to congratulate you on your achievements and instead focused on—"

"What I failed to do," Skylar rushed to say. "I know. I . . . if I could get a second chance, I'd—"

"Skylar, no." Vivica covered her eyes. "I'm so sorry. You shouldn't be lamenting the fact that you got into an amazing school. I didn't realize we'd made you feel like a failure by not . . . by not—"

"By talking about Brown like it's the only institution worth a damn." Elton scrubbed at his five-o'clock shadow. "Damn. I'm sorry, Sky."

"We're sorry," Doug said, sounding dazed.

Vivica nodded, seeming unable to speak.

"Do you want to forgive them, Rocket? Or think about it?"

"Forgive them," she said, her eyes welling.

Everyone converged on Robbie at once, even Madden, both him and Skylar absorbed in a group hug that couldn't have been more unnatural or awkward if it tried, but at least it was genuine. Skylar was getting the comfort and love she needed. That's what mattered most. That's what would *always* matter most. But speaking of her needs, his girl was shivering and that wasn't going to work for Robbie.

"I need to get Skylar somewhere warm. A shower. Now." He scooped her up into his arms, towels and all, pointedly ignoring her when she insisted she could walk. "No."

She started to argue, then visibly decided against it, her head flopping exhaustedly onto his shoulder. "Okay."

Skylar's uncharacteristic surrender got his feet moving, as well as his adrenaline. Again. "Was that lake cold enough to give someone hypothermia?"

"I don't have hypothermia."

"You say this while your teeth are chattering."

"That's partially due to the lingering terror."

Robbie stumbled a little on his march through the trees, almost like he'd blown a fuse, his human electricity flickering off and on. All because he was thinking of Skylar terrified. A cold sweat clung to his skin now and he had tunnel vision. Get her to the house, warm her up, tuck her into bed with some soup. That was the game plan. Oh God. Every time the adrenaline started to subside a little, the fact that his legs had gone weak became more obvious. "Partially?"

She blinked up at him and he could hardly decipher her expression. Was that . . . awe? "Maybe I'm shaking a little because I've never had someone see me as clearly as you do. Thank you, Robbie. For that."

A hat trick would no longer give Robbie the ultimate high ever again. Nope. This was it now. Skylar looking up at him like he was Superman. Someday maybe their kids would look up at him the same way. Like he could do anything. And suddenly, he could. This was another facet of being in love. It put a man in permanent beast mode.

"I can't wait to tell Mailer," he said to himself.

"What?"

"Nothing."

They were almost to the house when she reached up to brush her fingers against his jawline. "Thank God you came back."

His stomach bottomed out and he had to stop walking for a full ten seconds.

What if he hadn't come back?

"Sorry, I . . . maybe I shouldn't have said that." His arms were shaking around Skylar and she had the audacity to seem surprised about that. "I think maybe we both need that hot shower."

"Mm" was all he could manage.

This time, when she wiggled in his arms, he had no choice but to let her stand.

They walked up the front steps in a huddle.

CHAPTER TWENTY-TWO

Skylar had been shaken up like a martini at the Gilded Garden and dumped into a transparent glass, her feelings on full display. No hiding. No stiff upper lip. Was it residual fear or the immensity of her relief—or possibly a combination of the two—causing the giddy desperation that coursed through her body while Robbie worked the faucets of the shower, holding out his hand to test the water temperature?

She didn't know, but the need to touch him was so fierce, she put her hands behind her back. When had he become this . . . this rock? *Her* rock?

Over the course of the week, she'd started to depend on him. Of course she had. This was her teammate in the Page Stakes, not to mention her partner in a romantic deception in which they no longer seemed to be participating. Right? And Skylar had always been her own rock and in a lot of ways that would never, ever change, but God . . . Robbie's every action since he'd shown up this morning had been heroic. Decisive. Mature.

Scary.

This Robbie was *scary*.

In the sense that she was now experiencing a deep need to be touched by him. To feel his presence as closely as possible. His heat, his strength, his Robbie-ness that seemed to correspond to her emotional highs and lows intuitively. Was it possible she was romanticizing him because he'd quite possibly saved her from a watery death?

Did she love Robbie and not Madden?

Or was she just shaken up? Confused?

Was she letting her attraction to this man increasingly cloud her judgment?

Finally, Robbie nodded with satisfaction over the water temperature and made a no-nonsense gesture. "In you go, Rocket. Please."

She nodded and dropped the towel, immediately wrapping her arms around herself to combat the lack of warmth. Robbie made a gruff sound and ushered her into the steamy shower stall, releasing an exhale of clear relief when she stepped beneath the spray and moaned. After taking a few seconds to revel in the heat permeating her bones, she looked toward the still-open glass door to find Robbie watching her with his forearms propped high on the top of the shower frame, his chest dipping and rising slowly.

"You warm yet, Skylar? You feeling better?"

"Yes. I promise."

His eyes closed briefly and he let out a slow breath, relief softening his gaze when he looked at her again. "That bathing suit is so you."

"It's scientifically proven to add speed," she murmured into the shower spray.

His lips jumped. "Thanks for making my point for me."

Skylar turned a little in a shameless attempt to draw his attention to her butt—and it worked, his eyes going smoky, a muscle leaping in his jaw. "I have a cuter one I wear when I'm not trying to crush my competition and accidentally drowning instead."

He winced, paled slightly. "Could you stop bringing that up?"

"Sorry."

Robbie clenched his eyes closed and shook his head hard, as if trying to banish the last half hour from his mind. "What does this other bathing suit look like . . . and did you pack it?"

"I did pack it, actually. It's turquoise with white hibiscus flowers on it."

Robbie hummed in his throat. "I can't picture it. Going to need to see it in person, I'm afraid."

His gravelly tone caused a tautness in Skylar's lower body. A pull. "Maybe."

He simply made eye contact. The kind that made her sound breathless when she said, "I thought we decided you needed to warm up, too."

"I can't get in there with you."

"Why not?"

"It'd be a tight squeeze, for one." The muscles of his abdomen flexed and held, his gaze tracking up and down her thighs. "Two, I don't know what's going to happen if I touch you, but I doubt I'd be able to stop. And as bad as I want to get my hands on you, I've got an inconvenient need to know where we stand. Let's label this relationship, girl—"

"Get in, Redbeard."

"Fine. Coming."

He was right. It was very close quarters. The moment Robbie ducked into the shower, the available space in the stall shrank to almost nothing, but that was what Skylar's body wanted. At that moment, that was the only entity she wanted to hear from. News from her body, not her brain or her heart, both of which were getting their signals crossed. Robbie's bare chest crowded her into the corner of the shower, his hands planting themselves on the slippery wall above her head, biceps popping, a rocky exhale.

When he leaned down, when he would have kissed her—

every pinprick of her nerves celebrating in response, flashing hot and wild, rushing—he stopped before their lips could meet, searching her eyes with an intensity that blocked her next inhale.

"Tell me everything you want," he demanded, dragging their mouths together roughly. *Oh my.* "Tell me every fucking thing you want and need."

"Well, it's . . . Wednesday. It's blow job day. I thought we could—"

Robbie covered Skylar's mouth with his hand. "I'm not talking about sex. And . . . wow. Wow. I can't believe I just said that out loud. My hand on your mouth is actually preventing you from talking about sucking my dick. So yeah, I don't know, Skylar, but I think I'm pretty messed up over you. I want to know what you want in life. I want to make sure you get it?" He rolled their foreheads together. "I don't know. I don't know. My chest hurts, baby. Help me out."

She'd never experienced raw honesty from another person this up close and personal and it made her feel drunk. Stoned. That's what Skylar wanted, too. Didn't want to be in possession of a single faculty whatsoever. Just wanted to feel and not overthink what touching Robbie meant. Where his confessions might lead. "What I w-want in life?"

"That's what I said."

There was a list in the back of her planner, but in the steam with this big man pressing her into the wall, she could only recall a few items amid the hormonal rush. "I want to swim at the Great Barrier Reef. Pitch a no-hitter . . ."

"You haven't pitched one yet?"

"I have, but I want one at the collegiate level."

"Got it." His right hand dropped from the wall, fingering the strap of her bathing suit, waiting for her nod before he started slowly, slowly tugging it down her right arm. "Okay."

"And . . ." She snapped her mouth closed before she could say the rest.

"What?"

"Nothing."

A red brow arched. "Nothing?"

He yanked down the other bathing suit strap and it happened, it was happening, her breasts were uncovered. Out in the open. She couldn't help but look down to see what Robbie could see and wow, the view actually turned her on. Her arms were trapped at her sides thanks to the wet straps and that position put an arch in her back, lifting her breasts, her stiff nipples quickly growing wet with steam, her pulse accelerating at the way his eyes darkened, his huge hands coming up to cup and knead them, thumbing her nipples. Circling them with a featherlight touch and inspiring a slow tug between her legs.

A breathless glide of moisture. There.

She trapped a moan, but couldn't quell her shudder.

"That nice?"

"Yes. Yes."

"What was the third thing you were going to say?"

"I don't . . . I don't remember . . ."

Robbie lowered his mouth to her tight breast and gave a long, thorough lap of her nipple. "You're going to tell me what it is." The rosy bud disappeared into his mouth, the pad of his tongue rubbing, rubbing. Relentless. "Say it."

"A giant erasable calendar with everyone's sports schedules on it," Skylar blurted.

When she expected him to laugh or cringe, he only transferred his attention to her other breast, licking the entire thing up, down, and sideways, making her head fall back against the shower wall, her teeth making marks on her bottom lip. "Who's everyone?"

"Uh."

"Kids?"

"Yes."

"Is that a someday wish or a someday soon wish?"

"Someday."

He hummed again. It was a new sound for him, one he'd been making a lot today, like he was absorbing information about her or . . .

What.

Oh God.

She couldn't think with him giving her breasts so much . . . enthusiastic . . . attention. At some point, he'd lifted her off the ground with his forearm beneath her butt so he wouldn't have to duck down so far to lick and suck and kiss her there, breathing heavily all the while, like they were his last meal.

Where was this leading? What was going to happen?

Those unknowns led to her reaching for some control in the form of kissing. Threading her fingers into his wet hair and dragging him into a kiss that was even more intense than before, his hips grinding her butt into the shower wall in time with the stroke, stroke, stroke of his tongue, turning her brain into an impenetrable fogbank and more importantly, making her inhibitions go poof. Gone.

"I want to get on my knees for you," she gasped.

"No."

"You . . . no? But . . ."

"You were drowning less than an hour ago, Skylar."

"I didn't, though." She scrubbed a hand down between their bodies and massaged his erection through the soaked front of his trunks, forcing him to muffle a ragged noise in her neck. "You were there."

"I'll be there every time if you let me," he said, choppily. "The fact that I rescued you . . . is that why you want to kneel for me?"

She tugged open the string of his shorts and slipped her hand inside, gripping. Jacking him once, twice, three times, savoring the way his shoulder muscles tightened, the veins growing more prominent in his neck. "Maybe the fact that I want to suck this was subconscious until now, but Robbie?" She sipped at his bottom lip. Nipped it. "If I didn't want to get on my knees for you, I would never have put it on the schedule."

Relief, tenderness, and heat, combined with a heavy swallow, made him so endearing in that moment. Vulnerable. It was an admission that he'd needed to hear—that she'd been attracted to him all along. She kissed his cheek and lingered there, her grip staying busy on his erection until an uneven groan broke free from his mouth, his length stiffening further and further in her hold. The kiss Robbie gave her was wet, provocative, sexual. "Does that mean you've wanted to fuck me, too?"

Yup. "Don't push it," Skylar teased on her way down, her mouth open as it skated down his bare torso, her knees finding the shower basin with a gentle thud. And there he was in front of her, thick and protruding, straining toward her mouth in a subtle arch that she pumped in her hands, observing him from below until she judged that he breathed the fastest when her grip remained semiloose and moved fast. What else did he like?

"Teach me."

"Jesus Christ," he hissed, bracing a hand on the wall, cupping her face with the other. "You really know how to turn a spank bank obsolete, don't you? This is all I'm going to see from now on when I need to get off. Skylar on her knees with her nipples red from getting sucked, wanting me to show her how to fuck her mouth." His fingers twisted in her hair and fisted, not enough to hurt, but enough to make her back straighten, her attention captured. "Just so we're clear, I'm going to teach you how I like *my* cock sucked. Just mine. You don't need to know what anyone else likes." He guided his hard sex to her lips, rubbing the head along the seam of her mouth. "Nod or I'm not going to put it in."

It blew her mind that she liked being spoken to like this. In this moment, she wasn't a daughter or a pitcher or a sister or a student. All the things in her life that gave her performance anxiety or invited stress. She was just a half-naked woman who'd driven a man to a heightened state of arousal and he was letting her know it. Maybe later or tomorrow or next week, things would be different, but right now, she belonged to him. They belonged to each other.

So Skylar nodded, hot thrills running through her, overlapping, tripping over one another until she was a human beehive. Buzzing. "Teach me how you like it sucked."

Briefly, Robbie's head fell back, his Adam's apple prominent, throat flexing. Then he looked back down at her with glazed eyes. "Keep stroking me in your right hand. Use your left to hold my balls." She did as she was told, gratified to see his abdomen knit up tight like a drum, his hand fisting on the shower wall. "That's good. Fuck, that's good. Don't squeeze them, just move your palm front to back, give me a little friction, and . . ." He pounded that fist into the shower wall. "Like that. Like that. Yeah."

"When do I get to taste it?"

"You getting impatient?" he asked through his teeth.

"Maybe." She kissed his tip, teased it with the tip of her tongue. "Yes."

"Maybe I'm stalling because I know as soon as I see my cock in your mouth, I'm going to lose my fucking mind."

"Good. Do it," she whispered, burying her tongue in that salty slit, moving up, down.

"Oh goddamn, baby. Fine. Fuck it," he heaved, pushing his length into her mouth with a guttural grunt, her lips stretching to take him, that smooth invasion becoming a distraction from everything else, such as the actions she was supposed to be performing with her hands. All she could do was savor the new sensation of salty weight in her mouth, the act of being used for sexual pleasure and how excited it made her to exist—right now—just for this. "Look up at me, Skylar," he said raggedly. "Eyes up."

Her lids were heavy, but she forced herself to focus, to trace the muscular ridges and valleys of his body until mossy green connected with brown.

"Yeah, you love me in that mouth, don't you?"

He moved in and out for the first time, leaving her mouth until just the tip rested on her bottom lip, before tunneling back in, slightly deeper than before and that thick pressure passing between her lips and his subsequent shudder reminded her to tease his balls in her palm. To keep her other hand moving, fondling him in time with his slow fucks of her mouth that were starting to happen faster already, his breath rasping in and out, filling the shower stall and encouraging her like nothing else.

"Don't stop. Don't . . . ahhh. Good girl. Don't stop doing that. Fucking *Christ*." That fist in her hair grew more and more firm, the tug of her scalp causing a corresponding ripple between her thighs, a satisfaction in some part of her inner self she couldn't name. Joy of being possessed. Of making someone struggle with their own need, their own body. "Don't need to teach you shit. Sucking my dick is easy when you love it, huh?"

Skylar moaned, intuition telling her to twist her palm now, cup his testicles gently, and his response, his faster pumping and bit-off curse, told her *yes, keep going.*

"That's good, baby. Get sloppy now. Let's go. There should be spit all over your chin when this is over." Robbie took her mouth the way a man entered a woman's body—with firm, fast strokes—but he never went past the point that made her choke, not until she invited him to do it, loosening her throat and blinking up at him in a wordless signal that it was okay, and in the back of her mind, she understood that not everyone communicated as seamlessly as them and this was unique. *They* were unique. But the head of his engorged sex found her throat at that moment and she stopped thinking, stopped focusing on anything but him. The power she wielded with a mere swallow. The power in giving permission. All of it. "I'm fucked now. Oh God, I'm so fucked. You're . . . I'm . . . *deep.* I'm fucking your mouth so deep. Goddamn, Skylar."

She swallowed again, constricting her throat around his hard flesh. Moving on instinct, she jostled his balls, grazing the trunk of his shaft with her teeth ever so lightly, looking up at him in wonder as he started to erupt. Saltiness met her throat, and she coughed out of necessity, tearing up, but didn't stop. Couldn't. Not when he'd ripped his fist off the wall and pressed it hard to his mouth, barely managing to trap the strangled roar at the last second, his every muscle straining, his powerful lower body thrusting forward with low grunts, blasting exhales.

"I wasn't going to . . . I wasn't going to bust, I swear to God." He looked half incredulous, half delirious as he drove deep and held, more saltiness going down her throat, his entire body shaking. "You made it too good. Fuck, that was so good."

There was nothing to compare to the state she was left in. A daze, maybe, but her blood was pumping furiously, her sex beating like a heart. As soon as Robbie finished, doubling over to brace himself on his knees, sides heaving, Skylar lost her balance, too, slipping sideways onto her hip and leaning a cheek against the shower wall, a warm stream of water coating her cheek. With a swollen mouth and piping hot blood, her surroundings were a dream, complete with low light and the white noise of the shower. It would have been soothing if her body wasn't primed for more. More.

No sooner had she acknowledged her own hunger than Robbie knocked open the shower door with his elbow, wrapping his arms around Skylar and dragging her out of the still pounding spray, into the bathroom. Soaking wet and breathing hard, she was settled carefully onto the fluffy bath mat, but there was nothing careful about the way her bathing suit was stripped from her body.

Robbie loomed over her, steam glistening on his body, his face.

In that moment and every moment for the rest of her life, she'd consider this to be the most beautiful man she'd ever laid eyes on. The one who rubbed his face between her breasts without a shred of self-consciousness, his right hand shuffling her legs apart. "Not even going to lie, I thought that would end with me fucking your brains out, but I couldn't pull out of your hot little mouth to save my life." Briefly, he brought his right hand to his mouth and spit on it, before bringing it between her thighs. Pausing. "Can I give you head, Skylar?" He licked his bottom lip, pupils dilating. "Please, baby. Please."

She nodded so vigorously, she almost dislocated her jaw. "Yes. Yes."

"God, you're such a good girl, aren't you?" he muttered, his wet fingers sliding down into the split of her flesh, the friction to her clit like shock paddled to the system, and she choked a moan in her throat, heels digging into the ground, her hands flying to his shoulders, nails digging in, scraping up into his hair, core flexing. Flexing. "Yeah, that's what I thought. Drenched from making me come. She wears an innocent black bathing suit, but get the girl on her knees and . . . motherfucker. She's a bright pink thong girl waiting to happen, aren't you, Skylar? Never got off so fast in my fucking life."

Someone had blowtorched her nerve endings.

As a lifelong athlete, Skylar knew physical highs, but she'd never experienced anything like this. For one, she had total and complete trust of this man to be telling her the truth. She wasn't distracted by trying to read between the lines or judge his impression of her. She was free to feel—and feel she did. Everywhere. It was possible to be tense with need and languid with want all at once. She knew that now.

That tongue of his continued to skim back and forth on his bottom lip, but it paused as he looked down at her bared flesh for the first time, his hand tensing on her knee. "Damn, that's beautiful. I'd love to be riding it right now, but you had to be so good with that mouth, didn't you?" Robbie got down on his belly, releasing a hot exhale against her core with his eyes closed. "I'm good with mine, too. Drop those knees if you want to find out."

Did she drop them?

Yes, she did.

And good was an understatement. He licked some kind of S shape along her damp seam, then slowly pressed her open with the flat of his tongue, his thumbs skimming up and down on her inner thighs, giving her goose bumps, butterflies, all of it, before he finally started a gentle French kiss of her sex, introducing his tongue with shallow strokes that went deeper the more she started to shake, her whimpers lost in the pound of shower spray on glass, the steam enveloping them both, muffling everything except her body's overwhelming response.

"Can you . . ." she gasped.

"Bet."

His tongue met her clit and married it. That's what it felt like. A union. Two becoming one. He fused to her and stayed, groaning and holding her thighs wide while he raked his tongue up, down, and sideways on that sensitive bundle of nerves. "Oh my God," she managed, sounding throaty, like a different person, her fingers clinging to the strands of his hair, pulling him close. "*Robbie.*"

"Shhh. We're not the only ones in this house." He pushed two thick fingers inside of her, his expression vivid with lust over the way her hips lifted, grinding up against his mouth, her legs trembling. "Might have to drive us the two hours back to Boston just to hear you scream my name the first time we fuck." He kissed her clit, lapped at it with a savoring sound. "Don't worry, I'm going to be loud, too, hitting my tight girl."

He followed that raspy pronouncement with suction and she peaked without warning, her intimate muscles gathering in on themselves and spasming while she gasped for oxygen and attempted to absorb and fight the pleasure at the same time, because it was unexpected and too much. So much, she tore at his hair and shook, her body in a sort of divine shock, hot and fulfilled and relieved and sensitive.

Collapse.

Skylar wanted to marvel over the fact that she'd had an orgasm with a man for the first time, that Robbie was *not* all talk, but walked the walk. That she could, in fact, let her mind go enough to reach completion with the right person.

Was . . . Robbie the right person?

Had other girls ever wondered the same thing?

These feelings were coming on so fast and furious, she couldn't tell if they were a product of her and Robbie's close and continual proximity or if this glorious wrenching in her chest was authentic. If it was? God, that made her so vulnerable. Primed to have the rug pulled out from beneath her as soon as she let her guard down.

That startling train of thought was interrupted because she found herself limp, draped in Robbie's strong arms, being carried to her bed. He laid her down naked on top of the comforter and covered her in a throw blanket.

Then he stared down at her, brow creased.

"What are you thinking about?" she murmured, snuggling into the blanket, admiring his body that was still covered in a mixture of shower steam and sweat.

"A lot of things." He sounded dazed. "All at the same time."

"Hmmm?"

"Skylar, you're . . ." He trailed off with a swallow, raking a hand through his hair. "I've never seen or touched or tasted anything better than you. I want to go back and erase everything but you. That's mainly what I'm thinking." He paused. "The other is I want to get in that bed with you and sleep, because somehow, I know I'll sleep even better holding you than I would after a doubleheader. But I'm afraid you're not going to let me do it forever. I'm afraid to get used to it."

He's as defenseless as I am. "Get in here, Redbeard."

He laughed, pained. "Not this time. I'm feeling all vulnerable and shit."

It hurt not giving him the answer he wanted in that moment. To erase all doubt. But she wasn't ready to take that leap yet and taking back any promises later would be worse than leaving him hanging now, wouldn't it? "What are you going to do?"

Robbie traced the outline of Skylar's body with a conflicted gaze. "Jesus. I don't know. You look so soft in there."

"I am."

"*Baby.*" He raked his hands down his face. "No. I'm playing the long game. So, yeah. Guess what? You rest. I'm going to work on making your family fall in love with me while you decide what you want. While you *consider* me."

"I will," she said, her heart pumping even as her body continued to come down from its climax. "I am."

Did she really mean what she was saying, though? Or was she just shaken from what they'd experienced together?

No.

No, she was grappling with feelings for this man, but logic was the issue. Knowing his history. Still not quite ready to trust him with her heart, the way she could obviously trust him with her body. Even if she was beginning to wish she could. Beginning to wonder.

"Do you have a game plan to make them fall in love with you?" she managed, heart lodged in her throat.

"Not yet, but there will be alcohol involved." He raised an eyebrow at her. "Is your dad going to take one look at me and know I just blew his daughter's mind?"

Where was the lie? "You might want to put on a shirt, at least." Her face heated. "There are handprints on your shoulders."

Robbie looked at the prints in question and waggled his eyebrows. "My goal is to have some identical ones on my ass by tomorrow."

"The schedule says maybe."

"Right," he said dryly, pulling on a shirt and finger combing his hair. When he seemed prepared to leave the room, he just looked at her, his smile fading. "Are you sure you're feeling okay after what happened at the lake?"

"After you . . . did that to me on the bathroom floor?" Skylar buried her face in the blanket, a little giddy from the drop of adrenaline and the freedom to be so honest with him. "I don't even remember what happened at the lake."

"That's nice." Robbie shivered as he backed toward the door.

"Meanwhile, I'll have nightmares about it for the next five decades."

Halfway out into the hallway, he stopped.

Strode back to the bed and leaned down, drugging her with a kiss. A long, soul-searing kiss that closed her eyes involuntarily and squeezed the region south of her throat.

Oh dear.

"Consider *me*, Skylar."

CHAPTER TWENTY-THREE

Wipe the grin off your face, fool.

Robbie physically did just that on his way to track down Doug, dragging his palm downward over the lower half of his face. But damn, it wasn't easy to hide the satisfaction of having finally given Skylar an orgasm. A good one, too. She hadn't seen the intensity of it coming, if her unblinking eyes and flushed skin afterward were any indication, and all he wanted to do was get between those legs and give her more. Wanted her to chain-smoke pleasure until she was addicted to his body.

He realized he'd stopped walking halfway down the hallway, his dick telling him to go back. Go get in bed with her. With a wave of determination, though, he kept going. Because Jesus, he hadn't lied about feeling vulnerable. Had any of the women he'd blown off felt this way about him? *I hope not.* It was tough business wanting to mean something to a person and not knowing if they were interested in more than sex. If they were willing to give a relationship a shot. The ache was heavy. Unrequited.

As he walked through the living area and out onto the back deck, he spied Doug sitting in an Adirondack chair, staring out at the line of trees with a frown, hands limp and resting on his bare knees. Moved to silence by the same woman for a very different reason. Robbie couldn't help but feel responsible for forcing the family to make a breakthrough in the middle of their sacred yearly visit, although the fact that Skylar nearly drowned saved him from too much guilt.

"What's good, Doug?"

The older man shifted, sat up straighter. "Robbie." After a moment, he put his hand out for a shake. "It all happened so fast out there, I'm not sure I thanked you properly."

They gripped and shook. "My mom will be glad to know junior lifeguard camp wasn't a waste of money."

A subdued chuckle from Doug. "It sure wasn't."

Elton joined them on the deck, but he had a much stronger drink in his hand than wine. Whiskey, maybe. "How is Skylar?" he asked, leaning a hip against the wooden rail.

Damn, it felt great to be the one who knew the answer to *how is Skylar?* A beat-his-fucking-chest kind of great. "She's good now. Warmed up and resting."

"I don't think I've ever seen her shaken up like that," Elton said.

Doug let out a breath. "Me either."

Robbie's pulse was starting to race, just thinking about the moment he realized she was in trouble. "Maybe I should have a drink, too."

Elton disappeared into the house, returning a minute later with a second rocks glass holding a golden liquid, handing it to Robbie. "Bottoms up."

They clinked glasses and tossed back the liquor.

"You know, it's a kick in the ass to find out you've missed something important happening to one of your children. And Skylar might not be mine biologically, but she is my daughter."

"And she's my sister," Elton tacked on. "I should have seen it, too. She needed to be encouraged. Congratulated. And all I ever do is push for *more*. Bigger accomplishments." He tapped the bottom of his empty glass on the railing. "Meanwhile, my best friend is going to the Yankees and I'm sitting here inhaling his dust. Who am I to expect so much from her when my own goals are still so far out of reach?"

Doug turned in his seat. "Are you talking about Madden?"

"Yeah. He told me this afternoon. He got scouted at spring training."

"Son of a bitch," Doug murmured, pride arranging his features. "Good for him."

"Damn." As someone who knew the time and toil it took to reach the professional level of a sport—even baseball—Robbie couldn't help but give his romantic rival some credit. Even though it burned. "Being a pro was the one thing I had over him."

"Meaning what?" Elton said, raising an eyebrow.

Robbie coughed. "Nothing." Although, with both men opening up about their woes, he had the strange urge to share his own. This is what happened when three men drank on a porch. "Skylar isn't totally sold on me yet," he blurted.

Doug turned, dumbstruck. "*What?*"

Elton rolled his eyes. "Yes, she is."

"No. She's not." Robbie shook his head adamantly, but he stopped abruptly when Elton's protest really sank in. "Wait. Why do you think she is? Did she say something to you?"

"She let you carry her," Elton said, shrugging. "That's it. That's how I know."

"Okay, but I'm feeling vulnerable, so could you elaborate?"

"I'm feeling vulnerable, too!" Doug announced.

"Me three," Elton muttered.

Doug slapped his knee. "I don't like it."

"Can we go back to the significance of Skylar letting me carry her, please?"

"Christ, needy pants. Fine." Elton thought for a moment, then turned to lean back against the railing. "When she was twelve, we were all still getting used to our blended family. Dad and Vivica couldn't make one of Sky's games, so they made me take her. Cheer her on. And I went, but grudgingly. This was before she started with travel softball, so it was a baseball game." His gaze softened. "That's the day I claimed her as my sister. The guys were hard on her, but she kept her chin up. Kept pitching. But somewhere around the bottom of the sixth, she took a line drive to the stomach."

Nausea pitched inside of Robbie at the unexpected turn in the story. "No."

"Yeah. It took the wind out of her. Took her out of the game. And she was only twelve, but she still wouldn't let the coach carry her. My sister *crawled* into the dugout. She doesn't put aside her pride for anyone. Trust is even more sparing." He waved his empty glass in Robbie's direction. "She gave you both. Happy now?"

"No. Now I'm thinking about her almost drowning *and* with a bruised stomach."

"Oh yeah, it bruised. Eight shades of fuchsia."

Robbie glared at Skylar's brother.

"If Skylar has any doubts left, I'm sure she'll come around, son," Doug said, massaging the bridge of his nose. His hand dropped. "And Elton, the fact that Madden got pulled up before you is only encouraging. It gives you something to work for."

"I know. I'm proud of him. I wish I wasn't the kind of person that took someone else's accomplishments and turned them into my own failures."

"It's probably my fault." Doug dipped his chin. "I'm not as good of a father as I thought I was."

"Yes, you are," Elton and Robbie insisted.

Robbie reached over and clapped the older man on the shoulder. "Your adult children wouldn't continue to come back for this psychotic-ass competition if they didn't love and appreciate you."

"Thanks," Doug said dryly.

"You're welcome, man. All true."

"I think we all need another drink," Elton announced.

"There's nothing left," Doug said, coming to his feet. "I'll make a run into town."

Elton sighed, thought for a beat. "Maybe we should just have a drink *in* town? There's the pub, a wine bar . . . or that divey karaoke place off Main."

"Karaoke?" Doug's eyes lit up. "Is there a prize for the best singer?"

"Nope. It's done for pure enjoyment."

Robbie put an arm around Doug's shoulders and ushered him off the porch. "Come on. The lack of competition will be good for you."

An hour later, it became obvious that Doug would not have won, either way.

Unless they were crowning the most enthusiastic bad singer.

In which case, Skylar's dad was the champ.

But sitting in the dive bar, listening to a local sing "Paradise by the Dashboard Light" while getting better acquainted with the people who loved the woman *he* loved, Robbie definitely felt like he'd won.

Almost.

CHAPTER TWENTY-FOUR

Skylar was already fast asleep when Robbie finally managed to drag Elton and Doug home. Standing in the doorway of her bedroom with the doorknob in his hand, he found himself savoring the moment. Coming home to Skylar. Having the freedom to walk into her room and see her in a hoodie and flannel shorts, snuggled up with a pillow, her dark hair pluming in various directions, lips slightly parted. She'd left the lamp on for him, but he turned it off right away and started undressing, shoes first, socks, his jeans and T-shirt.

Getting into bed with her felt like the right thing to do. The invitation had been given, hadn't it? Still, sleeping in the same bed was couple shit and she might never want that with him. After this week ended, they might be nothing more than friends. If that was the result, he wouldn't be able to live a happy life knowing what it felt like to hold her while she slept. For now, they were still technically friends.

Friends who went up in smoke when they kissed.

Friends who'd gone down on each other.

If she decided against them, he'd be in love with a woman who didn't love him back.

Winded in the face of that reality, Robbie got down on the floor and started to make himself at home on the pallet, wincing when Skylar started to rustle around in the bedding. Had he woken her?

Damn, her ass looked juicy in those shorts.

Sadly, those squeezable buns were out of sight a moment later because she turned over onto her back, stretching, revealing her stomach. The low flannel waistband. And yeah, he didn't get hard over the thought of a whipped cream bikini these days, but he was definitely tenting his boxers over a girl in full-on pajamas.

She's not even awake, pervert. Go to bed.

"Robbie?" Skylar yawned.

"Hey," he blurted, coming up on his knees and walking to the edge of the pallet, his stupid pulse racing at the unexpected luck to talk to her. "Hey, Rocket."

She turned on her side, propped herself up on an elbow, and he tried not to sigh like a lovelorn poet as she blinked the grogginess away. "What time is it?"

"Just after eleven thirty." Try to stop him from smoothing her hair back, tucking it behind her ear. It couldn't be done. She looked way too soft. "Did you know your father has a secret karaoke fetish? We couldn't get him off the mic until last call. He was singing 'Yellow Submarine' to a bunch of empty tables."

Skylar's mouth dropped open. "You have to be talking about someone else's dad."

"I'm afraid not—and I'm pretty sure it's hereditary."

"Not Elton doing karaoke," she gasped.

"His poison of choice is 'It Makes Me Ill' by NSYNC. And it did. Make me ill."

She pressed her lips together to suppress a laugh, her eyes shining in the near darkness. "What about you? Did you sing?"

"Nah." He paused, let his head fall forward. "All right, maybe one."

"Which one?"

"Don't worry about it."

"I'm going to find out."

"Fine. Find out tomorrow. But I'll have a better chance of you letting me kiss you good night if you don't find out until then."

Maybe he *was* a lovelorn poet, because he'd never seen anything prettier than the moonlight on her blushing cheeks. Then Skylar whispered, "You have a pretty good chance already," and his cock went fully erect. His blood rushed south so fast he could only kneel there and attempt to regain his equilibrium while she scooted over to the far side of the bed. "Please share the bed with me. You deserve better than the floor after enduring dive bar karaoke."

"Jesus. You're not wrong . . ." Robbie's laugh was quiet and incredulous. "I'm lying, I actually enjoyed every second of it."

A dimple popped on her cheek. "Yeah?"

"Yeah. They're *your* family."

She softened into the pillow, watching him like she was holding her breath.

He needed something here. From her. What, though? He'd only admitted his feelings and declared his intentions to her that morning. She'd had less than twenty-four hours to start considering him as a possible love interest. A real one. Not a fake boyfriend or a sex instructor or substitute teammate.

Stop expecting so much so soon.

That's what logic told him.

His heart was another story. It wanted answers.

"Are you considering me, Skylar?"

"Yes."

He'd expected her to hedge or give him a noncommittal answer, so the single word affirmative made him lightheaded, a grin lifting the corners of his mouth. "Really?"

Instead of answering, Skylar sat up and removed her hoodie.

No shirt. No bra. Nothing. Just tits, all warm and rosy from bed. Robbie got in the fucking bed. "Get over here." She giggled when his knee got tangled in the sheets, preventing him from flattening her on the mattress and getting his mouth on those perky nipples. He could still taste them all covered in shower water. God. "Did I mention I've had a few drinks?" he asked, finally getting himself unstuck.

Lunging for her.

Pressing down on top of her with a shuddering sigh from them both.

"Should we wait until you're sober?" Skylar murmured against his mouth. "I don't want to take advantage of you."

He dove for her neck, razing his teeth in a circle below her ear, before kissing a path along the soft path to her collarbone, back up, gratified by the vibration that started to hum inside of her. Gratified that he was close enough to this wonder of a girl to feel her excitement grow. For him. "Drunk or sober, you have lifelong permission to take advantage of me, Rocket."

"Soon, Redbeard. Soon."

"Soon?"

"We've followed the schedule to the letter up until now, haven't we?" His mouth rode over hers, indulging his tongue with a sweep of her mouth, his hips shifting between her thighs. Humping her through their clothes, already obsessed with the firm heat of her pussy. *That's mine. I know it's mine.* "We should wait until midnight so it's officially Thursday. You know, just to keep the schedule intact."

He stopped kissing her long enough to witness the mischief in her eye. "Are you teasing me, Page? I didn't teach you that."

"Guess it just comes naturally."

"Yeah? I'd tell you to knock it off, but I love every fucking thing about you." His palm skimmed up her rib cage to cup her tit, his thumb brushing side to side across her nipple until she was squirming underneath him. "I remember what you told me on the car ride up here. How sex moves too fast for you. How you don't have a chance to find your rhythm, then it's over. I was planning on taking my time anyway." They breathed hard against each other's mouths. "I don't want to be in the same category as every punk who blew his chance with you. I want my own category."

"I . . ."

"What?"

"I want my own category, too. With you."

She seemed a little surprised by her own admission. Like maybe it worried her that she wanted something that her brain told her was too far-fetched.

It wasn't.

"You already have one, Skylar."

She chewed her lip.

Okay.

Apparently, he wasn't the only exposed one here. And there would be no sex until she was reassured. He needed to get it right the first time.

In an albeit painful mission to do just that, Robbie rolled off Skylar and onto his side, crushing her immediately to his chest because, lord, he could not fucking help it. Couldn't help rubbing his cheek on the crown of her head when she tucked it beneath his chin. Couldn't help sliding a hand into her flannel pajama shorts and gripping her gorgeous ass and dragging her close, needing to feel the sweet give of her pussy against his erection. Couldn't help memorizing the way her naked tits felt on his bare chest.

God, this was living. This was how he wanted to stay forever. Right there in that bed, connected head to toe with this person.

"You have more than one category and they're all pretty unique," he managed, though his throat was tight. "The only girl to remind me who I grew up wanting to be. The only girl I've ever dreamed of introducing to my parents. The only girl who can put me in my place and inflate my confidence at the same time . . . you know, I finally told one of the veterans to fuck off at practice. You were right, it needed to be done."

"That's why you have the black eye?" she asked into his throat, sounding breathless.

"Yup. Technically it's your fault."

"Hold on. I never condoned violence."

"We're hockey players. That's how we get our point across." Robbie locked the juncture of Skylar's thighs tighter to his arousal, moving her on it just a little to torture himself. "You're the only girl I'd compete with in the wilds of Rhode Island the week before playoffs. Only girl who'd make it worth sleeping on the floor. Skylar . . . you're the only girl. Period."

She was silent for so long, he leaned back to see her face.

When he saw the beginnings of a shy smile flirting with the edges of her lips, he started to hope. Hope he could maybe, actually be his person's person.

Keep her.

"Tell me I'm the only man—" On her nightstand, a ding went off on her phone. The kind that signaled a calendar reminder. Midnight. She'd set a timer for midnight. The schedule had just decreed it was time to fuck and, Jesus, that got him hot. She'd been wanting this as much as he had. "I'm the only man for tonight, at least, aren't I?" Robbie rasped into her hair, tugging her shorts and panties down, down to her knees. Hooking his toe in the garments and kicking them away, rendering her naked. *God yes.* "Tell me."

In the process of peeling down his boxers, leaving them circled around his thighs, she flushed to the roots of her hair. "You're the only man," she said, looking him in the eye.

Robbie waited for her to tack on the rest. *For tonight.*

But she didn't.

And there was no time for clarification, maybe he was even afraid to ask for it, because it might rob some perfection from the moment where he rolled an unclothed Skylar onto her back and fucked his tongue into her mouth, her thighs spreading open for his hips, their trembling intakes of breath so unique, so powerful to him. A sign there were depths there he'd never plumbed, but desperately needed to.

"Are we officially removing the 'maybe' in 'maybe fucking'?"

"I couldn't even spell 'maybe' right now."

He huffed an uneven laugh against her chin. "Was it ever a maybe, Skylar?"

"No," she whispered, fingers in his hair. "You were never a maybe."

Robbie had to bury his face in her neck, because he couldn't judge his own expression. Just knew it had to be too revealing on top of every confession he'd just made, especially when his body was so primed he could barely leash his response to her touch, her scent, the fact that she was going to let him inside of her.

Inside of Skylar.

"First things first," Robbie managed. "What kind of birth control are we working with? I have condoms in my bag. Are you on anything?" His forehead rolled side to side on top of hers. "Fill me in, because I'm going to have a real hard time thinking in, like, thirty seconds."

"I'm on the pill. And my parents made me get a physical before the Page Stakes."

"That's psychotic, but great?" He could hear the pain in his own laughter. "I'm all clear, too, as of last week if—"

"Yes."

"Really?" Robbie almost wept with joy. He'd never, not once

in his life, had sex without a condom, but he felt the pressing need for tonight to be different than anyone or anything else that came before. "No condom? You're sure."

Skylar nodded, her eyes full of trust that, frankly, humbled the shit out of him.

"Then let me get you ready, girl," he muttered thickly into her neck, his teeth locking around her ear, sucking the skin beneath while he eased to the side enough to get his fingers between her legs, using his thumb to slide down from the top of her slit to that wet bud, rubbing it gently, teasing it until it started to swell, her head throwing itself back on the pillow, lips parted on hot intakes of breath. "God. You get wet so fucking fast."

Eyes closed, she shook her head.

"Just for me?"

She nodded. "Yeah."

His chest crowded with flawed but honest male pride and he sank his middle and ring finger inside of her in response. *Deep.* "Keep it that way."

Skylar pulled him down for a kiss, part punishment for his being high-handed, part necessity because there was nothing else but each other in this moment, his fingers pumping gently but deep into her slick cunt, their tongues seeking deeper and deeper recesses of each other's mouths. His dick hurt in ways he couldn't have imagined, waiting to be buried in this girl, and he would, he *would* find out what it felt like any second, but he was growing addicted to the whimpers she made every time his tongue did a lap in her mouth, his fingers fucking her now a little on the rough side, but she liked it. She loved it. Bit his bottom lip and tugged, mewling, reaching down to press his fingers deeper.

"*Fuck*, you are so hot," he growled between kisses, hard sucks of her neck. "Can't wait to sit in the stands at your game. I'll be the only one in the crowd who knows how wide you open your legs to get fingered."

She moaned into their next frenzied kiss, before breaking away. Looking him in the eyes with glassy brown ones, her lips plump from being mauled. "Wait until you see how wide I'll open them when you fuck me."

Robbie couldn't remember a time in his life when he'd gasped. Like gasped *out loud*. But he did in that moment, because he almost busted. Had to slip his fingers out of her perfect heat and grab the headboard, bearing down on his lower body so he wouldn't finish on her thigh. He was that turned on by her pouty challenge—and that was it for his control. No more waiting and no fucking finesse.

He suctioned her lips with his own and pumped his cock home, muffling her cry with his mouth, gritting his teeth, and going still when he found her tighter than expected. *Oh. Oh my . . . God. Motherfucker,* that wet grip and clench she surrounded him with defied words. And then she rocked and whined, as if he felt good, but maybe too big, too deep too soon and his control nearly slipped then and there, because she was ringing his cock just by breathing. With every little shift or movement. *So good.*

"Are you okay?" he choked out.

"Yes. *Yesyesyes.*"

"Thank you, God. I need to . . ." Robbie drew back and dropped his hips again, digging his feet into the mattress to leverage himself and get extra deep. He couldn't get deep enough and yet the way she fit him was almost excruciating in its perfection. She was already snug, but she pulsed on top of that, milking his inches in a rhythm he'd feel in his bones for the foreseeable future. "I should flip you over and spank you for being so fucking tight. My *God.* I could come without moving."

"Move, though," Skylar whined. "Move."

"Okay, baby," he gritted out, easing into his typical starting pattern. Two pumps and a grind. Two . . . grind. Two what? The pattern dissolved along with any rational thoughts. His hips took over. There was no rehearsal for this girl; she was the only experience of her kind, gutting him with lifts of her hips, the brightening of awe in her eyes at how good it felt. Yeah, he didn't even have to ask—what was happening between them was unquestionable. The best they'd ever have. The best, period. "You've got me locked in here so good, you fucking angel." His stomach muscles started to seize up, one by one. "Might need you to ride me for a little while so I don't blow."

This girl practically threw Robbie onto his back without ceasing their breakneck pace, her hips on fire, hands planted on his chest, tits bobbing while she worked the drenched suction of her pussy up and down his length, giving no quarter. No time to breathe or recuperate or savor the mind-blowing sensations. His only option was to reach up and grip the slats of the headboard and watch the girl of his dreams buck her hips, sweat forming on her beautiful body, her breath beginning to hitch.

"I'm coming, Robbie." Skylar leaned forward, digging her nails into his shoulders and grinding—oh shit, grinding on his dick and contracting so swiftly, so repeatedly, his back arched off the bed. "You made me come. You make me come."

Now the girl was on her back again and he had no memory of putting her there. Only that her thighs were flat to the bed, her knees pointing at opposite walls and she was encouraging him by saying things like *that's it, baby, leave a mark* in his ear. *Use it. Use me.* And he was now a fucking bull in a China shop, grunting into sloppy sucks of her neck, his lower body moving at a demon's pace, flesh smacking flesh, the bed creaking beneath them, as if he could worry about something so inconsequential when he was seconds from letting go. This place, with Skylar, where he felt like his authentic self, giving up a part of himself because she was the right person, the only person, to trust himself with.

"Skylar," he said, gravity in those syllables, his body falling onto her like a beggar, gathering her close and rubbing his open mouth over her hair, across her forehead, moving on total and complete autopilot. "I'm in trouble, baby. I'm in so much trouble over you."

"It's okay," she whimpered. "We'll make it okay."

"*Please.*" Robbie choked on that word as he erupted, the release starting in the soles of his motherfucking feet and rocketing up to his groin, the pleasure so intense he yelled into the next kiss, his lower body rolling furiously, trying to get free of the pain, and it only subsided when she wrapped her arms around him and started planting kisses in random spots on his face, throat, and shoulders, as if she needed to do more when her cunt was seized up, throttling his body and his heart and everything that made him up. "Please, please, please," he kept chanting while the headboard cracked off the wall, no idea what he was begging for, only that she was the only one who knew how to give it to him.

And finally, he collapsed, a human in the form of vapor, no idea if he'd ever move again. But even in his replete—and frankly, love-drunk—state, the irony wasn't lost on him. He'd set out to teach her how to attract and keep a man, but she'd ended up teaching him about himself, instead. What he valued most. Who he wanted to be.

Where he wanted to be and with whom.

The answer to that had been obvious this morning, but now?

Now he had hope. A potential chance.

He wasn't going to squander it.

CHAPTER TWENTY-FIVE

Skylar woke up alone.

Her panic only had ten seconds to bloom, however, because Robbie came skidding back into her childhood bedroom in white boxer briefs, red hair wild, grinning like he had a secret. It all kind of happened in slow motion, the realization that she had fallen for him somewhere in the middle of this week's mayhem. Even before he'd shown up with Boston University swag, saved her from drowning, salvaged her father's pride, suffered through karaoke, and . . .

Blown her actual mind in bed.

Like, blown it into the next decade.

Was it crazy that she half wished he *wasn't* so good in bed? Because it was obvious he'd had *a lot* of practice. His hands and mouth and hips were confident in every movement. Knew exactly how to hold and touch and position her. She'd decided years ago she simply wasn't the kind of woman who could mentally relax enough to have an orgasm through intercourse, but, holy shit, her uterus was physically sore from how intensely Robbie had twisted her insides up and strained them with that blissful rush of release.

She was *hungover* from that orgasm.

Even more terrifying was the churned-up sensation in the dead center of her chest. How had the worst of it happened while she slept? Had his protective arms around her all night allowed her guard to drop and her growing feelings to spread?

"Talent show," Robbie stage-whispered, closing the bedroom door without a sound. "Your parents must have taken my rant yesterday to heart, because that's the final challenge. Talent shows have very low mortality rates. What are we going to do?"

Skylar couldn't answer right away because a wedge got stuck in her throat. Somehow on this giant planet, she'd collided with someone who got excited about her family's nonsense, too. This man was already very important to her. Did she have full confidence he'd always want mornings like this? Want a long-term relationship?

Not quite.

Not one hundred percent.

But maybe she could try to trust him . . . for now? See how it felt?

"Oh wow," she responded. "We haven't had one for . . . at least five years."

"I'm surprised they've ever planned anything that *wasn't* physically harrowing. What are we going to do, Rocket?" He clapped his hands together and rubbed them vigorously. "I'm a man of many talents, you know."

She stretched her arms and legs out as far as possible in the mess of sheets, yawning and wiggling her toes. "Oh, believe me, I know."

Robbie raised an eyebrow. "Wow. We're getting straight to the point this morning, are we?" He pressed one knee onto the bed, followed by the other, and prowled closer, laughing when she flipped quickly onto her stomach and tried to hide herself under the covers. Such behavior was ridiculous . . . and she didn't care. In fact, she coveted this freedom to act however she wanted in front of Robbie, knowing he'd respond in kind or simply be amused. *Look at me. I can be playful and sexy.*

The lessons had worked.

Skylar squeaked into a pillow when the covers were stripped off and she was covered, instead, by a thick blanket of hockey muscle, her butt fitting tightly into his lap like it had been carved specifically for that very spot and they both moaned over the way they locked together, her backside to his groin.

His warm, minty breath bathed her ear. "Since you brought it up, I'd love to talk about all the ways you find me talented."

Skylar made a conscious decision not to think of his talent in terms of how it had been honed, but instead how it had been focused on her. That mental trick wasn't easy to perform. She did it, though. She did it because their bare skin aligned in the morning haze was a heaven she'd never expected to visit and because she could still feel how tenderly he'd held her throughout the night. "You make me feel sexy," she murmured.

Robbie scoffed. "Because you are."

Heat bloomed on her cheeks, but she kept going anyway. "You make my body feel like it's the most desirable body in the world."

"*It is,*" he growled into her neck. "I promised myself I wouldn't give in to the male urge to say this, but I can usually go for hours. I'm lucky I lasted eight seconds with you." He let the weight of his lower body press down on hers, hips pinning hips, his bulge wedged between the cheeks of her backside. Rocking. Rocking. "There's no feeling like the one you give me. I don't know how I've been living without it."

"Me either," Skylar whispered, clutching at the bedding, wet warmth rushing to her center in a way she hoped/feared she would always associate with Robbie. "I'm wet, but I'm sore, but I want you anyway . . . ?"

"Thank you, Jesus. I'll go easy, I swear," he said hoarsely, reaching between them to tug down the waistband of his briefs, his breath growing more and more scattered, the force of it shifting her hair. "I'm sorry you're sore, baby," he mumbled into her neck as he pushed his stiff length inside of her, seating himself fully while she parted her legs a little, just inches apart, enough to allow him another sunken inch, his abs rolling up and over the curve of her backside, back down, up and over again, his flexed forearms coming to rest on either side of her face. Every thrust was a slow, deep journey of him pushing, pushing, *pushing*, bottoming out with a groan. "I'm sorry I made this soft little pussy hurt after everything it did for me." He licked a path up the side of her neck, punched his hips with some added strength. "It was hard to be polite after you rode my cock so rough."

"You loved it," Skylar said on a shaking exhale, finding she meant it. Was confident in that statement. Confident in herself.

"Loved it? My fucking life flashed in front of my eyes." Robbie wedged a hand beneath Skylar, sliding it between her sex and the mattress, her mouth falling open at the shiny new available option for friction there. There. There. She flexed her hips and bore down on his fingertips, gasping when he crooked the middle one just a little. Just enough. "Go on, baby. Help yourself come with my fingers. Please. *Goddammit.* You're already making my balls hurt. I'd be embarrassed if I could feel anything but you."

Her sensitivity from last night was almost too much, so much she wanted to shy away from it, but she was too turned on by the bold, hungry man on top of her to deny herself a chance to feel the pleasure he offered her with his rubbing fingers and grinding hips. Those digits rubbed and rubbed until her vision started to double, her teeth catching the meat of the pillow and biting down, her thighs scooting a hint wider of their own accord, the grateful, resounding rumble that went through Robbie serving as her reward.

"Bite down harder, baby. I need a few nasty pumps," he slurred, his hand flying up to her throat, holding it securely. "Oh my . . . *God.* Couple more. Okay?"

She nodded, moaned, lifted her butt slightly, her climax reaching its end, but not her need for him. For his touch. His union with her body. That would never run out.

Muscle smacked flesh, breath caught.

"Oh. *Shit.* I'm sorry." His hand slid up from her throat to her jaw, framing it, squeezing, pushing two of his fingers into her mouth. "I'm sorry, you're just so fucking good at taking my cock. I'm done. *I'm done.*"

She did something she never expected to do in her lifetime, then. She smiled like a smug feline as he jerked and shuddered behind her, his unintelligible words fumbling in her ear. His fingers were still in her mouth, so she knew he could feel the smile and she liked that, too. Liked who she was with Robbie.

They collapsed like two toys who'd run out of battery power, Robbie landing beside her in the pillows, looking nothing short of dumbstruck, his big back heaving up and down.

"I know what you're thinking," he said, winded, squinting up at her through one eye. "But we can't do this for the talent show."

They finally succeeded in waking up the whole house.

Thankfully, their laughter was the culprit.

"The talent show won't be until tonight," she said when their laughter died down, indulging her urge to reach over and twist a lock of red hair around her finger. "What do you want to do all day?"

"Anything, as long as it's with you."

Skylar hadn't held hands with anyone since a group movie date in seventh grade.

She tried not to be obvious now about stealing glances at her hand joined with Robbie's as they walked through town. After a quick breakfast with her family where she found herself unable to look any of them in the eye longer than half a second, Skylar dressed herself in a white tennis dress her mother had bought her for Christmas one year that had remained in her closet ever since. The form-fitting nylon and the attached short, pleated skirt had always seemed destined for someone flirtier and more feminine, but today, all the once-negative qualities of the dress were positive ones.

She'd left her hair in a barely brushed tumble, and that felt nice, too, not having her mane restricted to a ponytail for once.

Better than nice. It felt freeing.

And if Robbie's constantly pulling her into doorways and in between parked cars to kiss her was any indication, he liked the dress, too.

"Is it too late to buy this in nine hundred colors?"

"Probably. It's a gift from a prepandemic Christmas."

"Damn." They were in line at a deli now and he was using their joined hands to gather her in close, his lips grazing her forehead. "Does it have those attached panties? It looks like it does."

"Shh. No, I supplied my own."

He made an appreciative sound in his throat. "That's probably for the best."

"Why?"

"So I don't have to peel the whole thing off," he said, as if she was nuts for asking. He snarled into her neck playfully, nipping at her. "You think I'm going to last the whole day with you looking this hot? Nah, Rocket. Not happening."

Had she ever felt this light before?

Her stomach was floating somewhere in the rafters.

"Hey," she breathed, impulsively, a rush whipping through her blood at what she was preparing to ask him, but she wasn't scared. "Will you come to my home opener next week? If it doesn't interfere with playoffs?"

Robbie had already let go of her hand to fumble with his phone, swiping a few times until he pulled up what looked like the Bearcats team calendar. "What day?"

"Next Monday. It's a night game."

His mouth tipped up at one end. "I'll be there. I have away games Tuesday and Wednesday, but we're here on Monday, then a home game on Thursday."

They smiled at each other in the midst of the deli, Skylar's heart nearly punching through her chest. Had she ever felt this heightened brand of wild excitement for Madden? Or had she only ever been . . . *wistful* over her brother's best friend? Admiring? Because she knew for a fact she'd never had this sense of camaraderie or understanding or sexual anticipation. No, she would remember if she'd felt even a fraction of it. "Great."

"Will you come to my game Thursday?"

"Yeah."

"Okay." He laughed, crossing his arms, uncrossing them.

She laughed, too, because she was happy, and she didn't know what else to do. Also, it was their turn to order and they didn't realize it until someone in line cleared their throat. They got sandwiches to go (Robbie got three) and he carried the brown paper bag in his left arm, holding Skylar's hand with his right. If every woman with a pulse stopped and stared at him on their way down the sidewalk, Robbie didn't seem to notice and Skylar chose to ignore it. For today, she was just embracing the possibility of . . . them.

And ignoring the uncertainty that came along with it.

"You nervous about your home opener?"

"Definitely. First game as a senior. They're expecting a lot out of me." They reached the end of the row of shops and turned down a path into the park, shade enveloping the two of them. "But I know once I throw the first pitch, I'll be fine. Sometimes right before a game, I have this weird what-if moment, like maybe I'll get out there and my body will forget how to play and my arm will be jelly. Once muscle memory takes over, I just get further and further into the zone and I stop overthinking."

He hummed, brow drawn in concentration. "Just have to get through the first pitch."

"Yeah. How do you feel about playoffs?"

"Good. We have some momentum going in. Gauthier is at the top of his game and I'm trying to give him space without blending in too much." A few beats passed. "My problem was the opposite of yours at the beginning of the season. As a rookie, they mostly played me hoping I wouldn't mess with their chemistry. I think I've been so focused on not fucking up, I've forgotten to just play my game."

"Do you think that had a lot to do with the way they sometimes treated you off the ice?"

"Yeah. I didn't realize it until recently. Until you. But . . . yeah." Robbie traded their joined hands in favor of putting his arm around her shoulders and pulling her close, planting a kiss on the top of her head. "Who knows. Maybe the playoffs are when Corrigan comes alive."

"No." Skylar hip-bumped him. "They *will* be."

"You're right. They will be." Abruptly, he stopped walking, looking at her like he was seeing her all over again for the first time. "Hey, you. Skylar Page." His fingers delved into her hair and tilted her face up. "Just where the hell have you been all my life?"

A cool wind whipped through the trees, the clouds passing over the sun, leaving everything a shade darker momentarily. It was an odd event, almost like a rapid passing of time and she could see it, a glimpse of herself looking up into this man's face for years to come, almost like she was watching it happen from a distance. And she had no idea how to respond. Couldn't. Not with her heart in her mouth.

The light returned, along with sound and the movement of the branches above, his fingers still warm and anchoring in her hair. In response to his question, she wanted to say *I've been waiting for you.* It would have been a lie, though, because she never could have known to wait for this specific man, the polar opposite of who she'd envisioned for herself.

"I thought of our act for the talent show," she said finally.

His lips jumped. "I told you. We can't do that."

"Shut up." *My face literally hurts from smiling.* "It occurs to me we both know the original *High School Musical* soundtrack front to back. I mean, *I* haven't listened in a while, so we'll need some quick practice—"

"I practiced last night."

"You what?"

"'Start of Something New'?" He backed up and doubled over, as if his body couldn't handle the coincidence. "I sang it at karaoke last night."

"No. It's a duet!"

"I sang it with Elton. A duet was the only way I could get some airtime with those two hams."

"I played it so much growing up, Elton must have memorized the lyrics. Or downloaded it himself." She covered her face with both hands. "That's a lot to take in."

He lunged at Skylar, lifting her up off the ground. "Admit you still listen to it."

"*What?* No, I don't. I don't."

"Liar. You lie so hard. Show me your list of most-listened-to songs."

"You will *never* see that. Ever—"

He wrestled the phone out of her pocket and ran, his laugh

booming through the park when she sprinted after him and jumped on his back. "No password, Rocket? I could have been snooping while you slept this whole time?"

She gave up the useless task of trying to get the device away from him and deflated on his back, her chin coming to a hard rest on his shoulder, watching as he tapped his way into Spotify, blushing and hiding her face in his neck when he reached the list.

"No. No way, Skylar. No."

"Afraid so."

"'Get'cha Head in the Game'? You let me show you that video of me singing in the shower and wallow alone in my embarrassment when it's . . ." He barked a laugh. "Number *three* on your most played?"

"I was going to tell you when the time was right, when my Kit Harington diary entry wasn't still stinging." She jerked a shoulder. "It's a good hype song."

"The best."

"Hmm. Maybe not *the* best—"

"I'm talking about you. *You* are the best." Robbie dropped to his knees with her still on his back, swinging her around at the same time, so he could catch her and set her down gently in the grass, even as his sides shook with mirth. "You're going to kill me being so goddamn cute."

Skylar pushed at his shoulders. "I'm not cute. I'm intimidating. I can dribble and sing at the same time, as well as any Wildcat."

He lost it, falling face-first into the grass beside her.

Every time she thought they were done laughing, they started again and there were definitely grass stains on the white dress, but she didn't care. She didn't have a single care in the world as she giggled like a preteen in the grass of her hometown park, her second-most-embarrassing secret exposed to the man she was sleeping with, her feelings sprouting legs and running amok in a way she could no longer control.

Finally, Robbie handed back her phone and stood, helping Skylar to her knees, tugging her forward until she fell into his arms, where he rocked her in the shade. He pressed his mouth to her ear and started to say something, but a group of kids went careening past them carrying baseball gloves, a couple of them with bats slung over their shoulder, yelling at the top of their lungs.

"We bat first!"

"You batted first yesterday."

As they watched, the kids ran to the far end of the park and fell into formation, still shouting and disagreeing, but ultimately getting their haphazard game underway. It took two pitches for the first batter to get a hit, the ball soaring across the expanse of grass, bouncing once and rolling to a stop at Skylar's feet.

They traded a knowing glance.

"Do your thing, Rocket."

She picked up the ball, tossed it up once and caught it, then fired it across the park, right into the catcher's glove. Silence reigned in the park. But not for long. Everyone under the age of twelve started talking at once, each of them more animated than the last, but one voice stood out above the rest.

Or maybe he was just saying what Skylar wanted to hear.

"Can you pitch to us?"

SKYLAR LIKED TO think she rearranged a few young minds that day, at least where gender norms were concerned. After the kids got over the fact that *a girl could pitch*, they settled into a boisterous line, each of them taking a turn trying to get a hit off her. When one of them finally connected, the ball fouling off into the trees, the group of boys celebrated like their buddy had just hit a grand slam in the bottom of the ninth of the World Series.

"She's something, isn't she, boys?" Robbie called when the noise died down.

The next batter stepped forward, striking the metal bat off his shaggy pair of Jordans. "She's a lot cooler than *my* friggin' sister."

"Hey." Skylar wagged a finger. "No one is bad-mouthing any sisters on my watch."

"Sorry, she's the friggin' worst."

Robbie snorted around a bite of his third sandwich. "All right, you punks are hogging my girlfriend and I'm sick of it." He waved his pastrami and cheese on rye. "One more batter and we're out of here."

Skylar didn't outwardly react to Robbie calling her his girlfriend, even if her stomach flipped over like an egg being fried in oil. *Sizzleclap.* She tried to make the mental excuse that their actual relationship required too much explanation. Saying "girlfriend" was simply more expeditious. Except he was looking right at her now, chewing his sandwich with satisfaction and staring at her, as if to say, *Yeah, you're my girlfriend, what are you going to do about it?*

And she might have been smiling back.

The eggs in her belly scrambled together.

Oh boy. Was this happening? *Am I taking this leap?*

The only thing that could have broken the spell in that moment was one of the kids whispering, "Girlfriends are grosser than sisters," loudly enough to be heard in Cincinnati. Robbie threw back his head and laughed, startling a woman who passed by pushing a stroller. With her stomach still in chaos, Skylar fell into her pitching stance—and that's when she noticed the one kid who hadn't batted yet. He sat off to the side, his expression a cross between anxious and dejected. When Robbie stopped laughing, she watched him follow her line of sight over to the youngster.

"You want to bat, kid?" Robbie called.

The kid shook his head vigorously.

Robbie balled up his sandwich wrapper, threw it away, and walked over to the boy. Every eye was drawn to the conversation, turning the kid's cheeks red, so Skylar put two fingers in her mouth and whistled to distract them. "Hey. Who's my next victim?"

As she pitched to the final batter, she tried not to be obvious about listening to the conversation between the shy kid and Robbie, but she was too curious to ignore them completely. How was he going to handle this?

"What's your name?"

"Bo."

"Bo, you don't like baseball?"

"No."

"You have excellent taste. Neither do I."

Skylar rolled her eyes.

"Although it's definitely growing on me. Don't tell the pitcher."

She pretended not to hear that.

"All they want to do is play baseball, though. Every day." Bo shoved his hands into the pockets of his hoodie. "They make me play even though I suck."

"You suck less lately," one of the boys offered cheerfully.

"Hey," Skylar said. "Pay attention. Who's next?"

Eight kids shouted, "ME."

"Do you like sports at all?" Robbie asked.

"Yeah," Bo responded. "I'd just rather be inside."

Without looking over, she knew a grin was spreading across Robbie's face. "Have you considered hockey?"

As if to punctuate the moment, thunder rolled in the distance.

CHAPTER TWENTY-SIX

Robbie meant what he'd said earlier—and he meant it even more now. He wished he could go back in time and erase every single thing he'd done with women before Skylar. Every depraved act he'd committed. Every empty hookup. Because this . . . running home in the sudden downpour and getting soaked, forced to stop so they could laugh and kiss every hundred or so yards, sipping rainwater from her mouth . . . this was the definition of fulfillment. He'd fucking found it.

Due to the welcome heaviness in his chest and mind and nerve endings, his feet were barely working well enough to keep pace through the trees leading to the house. He just kept thinking, *She didn't correct me when I called her my girlfriend.*

What did that mean?

Was this once-in-a-lifetime opportunity really knocking?

"I know it's pouring and this makes no sense, but . . ." Skylar said, slowing to a stop, turning to him, her hair plastered to her face and neck, dress soaked, skin wet. If there was a chance he could call this woman his, he'd beat the game of life. Nothing compared to her. Nothing and no one could ever come close. "I don't want to go home yet."

"It makes perfect sense to me," Robbie managed, his voice like gravel. "God, you look so beautiful right now."

Her tits rose and fell. "You don't look so bad yourself."

It was darker than it should have been this time of the afternoon, but clouds had moved in and left the air heavy, slightly
humid. They stood in the electric atmosphere, their clothes absorbing more and more rain, but neither one of them caring or
taking notice. And it must have been the strange suspension
of time that made Robbie push. Made him reach for an answer,
even though he was asking too soon. Even though he hadn't
quite earned the answer he wanted yet. Even though he'd given
her barely any time to consider him.

"You going to let me be your boyfriend, Skylar?"

A smile flirted around the corners of her rain-slickened mouth,
softening the fact that she didn't say yes without hesitation. "I
need more information. Can you tell me what that relationship
will look like?"

"I can tell you what I *want* it to look like."

She pursed her lips. "That'll do."

"Okay." Robbie crossed his wrists behind his back and circled
in a slow pace around the girl of his dreams, trying not to get
distracted by the delicate line of her neck, her wet shoulders. Or
the fact that he could see her panties through the sodden material
of her skirt. That tight curve of her ass. He ignored the long, hot
tug between his legs and focused. "Once playoffs are over, I have
some time off. I'd like to spend all of it with you."

She flicked him a wide-eyed look over her shoulder. "All of it?"

"That's what I said." Too much? *Oh well.* He was in a magical forest with a girl who had doubts about him and honesty was
the only way to fix that. "I want to go to your games and watch
you pitch. I want to take you on millions of dates. I can't believe
I haven't even been to your apartment yet. I want to see it. And
I want my own side of the bed. Actually, fuck that. We'll both
sleep in the middle." He took a fortifying breath. "I'm probably only going to make it a week before introducing you to my

parents. Is it weird I want to show you where I grew up? I don't know. I need you to know me. I've never wanted anyone to know me so fucking bad and like what they see."

He'd circled back around to the front of Skylar now and found her looking as winded as he felt. Winded but strong, as if that made any sense. "I'm worried I'm making you change for me. I'm worried you'll resent me after a while."

"Resent *you*?" Surprise hastened Robbie forward, and he took her face in his hands, brushing away raindrops with his thumbs. "Skylar. Look at me. You're not changing me. You reminded me who I always wanted to be. Did you kick me in the ass? Yeah. *Good.* The best things in life kick you in the ass. And God, you *are* the best thing in this life. The best thing." Realizing he was shouting, Robbie dropped his forehead to Skylar's and rolled it side to side, lowering his voice to a rasp. "Forget the other guy and be my girlfriend. Please."

He groaned out loud when she slid her fingers into his hair. "I had no idea you were so romantic," she whispered. "That was really, really romantic."

That encouragement kicked the rest of his walls down and all the corny thoughts in his head came pouring out. "You haven't seen anything yet. I propose we get those bracelets you touch when you're thinking about your significant other and theirs lights up, no matter how far away they are. So if I'm in Montreal and you're in Boston . . . basically your bracelet is going to stay continuously lit."

"I've already forgotten the other guy," she blurted.

Robbie's heart nearly detached itself, it started pounding so furiously. "Yeah?"

"Yeah."

They were both laughing when he swooped in and caught her mouth in a kiss, but their mirth didn't last. It was eclipsed within seconds by lust so rough around the edges, he knew every sexual encounter from his past had been half-hearted, lackluster in comparison to what this person could do to him with a snap of her fingers. Hunger drove into his lower body like a Formula 1 car taking a curve, his cock full and aching, as if he hadn't fucked her twice already in the last twenty-four hours. Being inside this girl twice was laughably *not enough*. No number of times would ever be enough, but maybe somewhere around the ten thousand mark, he'd have taken the edge off?

Doubtful.

"I hate to break this to you, Skylar," Robbie said through his teeth, his hands creeping beneath her skirt to take those juicy cheeks in his hands, kneading them. "But we're probably going to end up canceling a lot of our dates."

Her head fell back as he attacked her neck, love biting every inch or so on his journey to her ear while she shivered against him. "Hmm. W-why?"

He gathered her panties in his fist, turning them into a thong and using the material to quickly yank her up onto her toes. "Because you've got this hot little slit between your thighs and I can't seem to keep myself out of it."

Skylar's eyes glazed over, her breaths beginning to sound more like gasps. "Maybe I don't want you to."

Robbie was already unzipping his jeans. "Maybe there's no way I could. How about that?"

This girl—this once-in-a-lifetime, mind-blowing girl who made him feel vulnerable and victorious at the same time—pulled her own panties down in one graceful forward bend. By the time she straightened, dangling them from her index finger and tossing them onto the forest floor, Robbie was in some kind of fevered trance and Skylar was the pocket watch swinging back and forth in front of his face.

"Come here," he said, shuddering when she lifted the front of her pleated skirt, letting him see her pussy. Teasing him with a side-to-side sway of her hips and Jesus Christ, he could already see the outline of her nipples through the wet dress, so he was done. Cooked. As horny as a man could get without dying. "Get up here . . ." He pulled her close by the cheeks of her ass, lifting until her toes were barely brushing the ground. "Or I'll put you up here."

With an expression of mock innocence, she wrapped her legs around his hips. "Like this, Robbie?"

I'm not going to survive. "Finally discovered your power over me, didn't you?" He reached behind Skylar, fisting his dick and dragging it down the rain-drenched split of her backside, earning himself a gasp and a jerk of her legs, a whimper when he finally positioned the head at the entrance of her cunt. "I have a little power over you, too, though, don't I?"

"You have a lot of it, actually," she whispered jaggedly. "More than you think."

Trying his best not to be overcome, Robbie tucked the sensitive tip of his cock into her perfect warmth and thrust up, hard, hips tilting to get himself as deep as possible while she struggled through the pressure of being joined at this angle, her thighs vibrating around his hips from the invasion, but loving it. Loving it. Her mouth told him so, giving him tongue and murmuring his name, even as she squirmed, driving him fucking crazy. "Tell me, then."

"I need you." Skylar wrapped her arms around his head, sobbing near his forehead as he started to bounce her, her rear end gripped tightly in his hands. "I need you, *I need you.*"

His pace picked up, because he couldn't help it. Couldn't help the raw upward slap of his hips or the frantic whirlwind in his chest, his belly, his head. He fucked her hard and fast, like an animal, in painful heat over the jiggle of her tits against his chest, the way his cock sounded like wet suction every time it entered her, his lips in a snarl against her throat. *Oh my God. Oh my God.* "I need you, too, baby. All the time. So goddamn bad. You're my girlfriend. You're *mine*."

These were not questions. They were statements. No one fucked like this, like their souls were bleeding, and left questions hanging in the air.

And when she said, "Yours. Yours," hot moisture pressed in behind his eyes and his knees almost lost their ability to function, gratitude hit him with such a blow. As it was, he stumbled slightly to the right before catching himself and going after her orgasm with a single-minded obsession, latching his teeth to the curve of her neck with a ragged sound he hoped, he prayed, she interpreted as a *thank you, thank you, I won't let you down.* But he never found out if she translated him correctly, because she said, "Come as deep as you can, *pleasepleaseplease*, I love the way it feels," and he nearly blacked out, every thought but one leaking out of his ears, especially when her thighs flexed and trembled around his waist, her cunt tightening around him like a motherfucking knot.

"Good. You're about to get some." He bit down hard on his bottom lip as the tremor started in his spine, his groin, everywhere, rattling him like windowpanes during an earthquake. "Every part of me, inside and out, is yours. Every fucking day of the week."

They shook through the end, trapped against each other as the release pitched and battered them, moisture from their bodies sliding down skin, mouths gasping and kissing, hands bruising, hips grinding, grinding, bucking, rain sizzling on their hot skin. She cried out and he knew that meant her thighs were going to drop, powerless, so he clutched her ass tighter and tilted his hips to compensate, bouncing her several more times to get rid of the pain, the perfect agony that came from being vulnerable with his person.

This is my person.

He'd known it the minute she'd mouthed *fuck you* at him at the baseball field . . . and shit, why was thinking about that making him emotional? Combined with the way she clung to him now, breathing so sweetly and erratically into his neck, he didn't stand a chance. Emotions were happening. Every last one of them. All for this girl.

He loved her, that was all there was to it, and he was never, ever going back.

He held her like that until the rain stopped, trying to shake the creeping worry that the storm wasn't completely over yet.

CHAPTER TWENTY-SEVEN

Robbie got the call as they were walking hand in hand up the driveway looking like they'd just survived a week in a tropical rainforest.

"Shit." He looked down at the screen of his phone. "It's one of the coaching assistants. Hauer. This dude never has good news."

"What could it be?"

"I don't know. Last time he called me, it was to set up a meeting with human resources over an offensive sweatshirt I'd been photographed wearing."

She raised a brow. "Offensive how?"

"Uh." He brought her tightly held hand to his mouth and kissed her knuckles. "Don't worry about it."

Skylar decided to let that mystery go unsolved for now. Her knees were still weak from what they'd done in the forest. Maybe when an orgasm was so intense it rendered a woman punch-drunk, she deserved a certain leniency. "You better answer the call."

"Yeah." He cleared his throat, brought the phone to his ear. "Hey, Hauer."

Skylar studied Robbie while he listened intently to whatever was being said on the other end of the line. Whatever it was, he didn't seem happy about it, although his body language was more resigned than angry. Then and there, she decided that whatever the call was about, she wouldn't let it disrupt this perfect state of . . . togetherness. Perhaps words spoken in the heat of the moment couldn't be deemed official, but it seemed like they were really doing this. They were on their way to being a couple, an outcome she couldn't have foreseen in her wildest imagination.

Robbie and Skylar.

Skylar and Robbie.

Together for real?

Yes, it seemed so, but . . . they *were* far removed from Boston this week. She couldn't help but hold on to some trepidation that they could make this work once they returned to real life, but she was there to try, dammit. She was there to give it her everything, because she couldn't envision a world where they went back to Boston and didn't see each other. Being near Robbie, talking to him, feeling his skin on her skin had fast become a given. He was well worth fighting the doubt. *They* were worth it. The thought of living a totally separate life from him after this week made her wet clothes feel colder. Icier.

Can't do it.

Even with the newfound confidence she'd earned this week throughout the Page Stakes, their family breakthrough, and her private lessons in love with Robbie, there was still the tiniest voice in the back of her head making her question how long she would be enough. Old hang-ups were hard to break.

Skylar shook herself free of the conflicting thoughts when Robbie hung up the phone. "Bad news. Coach called a last-minute practice tonight. Apparently, he's been living in the offices watching game tapes on the Oilers and he's mounting a new strategy. He wants us on the ice by seven."

"Meaning you'd need to leave . . ." She went up on her toes to read the time off the screen of Robbie's phone. "Like, now."

"Like, now." He let his head fall back. "No, Rocket. The talent show."

Having seen these regrets coming, she was already shaking her head. "Stop. We'll reschedule it or compete another time. You can't miss practice. Not right before playoffs." Ignoring the useless disappointment in her middle, she hooked her arm through the crook of his elbow and tugged him toward the house. "Come on, you can borrow my car again. I'll put together some snacks for the drive while you pack up."

"Who knows me like you?" She tossed him up a smile, but it dimmed when she found him looking down at her with unfiltered intensity. "You're not even going to make me feel guilty about leaving, are you?"

Surprise slowed her steps. "What? No. Of course not." Following instinct, she leaned in and kissed the valley between his pecs, which, thanks to his sodden clothing, were prominently displayed. If only the talent show were a wet T-shirt contest. They'd win by a landslide. "You play a sport. Competitively. Inconvenience . . . and FOMO is part of the deal. That's how we got to where we are. We missed stuff in order to practice."

"Missing stuff that involves you is different."

"I'm not going anywhere, Redbeard." Ignoring the subtle weight of uncertainty on her chest, Skylar continued. "If we're going to . . . to do this . . . us . . ."

Robbie's jaw flexed. "Oh, we're doing us."

"Okay, well, we're going to have scheduling conflicts. Probably a lot of them. Let's start being understanding about it now."

"Skylar." He seemed at a loss for words, tucking the same strands of hair behind her ear over and over, even when they had been well and truly tucked. "I don't know if I've mentioned that I'm fucking crazy about you."

"You have—"

He cut her off with a hard kiss. "It bears repeating," he said against her mouth.

"Could you two kindly stop Frenching in the driveway?" Elton complained on his way down the front steps, doing a double take when he saw their disheveled state. "How did you guys spend the day? Re-creating scenes from *The Notebook*?"

"Shut up, Elton," Robbie and Skylar said simultaneously.

Her brother only laughed. "Who's ready to get their asses handed to them in the family talent show? You won't see mine coming."

"Magic tricks?" Skylar drawled.

Elton gave her a death stare. "You ruined it. Happy now?"

"Obscenely." She could still feel Robbie staring at her profile. "Robbie got called back to Boston for a late practice, so we'll have to postpone."

"Oh shit." Despite the rocky start he'd gotten off to with Robbie, her brother couldn't hide his disappointment. "Sorry, man, that sucks." He looked at his watch. "Traffic gets heavy around . . . never mind, it's always heavy in Boston."

"Truth." Robbie reached out and slapped Elton on the shoulder. "Sorry to leave when the competition is heating up. On the bright side, this gives you an extra day to work on your magic tricks."

"Let's hope he's going to make himself disappear," Skylar teased.

Robbie chuckled, while Elton gave her a sour look.

"Listen, your sister is coming to my home game on Thursday next week. I'll try and hook you up for the next one." Robbie shrugged. "If you want to watch how a real sport is played."

"Hilarious." Elton rolled a grudging shoulder. "Yeah, fine, I guess I can suffer through it." He sighed. "I'll go break the news to Mom and Dad about the talent show. Pretty sure I overheard them practicing a reenactment from their favorite episode of *Blue Bloods*, so don't cry too hard over missing that."

The men engaged in some kind of ritualistic backslapping

routine that Skylar interpreted as a display of friendship, but she couldn't be sure. A minute later, she followed Robbie into the house, parting ways in the hallway so he could grab his things while she quickly put together a chicken salad wrap and a bag of multigrain chips, tucking the road meal in a reusable tote bag and waiting for him in the kitchen, still aglow from . . . everything. The incredible day they'd spent together. Robbie's truce with Elton. The fact that she had plans to see him again.

Skylar's phone vibrated in her pocket, pulling her from her daze. A text from Eve had her sitting up straighter. *Finally.*

> **Eve:** Hey. Could I bring the kids over for a while later?

Skylar let out a breath she'd been holding since the night at the Gilded Garden.

> **Skylar:** Yes. Please come now for dinner.

> **Eve:** We can't stay too long 😊 I'm working tonight. But I don't want to miss you before you go back to Boston. I'm sorry I didn't have more time, Skylar.

> **Skylar:** Don't apologize. We'll talk when I see you. Fair warning, my parents will be battling the whole time to come out on top as the kids' favorite.

> **Eve:** Spoiler: It's whoever has the candy.

> **Skylar:** Noted. See you soon.

Robbie emerged from the hallway—regrettably, in dry clothing—with his duffel strap over one shoulder, his gaze seeking her out at the kitchen table, expression warming. "Hey, Rocket."

"Hey, Redbeard."

"Walk me out?"

"Sure." She stood and he held up his left arm, wordlessly inviting her beneath it and she went, her shoulders settling into the warm nook of his body like she could never belong anywhere else. "But you should know, when you ask a pitcher to walk you, it has a totally different meaning."

His body shook with a quiet laugh. "I have an entirely new language to learn."

She kissed his shoulder, looked up at him from beneath her eyelashes. "Maybe this time, I'll tutor you in something. Do you think you'll be as good a student as I was?"

He made a sound that was part pain, part amusement. "See, this is why we're going to cancel dates. You going around saying shit like that. Now I'm seeing you dressed like a librarian, drilling me on softball terminology." He leaned down and caught her mouth in a kiss. "How am I supposed to drive?"

"Sorry."

"No, you're not."

"You're right, I'm not." They simultaneously hip-bumped each other.

They proceeded down the steps, stopping at the trunk of her car, Robbie popping it open and tossing in his bag. Gathering her back into his arms. "I'll call you tonight."

"Okay." Skylar closed her eyes as he kissed her forehead. "Eve is coming over. She's bringing the kids."

He pulled back quickly, brows aloft, and she could see he simply knew. During one of their many conversations in town that morning, she'd filled Robbie in on the fraught scene at the Gilded Garden and how the exchange had ended with the discovery that Eve was now caring for her sister's twins—although, for some reason, Skylar had left out the fact that Madden had also been there. That they'd shared a drink together. Skylar ignored the stab of guilt now, focusing on Robbie's sympathetic expression. He knew how much it meant that Eve had finally reached out. That they were going to see each other. "I'm so glad, Skylar. You'll let me know how it goes?"

She nodded, masking how shaky she felt over his imminent departure. "Drive safe."

Robbie pulled her into a bear hug and she gave in to the urge to wrap her arms around his waist, absorb the scent and size and strength of him. "Believe me, I'll be driving safer than ever from now on," he said.

A few minutes later, as she watched her car turn right at the end of the driveway, she was more certain than she'd ever been that her relationship with Robbie had the potential to be solid. But it wouldn't be long before she found a weak spot.

She never expected to be responsible for it.

CHAPTER TWENTY-EIGHT

Eve dropped onto the couch beside Skylar, visibly less stressed than when she arrived, probably because Douglas and Vivica had turned the kitchen into one giant art project station, several finger paintings already hanging on a line above the sink. In other words, the high-energy kids were occupied, and she was free to sip the after-dinner coffee in her hands.

Now that they were alone, Skylar was eager to address the elephant in the room and find out what had led to Eve's raising her sister's kids, but she knew from experience that Eve would drive the conversation around the block until she felt like parking, so she stayed silent and let Eve dictate the starting point.

"They're usually not so rambunctious, I swear," Eve said, sipping her coffee, her French manicure resting against the porcelain mug, the ends of her long, wavy blond hair curled against the curve of her waist. "They're probably just so happy to be somewhere besides my apartment or the office at the lounge."

"Are they in school?"

"Just registered them for pre-K at Cumberland Elementary. They'll be joining late, but it seemed necessary. I don't think they've been social with anyone but each other." A groove appeared on her forehead. "I've only made my way through one parenting book, but I know they need to be around other kids."

"I think if you've read an entire parenting book, you're already doing great."

Gratitude flickered in her eyes. "Thanks."

"Did your sister have them in any kind of daycare, or . . ."

"I didn't have a chance to ask." Eve smiled and shifted her position, a sure sign she was going to change the subject. "Madden mentioned you've been seeing someone. A hockey player? Serious enough to introduce to Doug and Viv? I thought he'd be here—"

As if the very mention of Madden's name had summoned him through the door, the Irishman was suddenly ducking beneath the frame of the entryway, his countenance carved from stone, as usual. He ceased to move when he saw Eve sitting on the couch, obviously surprised she'd finally decided to pay the Pages a visit. Eve stared at the floor, her knuckles white from being locked around the coffee mug.

Really? These two had one disagreement and stopped talking? If the Pages did that, no one would speak ever again.

"Do you want me to mediate this, or . . ." Skylar murmured out of the side of her mouth.

"No." Eve shook her head, turning to face Skylar more fully. Setting down her mug rather shakily. "No—and you're totally avoiding my question."

"I'm not!"

"Hockey player. Go."

Skylar felt parts of her heat that had no business warming up in the family living room. "Robbie. Corrigan. He plays for the Bearcats? Don't ask me what position—I've yet to learn anything about the sport, but he's . . ." Oh wow, her pulse was skipping like a stone going across a glassy pond. "He's going to teach me."

Eve studied her with a half smile. "I don't think I've ever seen you blush in my life the way you're doing right now."

"I guess you're forgetting the time I accidentally pantsed myself in gym class." Flustered over her best friend's scrutiny, Skylar gathered her hair into a ponytail, using the elastic on her wrist to secure it. "Robbie is . . . I didn't expect him."

"We never do, right?" After a beat, Eve laughed off what had seemed like a serious statement. "So, Robbie Corrigan." Eve's black satin envelope clutch sat nearby on the coffee table and she reached into it now, her movements ever graceful, taking out her phone. "Be honest. How much internet stalking have you done?"

"Oh, um. None?"

"I envy your willpower."

Skylar watched with growing pressure in her throat as Eve punched Robbie's name into Google and hit search, before she could protest. Everything that came up would probably be hockey related. No need for this urge to bat the phone out of her friend's hand or rush to explain . . . what? That she was already aware of Robbie's lifestyle?

Across the room, Madden and Elton had taken a seat at the dining room table across from each other, frosty bottles of beer in their hands, the wrinkles of tension between them evident. She tried to focus on that instead of Eve's thumb scrolling, wondering what she could do to help Elton. After all, she had a lot of experience feeling inadequate, especially when it came to sports. His time would come—

Eve darkened her phone and set it down in her lap. "How is the competition going? What sort of ass kicking did Doug and Viv serve up this year?"

"Wait." Skylar pointed at Eve's phone. "You're not going to say anything about the search results?"

"He's very handsome. And a *redhead*. Spicy."

"That's it?"

Eve opened her mouth, closed it. Reached for her coffee but

didn't take a sip. "I shouldn't have googled him. But I mean, come on. He's a public figure. Google anyone with a little fame these days and you'll find a reason the internet hates him."

Static popped in Skylar's ears, her arms tingling all the way to her fingertips. "Just tell me what you saw. I probably already know. He's kind of . . . a partier. But he's going to . . ."

Lord.

But he's going to change.

She almost said that out loud.

"I guess you have to meet him to understand," Skylar finished, lamely. "He's great. He saved me from drowning yesterday, for god's sake."

Eve's spine snapped straight. "He what? You almost drowned?"

"Just show me the phone," she blurted.

"Skylar."

"Eve."

"What's going on over there?" Elton called.

Madden frowned over a long pull of his beer, his scrutiny directed at Eve, as was Skylar's.

Skylar and Eve dove for the phone at the same time—and she had to hand it to the blonde, she was quick; but she hadn't grown up in a family of freakishly competitive athletes. It was no contest. Skylar had the phone in her hand in a blink.

"What's your password?"

"I'm not trying to keep what I found quiet," Eve strangle-whispered just for Skylar's ears. "I just wanted to show you later when you're alone and you can process it without everyone watching. Maybe you know about it already."

"Know about *what*?"

Eve sighed, hesitated, then punched in her four-digit password, lighting up the screen and revealing a blue-and-white list of search engine results. "There's a website where women share bad experiences with men, okay? It started off as a way to help women protect one another from violence, which we shouldn't have to take into our own hands, but here we are. There is also a fair amount of ex bashing, so it's not perfect. That seems to be what women are doing with Robbie, although . . . he appears to be an ex-boyfriend to no one. It never gets that far." Eve tapped through a few screens. "There's a whole page dedicated to him."

"Dedicated to who?" Elton wanted to know. "What are you talking about?"

"Nothing," Eve and Skylar shouted back without taking their eyes off the phone.

Even though Skylar desperately wanted to take the device and throw it in the lake.

Oh . . . my God.

Her eyes skimmed over rows of ugly words and phrases. *Serial player. Don't trust a word out of his mouth. Manwhore. Don't get played.*

Forgot my name after we slept together. Twice.

Holds weekly whipped cream bikini parties.

The worst part was the picture.

Robbie at what appeared to be a nightclub with two beautiful women on his lap, a third one pouring a shot of tequila directly into his mouth.

It was like someone had taken a shovel and scooped everything out of her chest in one go. Skylar could only hand the phone back with numb fingers and try to keep her features schooled, not sure if she should be more embarrassed or devastated. It was one thing to know Robbie lived an unapologetic bachelor lifestyle up until a couple weeks ago . . . and quite another to see it in vivid color on the internet. There was nothing wrong with being sexually active. That was his choice. But seeing the images, the words on the screen, only reminded her of how he'd bragged about his conquests. How content he'd seemed pursuing one-night stands, organizing threesomes on a whim. Could he be happy and fulfilled without those things?

"Okay," she whispered. "Um . . ."

"Look." Eve shoved the phone back into her purse. "Everyone has a past. You have to trust your own judgment of him."

"Yeah," Skylar forced past dry lips, her ears and face and throat on fire. "Thanks for showing me."

Eve started to respond, but the kids bounded over like matching whirlwinds, throwing themselves onto Eve, even as Vivica jogged in their wake shrieking for them to wash their hands before they touched anything. Before Skylar could rouse herself from what felt suspiciously like heartbreak to help her friend, Madden was there, plucking Landon off Eve, holding the child stiffly for a moment with his legs dangling, then settling him onto his feet with an awkward head pat. "Do you need help with . . . anything?" he asked Eve.

Why did she look so thrown by the simple question?

Was Skylar missing something? Had Eve's disagreement with Madden continued without her being aware of it?

"No, we're fine, actually. Better than fine." Holding Lark in her arms, Eve stood up, stooping with some difficulty, bending her knees to clutch her purse with a hand that was already semi-occupied. "But it is getting late, so I think we'll head out." She hustled Landon toward the door, nodding as he whined to be carried like his sister. "Thank you, Doug. Thank you, Viv." On her way out the door, she looked back at Skylar with undisguised regret. "Skylar . . . call me, okay?"

"Yeah," Skylar creaked. "Love you."

"Love you."

Activity took place around Skylar after that, but she was only partially aware of voices and movement. Dishes being dried. Art supplies being cleaned up. Madden pacing and looking out the window. Elton reading off dating profiles out loud to get Vivica's opinion. And Skylar just sat there, unable to feel her legs.

Am I getting played?

What am I doing?

If Robbie was there right now, she'd probably be reassured, but he wasn't. All she could see were those incredibly confident women on his lap, and the insecurities she'd made great headway in overcoming the last week started to bleed back in. If *those* women hadn't stood a chance with Robbie, how could she?

"Skylar," a deep voice prompted. In a way that suggested they'd been trying to get her attention for a while. Madden. He'd sat down on the coffee table in front of her, his hands clasped loosely between his knees. He tilted his head to search her face, his right knee brushing hers, maybe accidentally? She didn't know. Didn't know up from down in that moment. Only that she desperately needed a grounding presence and Madden was there now, taking up space. "I was wondering if . . . you want to get a drink with me."

Her first instinct was to laugh.

Really.

Really?

She'd carried a torch for this man since high school and he'd never done more than humor her, treat her like a kid. One he cared about, but still. Now that she was over him, he finally asked her out? The irony sucked on top of everything else. It was too much, but . . . maybe that's what she needed. Too much. To be overwhelmed and distracted and dammit, she refused to sit there in a pathetic fog of inadequacy and doubt, waiting for a man who up until very recently was throwing whipped cream bikini parties. And suddenly, she was dissecting everything he'd said about his last trip to Boston, putting together timelines and . . . holy shit. Was she setting herself up for this kind of constant worry?

No. Hell no.

"Yeah. I'll go get a drink, Madden. Sure."

CHAPTER TWENTY-NINE

Robbie sang at the top of his lungs to "Freak," by Doja Cat, even though he was in gridlock traffic and people in the surrounding cars were openly watching him, probably even taking pictures, if they recognized him. Robbie didn't care. He was in love. Even the I-95 traffic couldn't penetrate the golden glaze that coated him like frosting on a donut.

When the song ended, he reached into the bag Skylar packed him and took out the sandwich, unwrapping it and consuming half of it with one bite. "She even makes good sandwiches," he shouted around a full mouth. "I'm going to marry her." He honked at a middle-aged man in the Nissan to his right, leaning his head out the window. "I'm going to marry Skylar Page."

Dude tapped his horn. "Good luck."

"Thank you." He swallowed the rest of the sandwich without chewing, then regretted it, because he only had one Skylar sandwich in the car. "Dang."

His phone rang where it sat charging in the cupholder.

Robbie picked up the device and looked at the screen. "Hauer again? Come *on*." He answered. "What's up, Hauer?"

"Corrigan. Sorry for the last-minute scramble. Practice is off."

"What? I just drove from Rhode Island."

"Yeah. Apologies. All this rain, there's some issue with a leak at the arena. It's not even near the ice, but there's some liability bullshit that says we can't be in-house while they're making repairs."

Hope and anticipation sparked. "Does this mean I can go back to Rhode Island?"

"Yes, but stand by for a possible practice tomorrow."

"Ten-four, Hauer. Over and out."

Robbie had barely ended the call when he started looking for the fastest way to turn around. To get back to her. He almost sideswiped a minivan in his haste to reach the exit ramp, already imagining the softness of sleepy Skylar beneath him when he crawled into bed with her. How she'd snuggle into him in those flannel sheets and breathe against his throat. God, he never wanted to sleep any other way. He should stop and get flowers or something. No, forget flowers. He'd buy her some of those gel pens for her planner. They carried those at gas stations, right?

He stuck a hand out the window, a silent plea to be allowed to cut in front of a truck in his quest to get off the freeway. "Excuse me. Thank you," he called to a driver in the next lane. Over and over until he was finally free of the traffic and free to loop back in the opposite direction. Toward Skylar. The only direction he knew anymore.

Skylar had made a huge mistake.

Upon climbing into the passenger side of Madden's truck, her heart lurched.

She tried to remind herself about what she'd seen on the website. How many women Robbie had probably made feel insignificant when they were anything but. He hadn't even taken the time to learn their names or see them as anything but bodies. She didn't doubt that he had serious romantic feelings for her. He did. But could a man go from having so much freedom to sow his oats to . . . sowing them with one person?

Logic told her that was unrealistic.

Her chest told her yes. Yes, he could. He *had*. When they were in each other's arms or looking each other in the eye, she had full faith. In remembering how perfectly her soul felt complete around Robbie, she felt sick as Madden slowed to a stop at the first stoplight on the way into town. To her left was the deli where she'd gotten sandwiches with Robbie. The sidewalk where he'd held her hand, made her feel protected and special.

He makes me feel so special.

"Is the air on too high? You're shivering," Madden pointed out.

"No, I'm fine, I just . . ." She couldn't deny the sudden urge to bring Robbie into the conversation somehow. To make him present. "Just wondering if Robbie made it to Boston yet."

Madden was silent while accelerating through the intersection. "Do you want to call him and ask?"

While I'm on my way to have a drink with another man? Probably the only man who could cause Robbie to feel insecure?

Wasn't that the point?

Nausea roiled in Skylar's stomach. "No, it's fine. I'll call him later."

Madden said nothing for the rest of the drive, his silence doing nothing to decrease her nerves. After they reached the lot of the bar and he parked, he circled around the back bumper and opened the door for her, holding out his hand to help her down. There was no tingle, no leap of her pulse when her fingers slid into his palm, when he gripped her hand. There was nothing. Not that she'd expected there to be electricity. Not anymore. But the total lack of anything resembling attraction only brought home the fact that she'd come on this date for some kind of vindication. And she hated herself for it.

"Madden, I think I have to go. Can you take me home?"

His brow furrowed. "Is everything okay?"

"I just . . . I don't think I should be on a date with you when I'm supposed to be with Robbie." Skylar squeezed her eyes shut. "No, not supposed to be. We are. I decided to trust him and I let my insecurities get the better of me at the first whiff of doubt and he deserves better than that. He really does."

Madden's energy slowly shifted into what could only be described as rigid discomfort. "Skylar, I think maybe you got the wrong idea about this. It's not a date." He stared off down the row of cars, visibly searching for the correct words. "You're a wonderful girl. The best. But I think of you as . . . family, I suppose." He shifted right to left and crossed his arms over his middle. "This is about Eve." His blue eyes lifted to meet hers. "To me, everything . . . is about Eve."

Clarity was a bitch.

Her confusion gave way within seconds, parting like dark storm clouds to reveal the brightest clear blue sky imaginable, a sun glaring at her from the very center.

Madden was in love with Eve.

Suddenly the way they looked at each other had new meaning. The way they'd looked at each other *since high school.* Which meant Skylar had been in love with a man who was in love with her best friend. For years.

Skylar held her stomach to keep it from imploding. Not out of jealousy or sadness or anything like that. She simply couldn't accept such stupidity from herself. Such a glaring lack of awareness. "Oh my God."

"You didn't know?" Briefly, he ducked his head. "I thought I was being so obvious."

"Not to me." Skylar marveled over the fact that in the space of a few minutes, Madden had gone from unwanted date to a man clearly lovesick for someone else. It hurt in a way she couldn't have expected, because she knew what he was experiencing, she'd been there herself, and unrequited love equaled agony. Although her technicolor feelings for Robbie made her wonder if she'd ever truly been in love with Madden in the first place. "Have you told Eve how you feel?"

"She'd have to let me close enough first." His throat moved with a swallow. "She *runs* from me."

"Why?"

"If I had the answer to that, I'd do something about it." He paused for a good ten seconds, his tongue tucked into his cheek as if he was working up to something. "The reason I brought you here is to ask for your help. Eve has these two children in her care now and she's struggling to keep the club. The health insurance alone for three people . . ." He shook his head. "If she took my name, they'd have it for free. My contract with the Yankees isn't on par with some of the more established catchers, Skylar, but it's a damn good beginning. I could help her. I could provide for her. For them."

Skylar took a moment to process all that, suddenly feeling very young in the face of the gigantic problems facing two people she cared about deeply. And very silly for going out with Madden for a selfish and immature reason when she should have just talked to Robbie about what was bothering her and resolved it like an adult. "I'll talk to her for you, if that's what you want."

Madden tipped his head forward on an exhale. "Thank you, Skylar. God knows she won't talk to me these days." After a beat, he nodded at the car. "Should I take you home now so you can give your fella a call?"

"Yes." Relief permeated her blood. "Yes, please."

Skylar assumed everything would be fine. They were home in a matter of ten minutes and she already had the evening mapped out. Shower, get into her pajamas, and spend some quality time with her planner while she waited for Robbie's practice to be over. Then she'd call him and hear his voice and set about forgiving herself for slipping up.

But the night ended much differently, because when Madden pulled them into the driveway, Robbie was waiting for her on the porch steps.

CHAPTER THIRTY

In a way, I deserve this, don't I?

That was Robbie's first thought upon seeing Madden and Skylar come down the driveway in Madden's truck, the fact that they went out together confirmed by his own eyes. When he'd arrived after a surprisingly traffic-free drive back to Rhode Island, he'd found Doug and Vivica in the living room watching *Under the Tuscan Sun.*

"Robbie, you're back," Doug had called, sitting forward with a glass of white wine cradled in his hands. "What happened to practice?"

"It got canceled because of some leak at the arena." He'd jerked his chin toward the back bedroom. "I'm going to see Skylar."

"Oh. She . . ." Vivica had looked at her husband. "She went out for a drink with Madden a little while ago."

At that point, Robbie's stomach had turned to fucking lead. "*Just* Madden?"

Vivica must have sensed the storm brewing inside of him because she laughed and tried to make light of the situation. "Just having a friendly chat, I'm sure."

Maybe.

Yeah. Maybe that was true or maybe Vivica was wrong and they hadn't gone alone. They could have met some old friends. There were a million possible explanations, but none of them stopped this ugly, oily jealousy and panic from bubbling in his gut. And now, when he saw her sitting in the driveway in Madden's truck, the sensation amplified itself until he felt ill. Because Skylar didn't look happy to see him. Nah, she looked guilty. Like she'd gotten caught.

Robbie tried to make his legs work when she hopped out of the truck, but he couldn't, so he just remained stuck, staring at her. Waiting to find out what could put that expression on her face.

"Hey," Skylar said, sounding winded, swiping her palms on the legs of her jeans. Observing him through owl eyes. "You're here." She attempted a smile and couldn't hold on to it, spreading the panic inside of him. "Practice didn't happen?"

"There's a leak," he responded, lips stiff.

"Oh."

He swallowed a fistful of gravel. "What is this? A date?"

"No," she breathed, waving a hand. "Not at all."

"Then why do you look like you want to cry?"

Skylar didn't answer.

Several moments ticked by, the silence broken when Madden stepped out of the vehicle—and Robbie had never wanted to kick someone's ass so badly in his life. As a hockey player, that was saying something. Ironically, he wanted to kick Madden's ass for being too blind to realize Skylar was perfect, while he also wanted to kick his ass for noticing. Oh yeah, the latter way more than the former. "Robbie, I can see you're upset, but there's no reason to be." Madden scrubbed the back of his neck. "I'm sure Skylar will explain it to you, but this was only meant to be a drink between friends."

"You can get back in your truck now," Robbie managed to say despite the manacle around his throat. "And I'd suggest you drive away fast."

Skylar's expression was one of shocked reproof. "*Robbie.*"

Robbie pointed at Madden. "You fucking heard me."

Madden held his ground. Robbie would give him that. The guy probably would have been a decent fight, too, but the Irishman chose to diffuse the situation by finally getting back in his truck and backing down the driveway, although not as fast as Robbie would have liked.

"Why do you look like you're going to cry?" he asked Skylar again.

"Because. I know how I would feel if I saw you out with a girl you used to love. I know it would probably feel terrible."

"It does."

She closed her eyes. "We didn't even have a drink. We only made it to the parking lot and I asked him to bring me home."

"Why?"

"I felt guilty."

"If it was just a drink with a friend, why did you feel guilty?" A seven-hundred-pound weight sat on his chest. "Were you curious to see if your feelings were really gone?"

"No. I know they're gone. They were never even as deep as I thought they were."

"Then I'm still in the dark, Skylar. Why do you feel guilty?"

"Because I saw . . ." She took a long, shuddering breath. "Eve googled you and this website came up that she showed me. It has details, like really specific details about you a-and women you've been with. There are pictures of you and you look so happy like that. It just blindsided me."

This was his first time hearing about a website with pictures and intimate information on it that pertained to him, and his first thought was *Time to grow up and get a good lawyer, bro,* but he'd worry about that later. Right now, he was quite simply sick to his stomach just speculating on what Skylar might have seen or read. God, that must have been hard for her. If the shoe were on the other foot, that kind of imagery would kill him. At the same time, he couldn't change the past.

Maybe he'd been naive to try to change her mind about him in the first place.

His actions and words were all he had—and they obviously weren't enough. "I'm sorry you saw that," he rasped, in a tremendous understatement. "But I can't change the things I did before I met you."

She took a step forward and stopped, her tone sincere when she said, "Of course not. And I wouldn't want to change any part of what made you this Robbie. I fell for that Robbie."

He only half heard that statement, because the pieces that formed tonight were coming together. "And yet you saw this website and decided to go out with Madden, anyway. Was that to spite me, Skylar?"

Her face was already in her hands.

"Wow."

A huge part of him had expected her to say no. To give another explanation.

There wasn't one, though, and now a hook twisted inside of his chest cavity, making it very hard to breathe. Anger and resignation and regret caught him in the chin all at once. "Well," he managed, staggering to his feet, getting his phone out of his back pocket and opening the Uber app, ordering a ride, so he wouldn't have to borrow Skylar's car. "Who's the one who can't be trusted now, huh?"

She came closer, looking down at the screen of his phone and starting to breathe faster. "Please don't go. I want you here."

"I want to be here, too, of course I do, because I love you. I love you, Skylar. But I'm fucking mad. And I feel empty and sick right now and *you're* the one. *You* taught me to trust what I'm feeling and stop laughing everything off. So I can't laugh at this.

I can't pretend I'm not feeling judged and punished when I just came here to *love you.*"

"I'm so sorry," she whispered, hands pressed to her cheeks.

The sheen of tears in her eyes almost broke him in half.

He wanted to get on his knees and crawl to her, ask her to forget everything and go inside and make love and wake up tomorrow like nothing happened. But would this happen again? Could he live worried that she'd punish him every time an unsavory detail emerged from his past? And he meant what he'd said. Skylar had shown him how to express himself openly and now that he'd experienced that growth, going backward was impossible. The fact that this girl had made him a better person and he had to leave her there crying was the worst insult to injury imaginable, but right now, he had to.

His hurt was valid. He wasn't going to disregard it.

Ignoring the agony in his middle that came from walking past the girl he loved without drying her tears, Robbie picked up his bag and strode for the end of the driveway to go meet the Uber that would take him back to Boston.

"Maybe I shouldn't have left," Robbie slurred on Monday as he bit into his Stouffer's lasagna. "Maybe I should have stayed and fought it out. She was *crying.*"

"You shouldn't cry and eat at the same time, man," Mailer said, handing him a napkin. "You're going to choke to death."

"Good."

Mailer reared back, alarmed. "You don't mean that."

"I fucking *do* mean it."

"Ah, she'll come back around," Mailer said, recovering from his shock enough to slug him in the shoulder. "They always do, am I right?"

"No. That's what I've been telling you. She's not like anyone else." Robbie stood and lumbered to the refrigerator, searching through various frozen meals for another lasagna. Not that he could find anything he was looking for when his brain was only showing him visions of Skylar. Practicing flirting with him at that rest stop. Pitching to those kids. Her face covered in raindrops. "She's Skylar."

Mailer groaned up at the ceiling. "You know, everything was fine when we were having empty sex with strangers."

"*Was* it, dude?" Robbie shouted.

"I don't know anymore." They sat with that statement for a while, the modern kitchen feeling sterile and cold. Then Mailer said, "This is out of my depth. I'm calling Burgess and Sig."

"*No*," Robbie shouted, jabbing his fork in the air in front of Mailer's face, before his arm gave up and dropped like he was holding a bowling ball. "Okay."

Robbie lay face down on the couch while Mailer talked on the phone in the other room. He couldn't make out the conversation, but he overheard the phrase *he smells like cheese and ass*. After that, he must have passed out, because when he woke up, Mailer was presenting him with another lasagna piping hot from the oven and someone was knocking at the door.

"That's Sig and Burgess?"

"Yup," Mailer confirmed, striding across the floor in his socks to let in Sir Savage and Sig—and they weren't alone. Chloe, Sig's future stepsister, breezed in with a beaming smile and Tallulah, Burgess's girlfriend, entered more slowly and cautiously.

Burgess took Tallulah's hand and guided her to a leather chair across from Robbie, grunting quietly for her to sit down, then proceeding to stand behind her with his arms crossed like a bodyguard. Meanwhile, Chloe took a while to stop flitting around the apartment checking everything out—the view, the mini beer fridge in the corner, a framed poster of Bobby Orr. Sig leaned against the wall and watched her explore with hawkish intensity, then tugged her into his side like he couldn't stand the separation anymore.

Which was new. They usually just made blistering eye contact.

"Oh," Robbie croaked. "Did you guys finally get together?"

"Yes," Sig said in a hard voice.

"Yes," Chloe bubbled.

A month ago, the kind of behavior currently being displayed by his two teammates and their significant others would have made Robbie roll his eyes. He got it now. Man, he completely understood. Finding your person was a miracle and once you did, keeping them close was pure necessity, which was probably why he felt drained of his will to live right now.

Sig stroked a hand down the back of Chloe's hair. "Anyway, we called in the big guns to help you out."

"So watch your language," Burgess tacked on.

"And put on a shirt."

Mailer disappeared into Robbie's bedroom and came back with a gray Bearcats T-shirt, tossing it to him. And obviously he was on the verge of a nervous breakdown, because the sleeve dipped into his lasagna and he almost started crying, but he managed to set aside the cheesy masterpiece and don the shirt. "I appreciate you all coming, but there's nothing anyone can say or do to help the situation."

"There is always a way to help, Robbie," Chloe said comfortingly.

She started toward Robbie, as if planning to sit beside him on the couch, but Sig caught her around the waist and tugged her back. "Nope."

"See?" Robbie threw a hand out. "This is the problem. My

reputation. Sig won't even let his girl sit next to me when I smell like cheese and ass."

Mailer winced. "You heard that?"

"It's not just you, Robbie," Chloe rushed to say. "He doesn't even like me sitting next to my coworkers—and I'm in an orchestra. It's part of the job description."

Sig shrugged.

"Why don't you tell us what happened, Robbie?" Tallulah prompted. "I'm sure we can piece together a solution. It's probably a matter of simple communication."

Burgess put a hand on Tallulah's shoulder and nodded.

Robbie took the final bite of his lasagna, no recollection of when he'd wolfed down the entire tray or how much of it was in his beard. "Well, she hated me in the beginning because she overheard me bragging about my nocturnal activities. Honestly, I think I was too blown away by her to realize I was fucked from the start."

"Language," Burgess chided.

"Sorry." He sighed with his entire aching body. "Anyway, she was in love with her brother's best friend, who is this big, quiet guy with an Irish accent, as if I'm not already at a disadvantage. I offered to pretend to be her boyfriend to make him jealous . . . and teach her a few tricks while we waited for him to notice she's a goddess walking among humans."

"Tricks?" Chloe asked, nose wrinkled.

"You know . . ." Robbie put aside his empty lasagna tray with a heavy hand. "Flirting, kissing, going on dates . . . other stuff." *No big deal, just the most incredible sex of my life.* "It had been established that I'm the master. She wanted to learn from me."

"So . . . the whole time, you were essentially reminding her how skilled you are with women," Tallulah deadpanned. "Go on."

"Well, *that* recap stung, thank you very much," Robbie said, rubbing at his chest. "She didn't even need the help. She's perfect. She's so . . . *perfect*. Funny and driven and honest and encouraging. Beautiful as sin. Competitive like me." He pinched his fingers together. "She has these little stickies for her planner and she looks so serious while she's writing in it. She can't stop messing with her ponytail when she's nervous. She doesn't let me breeze through uncomfortable conversations. She makes me talk them out. I feel like knowing all these things about her is going to kill me. I can't forget them."

Chloe sniffled.

Sig turned her face into his shoulder and started to rub her back without missing a beat, gesturing for Robbie to continue.

"At some point, it stopped being about making him jealous and it started being about us. Everything was going great, you know? At least I thought so. The second I turned my back, she went out with him. And his accent. I probably never would have found out . . ." He trailed off, shaking his head. "No, that's not true. She would have told me eventually. She's not a secret keeper. There isn't a deceptive bone in her body."

"Why did she go out with him?" Burgess asked. "And why did you let him live?"

"It wasn't romantic. Don't get me wrong, I'm jealous as hell, but I think Skylar just wanted to . . . emotionally bodycheck me after seeing some garbage about me on the internet."

Mailer stepped forward with his phone aloft. "I have the website in question right here."

"Dude." Robbie kicked his roommate in the back of his leg. "What the hell."

"They need the full picture."

"No, they don't!"

Burgess plucked the phone out of Mailer's hands. "Yes, we do." He went back to his post beside Tallulah, scrolling with his thumb. "Jesus Christ, Corrigan."

Robbie doubled over, dropped his head into his hands, and groaned loud enough to shake the windowpanes.

Both women scrambled out of their respective spots to look over Burgess's shoulder, which was physically impossible, of course, so he handed the phone to Tallulah. The twin gasps arrived five seconds later.

"She *saw* all this?" Chloe whispered.

"I assume you've contacted a lawyer," Tallulah said.

"You're not going to want to hear this, Robbie," said Chloe, "but I would have gone on a date with an Irish guy, too. Ten of them. And I would have thrown in an Aussie."

Sig did a double take. "How about you don't put that image in my head, Chlo?"

"Only kidding!" She looked at Tallulah and mouthed, *I'm not kidding.*

"Look . . . I haven't done any of that shit since I met Skylar. I don't *want* to. But I can't be looking over my shoulder waiting for her to doubt me again. It's going to be painful every time. It hurts to be doubted by someone I'm so goddamn in love with. I'm mad, all right? I'm fucking mad and . . . devastated."

Tallulah's expression had gradually turned sympathetic. "Did you tell her all this?"

"Yes."

"And?"

"She said she was sorry." His chest erupted with a fresh wave of pain. "She was crying when I left on Thursday night."

"Making your woman cry." Burgess shivered. "It's worse than two broken legs."

Tallulah reached up and threaded her fingers through Burgess's, squeezing.

"Let me ask you a question, Corrigan," Sig said. "Let's say she gets on a plane tomorrow and moves to . . ." Momentarily, he eyeballed Chloe. "Ireland or Australia. And you're never going to see her again. How do you feel about that?"

Robbie's ribs almost cracked from the sudden pressure. "What?" he wheezed.

"How. Do you feel. About that?"

"Like I want to die." Even that was an understatement.

Sig dipped his chin. "Then guess what? You're a lucky son of a bitch, because she lives *in your town*. And she might even still like your ass. So quit wasting time."

"Sig, you're so smart," Chloe said, hands tucked beneath her chin. "I wouldn't leave you for all the Australians or Irishmen in the world."

"Now you tell me."

"Hold on, though," Tallulah broke in with a wave of her hand. "He can't just get back together while he's holding on to this feeling of betrayal and judgment. Although . . ." She held up the phone Mailer had given her. "If anything deserves a bit of side-eye . . ."

Robbie threw up his hands. "We were all consenting adults."

"True." Tallulah tossed the phone back to Mailer. "Rebuild the trust before you jump back into the relationship. Spend some time with her on your terms. Decide if your feelings are the same or if they've changed—"

"My feelings for her are never going away," Robbie rasped, visions of Skylar flipping through his mind like the pages of a glossy magazine.

"Then work your way toward a better place. Take your time."

Being encouraged to go see Skylar was like being handed the keys to a golden kingdom. That was exactly what his heart urged him to do and God, he was grateful to have that feeling seconded. "Go see her," Sig enunciated.

He stood up and walked straight to the front door, his pace accelerating as he went. "Okay. Her home opener is tonight."

Mailer blocked his path. "Maybe a shower first, buddy?"

CHAPTER THIRTY-ONE

With one hour to go until the home opener, Skylar sat in her car staring at the license plate of the SUV parked in front of her. BUBOUND read the license plate. On the glass, just above the stationary windshield wiper, were various boasts. *My kid graduated with honors from Sun Valley High School. Sun Valley Honors Society.*

How many kids did this person have? Surely it couldn't all be the same kid.

What kind of bumper stickers would she and Robbie have on the family car? Hypothetically, of course. If she hadn't blown the whole relationship to smithereens.

He'd definitely have to slap something hockey-related on there.

Our kid ate your honor student. Easily.

She'd let him put whatever bumper stickers he wanted on the car with the caveat that she be allowed to get her dream license plate. 3XUROUT. If their kids turned out to be competitive freaks like their parents, that car would always be parked outside of arenas and gymnasiums and fields, just like the one in front of them.

Thinking this way was pointless. Premature, too. Skylar hadn't heard from Robbie since Thursday night when he left Rhode Island in an Uber, and she didn't even know if he wanted children. These tales she'd been weaving in her mind since that awful night were a form of self-punishment and she couldn't seem to stop doing it. Upon waking up every morning, she opened her eyes and thought, *What would Robbie say if he was waking up beside me right now?*

I'm starving was usually the front-runner.

Skylar rubbed her weary eyes and dropped her head back heavily against the rest. "Get out of the car," she urged herself, hyperaware that she only had ten minutes before she was due on the field for warm-ups. "Go to the locker room. Change. *Wake up.*"

Not so easy, it turned out. Her legs didn't want to work, let alone her pitching arm.

Instead of exiting the vehicle, for the one-millionth time she went into her Notes app and read through the various text messages she'd drafted to Robbie. None of them were good enough to send. He'd probably already moved on in spectacular Robbie fashion, anyway, and she couldn't blame him. At some point, she'd have to do the same, but . . . she didn't want to. That was the problem. She wanted to stay right where she was.

In love with Robbie Corrigan.

That's where she was supposed to be.

Skylar turned off the engine with a choppy grab, using the back of her hand to swipe away the excess moisture in her eyes. She stepped out into the cool spring evening, popping her trunk to remove her equipment bag, settling the strap on a shoulder that only wanted to droop.

After securing the trunk lid and locking the car, she closed her eyes and took a deep breath, beginning the shaky walk to the locker room entrance. As she approached, the voices in the distance grew louder. Her younger teammates and their loved ones exchanged final well wishes before the players disappeared into the red double doors. Her parents never walked her to the entrance on opening day, though she'd always wished they would—

Skylar slowed to a stop when she heard her father's unmistakable chuckle, followed by her mother's high-pitched titter. Elton's sarcastic tone. They were waiting outside the locker room? Really? She'd known they were coming to her home opener, of course, but they usually just went to their seats and waved to her during warm-ups.

As she got closer and noticed they were in the Boston University T-shirts Robbie had bought them, Skylar almost turned around and ran back to her car, because everything north of her belly button tightened at once, her neck tendons turning like cranks, her tear ducts burning. But she couldn't turn back now, because Elton had spotted Skylar, giving her that smug/dry smile reserved only for siblings.

This is what she needed. A boost from her family.

She'd take it, then do her best to get focused.

"Well, if it isn't legendary pitcher Skylar Page," Elton said, too loudly. On purpose.

"Hey," she called back, forcing a smile and reshouldering her bag. "What are you guys . . ."

That's when she noticed the man standing beside Elton. He'd been crouched down tying his shoe. But he stood to his full, impressive height now, red hair visible around the edges of his Bearcats cap, his gaze cutting through the agony of the last few days and stopping Skylar in her tracks. The bag slipped off her shoulder and landed with a *shoof* on the ground, her pulse flying into a chaotic sprint. She couldn't find any words, probably because they were all twisted around her vocal cords and squeezing.

"Hey, Rocket," Robbie said, levelly.

Still mad at her. Still mad. "You came?"

"Didn't I say I would?"

She zipped her gaze to the ground and left it there while she tried to swallow the emotion in her throat. Looking at him was too hard when she needed to be composed. Focused. When she finally gathered enough wherewithal to lift her chin again, though, Robbie was standing directly in front of her, his broad shoulders blocking out everything behind him.

"Hey," she said, lamely, unable to meet his gaze. Staring at the slight cleft in his chin, instead. Or was that a dent from a puck?

"Hey," he said, pausing for a moment before taking off his hat, dropping it to his outer thigh. "You going to look at me?"

"I can't."

"It's bad enough suffering through hour after hour without you, Skylar." His voice turned gruffer as he spoke. "Knowing you're in bad shape, too, might be the death blow, you know that? Look at me."

Suffering? Her eyes lifted of their own accord to search for signs of misery and . . . God, she found them. His eyes were bloodshot and sunken deep, creases on his forehead that hadn't been there before, the corners of his mouth turned down.

"Yeah," he rasped. "You see what life without you does to me?"

Her breath caught. "Did you come here to tell me you're miserable?"

"I didn't know what I was going to do until I got here and saw you."

"And?"

His Adam's apple lifted. Stuck. "You have a ball and a couple of gloves in that bag?"

"I always have a ball and a couple of gloves," she whispered, aching with the barely controlled need to throw her arms around him and inhale his scent. "Why?"

"You told me the first pitch is the hardest. That once you throw the first one, you settle into your game." He toed her fallen bag with his boot. "Why don't you throw it to me before you go in? Get the nerves out of your system."

I love you.

I love you I love you.

The gesture wasn't necessary. They both knew the true first pitch wouldn't start until she stood on the mound. *That* would be the one accompanied by ten thousand mosh pitting nerves. His offer was simply proof that he knew her so well. That he still cared. That he had been listening and paying attention and learning her.

It meant the world.

"Okay," Skylar said quietly, surprised when her agreement seemed to drop Robbie's shoulders with relief, his chest expanding. Trying not to read too deeply into his presence, his actions, she got out the gloves, handing him one. As he backed up along the edge of the stadium, Skylar saw that everyone else had left, including her parents and Elton. It was just her, standing with the ball, and Robbie, dropping into a catcher's stance thirty yards away, his hat turned backward, waiting, the sounds of the parking lot beginning to hum with early arrivals.

She expected the pitch to be a formality. A quick show of goodwill that she probably didn't deserve. But that's not what happened at all. As she stood there, preparing to throw, his unwavering gaze slowly started to calm the choppy ocean surface inside of her. His lips weren't moving, but somehow, she could hear him, feel him on every side of her, his presence a reassurance. Everything was currently *not* all right, but the longer she took to throw the ball, the more his expression changed, becoming one of naked vulnerability, the knot in his throat getting trapped beneath his beard.

Skylar wound up and pitched, hitting the dead center of his glove.

He smiled at her, stood, and removed the glove while shaking out his hand.

"Nerves." Robbie winked at her. "What nerves?"

She threw her glove down and ran to him. And it was a singular kind of euphoria knowing that even though things weren't perfect or back on track by any means, he'd still catch her. He'd still show up. Halfway to his open arms, she knew she could trust this man with her heart. Trust him, period. It was right there in the unwavering dedication in his eyes, in the way he didn't budge an inch when she landed against him, his arms catching and holding her there. Squeezing her tight and rocking her, neither one of them seeming to breathe.

"I might still be hurt and angry that you doubted me and went on a revenge mission after I went all in on us, Skylar," he said, hoarsely, "but I'm painfully in love with you, too, and that's not going to change."

Heart elevating, she made a choked sound into his neck. "I miss you so much."

"God, I miss you, too. Every fucking second."

Tell him you love him.

Skylar needed to say those words, but they wouldn't come out. They remained locked in her most stubborn of recesses, refusing to be uttered until she earned the right to say them. When she did, when she allowed herself to make that declaration in return, he needed to know she meant them with her entire heart. Right now, he still doubted her, the way she'd doubted him—and the turnabout sucked, but there it was.

There they were.

Robbie set her down with palpable reluctance, holding her against his body, his breath accelerating against her temple when she shifted against him, lifting on her toes and letting him feel her breasts and belly and the gap between her legs, trapping a moan when he braced a forearm against her butt and rocked her closer, his mouth finding hers in a groaning kiss, a melting, hungry one that at once satisfied and starved her even more. The kind of kiss someone gave their partner before sending them off to war, but it was coming from both sides, so much passion in the single melding of tongues and lips, she grew dizzier and dizzier in the sunlight. Gloves and ball were dropped in favor of his fingers digging into her hair, while Skylar traced the grooves of his ears, his neck, his shoulders, simply needing to reacquaint and memorize.

A car door slammed a few yards away and they still couldn't stop kissing, not right away. It was more of a gradual slowing down out of necessity, both of them pulling back, dazed while trying to catch their breath.

"There is no one in this world for me except you," he said, looking her in the eye. "Go in there and pitch the lights out. I'll be there. I've got your back."

Skylar's heart rapped wildly in her chest. "I know."

He swallowed hard as he backed away. "Good."

That was the last time she saw Robbie until he was sitting in the stands, wedged in between Elton and her father. Eating a foot long chili dog. Obviously.

Everything was going to be all right. That belief was unwavering.

Robbie had made himself clear by showing up. Declaring himself so lovingly.

Now she had to find a way to do the same.

To give him the same faith and security he'd given her.

A grand gesture.

An idea would come to her . . . but would it be a good enough one?

That was a different story.

CHAPTER THIRTY-TWO

Robbie knew the exact moment he wasn't mad anymore.

Skylar sat down beside his mother in the stands on Thursday night wearing a Bearcats hoodie and he almost jumped through the glass to get to her. Thing was, Skylar didn't even *know* those were his parents. But his parents knew damn well she was Skylar because he'd told them everything over dinner last night when they landed in Boston and now, he could barely focus on his stretching routine, he was so riveted by that first interaction.

His mother snuck a peek at the girl beside her and smiled like a cat who'd got the canary, giving Robbie a covert double thumbs-up. Skylar didn't notice, because she was observing a trio of bare-chested fans with furry cat ears screaming, "*Bearcat Nation yeahhhh*," into a live television camera several feet away.

Robbie watched without breathing as his parents introduced themselves and Skylar froze, before leaning forward and hugging his mother, making her smile like he'd never seen before, not even when everyone complimented her shepherd's pie. Yeah. He stopped being mad at Skylar probably forever in that moment— and became well and truly pissed at himself. How had three fucking days passed since he'd kissed her in the parking lot before her Monday night game? How had he stayed away?

How?

For one, he'd been traveling for the first two games of the series and had been in and out of team meetings, media sessions, and workouts. On top of that, he'd been on the phone with a real estate lawyer trying to put a down payment on a condo in Brookline that had been easy to find because it was owned and advertised by the same management company that owned his current building. Still, he could have called Skylar. No, he *should* have called, except his heart had still felt raw and beat-up. Until now. Now it was bleeding for a different reason. He needed his girl. It was bullshit that he didn't have her.

She'd hugged his mother.

"Hey," Sir Savage barked, knee-deep in his back stretches beside Robbie. "Series is tied. Head in the game." The soon-to-retire team captain coughed. "That does make a nice picture, though. Is that their first time meeting?"

"Yes," Robbie managed, feeling ridiculously winded over having his idol acknowledge the important moment out loud. "I probably should have warned Skylar that she'd be sitting next to my parents, but I didn't want to spook her."

"So you blindsided her, instead," Sig said, grinning on the other side of Robbie. "Good call."

"Looks like it's working out fine, doesn't it?" Robbie shot back.

"Sure does, buddy," Mailer said, patting him on the back as he skated by. "What do you think they're talking about?"

"Me, obviously."

Sir Savage grunted. "All good stuff, I'm sure."

"Yeah." Robbie picked up his stick and stood, suddenly determined to have the best game of his life. "Would it be crazy if I ask her to move in with me?"

"Yes," they all said at once.

"I don't care. I'm doing it. I'm going to marry her, too."

"Why the rush?" Mailer wanted to know.

Sig and Burgess both opened their mouths, seemingly to second Mailer's concerns, but they snapped them shut just as fast, their attention drawn to the family section where Tallulah and Chloe sat side by side, waving at their boyfriends.

"I get the rush," Sig said gruffly.

"Same." Burgess sighed. "Ask her. Tonight. Don't waste a second."

But Robbie wouldn't get the chance to ask. Not until much later.

Sensory overload.

Until tonight, Skylar hadn't known about hockey stretches. But oh, she knew now. Try talking to the mother of your sort-of boyfriend while he humps the ice one hundred yards away. It isn't easy to concentrate. She'd been so startled when Angela introduced herself, she'd gone in for the hug, which, frankly, had felt like the right thing to do. Her first impulse. And Angela hadn't seemed to mind.

The reality was, Skylar wasn't Robbie's girlfriend, though. Not really. She'd shown up at Boston Garden tonight unsure if he'd even left a ticket at the box office. There had been no communication between them since their kiss in the parking lot, a kiss that she could still feel wash over her body every time she closed her eyes. Maybe waiting for Robbie to stop being mad was hopeless. Maybe love wasn't enough when two people had doubted each other the way they had.

Or maybe she needed to make a gesture. Something more than showing up at a game and sitting in a seat. She'd spent the last three days trying to come up with an act of love to show she'd been paying attention, that every moment they'd spent together had been important, the way Robbie had done when he'd offered to catch her first pitch in the parking lot. As of now, she was still drawing a blank.

"I hear you're a big-time pitcher," Angela said, smiling, her

Long Island accent offering the pronunciation *pitcha*. "Robbie says you're a phenom."

An embarrassing level of heat pressed behind Skylar's eyes. *He talked to his mother about me.* Maybe this wasn't so hopeless after all. "Yeah, I am pretty good," Skylar murmured without thinking.

Robbie's mother cracked a laugh. "I love that confidence!"

Skylar smiled through her flush. "That's how I met Robbie, actually. Did you know the Bearcats have a rivalry with some local baseball players? One of them is my brother. Imagine my surprise when I was dragged out of bed on a Saturday morning to pitch against a professional hockey team."

Angela shook her head, only mildly astonished. "I'm sure my son was the ringleader. He's a good boy, but wherever he goes, trouble follows." Quickly, she reached over and squeezed Skylar's hand. "Not that you have any reason to worry."

"I'm not worried," Skylar reassured her, meaning it. One hundred percent meaning it. She trusted that man down on the ice with her life. Her heart. "He'd probably say he's the fun kind of trouble."

"You're right, he would say that." Angela gave her a once-over. "Why aren't you wearing his jersey?"

"Oh, I . . ." Skylar trailed off, not knowing what to say. She ended with a jerky shrug, giving Angela an apologetic look for not having an answer.

Robbie's mother scrutinized Skylar's expression and made a sound of understanding. "You're unsure about where you two stand after your little tiff, is that it?"

God, this woman got to the point fast. "It wasn't so little."

"Well, it couldn't have been that big, either. He talked our ears off about you all damn night." She elbowed her husband in the ribs, sloshing his beer. "Didn't he, Clark?"

A long-suffering sigh. "Yup."

"Robbie has *never* talked to us about a girl before. Suddenly, there he is getting choked up talking about the little gold flecks in your eyes. Fight be damned, all right?"

"All right," Skylar responded, grateful for the insight even though it made her heart all the heavier. If he was so enamored of her, why hadn't he called? Texted?

He needs that gesture.

You're blowing it.

"Dinner was gorgeous, by the way. Have you been to Mamma Maria? I had a chicken piccata that was well worth the heartburn, let me tell you. My ankles are swollen from all the salt."

"Here we go again with the ankle talk," muttered Robbie's dad—and maybe Skylar had no right fantasizing this way, but she could only imagine the hilarity that would ensue when these people met their polar opposites in Vivica and Doug.

"Robbie kept getting phone calls during the meal from his real estate agent, but all in all, a lovely night."

Skylar's ears perked up. "Real estate agent?"

"He's been planning a move for over a week. He didn't tell you?"

Over a week? Skylar was almost too stunned to respond. "N-no."

"Don't worry, sweetheart, it's not like he's leaving Boston." She patted Skylar's knee. "He just wants a place of his own."

Skylar stared straight forward, pulse tickling her wrists, trying to process that information. Robbie was moving out of his bachelor pad with Mailer? Was it possible, even just a little, that he was doing that for her? For their relationship?

No. No way.

Right? Wouldn't he have told her, if that was the case?

Hypothetically, however, if he was moving out of his party palace and into his own apartment to show he was serious about their relationship—and she'd *still* gone out with Madden for that drink—she was an even bigger asshole than she'd realized. Plus, she was falling even further behind on Big Gestures than she thought.

"Forgive my son if he's taking a little while to straighten things out between you two. You see, Robbie used to get most of his advice from his grandfather. *My* father." Angela crossed herself. "If he was still alive, he'd be sitting next to you with an extra large Coke giving you statistics for everyone on the ice. He was a big character."

"I've been told a lot about him," Skylar managed. "I heard he loved to fly kites."

"That's true. That big yellow one . . ."

The static rush in Skylar's ears drowned out the rest of what Angela said. Yellow kite. The one that was stuck in the tree that Robbie couldn't get down because of his fear of heights. Robbie's words drifted back to her while she watched him finish warm-ups and leave the ice, presumably preparing to be introduced and start the game. *It's ridiculous, but as long as his kite is stuck in that tree, I'll have this weird sense of things being unfinished. Or unresolved. Like he's out there somewhere missing that damn kite.*

Skylar didn't have a fear of heights. She could get him that kite.

She could do this thing that was important to him and earn her right to say *I love you.* Maybe then he'd be ready to start dating her again. Because she couldn't stand being trapped in the uncertainty anymore when she was so sure of Robbie, she felt him in her bones.

"Where exactly is this yellow kite that got stuck in the tree?"

ROBBIE WALKED INTO the friends and family waiting room ready to propose.

No bullshit.

Don't get him wrong, he'd concentrated as much as possible on the game—and they'd secured the W, bringing the series to 2–1—but he'd be lying if he said he didn't sneak approximately ten thousand looks at his beautiful girl sitting in the stands with his parents. At this point, his heart was going to tumble out of his fucking chest if he didn't kiss Skylar and sleep in the same bed as her tonight. *Tonight*.

No more screwing around. This was serious. He felt ill.

So why didn't he see her anywhere? Wives, girlfriends, parents, assorted family for the entire roster, down to the equipment manager. No Skylar.

"Where is she? Where's Skylar?"

His mother drew him down for a kiss on the cheek. "Nice to see you, too. What a joy she is, Robbie. Pure joy. So much heart and sincerity for such a young girl. She left."

Robbie's entire chest lurched, like a semitruck slamming on the brakes. "What do you mean, '*she left*'?"

"She said she had something to do."

Something to do?

Like a date?

Nope. Absolutely not. That was irrational.

Unless he'd waited too long to get his head out of his ass.

Robbie dropped his equipment bag to the floor with a thud, raking a panicked hand through his hair, the pulse in his neck sprinting like a mailman trying to outrun a Doberman. Crouching down, he riffled through the front pocket of his bag, freeing his phone and calling Skylar, his chest seizing at all the heart emojis he'd added to her contact profile when he was drunk on lasagna. He was going to add more later.

She couldn't have gotten far, right? She'd still been there at the end of the third period. He'd simply ask her to come back, they'd resolve the remaining divide between them and put a permanent end to this separation. That would be that.

Voicemail.

Fuck.

"Skylar, could you please stop whatever you're doing and come back here, please? Don't make me look at you all night and not even kiss me afterward. What the hell is that?"

He hung up, stared at his phone. "*RING*," he bellowed.

"Robbie, that was a terrible message."

"Ma, please, I'm in the middle of a crisis. Did she say where she was going?"

"Don't you think I would have told you by now?"

"She was asking an awful lot of questions about that kite," his father drawled, still holding a half-drunk beer in his hand. "Wanted to know directions. Logistics. For chrissakes, Angela, you drew her a map on the back of a bar napkin."

"The kite?" Robbie stood up slowly, but his legs were starting to tingle. "Why did she want to know all that?"

"When she kissed me goodbye, she said she'd see me on Long Island." His mother laughed, clearly not grasping the gravity of the situation the way Robbie was beginning to do, his stomach squeezing like a lemon. "Maybe she meant sooner than later."

He called Skylar again, but this time his hand was shaking.

"Hey, Rocket . . ."

"Honey, he calls her Rocket," whispered his mother, hands clasped beneath her chin. "How adorable is that?"

"Listen," Robbie continued, his vision starting to turn an ominous shade of gray. "I know this is a long shot, but you wouldn't be on the way to Long Island, by any chance? Right? To get a kite down out of a tree? No. *Right?*" His throat was shrinking down to the size of a cocktail straw. This wasn't an average person he was speaking to. His girlfriend was highly competitive and well versed in challenges just like this one. She'd absolutely make this attempt. Oh my God. "Because that would be a very bad idea, Skylar. That tree sticks out over the edge of a cliff. *A cliff*, okay? It's a big drop with a lot of rocks . . . and I'm suddenly very positive that's exactly where you're going. But you can't. You cannot try and get that kite down, please, because you could get hurt and I won't . . . I can't even conceive of that without getting dizzy. If something happens to you, it happens to me. Stop the goddamn car, Skylar." He jabbed his thumb into his eye socket, pacing in a circle. "Okay, I know you won't. I'm right behind you. I'll stop you myself."

Robbie hung up, fumbled his phone back into the bag with quaking hands, slung the strap across his chest, and ran for the exit, his parents hot on his heels.

CHAPTER THIRTY-THREE

A faint glow of sunlight was just beginning to show itself on the horizon when Skylar reached Long Island. Even in the wee hours of the morning, the traffic going through the Bronx was backed up, due to the abundance of delivery trucks ferrying goods to Manhattan and the outer boroughs. Bridge traffic flew, however, the majority of cars heading in the opposite direction as she was welcomed by the nicer roadways and greenery of the island.

She didn't have a plan. She only had a goal.

There was a good chance this idea made her psychotic. Point the finger at the asylum where she was raised. Courage had always been rewarded. Accomplishments. And while the Page family had made some serious strides recently in expressing their feelings to one another in a normal, healthy, non-life-threatening way, retrieving the kite from the tree was the biggest expression of love she could come up with. It was a tangible thing that she could understand, and Robbie would hopefully recognize, so she was trusting her gut and going for it.

Skylar would include words, too. Words were important. Maybe they would be enough on their own, but she couldn't hand him the heart out of her chest, so this was the next best thing. It was real, proactive. Like Robbie moving into a new place. Or showing up with Boston University sweatshirts. Or taking her first pitch.

And at the very root of this possibly risky adventure was this:

she loved him and wanted him to have the fucking kite. It was *important* to him.

Therefore, it was important to her, too.

Skylar had listened to the voicemails. Five times each. She didn't like the panic in his voice, but apparently this need to prove how much he meant to her was making Skylar more stubborn than usual, because she kept driving, checking the rearview mirror every few minutes, searching for a car that might belong to Robbie's parents.

She reached Sands Point Preserve at 5:15 A.M. It didn't open until nine.

Too bad.

She parked on the side of the road and walked along the metal fencing until she was out of view of the security camera, then she used the trunk of a tree to hop over into the Preserve, offhandedly wondering who she would call with her one jailhouse phone call. Ironically, it would be Robbie. But she wouldn't mind swallowing her pride if she had the yellow kite. Something to make him believe in her again. Trust her with his heart.

At this time of the morning, the air had a distinct chill, making her grateful for the Bearcats sweatshirt. Wind whipped the tree branches overhead and untucked hairs from her ponytail as she found a hiking path and took it west, using her iPhone flashlight to illuminate the way, until she reached a wooden sign that pointed her in the direction of the cliff overlook. She broke into a jog; the closer she came to the cliff, the heavier the wind, and the more her stomach muscles started to tighten.

It took her fifteen minutes to reach the cliff.

And less than ten seconds to lose her courage.

In her mind's eye, the cliff and the beach below had rendered itself almost like a drawing. The reality was so much more intimidating. The sun was halfway risen over the Atlantic now, as if wanting to illuminate exactly how foolish she'd been to believe she could attempt this retrieval. The cliff was *high*. Very high. It took her a good five minutes to pinpoint where the kite was stuck and when she saw it, a hysterical laugh bubbled in her throat, carried off by the wind.

Nope. Not a chance. She'd either need a crane . . . or she'd have to shimmy her way out along a single medium-sized branch that didn't look like it could hold her weight, simply hoping it wouldn't snap and send her crashing to the rocks below. The kite was too far out to grasp with any kind of instrument from her position on the cliff, even if she had something that would do the trick, which she didn't. It had quite possibly picked the most unreachable spot in this preserve to make its final resting place.

Skylar sat heavily on the ground, gathering her knees to her chest, and watched the rest of the sun creep into the sky, though the gray clouds kept the breeze heavy, the water choppy. She took out her phone, intending to call Robbie to let him know she'd aborted the mission and he could stop worrying. There was no reception and the call didn't go through, however, so she stood and started walking back the direction she came—

"*Skylar.*"

Robbie's voice stopped her progress, her heart taking over, seemingly going from dormant to hammering within seconds. "Robbie," she called, but the rustling tree branches drowned her out, so she tried again. "*Robbie.*"

"Skylar." He came into view the way a warlord might charge over a hill into battle, his visible relief when he saw her causing him to stumble. "Don't fucking move," he wheezed. "Don't."

"I'm not. I won't."

"Don't you *dare* try to get that kite. Back away from the tree."

Skylar put her hands up, feeling weary and overwhelmed and bolstered and elated by the sight of him, all at once. "Okay. I'm not going to do it. I can't. It's impossible."

"*No kidding.*" Robbie reached her then—and she wasn't sure what she'd been expecting, but it wasn't to be pulled into his embrace, his mouth stamping furious kisses all over her forehead and cheeks and hair. "What the hell am I going to do with you, Skylar?"

"I was just hoping you'd keep me," she whispered, accepting more kisses to her hairline, her neck and chin. "The kite is a lost cause, but we're not. *We're* not, right?"

Robbie went from kissing her to shaking her. "No. *No*, we're not a lost cause. How could you think that for a second? Do you think I could walk away when I love you so much?" Haunted eyes ran circles around her face, his thumbs fanning up and down her cheekbones. "I'm done being mad. I'm done being without you. I'm *done*."

A lump expanded in her throat. "Robbie."

"Yeah?"

"I love you." She sucked in an awkward breath. "And you're the first man I've loved. I didn't know what this . . . this beautiful weight felt like until you."

He choked on a cough. Closed his eyes. "You know, you could have just said that, instead of giving me a lifetime of nightmares," he rasped, kissing her mouth hard. "You'll be lying beside me at night when I have them. That's the silver lining."

She was already nodding, but couldn't speak just yet, the confession having taken so much of her on the way out. It felt as though she'd literally handed over her heart.

"I should have called you sooner. I just wanted to get this new apartment. Show you how serious I am. And then I saw you with my mother last night and I realized I've barely been breathing since the last time we were together." Robbie rolled their foreheads together. "I don't want to fight ever again, all right?"

Skylar's laugh was watery. "We're definitely going to fight, Redbeard."

"*No*." He slanted his mouth over hers, both of them moaning at the contact. "No. And I get to win this argument, because I just drove five hours thinking you'd be dangling over a cliff when I got here."

"I'm sorry for being dramatic. I'm dramatic over you."

"Fine. You win the argument." He shook her a little. "God, I love you."

"Robbie, I love you so much."

He searched her eyes. "Enough to move in with me?"

"*Already?* That's . . . that's crazy . . ."

A low grunt of frustration. "How about your own set of keys and a giant-ass closet?"

"Still crazy." A blissful laugh burst out of her. "But I'll make a pro-con list in my planner."

"Great. Let's do it right now. We'll start with the pro side. If you have clothes at my place, you're more likely to sleep over. Which means I'll get to hold you at night. *God*, I miss holding you. I thought I knew how much I would, but it's worse. I can protect you, too. You know how seriously I'm going to take that job? I'll walk you home, all the way to your door. I'll kiss you when you've had a bad day. Make you laugh. And I know, I *know* you're going to do all that for me, because you're a fucking wonder." Robbie's mouth worked hers roughly, breaking away to race up the slope of her neck while he took her hand, bringing it to the growing bulge between his legs. "One more pro. The more time you spend at my place, the easier it'll be to get this inside of you. You just have to ask."

"Definite pro," she breathed, stroking him firmly through his sweatpants. "I want you so bad."

He hissed like a teakettle. "Have me, Skylar. I plan on having *you* for the rest of my life." Skylar was so overwhelmed by the shimmer and dive of hormones and the way Robbie unzipped her jeans and slid his hand inside the opening to grip her sex, hard, kneading her flesh through her panties like he owned every inch, she almost let that statement get away.

She caught it at the last second, however, before it could fade into the ether, holding on to it like a treasure while she toed off her shoes. "I like the sound of that plan."

"Good." He bent forward long enough to remove her jeans entirely, tossing them to the leafy earth. "It's the *only* plan."

He backed them up until he could sit down on a boulder, pulling her down into a straddle on his lap, their mouths opening and exhaling when her softness met and pressed against that swelling part of him. "I don't remember you being this demanding," she gasped as he yanked her panties to the right and guided himself to her wetness.

"You don't understand, I've been a mess needing this pussy. Got me so *addicted*."

He shuddered violently.

Licked at her panting mouth. Whispered her name. Pressed one thick inch inside of her. Two. Making her whimper, nails sinking into the meat of his shoulder.

"Maybe I'm demanding now. Maybe I'm not myself when I've been without you." Gritting his teeth, Robbie punched his hips upward, shooting delicious shock waves to every corner of Skylar's body, the pressure so welcome it made her eyes water, made her immediately start moving, writhing, clinging to his broad shoulders while she ground and bucked her hips, thighs quaking. "I refuse to be without you anymore. Take the keys. Take the closet. Take half of everything I own."

She rode him, thighs wide, reveling in the spontaneity of the moment, the perfect connection of their bodies, his warmth and size and heart. Yes, his heart. She could feel it thundering against her breasts, experienced his love for her everywhere. In the air, in her blood. "We've barely started the pro-con list—"

A snarling gust of wind ripped across the cliff, so intense she ducked her face into his neck, his arms coming around her at the same time and crushing her close. When the gust died down, they looked at each other through eyes made glassy with hunger, Skylar's lower body beginning to roll and press and scoop again, their mouths whispering words of praise in between kisses, woven in and out of groans of each other's names.

And Skylar could read it—the future in Robbie's eyes. Could see how unwaveringly he believed in that future. How much he wanted and needed it with her.

She would give it to him.

When they finished, they did it together, Robbie's hands bruising on her backside as he yanked her tight, tight to his lap and cursed gutturally, telling her he loved her while she shook, following just seconds later, his eyes losing focus, head falling back, neck muscles so stark, bathed in the morning light while she circled, circled those final times, making him jerk with a renewed wave of pleasure, finally collapsing into the arms that were now her home. And she wrapped her arms around his neck and offered him one back.

"Skylar," he whispered a few minutes later, sounding . . . still dazed?

"Mmmm."

He took her chin in his hand, turning her face to the right.

They both stared open-mouthed at the yellow kite sitting sideways on the earth, not five feet away, trapped in some tall grass.

"No way," she said, moisture flooding her vision.

Robbie dropped his face into her neck, his voice hitching. "Holy shit."

Whether the dislodging of the kite was an act of nature, pure coincidence . . . or a message from a loved one on the other side, Skylar decided to interpret it to mean they weren't there in that moment on that exact day by coincidence. Not a moment of their time together had been an accident, since the morning of the baseball game until now. Every word, every decision had led to here . . . and she couldn't imagine being anywhere else.

With anyone else.

"Okay, Robbie," she whispered. "I'll take that set of keys."

His parents ever so faintly heard their son's cheer of victory from outside the fence of the Preserve. They high-fived. "We'll offer to split the wedding with her folks, I think."

A gusting sigh followed, but there was a smile behind it. "Fine."

EPILOGUE

Five Years Later

Robbie inhaled the scent of fresh cut grass, closing his eyes while he absorbed the music of life happening around him. The soundtrack had changed drastically since he'd met Skylar. Become richer and more fulfilling. And it changed again every year, adding new voices, new life, but one thing never, ever changed and that was his devotion to her.

His wife.

It had only been ten seconds since the last time Robbie looked at her, but that was ten seconds too long, as far as he was concerned. Especially now, when she was in her element, dressed in white shorts and a Bearcats hoodie, preparing to throw out the first pitch of their once-a-year Saturday morning game.

Bearcats vs. Baseball.

An excuse to get friends and teammates together, sure, but secretly, it was their way of remembering their very first meeting, which Robbie privately referred to as the day his life truly began. Who could have guessed the girl whose first words to him were *fuck you* would end up becoming his everything?

Robbie. He'd known. Looking back, he recognized that boot in the gut and what it had meant. He'd found his soulmate that day.

As if Skylar sensed the direction of Robbie's thoughts, she

turned and he had the pleasure of watching unconditional love wash over her features.

After which, she stuck her tongue out.

Some things never changed. Thank God.

But some things did.

For instance, the Page Stakes were never held again.

The rain check had been cashed five years earlier when Robbie and Skylar returned to Rhode Island, smashing a rendition of "Get'cha Head in the Game" complete with synchronized basketball dribbling. That video would go on to be played at their engagement party six months later, Mailer helming the projector, laughing and crying at the same time.

Another half a year later, their wedding was held at the baseball field at Langone Park, in the very spot where they met—and where they now stood, preparing for a showdown. On their wedding day four years earlier, they'd exchanged their vows on the pitcher's mound and immediately broke into a nine-inning baseball game as soon as they said "I do," starring the wedding party and a few of the athlete/guests, Skylar pitching in her wedding dress while the Bearcats got progressively champagne drunk, so they'd have an excuse for losing. Not that they admitted it out loud.

And thus began a new annual tradition, the yearly hockey versus baseball player throwdown in the park, brought to you by Rocket and Redbeard. Nobody ever won or lost, because someone usually incited a brawl or there was a collective decision to quit and go eat tacos. The Bearcats pretended to merely tolerate the baseball boys, but in truth, they'd become grudging friends over the years and even attended each other's games.

They drew the line at wearing merch.

"Hey," Skylar said, jogging over to Robbie and falling straight into his arms, nuzzling his chin with her nose. "We were in such a rush to get out of the apartment this morning, I don't know if we wished each other happy anniversary."

"Petition to make the game a day after our anniversary next year."

"I'll take it up with the board of directors." She smiled over at their yellow Labs, Gaby and Troy, who were sitting in the visitors' dugout wearing yellow scarves around their necks made from a certain yellow kite, dutifully receiving scratches behind the ears from everyone who passed. With Robbie at the height of his NHL career and Skylar busy traveling between East Coast schools as a freelance pitching coach, kids were still a someday discussion, but the pooches kept them busy enough. "I hear they can be bought for the right price."

"I'll bring the Pup-Peroni."

"That ought to do it."

Skylar started to turn around, but Robbie didn't want her to see what was happening on the field behind her back, so he snagged her chin and kissed her, gratified to the soles of his feet when their mouths locking together had the desired effect. Her knees wobbled and she melted against him, setting loose a contented sigh in her throat. The baseball in her hand dropped on the ground behind him and damn, she parted those lips and wished him a little too happy of an anniversary while in public, because you guessed it, Robbie started to get real hard, real fast.

"Too late to cancel the game?" he said hoarsely when they broke for air.

Her sunlit eyes shone with happiness. "Ah, come on. We love this yearly showdown."

"I love anything as long as we're doing it together, Rocket."

And, damn, did he mean every word of that. Whether they were icing injuries in front of the television, grocery shopping, talking until the wee hours of the morning, volunteering, walking the dogs, relaxing on vacation, or fucking like fiends in his hotel room during a road series, Robbie was always, always in the best place. At the side of his best friend. His wife. His other, better half.

Skylar "Rocket" Corrigan.

Living without her would be like asking someone to run full speed in outer space. A total impossibility that he didn't like to think about at all, frankly, and he never took the fact that she'd chosen him for granted. He could even laugh now about their relationship starting with a scheme—and laugh he did, especially since Madden had found his own hard-fought happy ending. In fact, he and Eve both were in today's lineup.

Skylar's hand ventured beneath his T-shirt, and she rubbed a single knuckle slowly down the length of his happy trail, causing several brain cells to snap in half. "How many Pup-Peronis would it take to persuade the board to postpone *this* year's game until tomorrow?" Robbie caught Skylar's bottom lip between his teeth and tugged her into a kiss, growling, "I'd really like to be celebrating alone with my wife."

"We're playing this game, Redbeard. I already warmed up my arm."

"I love your arm." He ducked his head to kiss her neck. "And your knees"—kiss—"and belly"—kiss—"and toes. All of you. That's why I want a rain check. Come on. We're good at those."

Based on her smile, she was enjoying this. Torturing him. And, apparently, ignoring his plea. "Should we place a side bet for old times' sake?"

He pulled her back into his arms, making the universal sign for *hurry up* behind her back. "What are the terms?"

"If the Bearcats win, I'll go topless in the apartment for the whole night."

His tongue tied itself together. How had this woman ever

come to him for advice on seducing a man? If she so much as batted her eyelashes, he rolled over and panted for belly rubs, just like one of their dogs. "You'd . . . do that? You'd please do that?"

She laughed, the sound full and happy. "And if team baseball wins?"

"I go without pants?"

"You do that anyway." Skylar tilted her head back, swaying side to side in his arms. "I was thinking more . . . I'll let you eat lasagna on the couch."

Robbie blinked. "Wait, so I win, either way?"

She gasped. "I must love you or something." Before he could question his luck, Elton—one member of the crowd standing behind Skylar—signaled Robbie.

Showtime.

He turned his wife around in his arms, pulling her back against his chest so he could watch her profile while she reacted to over a dozen of their friends wearing eye black, holding softball mitts, and sporting brunette ponytail wigs, all of them doing their best impression of Skylar on the pitching mound. "Happy anniversary," they yelled, loud enough to be heard on Long Island. Skylar looked up at him, stunned, tears of mirth forming in her eyes, but instead of asking him how long he'd been planning the anniversary surprise, she took Robbie by the elbow and turned him around . . .

Where he encountered the rest of the game's attendees standing behind him with false red beards and mouthpieces.

"Happy anniversary!"

Robbie and Skylar fell sideways into the grass, laughing until their sides were on fire, and only when their amusement died down did they look at each other and mouth the words *I love you*. Words that would be echoed every day after that for the rest of their lives.

ABOUT THE AUTHOR

#1 *New York Times* bestselling author **TESSA BAILEY** can solve all problems except for her own, so she focuses those efforts on stubborn, fictional blue-collar men and loyal, lovable heroines. She lives on Long Island, avoiding the sun and social interactions, then wonders why no one has called. Dubbed the "Michelangelo of dirty talk" by *Entertainment Weekly*, Tessa writes with spice, spirit, swoon, and a guaranteed happily ever after.

 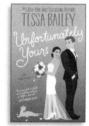